RUNNING The SY
Part IV

by Mark Cunnington

Trio Publishing

Also by Trio Publishing

The Syndicate
The Syndicate 2nd Edition
The Syndicate (R.I.P.) Part II
Return of The Syndicate Part III

First published 2004

Published by Trio Publishing
50 Gillsman's Park
St. Leonards on Sea
East Sussex
TN38 0SW

ISBN 0 9537951 3 6

Printed and bound by Chandlers Printers Ltd
Bexhill-on-Sea, East Sussex

INTRODUCTION

Human relationships are central to all of our lives. The wires that connect us to our friends, our family and our lovers also connect us to the friends, families and lovers of new people we meet. Sometimes, when the wires cross and get tangled, things can become extremely complicated. Even more so when there are lines out for carp!

Our story starts from where we left it.

Chapter 1

The wooden clubhouse was already open. To myself, courtesy of the passage of time, it was now familiar and unremarkable, a simple single-storey building of six rooms complemented by a few basic amenities. It had a small kitchen complete with old cooker and stored, electrically heated hot water, two toilets in working order, a shower-room with a mains-fed 8.3kw shower that contravened the current electrical regulations by not having a pull switch and dedicated RCD breaker (remember I am an electrician, *was* an electrician), an office and one large room. The large room covered around three-quarters of the total square footage of the entire building and was at the end of a tiny corridor from which the other rooms branched off. The exterior comprised a lockable lean-to for housing various gardening tools and a couple of lawn mowers, a sturdy front door – the one I was soon to be walking through – and was constructed of vertical timbers clad in creosoted shiplap wood with various single-glaze windows at strategic points. The roof was flat, covered in mineral felt, and not leaking. The clubhouse had no surprising facets at all, apart from the bit about the flat mineral felt roof not leaking and the minor detail that the whole structure had been built by a murderer who, when his hideous secret had finally come to light, had topped himself. From now on things do get rather remarkable.

The manner in which the murderer had ended his life was not commonplace; I could vouch for it first hand because I had been there, at the death as they say. In truth I suppose the suicide would be classified as unusual, bizarre even, but by way of its abnormality it had at least shown a little more originality than merely bolting down hundreds of sleeping pills, chucking oneself in front of a train or jumping off a bridge spanning deep, cold water. Death by portable 70/30 butane/propane cooking stove, aided and abetted by an almost hermetically sealed bivvy, had a certain air of the outlandish. Although not for long, the air had soon run out. Michael's final, successful oxygen-consuming act had been his choice and his alone and it had gone exactly according to plan. He had zipped it and lit it so to speak and the laws of combustion had done the rest. The reason? In short it had been an irrevocable act of repentance.

Via the cooking stove of doom he had finally alleviated the festering guilt ravaging both his mind and body ever since the day he had taken another's life. Mind you, it had been a long time in coming. It had needed Rambo and myself to confront him with the murder weapon and the ring of his victim to ultimately drag the suicide out of him countless years after the macabre killing. Without our intervention he would have coped with his feelings and would still be running the syndicate even now, suppressing his guilt and self-loathing in the name of monster carp, an aesthetically perfect gravel pit and, let's not forget, a functional wooden clubhouse.

Running parallel to our disclosure of hammer and ring – adding salt by the skip-load to the wound I should add – was the other tale of skulduggery. Without us kindly informing him at the same time as we had revealed our knowledge of his grim deed, he would have been blissfully unaware of being ripped off by his long-time best friend, Hollywood, the obnoxious Rocky and the sly Darren. All three of them had been involved in a fish stealing cartel culminating in selling large carp back to the original fish farmer who had supplied them to Michael in the first place! What goes around comes around!

And what had been the consequences of detonating this gruesome double cluster bomb right under Michael's rat-like nose? Well, he had ended his life but not before he had signed the relevant paperwork and left his life's work to me. To *me*! He had left Hamworthy Fisheries to me! All of it!!! Exclamation marks by the ton! The pit, the massive carp in the pit, the surrounding land, all the monies in the syndicate's accounts, the access track from the main road *and* the functional wooden clubhouse were mine. No wonder I was an ex-electrician. Fairly recently I had been a part-time electrician, an unemployed one before that and a proper one way back in the mists of time long forgotten. Not now. I owned land now. And water. And property, albeit only a functional wooden clubhouse, you see, Michael's house had been rented.

Michael's death by carbon monoxide poisoning had been a case of misadventure – officially – with regards to the report recorded by the coroner. As far as the world was concerned Michael died through his own ignorance in a tragic accident. There was no suicide to consider because to the rest of the world there had been no reason for suicide because there had been no ghost because there had been no body because there had been no murder because there had been no terrible act of betrayal. But there *had been* a suicide and a reason for it. There *had been* a ghost and a body and a murder and there *had been* a terrible act of betrayal. This was my dark secret. Our dark secret. A secret jealously guarded by Rambo, Sophie and myself. Others might have had, indeed might still have, some gut feeling of oddness, some inner doubt concerning the strange way Michael had died but we were the only ones who knew the truth. But come on! Who would believe such a truth? Who in their right mind could contemplate a truth so radical, so frightening, so laden with implication? Best let it all wash under the bridge for all our sakes and try not to ponder on it too heavily. Easier said than done I can assure you.

Michael had died all zipped up in his bivvy with the forty-pound carp, Swansong, swimming around the pit whilst attached to one of Michael's rigs. The Delkim head and sounder box had announced his death, if not to all and sundry, then to those of us in earshot. I often looked at the photo we had taken of Michael 'holding' Swansong with the hidden Rambo holding his lulling head straight – Michael's head that is, not Swansong's – and wondered if we weren't all utterly raving mad. What on earth were we thinking of photographing a dead man 'holding' a large fish? Feebly, in my defence, I explained to myself that you really had to have been there at the time to understand why.

It wasn't a photo I showed to many people but every now and then I did. When I felt the strange compulsion to show someone, I never told the person the human in the frame was a stiff. I wanted to see if this new viewer could see the awful truth for themselves. They couldn't. No one ever mentioned it and I don't think they were held back by social convention, they simply never twigged it. They never said; 'Huh! The bloke in the picture's dead, isn't he?' or 'Why did you snap the corpse with the big mirror, then, Matt?' It simply never crossed their minds. It does mine. Every time I look at a photo, any photo, I peruse it for evidence of death and mortality.

To be fair you couldn't have guessed Michael was dead from the photo. You might have thought he looked a little odd or not very photogenic and, if you were prone to being unkind, you might have thought he had some sort of mental deficiency. But not dead, after all 'the camera never lies'. As someone once said; 'How do you snort in print?' What a load of complete bollocks! The camera is one of the most dishonest implements on the face of planet earth when it wants to be. In skilled hands it is the smoothest of prevaricators. Even wielded by my inexpert hands it was still a brilliant bullshitter. With digital enhancement, airbrushing, staged poses and such like the advantages the camera held over the observer of its work meant you were well and truly stuffed. Your perception was a pathetic jack-high hand compared to the camera's running flush of tricks and smoke and mirrors. When it wants to, you only see what the camera *wants* you to see. Advertisers know this.

Why you would have had to be psychic to know Michael was dead from the photo alone. I knew he was dead because I had been there, behind the lens, but was I ever so slightly psychic? Ah… just one of the many million pound questions which had erupted to the fore since I had joined Hamworthy Fisheries and became embroiled in ghosts, death, life and the shades in between. Unfortunately there were no multiple choices, no phone-a-friend, no ask-the-audience, no 50/50 and no guiding coughs from the audience on this ultimate enigmatic question. I can scan my history for clues to the answer, though. The mind-meld with the fifty mirror at Lac Fumant admittedly drug-induced and the contact with the ghost? It seemed I had something. It had been me after all, not anybody else, who the ghost had contacted. Apparently she had tried Alan and failed before I was around, yet she had called to me on my very first night at the pit. And I had heard her. She must have known or at least had an inclination I would be able to hear her. Did I possess a buried talent? If I did it was fucking deep because I couldn't pick a horse, get a hunch, read a person's thoughts any better than I could years ago before my supposed revelations.

Only the other day I had tried to read the mind of my five-month-old daughter, Amy. I had held her under her little arms so her head was slightly higher than mine and I had stared deep into her large brown eyes. With furrowed brow I had concentrated deeply, my mind reaching, stretching out to hers, desperately scouring my conscious for contact with hers. And what had happened? She had puked on me! I hadn't even seen it coming. Maybe I was a part-time psychic or my powers had peaked and were on the wane. Maybe I was full of crap. At the time I was definitely covered in vomit.

Michael was now dead and buried and so was the soul of the ghost, still encapsulated in the ring and so – continuing nicely with his own separate game plan – was Rambo. The ghost's bones had long been disposed of. It had been the first act of my syndicate leadership, to get them off the island and away from the likes of Noel and Alan who might have one day braved a look for themselves. The ring was now buried in Rambo's pseudo-grave along with whomever it was he had put in his coffin to give weight to his fake death. The very death he had so carefully contrived to rid himself of such tiresome burdens as paying tax, paying for goods already received and disappearing from all the people he had stitched up in the fabulous, fascinating arms dealing market. Were our lives for real? You had to try and laugh at it, the massive improbability of it all.

At night, lying in bed – another million quid ask – I had pondered on my life being a figment of someone's imagination, a play, a television show or a book. Was I a mouthpiece for some person's thoughts? It couldn't be real could it? All the things that had happened to me because of my love for *carp fishing* of all things! From vicious competition to rich fishery owner via degradation, violent acts, prison, lottery wins, holidays, drug-trips, mind-melds, Rebecca, amazing captures, contacts with the dead, contacts with the unborn via the dead, murder, suicide, inheritance… where would it all end? Had it all ended? Were my failed, naff attempts at reading Amy's mind proof of the end of my amazing story? Could I look forward to an unexceptional life from now on, one embedded in normality? Did I want one? Or did I want to carry on riding the wave of the implausible like a whacked-out surfer-dude, there for the crack, not caring if he got smashed into the ocean's depths? In answer to the original question Amy's nappies smelt real enough, the buzz from hooking monster carp felt about right as well. All emotion seemed present and correct, physically everything looked pukka. No, it was real all right. I was keeping it real. I daresay death would be real enough when it came.

Another million pound trickster. What happened after death? In Rambo's case it was straightforward enough, another life significantly less complicated, more affluent than the first. His wasn't a proper death, though. What would happen to me when I exhaled my terminal breath? I pulled a grimace as I climbed the four steps leading up to the clubhouse front door. Now was not the time to start trawling for the nth time through my giddy head for a precise answer to an age-old conundrum which I, apparently, had more insight into than most. Was there a GA? Ghosts Anonymous. A sad little group of deluded souls who reckoned they had genuinely met some.

If Rebecca had haunted my thoughts for some while after coming back from Lac Fumant on the first occasion, then the ghost, and all its incriminations seemed destined to, well, not haunt me, we had taken care of the ring as she had asked, but let's say 'live' with me forever. It felt a heavy burden to shoulder; 'Dear Deirdre. Some time ago I was visited by this ghost, no it was a ghost, honest, and it asked me to help sort out the bloke what done her in. Now, in the meantime me Missus joined the club, don't ask how, that's another letter all by itself, and this ghost then told me that the sprog wanted to be called Amy, so anyway that's what the Missus did want to call it, although she didn't know that I knew that, but in the meantime I had found this hammer and it gave me a sort of a jolt and made me remember something this mush had said to me...' and so on and so on. It wasn't something you could easily seek help about or casually drop into conversation.

I carried on through the door and into the short corridor passing other closed doors to smaller rooms until I came into the most sizeable room of the clubhouse. Oddly the room was devoid of human life so my eye fell heavily on a line of padlocked chest freezers.

"The four white elephants," I said quietly to myself and smiled wryly.

In theory they should have been brimming, bulging, bursting and bristling with bags of blended, boisterous but above all bulky boilies. But they weren't. Perhaps two at most were half-full of boilies, the rest were stuffed with cold air and frost deposits. Rather stupidly I viewed the four freezers as a barometer of my syndicate leadership. Loaded freezers would have signalled acceptance of it, whereas two virtually empty ones and the other two being as full as you would expect from a tight-arsed, non-sponsored, unemployed baiting team of two, signalled an undoubted thumbs down. As far as I was concerned full freezers equalled fulfilment. Fuck all in the freezers equalled, let's say, to give it a very bland handle, 'a certain resentment'.

I had bought the four new freezers myself as an introductory 'gift', for want of a better word, to try to placate the members and deal with my feelings of culpability for being given, because that's what it boiled down to, the whole fishery, lock, stock and functional wooden clubhouse. Their emptiness reflected how the members had viewed my gesture and therefore my standing as new syndicate leader. I had hoped, as an alternative, that it had proved the bastards were really an untrusting lot frightened of giving away their bait secrets. Who was I trying to kid? Myself, basically. Being candid, if I thought the latter was true then there was no doubting my being in denial; I was *not* a popular bloke. How could I be? Less than eight months in the syndicate, a newcomer unknown from Adam, and then – light blue touch paper and stand well back – there you are, mate, have the whole lot on a plate. Have it! Go on, it's yours! Cue such adjectives as jealousy, incredulity, bitterness, envy, spite... to name but a few. Overall it was clear there was 'a certain resentment'.

Then, just for good measure and to add to the general picture of malcontent, add a hefty dollop of apprehension; A, for the new broom and B, for the scary nuclear weaponry (i.e. Rambo, right-hand man of new syndicate leader) at its disposal. From their perspective how else *could* they feel? Who would care, you might say?

5

Fuck'em you might say but I couldn't easily say it because of how *I* felt. Sir Alex Ferguson I most obviously wasn't and it was clear to myself that the special human traits of management weren't my forte. Without Rambo to bolster and cajole me I doubt I could have coped despite Hamworthy being everything someone like myself could possibly dream of. Rambo had told me time and time again I had deserved it, earned it even, what with my dashing exposé of Michael and the fish stealing. However, mad as it might seem to an outsider I wasn't as comfortable with my new gift as I would have like to have been. I loved it, of course, I loved the financial security it gave me but me being me I couldn't accept it solely for what it was. I couldn't forget about how and why I had acquired it and I felt uneasy with the prospect of being the person who would have to deal with running it.

In the five months since I had suddenly been catapulted into fishery ownership via the powerful elastic of Michael's Will, I had sensed a 'certain resentment' from the others and the freezers had been my rather puerile – even I have to admit it now – attempt at appeasement/pacification/bribery. I should have known it was impossible to buy respect or pay off 'a certain resentment'. I had known about it not being able to pay for love or purchase grief but I was on fresh ground and another steep learning curve. It had been a knee-jerk reaction, one taken and implemented on my own a mere fortnight after taking over Hamworthy Fisheries. It had been a dumb thing to do, with hindsight, and I told Rambo it had been caused by sleep deprivation, which in turn had been caused by the bawling, milk-deprived Amy.

The fateful night of the reading of Michael's Will by the balding Mr Furlington had not been an easy one for all concerned. Before he had even started the reading there had been an underlying tension within the membership caused by Michael's death, the power vacuum it left and therefore the uncertainty it had created. You have to realise how paranoid everybody within the syndicate had become and how frightened they were of losing their places. We are talking of the best syndicate in Britain after all and anything that could alter the status quo had understandably been viewed with fear and trepidation. Much like you would view the group of the same name, come to think of it.

Although on the night nearly everyone had subscribed to the idea of Hollywood being the new owner, the unknown allegiances he might have forged must have left many with a feeling of being out on a limb. Seemingly Rambo and I, as the last two in, were undoubtedly at the toenail ends of an already dismembered, 42" inside leg. Rocky and Darren loathed us for having the temerity to breathe and wear camouflage clothing – Rambo of course, not me – but I was his mate. We were disliked by Noel and anyone else he had told for getting away with our outrageous night-time sortie on the island with boat, flippers and wetsuits. Lastly, the others distrusted us as we were new, possibly dangerous faces and had been *the first pair* to be admitted into the syndicate. Naturally none of the others knew Michael's dark secret, which in turn became *our* dark secret.

Michael's clever membership policy had made the syndicate a largely fragmented and splintered affair. His code of isolationalism, for want of a better word, bred doubt and dilemma and his autocratic style and absolute authority, backed up by rules and regulations had kept things on a very level keel. And now, suddenly, he was gone. If you were feeling exceptionally full of yourself and were up for the odd piece of pseudo-intellectualism and questionable analogy, you could liken the syndicate to any country previously run by a power-mad dictator, which all at once, for some reason or another, suddenly isn't. The ambience, therefore, on the evening of Mr Furlington's revelations, had hardly been conducive to a relaxing evening. In fact it was more akin to being as strained as a well-endowed, ex-heavyweight, now super heavyweight lifter's two-year-old jock-strap which, halfway through a world record lift, had suddenly and inexplicably been subjected to a thumper of a hard-on.

When Mr Furlington had handed Michael's entire estate to myself and then, just to give the proceedings an extra edge, had kicked out Rocky, Darren and Hollywood on the fish-nicking rap, all hell had broken loose. Rambo had busted Rocky's arm to bits after a short but violent struggle, Hollywood had broken down in tears before he could smash me in the mouth and then I had disappeared, after a mobile phone summons, without so much as a 'thanks for the fishery', to be a waste of space at the birth of my first child. All in all, to say I hadn't got off to a promising start with the remaining syndicate members was an understatement so massive it compared favourably to the pilot flying the Enola Gay over Hiroshima saying; 'Some people are going to suffer a little discomfort when I push this lever'. As to the ex-members, well you didn't need to have a degree in interpersonal relationships to suss how they felt about me. On the Richter scale of hate I was off the end of it. Luckily we had seen neither hide nor hair of any of them to date. This, rather perversely, made me worry even more because I wondered what the hell they were going to get up to and when they would get round to doing it. I was sure there would be some hateful response at some time or another. I waited for it like I waited for a run, not knowing when or even if it would eventually come, but the thought of it filling me with dreaded anticipation. It was another pressure to deal with and one I could have done without.

So, there I was, presented with this remarkable legacy of one man's vision, half elated at what was now mine but also dispirited at the negative aspects of how I had attained it. It wasn't as if I could tell them all the truth. From their perspective it must have stank and stank big-time. How bad? Try to imagine a metal dustbinful of rotting herrings, dog shit, cat vomit, a gross of cracked bad eggs, 10,000 ejaculations-worth of two-week-old semen and 5ml of Secret Agent left out in the sun on a hot day in summer. Got that? Then you lift off the lid of the bin, give it a quick stir with an old nine-iron… and add *another* 5ml of Secret Agent.

So what had I done? What cunning plan had I come up with to start to bring everyone around in a shrewd calculating contrivance to negate the circumstances that had united all the members against me? I had bought four fucking freezers; four fucking padlocks and lined them up against the wall of the largest room in the clubhouse. There you go fellows… enjoy! And, having done that and subsequently realised it hadn't been a good idea, I had crawled back into my shell and kept myself low-key and tried to pretend I wasn't the man in charge. I had let things run their own course, fished a bit and tried to act as if I was exactly the same member I had been before Mr Furlington had chucked what…? A million quid's worth of collateral at me, or was it two million? Yet another million pound question. Did anyone do postal courses in man management? Section one. *Trying to run with the hare and the hounds*. Why this is a really bad idea. Discuss.

It was a futile attempt on every front, especially the bit about trying to be as I had been beforehand. Becoming a dad had changed me for a start. The weird concept of having this thing, this child, which you loved more than your own life itself gave another altogether different perspective. The child was so dependent on you, it was real responsibility and the world seemed a much more worrying and dangerous place because of it. Maturity? I'll come back to you on that one. And then there was the ghost. Who could live through an episode in their life like I had and not be fundamentally shocked and rattled by it? Everything you had ever believed in or maybe more pertinently, *hadn't* believed, called into question. Sophie had been deeply affected by it and even Rambo, although he did his macho best to hide it, had been stunned. To the remaining members, who didn't give a toss whether I had one kid or eight of them and had no notion of the ghost, I was this jammy, fucking son-of-a-bitch who had been handed the most precious of precious gifts. They were all Gollums and I had the one fishery to bring them all (I *have* seen the films now, Sophie kept nagging…) and, apparently, in the darkness bind them. Well, I was *keeping* them in the dark, at least.

They would talk to me, when the occasion arouse, be really friendly, but it couldn't mask their dislike. It was only their fear which held them back. They knew I had the power to rip them away from what they held so very dear, hence their two-faced posturing. They didn't like me but couldn't dare risk showing it so they concealed it, or tried to, behind a wall of superficial sycophancy and false bonhomie. It was blatantly transparent to me what was going on, and no, you didn't need to be psychic to see it. There was 'a certain resentment' amongst the members as I have said and I seemed powerless to change it.

"Don't worry about it, boy," Rambo had said. "Anyone who's got anywhere in life has to put up with all that kind of old crap."

"Yeah," I had answered. "But who has got to the anywhere the way I have?"

He didn't reply.

Maybe only Alan out of them all didn't begrudge my inheritance but I tried to avoid him, or cut him short when I couldn't, because I felt sure he was going to start banging on about how the ghost had murdered Michael and I simply couldn't face it. He soon got the message and I managed to successfully alienate the one member who didn't despise me within a couple of months. Not bad, eh?

I heard a toilet flush. It explained the empty room.

Today though, was my first big move as syndicate supremo, today was the day when, at last, I started to grip the bull by the horns. Over the last month or so I had come around to Rambo's line of thinking and today was show time. He had kept going on and on to me how, given the circumstances, I was not going to be Mr Instant Wonderful Syndicate Leader. Accept it, had been his advice and in time with solid leadership I might earn grudging respect.

"Yeah, right," I had said.

"Look, boy," Rambo had stated with a touch of exasperation in his voice. "You can't keep beating yourself up about how you got the place. They hate me as well, I'm getting a fee from their subs remember. You see it's *yours*! Fuck the others! If they don't like it they can fuck off out of it! You won't get many go believe me. Anyone in any position of authority who has to make decisions will be unpopular. Fact of life. Anyone who inherits large amounts of cash or anything that is worth something is going to be loathed by someone. Big green-eyed monster, fact of life number two. You haven't got to do anything here. Keep it ticking along as before, same rules, same fishery management and the place will look after itself. The only spanner in the works will be whether we can keep a lid on the place publicity-wise what with our three reprobates now loose canons in the rest of the carp fishing world. The only thing you have to address is the replacement of them and Michael and maybe just *one* sensible rule change."

Rambo had sidled up to me and clasped my shoulder with his massive right hand. I had felt my flesh compress and knew internal bleeding was occurring that would manifest itself in a nice blue-green bruise.

"I mean, come on, boy! Have you landed on your feet smelling of roses, or what? The best carp fishery in Britain, beautiful, healthy baby girl and beautiful partner plus on paper you're a millionaire! What could be better than that? Sure there's a bit of resentment, if Hollywood had been given the place there'd still have been some, it's the way we humans are made. Keep it all on the rails, be firm but fair with them all and soon they'll have forgotten about Michael or worrying about Matt Williams getting mega-lucky. When they keep hauling in those fifties and when the pit does a sixty or a new British record they won't care if George Bush, Saddam Hussein or Mickey Mouse is running the syndicate."

I had nodded. "Mickey Mouse. Whoa! Frightening."

Rambo had nodded. "Globalisation pirates and international brainwashers the Disney mob! Anyone who can persuade the world it's cool to wait in line *and* pay top dollar for the experience, *plus* convincing you at the same time to buy into their corporate dream of stripping your wallet via overpriced food and Chinese-made merchandise really *is* frightening."

"Pay per queue," I had said rather pleased with the coining of the phrase. "Oh… One more thing," I had added.

"What's that?" he had asked.

"What if *I* catch the first sixty or smash the British record?"

"Then *I'll* fucking kill *you* and you won't have anything to worry about." And he had laughed and turned away.

"One other last thing," I had said.

"What?" he had said.

"What if I come back and haunt you?"

Rambo gave me a menacing glare. "Even keel, steady-as-she-goes, replace the four missing members, one sensible rule change. Okay?" He had said while chopping a flat palm slightly downward through the air.

I heard a door open and was rushed into present reality. I turned to face Hamworthy Fisheries' Lieutenant Rambo, resplendent in full camouflage regalia.

He gave me a look of mock astonishment. "You're here, then! Bit of a shock. Not been abducted, then?"

I rolled my eyes. "No. No alien abduction yet."

This was Rambo's latest running line of enquiry, the one that had superseded the Rebecca one. The one about whether I had had sex with her after heroically proving everyone wrong having caught the mind-meld fifty mirror at Lac Fumant (1st time) an hour earlier.

"You could have been abducted and to hide it they've wiped your memory," Rambo theorized with a look of 'gotcha there, pal' on his face.

"Well… yes, obviously." I conceded.

"It's the last thing you need to have happen to you, then you've pretty much got the full set," Rambo explained.

I waved a hand at him. "Huh! There are loads of things I haven't experienced. Like Hollywood's two stunning looking, lap dancing, ex-international gymnasts, who were also bisexual nymphomaniacs, for a start," I informed him.

"Abnormal things. Things of myth and legend, things the rest of the world can't prove even exist. Those kind of things," Rambo explained. "Not humdrum, mundane things like a ménage-a-trois with stunning looking, lap dancing, ex-international gymnasts, who were also bisexual nymphomaniacs."

I looked at Rambo from underneath lifted eyebrows. "You're talking bollocks, you know," I said in mock gravity.

He laughed. "Would you have ever said that to me when we first met, when I first asked you to come in on a bait with me at the old SS syndicate?"

It was my turn to laugh. "Christ no! I'd have been too frightened."

Rambo looked out one of the windows and avoided my eyes. He grunted and pushed air down his nose. "We've been through a lot together over these last few years…" his words faded away and left a hanging silence.

"Tell me about it," I concurred.

"… And on it goes," he added. "Right then," he said sounding business-like, his few seconds of retrospection over. "Let's get the table and chairs sorted so we can look through the CVs of these prospective syndicate carpers."

Today was show time, all right. I would review, along with Rambo, the list of possible members who had been forwarded by our reliable bait-mate, Pup. Once we had done that we would send out four letters asking each angler to come and be interviewed at my house, just like Michael had interviewed us. I would also propose a new rule change to go out with all the existing members' renewal application forms. It was a new era and I was at last getting my head out of the sand, or at least having it yanked out by Rambo, and getting on with it. At least I should have four blokes who should be pretty happy with my style of leadership.

Chapter 2

Rambo dragged the large table out from its usual corner-hugging, space-saving position and placed two of the clubhouse's tubular-legged plastic chairs under it. The last time the table had been used, to my knowledge at least, was when Mr Furlington had broadcast Michael's Will to the Hamworthy syndicate members. His briefcase and sheaf of legal papers had been neatly and precisely placed on the very chipped and scored surface that Rambo was now giving a cursory wipe with a camouflaged sleeve propelled by a formidably muscled forearm.

"How many candidates has Pup put up then?" I asked. What the hell did I know? I was simply the bloke who supposedly owned and ran this whole thing.

"Six," came the reply. "When I went down to his house to pick up our last lot of bait he gave me the CVs, as it were, of these lucky boys. He asked them all to write a paragraph or two by way of an introduction. A sort of 'why you should let me into your syndicate' piece."

Now it was Rambo's turn to lay some papers on the table, only his manner was somewhat less dignified than Mr Furlington's. Rambo plonked a folder of A4 sized paper onto the table with considerable force. Little flecks of dust glittered in the sunlight as they were wafted up into the air on the draught caused by the folder. Sidetracked, I wondered if I ought to hire in a cleaner, or even better, a private detective who could fingerprint the four white fridges to find out who was using them so I knew who *wasn't* using them. My eyes re-focused from the dancing dust particles and I stared at the folder. Four from six? But maybe it would be *none* from six if we thought they were all unsuitable. Inwardly I shook my head. Pup wasn't daft, he knew what type of carp angler we were looking for and his ever-growing bait business must have been supplying him with plenty of possible candidates.

Just to go back a little, it had been Rambo who'd had the forethought to enlist Pup's help in filling the void left by Michael, Hollywood, Darren and Rocky. I had still been marooned in a world of bemusement, guilt and insecurity while Rambo had moved on into a world of practicalities, pragmatism and picking up some more pop-ups. Michael had trusted Pup with our membership aspirations before qualifying them himself, although perhaps with hindsight he might not have been so keen if he had to live his peculiar life again. (Reincarnation? Don't even go there! Die, come back as a carp – one that gets caught by anglers – die again, reincarnate back to a human once more and tell all the animal welfare activists you truthfully couldn't feel a thing! *If* you could remember. Rather inconveniently for such theorists you rarely could).

"How come you were so on the case to start thinking about getting new members?" I had asked him when he had told me what he had in mind to do.

The reply had been quick-fire and without inhibition. "Because I'm on ten percent of the annual subscriptions. That's how come, boy!"

"How mercenary," I had said rather haughtily, half-joking and half-meaning it. Deep down I knew he didn't need the money but I wanted him to have it. Christ, he had baled me out enough times.

"It's what I used to do," Rambo had reminded me. "Only getting hold of a few punters' names is a lot easier than fighting a war for someone."

"I can imagine," I had said truthfully.

Who needed war? I had thought rather ruefully having been led into contemplating such a horrid concept by Rambo's words. The answer was as grim as the notion – rather a lot of people – when you stopped and analysed it for at least a second. There was always somebody somewhere trying to blow up somebody somewhere else and each time one succeeded, the other re-doubled their efforts to do the same back to the people who had started it in the first place. In today's world, war was less likely to be whole nations pitched against each other as in the past, but would manifest itself in the form of small groups of terrorists reeking havoc on civilian targets. In long-standing disputes, I could imagine the original reason for the violence easily being forgotten, and the spiral of evil deeds becoming a self-perpetuating force fuelled by hatred and revenge. Retaliation, tit for tat violence, the taking of an eye for an eye all phrases for the cycle of violence. Still, on the up side, Rambo had done all right out of it financially, and by way of his success in both fighting and supplying the tools of destruction, so had I. Especially when I was gulag-wise and he was squaring the mortgage for me. Every cloud has a silver lining, even the clouds of war.

I had asked myself if anyone would want revenge against me? In fact I still asked it every day, as I waited for the run of revenge to arrive from the expelled members. It only took another one-second analysis. I could think of at least half-a-dozen off the cuff, all people who had been distinctly upset with me and all of them carp anglers. Carpwars. I ask you! The names rattled into my head with the ease of machine gun bullets on a similar mission.

"I bet Pup was shocked when you first told him Michael had left the lot to me, wasn't he?" I said as I parked my arse on one of the plastic chairs. It was like being back in school assembly.

"You could say that," said Rambo shoehorning himself into the other. "He couldn't believe Michael had been so stupid, to zip himself up like he had, with the cooker belting away."

I gave Rambo a wry smile. "Bloody hell! What would he think of the truth?"

Rambo gave a small shake of his head. "Don't. What with Michael's death and Hollywood's unfathomable fish stealing scam I could almost smell his brain going into meltdown trying to work out the reasons."

"Blimey!" I exclaimed laughing out loud. "If you could smell anything other than boilie flavours in his house, it *must* have been bad!"

Rambo smiled. "You really ought to go and see him you know. You haven't seen him for over a year. It's always me who goes and picks up our bait and besides, in another two weeks he'll be married. If it wasn't for *him*, *you* wouldn't be sitting pretty on the best syndicate in Britain."

I avoided Rambo's earnest stare. "I'll see him at the wedding. I'll have a nice long chat with him there," I said trying to dismiss the matter.

Rambo was right, I should have been to see Pup but what with Sophie being pregnant, us getting into the syndicate, then me getting the syndicate and Amy being born I had never quite managed it. And now he was getting married. Why did I find the concept of Pup getting married so incredulous? I guess it was the whole idea of this stinky bait-nerd having an interest outside that of the mixing and rolling and flavouring of boiled baits which totally threw me. I'd had Pup's whole existence revolving around boilies to the absolute exclusion of all else. Secretly I was flabbergasted he could actually find a woman, a real live one, barking enough to marry him, find him sexually attractive and, obviously, er… have sex with him. But not necessarily in that specific order. Times have changed.

Then again perhaps I was missing something. My cynical mind turned to the possibility it was a marriage of convenience. Now there was a thought. Perhaps she was an asylum seeking refugee or an impoverished Eastern European who, having been used to working in a freezing sweat shop – a nice oxymoron if ever there was one – was only too glad to ship out and wed Pup. A mad, boilie-making, one-man freak show, true enough, but a mad, *Western*, boilie-making, one-man freak show with *assets*. Namely, a mad, one-man boilie-making business and a multi-flavour impregnated property. It could turn a girl's head. Well, it would do the minute she stepped through the door and a few molecules of the house's uniquely charged air wafted up her Slavic nostrils.

"What's she like, this girl he's marrying?" I eventually asked as I flicked distractedly through the six CVs. On the top one I read the words, 'although catching carp is of extreme importance to me, carp welfare and protecting the environment are never usurped by the former. In all my years as a carp angler…' Fucking liar, I thought, moving my eyes up from the writing to meet Rambo's and engage his answer to my question.

"I've never actually met her. She's never been around when I've been at Pup's," Rambo admitted. "Apparently she's a local girl, late twenties, blonde hair and well fit." Rambo's voiced turned slightly sceptical. "At least so *Pup* says." Rambo's voice changed again and was upbeat. "Mind you, she can gobble cock like a hungry dog eating a saveloy *and* get the whole lot in, in one go!"

"Christ!" I sneered. " Did Pup tell you that as well?"

"Nah," admitted Rambo. "I just like putting women on an unobtainable plateau of perfection. She definitely does help roll his bait, you know."

"Rolls his sausage, does she?" I enquired sarcastically.

"No! She really does help him roll his bait. I reckon he's only marrying her for her female pheromones."

"'Marrying her for her female pheromones'. Well that's a euphemism I've not heard before." I said caustically. I stopped and rubbed my chin. "How on *earth* did he ever get to meet her? He hardly ever leaves his boilie palace does he?"

"Oh, he told me how he met her," Rambo assured me.

"Come on then, let's hear it. I could do with a laugh. Where was it, at a throwing stick convention? The annual catapult manufacturers' summer fair?" I demanded.

"You're a few steps too far on in the process, boy. He met her in Tesco. He had a trolley-full of eggs as he trundled up and down the aisles and she was obviously the kind of girl who took an interest in other people's purchases. While he lingered at the meat section, paralysed by the choice between a joint of silverside and a piece of rump steak, she appeared alongside. Their trolleys touched, static electricity was discharged and chemistry permeated the air. She recommended the rump because she'd had a bit last week and it was well tender. She looked into his eyes, asked why he had a trolley full of eggs and bingo! A relationship was hatched!" Rambo gave me a silly grin and shifted his eyebrows away from his eyes.

"So she *does* eat meat! 'Hatched'. The eggs. Very good!" I said, giving Rambo a ripple of applause. "They met in *Tesco*! And they say romance is dead."

"No, but the fucking cow which donated the bit of rump is," Rambo assured me deadpan. "The one that gave the silverside is still in intensive care," he added.

"Does she smoke?" I asked. I had no idea why.

"Only when she's on fire," Rambo stated dryly. He continued. "Yes. She does, I can remember Pup saying he was worried about nicotine getting into his mixes. Yeah, that's right, he made a joke about it saying that she's similar to him in respect that she rolls her own as well. Melissa the Rizla Queen, I'll call her."

It was my turn to be dry. "If Queen Melissa rolls as many fags as he rolls bloody boilies she'll be dead from lung cancer by Christmas!"

While Rambo chortled at my little joke I allowed my eyes to roam back down onto the CV I had read from before; 'Although I am a well-known angler, a name as such, I can assure you of my complete discretion when it comes to the publicising of the fish I'm sure to catch from your wonderful fishery…' Pass the sick bucket. I flipped over the CV to see who it was. Holy shit! Five out of six, no messing!

"Did you know *he* was applying to join," I spluttered, chucking the small wad of papers to Rambo.

He nodded, laughing. "And?"

"No way! That prick! I can't stand him even though I don't know him and haven't ever met him!"

"Pup reckons he's okay, he just comes across poorly in his articles. A bit 'God's gift to carp angling'."

I was not impressed and my face must have reflected my resolution. "God's gift to bullshit, more like!" I said spitting the words out with venom.

"Bin him, then?" Rambo asked.

"Bin the bastard!" I told him emphatically, the power of my position coursing through my body.

Rambo screwed up the papers belonging to the person of my, I suppose, illogical hatred, into a ridiculously tiny ball and plopped it into the metal bin a few yards to his right.

"Feel good?" he enquired. I nodded back enthusiastically. "See. On a personal whim you've wiped out the entire aspirations and hopes of a carp angler."

I shrugged. "Well in his case, fucking good job!"

Rambo gave me a 'thumbs up'. "Good, boy! *Now* you're starting to run the syndicate."

The pair of us spent the rest of the morning chatting about this, that and the other while occasionally getting to grips with the task in hand of picking four punters for interview. One of them was to be Pup's best man at the upcoming wedding and I wondered how Pup would feel if I denied his mate a place given the circumstances. Rambo had been spot on. If it hadn't have been for Pup I wouldn't be the grand owner of the Hamworthy Fisheries Syndicate. As it transpired, fortunately, Pup's best man, Steve, seemed a decent sort of bloke, had family responsibilities and a good job, much like three others from the remaining five. The odd one out was the unlucky candidate who was much younger, being only in his very early twenties, and was single. It was this fact, rather than his age alone, which put the nails in his coffin. Without the ties of a family he might have a lot more disposable time and although I didn't particularly want to mirror Michael's style of leadership – killing women not being one of my hobbies – I did want to maintain the pit's lack of fishing pressure as much as I could.

To be honest if someone had told me a pit, with the size of carp in it and costing as much as it did to be a member, could remain as relatively lightly fished as Hamworthy was, I would have called them a liar. Yet, I had seen the evidence first hand as an ordinary member and now as the owner. Whatever I thought of Michael as a person, his meticulous weeding out of prospective members had been an unprecedented success in terms of the desired outcome. I desperately wanted to try and carry on his work in that respect at least. Anyway, it meant the youngster got the flick along with Mr Famous Carp Angler (in his head) and the six became four. Provided they came across okay in the upcoming interview my syndicate would be back to full strength.

Naturally, on another whim, I could have decided *not* to fill the spaces. It was an option but Rambo had pursued the vacancies via Pup while I was stuck with my head in the sand and who was I to deprive him of his ten percent? More pertinently, who was I to deprive myself of ninety percent of £5000 (my cut of four new memberships @ £1250 a throw – come on keep up) plus the interest on four new 1st deposits (4%

approx of £10K per annum). The spondulicks probably had something to do with my decision.

You see, I had more money now than I had ever had, but circumstances had changed. It was *my* turn to contribute and somehow the thought of letting around 5K disappear seemed mad. Coupled with Rambo's actions, my wanting to repay him for the past and keeping up my financial side of things for Sophie meant losing four members was a non-starter. Call me a carp fishing capitalist if you like, I don't care, I can fit into the crowd and it's quite a commercial crowd believe me!

Money opens doors, particularly in education, and Sophie had already contemplated sending Amy to Benenden at Christ knows what per term when she was old enough. *And* she had joined the most expensive gym in the area a couple of months back, in order, as she had put it, 'to get my figure back'. I had asked her what the figure was to get her figure back but she had just told me to go figure it out for myself. I had said; '40 - 24 - 34'. She had said; 'Dream on, I'm a silicon-free zone, go check out your adolescent fantasies on Television XXX'. When the icy hand of reason grips you, a woman's icy hand of reason, there's little point fighting it.

Let me quickly explain about the gym. The gym was one of a few symptoms indicative of an interesting development in Sophie and mine's relationship. Basically, what it boiled down to was the spending of money after a radical shift in philosophy. Whereas before, prior to my gaining the syndicate, it had been her mother who had won the lottery and ladled a nice little lump of it our way, now I, as an individual, had since been ladled an even bigger lump by Michael. He had left Hamworthy to Matthew Williams and nobody else.

Although as couples go we were very secure about money, it all being in joint accounts with either to sign – it was 'our' money rather than either 'mine' or 'hers' – I had always been very aware of the past discrepancy in contribution. I had been in prison and earning nought, getting by thanks to mortgage man Rambo and the continuing popularity of war in its many and differing forms. When, almost immediately after I had been released, Sophie's mum had become an overnight millionaire. Thanks to her generosity we had suddenly become well off but it had certainly not been down to anything I had done. More to the point it had not been down to anything or anybody connected to *me* by a bloodline. It had been *her* mum who had given us the money and that was the crux of the matter.

Consequently, in due course, Sophie had permitted the two of us a small indulgence, a little spend-up to celebrate our new wealth. It had manifested itself in her spending spree on clothes and my first trip with Rambo to Lac Fumant, accompanied by loads of new tackle purchased before the off. The rest had been tucked away into a now very healthy joint account. I had been more than happy with this state of affairs and although I had promised to try and build up my electrical business I had regarded the nest egg, rather presumptuously I guess, as my 'peace of mind fund'. It would give us, or in truth in my head, give me, security, freedom from pressure of work and a long leash in terms of going fishing.

Sophie had been insistent on not eating into the capital and was determined not to sponge more money off her mum, hence her attempts at trying to get me to build up my electrical work and her decision to carry on working. When she had became pregnant and it had corresponded with me getting the nod to get into Hamworthy, she had only agreed to let me have the joining money if I promised to pay it back from the business. Although it was our money in law and I had equal rights – either to sign as I mentioned earlier – Sophie called the shots because of the nature of the way it had arrived into our joint account. Being the honest, fair-minded gem of a lady she was, she had put equal constraints on her own spending as she had put on mine. In fact to be categorical about it she had let me get away with far more than she had ever allowed herself. There had never been a chance of her saying; 'Well I lent him around four grand to get in the syndicate so I'm going to spend four grand on myself'. She was too whole and self-less for such childishness, too responsible, too decent. I, for my part, could never have been reckless with the money because I owed her too much, for all she had put up with in the past. However, now things had changed big-time and the goalposts had been dug up and moved to the middle of the rugby pitch.

Her mum had become a millionaire overnight and to all intents and purposes so had I. I wasn't as cash rich, she had won nearly two million after all, but this was simply because the bulk of my inheritance had the wealth tied up in the land and pit itself which comprised Michael's estate. Whatever, I was a millionaire all the same. The amount of money in ready cash of which I had suddenly become the custodian still ran into six figures, not including the huge wad of 1st deposits, the interest from which, was paid back annually into the main account where the ready cash was stored. Of course there was also the not unsubstantial amount of three 1st deposits becoming lost deposits. These had belonged to the expelled Hollywood, Rocky and Darren and therefore, as the rules clearly stated, their initial £2500 signing-on fee had been forfeited. Another £7500 back into the main account with another £10000 soon to be winging its way back courtesy of the four new members.

Then there were the annual fees, twenty members, less Rambo and myself; eighteen times £1250 equalled a thumping £22500 income. Mr Ten Percent took his lieutenant's fee and I was still earning a good wage for doing not a lot. In any case I still had the option to sell the lot in five years if I desired, if I wanted to 'cash in my chips'! Mr Furlington had said so, so there! To put it bluntly, I was fucking laughing. Or would be if I could stop counting my guilt and start counting the dosh.

This rush of money from my side had suddenly freed Sophie from her self-imposed austerity and if the truth was known, the deep psychological effects of the ghost and becoming a mother had also contributed hugely. With ample money available to her, although legally 'ours' but in the unspoken view of us both more 'hers', and not feeling duty bound to save it due to *my* money, she let herself go slightly. In her mind we had clearly passed the point where she needed to be as frugal as she had previously insisted. While I remained stupefied by my negative thoughts of how I had acquired my inheritance and how I was going to deal with running it, Sophie had no such qualms. Something in her mind clicked, undoubtedly caused by a combination of a ghost, a baby, a double windfall, post natal whatever and a regular monthly period, and she started to spend some chunks of the money how many would have from the second the cheque from her mum had cleared.

Although her release came from many quarters the most powerful, shackle-breaking one was the demise of the young woman who had become the ghost. She had been in the prime of her life and suddenly it had been snuffed out by Michael's horrific act of barbarism. In Sophie's mind, she had told me it many, many times while we had laid in bed and talked and talked and talked about our dark secret. It had moved her incredibly. One mortal life. It was all we got and although the premise of an afterlife for some left a huge vertigo-inducing hole of unanswerable questions to fall into, this one theme shone brightly in Sophie's head. (Ironically she sounded like Rebecca had when she had visited her poorly best friend and was hinting at seduction.) One life, one go at it, one chance to seize the day and make the most of it. That was her mission and as if to underline the precious nature of life there was our new contribution to it, Amy, our dearest daughter for whom nothing was too good. 'I wonder if she'll end up getting spoilt?' I had asked myself. It was a rhetorical question.

So Sophie's slant on the world had changed, the beauty of it being we could now live for the day and still have money set aside for the future. I gladly let her spend what she wanted, she deserved it. Firstly she had indulged herself in a new car on the vague pretence of the new one being far more child-friendly and having a better crash rating than the old one, which was two years old. I say 'pretence' which is unfair because the car *was* better than the old one for the reasons I've said, but how much better? It's all a game of self-kidology and nearly everyone alive is susceptible to it. It's like buying new rods, a new TV, anything, in fact, which replaces a perfectly serviceable bit of kit you already own. You convince yourself that the new product will be so much better than the old one and you strive to find the reasons why it will be so much better. Most of the time the actual differences in the real world, as opposed to the brochure, are small but they all help reinforce the ultimate reason. And what is the ultimate reason? The ultimate reason is purchasing pleasure. Buying something new makes you feel good and when it's a case of cash up front with no nasty downer of a credit card bill or loan interest rate to hit you once the euphoria has gone, it's even better. Money burns a hole in most people's pockets; surplus money has a little oxy-acetylene pack on its back with a large blowtorch blazing away at them. Sophie's willpower-forged denial had lined our pockets with an asbestos mat but now both were gone. Fate, it was a long time since I had thought hard about fate, not since I was outside Rebecca's bedroom door, had created the conditions for Sophie to dispense with asbestos.

So, initially she had bought the car, no end of things for Amy and loads of luxury goods for the home. Then, gradually returning from zombie-land as Amy, at last, started to sleep the night, Sophie turned to thinking a little about herself and her appearance. The loss-of-sleep, haggard, still-in-pyjamas-at-lunchtime look went out the window and the new refreshed Sophie joined the swanky gym and bought a multitude of quality designer training clothes to look great while she exercised. And she did look great. Her body soon shifted from its slightly saggy state to that of a woman, a fit woman, in her late twenties. Sophie would go to the gym during the day, sometimes in the evening, up to three times a week and I could tell she revelled in her new pastime and the determination to live her life to the full.

Health and vitality radiated from her. Her life force became even more prevalent than it had before. It was stronger than when she had put up with my mad battle against Watt, stronger than her wait for me while I was in prison, stronger than during her arduous birth of Amy. She had always been vivacious, feisty even, but now she had come to terms with a part of the dark secret all her positives were magnified.

When she was at the gym I would do the honours looking after Amy most of the time. If I could fight off the grandparents that is, Sophie's mum (her dad had died long ago) and my mum and dad were all keen to look after her. If it coincided with me wanting to go fishing I let them have her, naturally enough, but she had been born in October and we were only into the middle of February so my fishing hadn't been much of a factor. Besides I could really try and get inside her little head when it was only the two of us, or not, as was the case, and get covered in puke.

All in all it was a wonderful life for us both; plenty of dosh, plenty of leisure time and minimal inconvenience in terms of duties to be done. The only shadow was the one left by certain aspects of the dark secret, the negative thoughts I had concerning the syndicate and when the blow of retribution from Rocky or one of the others would come and in what manner. My inheritance had set the scales of our relationship to a more equal balance and Sophie was thriving in the new freedom and philosophy the situation had allowed her to give herself. Looking on from the side as she emerged from the trauma of a difficult birth into motherhood, via the knowledge of the brutalised woman who had been the ghost, it was obvious she had become more aware of mortality. The lesson that death could pounce on you at any time and from any angle, even from the most unlikely of places, was a timely one. But whereas most were in no position to change their outlook we had the opportunity thanks to money and our good health.

As I sat next to Rambo, a decision made on the four prospective members, a sensible amendment to the rules safely made and all the old members renewal forms ready for posting, I felt as if, at last, I was getting my head around running the syndicate. I would take Rambo's advice, steer the steady path and let the capture of large carp weave their magic.

Eventually we were back to talking about Pup's wedding.

"He's not having a stag night, you know," Rambo informed me. "I don't know why, he just doesn't want one. It's going to be a civil ceremony for close family and friends and then an evening reception at the Beauport Park Hotel."

"I know. I *did* get an invitation." I pointed out.

"Did you know some of the Lac Fumant gang are coming?" said Rambo smugly. He knew I didn't.

"No!" I exclaimed in total surprise. "How come they know Pup?"

"It's all your fault, boy," Rambo informed me.

"My fault! How can it be my fault?"

"When you caught the mind-meld mirror on a pop-up…" Rambo intimated, winding his hand in a circular motion.

"…They all wanted to know what the bait was," I finished for him.

"Exactly!" Rambo confirmed.

"How'd they find out?" I asked.

"It was a catching bait and they were fucking carp anglers. They'd find out somehow wouldn't they?" Rambo teased.

"I don't see how," I scoffed.

"Well, just between you and me… *I* told them."

"*You* told them!" I parroted, somewhat shocked. "You've kept that quiet for a long time."

"I told Alistair anyway and you know how he can gas. It wasn't until the second trip, in any case," Rambo added by way of an explanation.

"A bit unlike you to be so loose-mouthed even if it was a bit late in the day." I said, giving Rambo a sideways look.

"Yeah. I suppose it was. I was probably feeling a bit generous." Rambo paused. "You know, what with the place fishing so poorly, it didn't make much difference what bait you were using."

"I hope you read that it's strictly formal morning suit for the ceremony," I said changing the subject.

"I know. I *did* get an invitation." Rambo pointed out.

"It'll be the first time I've ever seen you *sans* camouflage!" I was the smug one now.

Rambo's face clouded and his eyes averted mine.

"You can't not come," I informed him.

"Oh, I'll be there, boy. Don't you worry about that."

Chapter 3

"Good morning, Steve," I said to the man who was going to be Pup's best man in three days' time.

Rambo, who had answered the doorbell when it had rung while I had remained seated behind the dining room table, showed Steve to a chair. I noticed Steve's comprehending take of the scene before him and tried to ignore it. Amy, who was cradled on my lap guzzling warm milk, easily overlooked Steve and concentrated exclusively on devouring the bottle's contents. The little slurping noises she made punctuated an awkward silence while the three of us tried to get our heads around the unlikely scenario I had allowed to happen. Not one of us, including myself, had thought a five-month-old infant would play any part in an interview, the purpose of which, was to pass judgement on the applicant wanting to join the country's ultimate carp fishing syndicate. Rambo, who had spent his life dealing with unlikely scenarios, usually of the intensely ultra-violent kind, shoved a finger in an auditory canal and waggled it. Little babies unnerved him, I could tell, sub-machine-guns and rocket launchers, not a problem, bitsy little bub-bubs – a different matter altogether.

At last one of us managed to snap out of the all-embracing bemusement.

Steve gave me a knowing smile. "Morning, Matt," he said. "I can remember doing all that a few years back."

This *wasn't* how I had envisaged my first Hamworthy interview.

"I've got four lads coming over for an interview today," I had informed Sophie at breakfast.

"Fine. I'm going to Bluewater with Sarah all day to get a new outfit for the wedding. Remember me telling you?"

"Oh, yeah, that's right," I had fibbed, having totally forgotten. "Good, that'll work out fine. Me and Rambo can have the place to ourselves…"

"I'm not taking, Amy," she had interjected with a statement of fact. "It's a long way in the car, none of the stores are especially buggy-friendly and she'll be much better off staying here with you. A bit of one-on-one with her daddy will be nice for her. And for you."

"Except it won't be one-on-one because I've got these four lads coming over for an interview," I had reminded her with a hint of exasperation.

"So?"

"I can't look after her *and* do an interview," I had explained fitfully. To try and emphasise the point I had then gone into a rambling monologue. "Oh yes, let me tell you a bit about the syndicate, pass that clean nappy, it's about twenty-nine acres in size, hold on while I change it, you might want to pinch your nostrils together... it's an old gravel extraction pit, hold on she's still crying, she's probably hungry, now look the milk needs to be made from water where the kettle's been boiled only once because the evaporation of water when steam is made from boiling can cause an over-concentration of minerals, and stuffed full of bloody great carp, yes four level spoons of milk powder in the bottle, many of which are over forty pounds."

Sophie had been unimpressed. "It's called multi-tasking, dear. Ask any woman, she'll tell you all about it." Sophie had drunk the last remains of her tea. "And *don't* let Rambo hold Amy. The big lummox is too heavy-handed."

"So, I'll look after her *and* do the interviews, then?" I had said to make sure I had got it right.

Sophie gave me a kiss on the cheek and wrinkled her nose. "Absolutely."

I gave Steve a rather self-conscious smile. "How many have you got? She's our first one."

Steve's eyes glazed over and a wistful look appeared on his face. "Four now, the last one turned out to be three which was a bit of a shock to say the least. All four are boys, the eldest is aged eight and the triplets are six." Steve's head lowered to the floor and he gave it a slow and gentle shake. "It's like Armageddon in our house. You can't see the carpet for toys, there's constant fighting and meal times are like a chimps' tea party." He raised his head back up to make eye contact with me. "A chimps' tea party where the keeper has secretly laced their drinks with amphetamines." He threw both of his hands away in a gesture of mild despair. "As for trying to get all of them to bed... well, it's about as difficult as trying to get all of them up in the morning. At night you need a baseball bat to subdue them and in the morning a scaffold pole to prise them off the mattress. Life is a constant battle to get everything done and cleared away before the next instalment ruins what you've just achieved and you have to start all over again." Steve turned his attention to Rambo. "And she wonders why I like to go fishing."

I was still recovering from hearing Steve and his partner had done three at once and could only wonder at the state of permanent pandemonium prevalent at his property. "Triplets!" I cried. "Were you on some sort of fertility treatment?"

"No, amazingly enough. It was all perfectly natural, or rather *unnatural* if you ask me." Steve confirmed.

"Blimey!" I conceded. "How do you account for three at once?"

Steve puffed out his cheeks. I could tell he had given this one a lot of consideration over the years. "I put it down to turbo-charged sperm, freak multi-ovulation and bad luck. Don't get me wrong, I love the boys to bits but it's been horrifically hard work. I even checked the marriage certificate to see if there was any hidden clause that would allow me to sue the wife. She tried to tell me there was no way I could sue her for producing three beautiful, healthy boys. I told her it wasn't so much what I'd gained so much as what I'd lost. My life for a start." Steve looked rueful. "I'm only joking but many a true word said in jest, eh? Can you imagine getting up in the night to feed *three* of them? If God had meant me to feed three babies at once he'd have given me an extra arm *and* taken away my sense of smell so it wasn't so bad when it all came out the other end. And that was just the start of it! As they grow older different things become more problematical, as one issue wanes then another pops its head up for you to contend with. It's a continuous battle of attrition, I can tell you. I like to think of it as trying to keep the lid down on a huge suitcase full of the nuts and bolts of life; clothes, meals, washing, cleaning, earning money, being at one place at one time and another place at another time, all those kind of mundane chores, and they're all trying to burst out because they've been placed on top of two massive, compressed springs. Lose concentration or stop pushing down hard enough and the whole lot gets twanged all over the place and it can take days to get it all back in and under some semblance of control!"

I blinked over wide eyes. Just doing Amy, a single little soul, had been hard for us as first time parents, but *four*, three the same age, was serious graft.

"Do you know," Steve continued warming to the big theme of his life, "originally she even tried to tell me that if I was all right getting up to hit three runs in the middle of the night, I should be perfectly fine getting up to feed three of my offspring at a similar time. Firstly I told her I'd *never* managed to get three runs in a night and when that didn't wash, I told her she should have the boys operated on to have their vocal chords removed and replaced by bite alarm speakers. *Then* I might respond a bit better. As I explained to her, I simply never heard the little mites when they were crying." Steve touched his nose twice with his index finger and surreptitiously looked left and right. "Selective deafness," he whispered, "even when pretending to be asleep, is a wonderful thing." His face turned into a scowl. "Trouble is, the bloody kids themselves have cottoned on to it and choose to ignore what they don't want to hear. Must be genetic. Still, there won't be any more, I'm pencilled in to have the snip." Steve suddenly looked embarrassed. "Um… Not really what we're here to talk about. Sorry," he said in a stilted manner.

I laughed. I had taken to him already. "Have you got your speech ready for the big day?"

Steve seemed relieved to be moving away from talking about his large family, especially now that he had let it slip about his snip. "Pretty much. Most of the people going are connected to carp fishing so there's plenty of common ground, which should, in theory at least, make life easier."

"What's this Melissa like?" I asked eagerly.

Steve looked at both of us and his tongue quickly came out and flicked across his top lip. His relief had gone in an instant. "She's very nice…" he began.

"Never mind all that!" I said sensing a fudge. "What's she *really* like?"

Steve gathered himself for a more truthful answer while I lifted Amy up to be winded by facing her over my shoulder and rubbing her tiny back with my right hand.

"She is very attractive," he admitted. "She's very much in the mould of your average bloke's stereotypical looker; dyed blonde hair, nice face, good body and big tits. She's late twenties, smokes roll-ups, believe it or not and she's not what you would call classy, but to be honest I don't think she cares one way or the other. But, and it's a big but, in my humble estimation she *does* suffer from what I would regard as a rather peculiar mental kink."

Steve paused and looked agitated. He was probably not helped by the way Rambo and I were like a couple of scrap yard dogs straining on their leashes, eager to rip apart the new revelation that was going to have to be tossed their way. He knew he was in a conversational cul-de-sac and the only way out was to tell all.

Steve rushed over his next few words. "Now, don't get me wrong when I say this or take it the wrong way. I'm not trying to offend anyone here in any sense whatsoever," he blurted speedily. An expression of disquiet came over his face. "Christ, I'm digging my own grave here. Look, here it is, right. Melissa, *genuinely*, *honestly* finds carp anglers and carp angling sexually stimulating and exciting."

There was an even larger awkward silence than there had been ten minutes ago.

I held back my instinctive response. My instinctive, sarcastic response to try and wind Steve up by saying something like; 'And what's so odd about that, then?' Instead I looked at Rambo who looked back at me and then the pair of us turned our cumulative gaze on Steve who was going paler by the second.

Rambo ran an index finger underneath his nose, once forward and once back and put his hand down. "As much as I'd like *not* to say it, because of the implication, and as much as I wish what you say *was* true… you *cannot be fucking* serious!" Rambo immediately held up a hand and mimed a 'sorry' towards me. If Amy started to eff and blind before saying 'mumum', Uncle Rambo could take the rap for it.

Release temporarily flooded through Steve as he realised he wasn't going to get hung, drawn and quartered. He shrugged apologetically. "It's true, lads. Honest."

"Perhaps it's the unkempt, unwashed vagrant look coupled with the sensual smell of carp slime and Monster Crab flavouring which does it for her," I ventured. I paused and then blustered. "Come on! You're extracting the urine!" Normally I would have said 'piss' but I'm a good daddy.

Steve waved a couple of Al Johnson 'Mammy' hands at the two of us and repeated himself. "Honest, lads. It's true. Some anglers really get the hump when I start telling them about this mad girl who finds carp angling sexually stimulating. They take it as a personal slight on their ego and male machismo, but surely even the blindest of the blind would see the truth for what it is. Wouldn't they? Don't you?"

The last question was virtually pleaded as Steve struggled with his renewed internal doubts as to whether he had offended us and blown his chances of getting in the syndicate. Meanwhile I pondered on whether I should tell him that I had considered the poor girl barking on the grounds of finding Pup attractive in the first place let alone have sex with him and be willing to marry him. This was before, I would like to point out, having to accommodate the information that the girl had desires wide enough to classify carp fishing as a whole to be a sexually exciting genre. A woman might find 'Playgirl', or even 'Bondage Monthly' titillating and arousing but 'Carpworld'? Do me a favour. My mind leapt to a vision of a buxom, blonde-haired girl moaning in ecstasy as she expertly fingered herself while leering at a step-by-step PVA bag set-up article. I teetered on the brink of insanity. Mental kink, more like a mental switchback with three-sixty degree loop and twist. What could you possibly say to such a remarkable statement? Offer to buy the girl a strait-jacket? Pay the psychiatrists fees? You would be in debt for life. Or just chuck her twenty 'Crafty Carpers', or whatever it's called now, and get the video camera rolling?

In the end I decided upon tact. "Although hardly an expert on the female psych," I said to Steve, "its yearning and desires, I would reckon she slips into the classification of being, let's say to be generous and not overly sensational, a bit bonkers. Certainly she would be a bizarre statistical anomaly in any female magazine poll conducted on sexual turn ons. All the women I know put up with their other halves going fishing, I can't think of one off-hand who considered it added to their partner's sexual or physical attractiveness," I said truthfully. "She must be the exception that proves the rule, to quote a cliché," I said. "A real one-off and totally unique, sadly for us." I started to think aloud. "Fishing isn't really that sort of thing, is it? It's not like being a footballer or a rugby player. Going skiing, yachting, being a racing driver or motorbike rider, *they* all have a type of glamour associated with them. Participating in one or several different sports can add to a person's charisma, especially when you happen to be really good at them, but fishing? I mean, what sport, if we are a sport and not just a hobby, are we on a par with in terms of glamour and coolness. Darts? Pot-holing? Model railway enthusiasts?" I ran out of ideas pretty quick.

Good job, I thought, they weren't making our beloved obsession sound any better. You had to be realistic, though. Get seriously objective about the mechanics of a three-day carp session and it was hardly riveting stuff to those who hadn't had their arse bitten by the bug. People I had spoken to over the years saw it all as pointless, especially when you told them the fish sometimes had names and then you put them straight back once you had caught them. Two runs in three days. That's action every thirty-six hours, lasting what – ten minutes? How boring. I used to tell them they would like to be doing as well when it came down to having sex. That used to shut them up. Sex. It was all linked to sex. Freud might have been right after all. He was a bit of a nutter – all psychoanalysts are.

"Still," said Rambo, "maybe she's just the beginning of a new female attitude towards carp anglers. One where the chances of you doing a night without getting shagged senseless by the lake's local horde of raunchy groupies are somewhere between slim and zero."

"Look, mate," I told Rambo, trying to keep a straight face, "I know you were on about putting women on an unobtainable plateau of perfection, but you're way out on this one."

Rambo looked crestfallen and his head drooped. "I know, I know," he muttered. Suddenly he lifted his head and his eyes burned with a new enthusiasm. "So," he said positively, rubbing his hands together vigorously. "Has she got a sister then, or what?"

In an instant I could see where he was coming from. Eagerly my brain put two and two together. This sexual attraction to carping may well be a genetic trait, like Steve's kids' selective deafness, passed on in equal measures to all females of her generation sired from the same gene pool. Even I – fuck knows why or on what level, I couldn't begin to analyse it, help me Sigmund, interpret my dreams! – stared expectantly at Steve.

"Yes!" he confirmed. "*Two* in fact. One two years younger, the other two years older and they're *both* going to be bridesmaids at the wedding."

"And are they of a similar persuasion to Melissa, shall we say both physically and mentally? " I asked, my heart beating a little faster than it should. I noticed the light catch Rambo's eyes and they gleamed in their wideness.

Steve was upbeat. "They're both cracking looking girls, I can assure you," he confessed, nodding vigorously. "Very sexy in an in-your-face kind of way."

"*On* your face!" remarked Rambo leering.

"And the other part?" I said. It came out a bit desperate I had to admit.

"No," said Steve dourly, deflating like a punctured football. "I'm afraid *they* both think she's got a bit of a mental kink as well. Both Melina *and* Melloney can't see what the attraction is unfortunately. Not in Pup necessarily, I think they quite like him as a person, they think he's sweet in an oddball kind of way, but the fishing thing in general. I'm convinced Melissa wouldn't have ended up marrying Pup if it hadn't been for the extra rush from his fishing involvement."

"I wonder how it all originated?" Rambo asked. "What caused such an unusual trait?"

I was onto a new line of thought. "Melissa, Melina and Melloney?" I queried. "Sounds like she gets her warped sense of judgement from her parents!"

"Chronologically it's Melloney, the youngest, Melissa in the middle and Melina is the eldest," Steve informed us. "You can tell they all come from the same mould, similar features, same hair colour out of the same bottle. Given the choice of any one from three I'd be hard pushed to choose on a purely physical attraction level." Steve stopped and thought. "Except when I got out one of my sliding 'D' rigs and Melissa started to paw me all over, that'd help focus my choice. Apparently she's always found anglers attractive, right from an early age, Rambo. I guess Pup, although he doesn't fish as much as many because of his boilie business, simply fitted her bill and her time scale to find a bloke and get hitched. It's ridiculous isn't it? Until I see her all over him like a rash, that is."

"Melissa in the middle? Great name for a TV show," I said picking out Steve's earlier statement. Rambo and Steve gave me blank looks. "'Malcolm in the Middle'?" I asked.

"You've lost us on that one, boy," said Rambo, winding an index finger up to his temple and pulling up one side of his top lip. It was the same finger he had shoved in his ear.

I was about to explain when Amy gave an almighty belch and I felt a warm sensation ooze through my tee shirt and onto my skin around the area of my shoulder blade.

"She's just been sick, boy," Rambo helpfully pointed out.

The smell of milk with just a subtle hint of bile had already reached my nose. "You don't say," I answered disparagingly.

I eased Amy off my shoulder and held her at arms length, my two hands under her little armpits. She gave me what could have been construed as a smile but was most likely a facial distortion caused by the effect of wind. A watery bit of milk dribbled down her chin. I needed to do something. Usually this meant off-loading her to Sophie but instead I went to pass her to Rambo, then, bearing in mind her dire warning, I gave Amy to Steve instead.

"I'll go for experience," I said by way of an explanation for the snubbing I had given Rambo.

"Too right you will, boy. This is my third best camo jacket," Rambo warned.

"Look, I'm just going to change my tee shirt. Fill Steve in on the financial details of joining the syndicate and I'll be back in a few minutes. Okay? You're in, mate," I said directly to Steve, giving him a discrete bob of my head and a screwed up nose, all graciously free of charge. He would be paying for the rest.

I left the room and the beaming Steve and went upstairs, changed my tee shirt and reflected upon my first new syndicate member decision. Steve seemed a good bloke. I couldn't see there being any problems in the making and with four kids to sort out I didn't envisage him being a time bandit, exactly the opposite, in fact. When I came back down Amy was fast asleep on Steve's lap and he had written out the two cheques, one for his 1st deposit, and the other for his annual subs.

"Nice touch!" I commented motioning towards the sleeping Amy.

"Been there, seen it, done it, got puke on the tee shirt," said Steve, laughing. "Where do you want her?"

"Do you think you could get her upstairs into her cot with out waking her?" I asked.

"No worries."

And there weren't. Steve was a pro. I turned on the baby intercom and the pair of us went back downstairs.

For around another hour we sat and chatted about how Steve had first met Pup, how many big carp there were in the pit, the three 'M's as Steve called Melissa, Melina and Melloney and loads of other syndicate related stuff. I showed Steve the latest forty-pound carp wall chart which Alan had produced, rather grudgingly I have to admit, (who could blame him after my awful treatment of him) and he was well impressed. I gave him the revised set of rules that had gone out to all the existing members for his perusal and pointed out my one new sensible rule change.

"It concerns the one about sacking fish for fifteen minutes to set up photographic equipment and the one about all fish below twenty-five pounds going into the stock pond and the stock pond logbook," I pointed out. "You see, previously the combination of the two rules meant anyone catching a fish below the twenty-five pound mark would have to take it around to the stock pond almost straight-away because you weren't allowed to sack up fish for more than fifteen minutes. Now if you've just had a take and it's a feeding spell you're not going to want to wind in and cart the fish around to the stock pond there and then."

"Not unless you could get to the pond and back inside twenty seconds, of course," Rambo noted, referring to the unattended rods rule.

"I carry too much gear to get the transporter in the rucksack as well as the scales," I said, unfazed by Rambo's little joke. "I broke the original rule with my first ever Hamworthy carp because of those very reasons. Anyway, so *now* fish above stock pond size *still* have to be photographed within the fifteen minutes but fish for the stock pond can be sacked for up to six hours and *then* moved."

Steve was complimentary. "Yeah. Much better idea."

I felt buoyed by Steve's total acceptance and wondered if running the syndicate was going to be so bad after all. Perhaps if I got Rambo to shoot all the old members I could feel this confident and relaxed all the time. On the other hand there was a lot to be said for keeping the murder count down to one, so mentally I put a stay of execution on the remaining existing members.

"So which one of these carp is the one that Michael had hooked up while he was already dead?" Steve asked looking at Alan's chart. "Pup's told me a little about the weird way that Michael died. I'm guessing you must have told him how it all happened," Steve said to Rambo.

"Yeah. I phoned Pup the day after it all happened," said Rambo. "I felt as if I should tell him as it was because of him the two of us were in the syndicate in the first place. This was some time before we knew he'd left it all to Matt, of course."

Steve nodded slowly as if he was grinding something over in his mind. "I still can't believe someone would be daft enough to light a stove and zip up," he said incredulously.

I had a sudden thought. "How come Pup has never applied? Come to that, why hasn't he ever put you up for membership before? Before he did us? You're his best mate after all." And swiftly another. "Or had you already been to see Michael and been turned down?"

Steve grinned. "No! I never had enough money to afford this place up until now. I got promotion a few years back and an increased salary that's allowed me to scrape enough together to afford the dreaded 1st deposit. Pup knew how much it was, he and Michael were, well, not exactly close, but Michael did trust his opinions on anglers and had his bait rolled by him for a number of years. Pup's nominations, for want of a better word, gave him a starting point. Yes, I've got a well-paid position *now* but he knew I could never afford it beforehand. As to him never joining, I think Pup has rather strong views on syndicates, he feels they are a breeding ground for trouble and internal squabbling. I know he also thinks they are too elitist and deprive others the chance to fish the best waters, a bit of a generalisation, but it's the gist of how he feels."

"Fair play to him for sticking to his beliefs," said Rambo. "If I'd have been in his position I'd have harassed Michael into letting me in yonks ago."

"Hold on a second," I said, "I want to show you something."

I went out the room and got the photo of Michael with Swansong and brought it back and gave it to Steve.

"That's the forty, Swansong. And there's Alan's painting of it," I said pointing to the third to last fish on the chart. There had been two more forties since. The delightfully named Dumptruck and the slightly more poetic Starcluster.

Steve's brow furrowed. "I thought Pup had said he was already dead and one of you two landed it when the buzzer went off?"

"That's right," I said.

Steve's brow was even more furrowed now than it had been earlier. "So what's he doing holding a carp?"

"Look closely," I told him. Steve obediently held the photo up close to his face and tilted it to the light. "You can't see it can you?" I asked, pleased the six by four lie in front of him had gone undetected yet again. "No one gets it when I show them this."

Out of the corner of my eye I noticed Rambo looking agitated and it registered he was not impressed by my sudden inexplicable desire to show Steve the photo. Why was I drawing him into thinking about an incident I should be glossing over? I was being a complete jerk all because of some silly game I had in my mind about camera tricks.

I took the photo away. "It doesn't matter," I mumbled weakly. Both Rambo and Steve gave me a hard stare.

"Why did...?" Steve began. "Forget it. None of my business."

"What? What were you going to say?" I said.

"No, it's nothing," said Steve.

It clearly was something. "Go on, you can ask?" I told him, trying to keep my voice as calm as possible.

Steve shrugged and looked ungainly. He was struggling. "How come Michael left the syndicate to you? You'd only been in it five minutes. I'm not being funny, it just seems an odd thing to do, to leave it to the last member to join."

"You're right. You'd think he'd be the last person to leave it to, wouldn't you?" chipped in Rambo who obviously thought things had gone far enough and needed his input. "We've talked it over for hours and hours, haven't we, boy? And do you know what, Steve?" Rambo stopped for a couple of seconds to increase the impact. "We haven't got any idea either." Rambo waited again. "Having said that, you do know fish were being stolen from the pit by three ex-members while Michael was still alive, don't you? One of those three members had been helping Michael from the very start and was the person who everyone else thought would be given the syndicate when Michael died. You must understand that because of Michael's poor physical condition and the fact he always looked as if he'd never see out another pair of clean pants, the next owner of Hamworthy was given more consideration than you might imagine."

"No, Pup didn't mention any of the fish stealing stuff. I knew a bit about Michael and Gary. I presume you mean Gary." Steve was staggered. "Gary was stealing fish from Michael? Wow! That doesn't make any sense either."

"You see it was Matt who uncovered the treachery and had the decency to tell Michael about it even though we never had actual physical evidence. It took guts, if Michael hadn't been able to verify the truth of the allegations how long do you think Matt and I would have been in the syndicate having accused Michael's best friend? I can only suppose Michael felt so deflated about being back-stabbed once he *did* find out the truth, and being very aware of his poor health, altered his Will to favour the one person who had shown true integrity. Matt. And then with terrible timing and a big bucketful of irony he dies! Perhaps he was so distracted by the recent events it contributed to his unfortunate death."

"Either that or he killed himself," said Steve without a hint of humour.

"If you owned Hamworthy would *you* kill *yourself*?" Rambo asked trying to crush Steve's preposterous supposition in its infancy.

"No *way*!" admitted Steve. "I'd have killed Gary before I'd have done myself in!"

Chapter 4

That night in bed, having interviewed and later given places to the remaining three applicants, sleep had been an elusive commodity. It had been as elusive as a January take on a floater, as rare as a piece of steak cooked on a petrol stove filled with diesel when you had run out of matches and lost your cigarette lighter, and as scarce as a black carp angler.

Just to go off on a tangent for a second, it was odd to think I had never met a single, solitary black carp angler. In all the years I had been wrapped up in the pursuit of carp, not one of my fellow carping comrades had been black. Some had been very hairy – the hirsute in pursuit of carp – but not black, black haired maybe, but not black-skinned. Some had no hair at all; some had been short *and* had no hair – a bald-headed runt on the hunt for carp. In fact the spectrum of carp anglers I had met had been very wide-ranging in terms of physical, social and intellectual bearing but they had *all* been white-skinned. Although black athletes and footballers were in abundance there were no black carp anglers, to my personal knowledge, to be seen at any waterside. As for gay, black carp anglers, or come to that gay, *female*, black carp anglers well, was there one in the entire UK? There had to be a few in the US, surely, but not on this side of the pond. A pity really, imagine the politically correct kudos a few thousand gay, black female carp anglers would give to fishing. Christ, they would be throwing lottery money at us at a rate comparable to snowballs in a kids' playground covered in six inches of snow during the lunch break. We would be untouchable, fishing would be loved by the luvvies and if the odd otter or two had the temerity to start taking fish, why we would just march out our supporters to wipe *them* out.

Stopping the oppressed ethnic and sexual minority catching carp? We couldn't have that! Why there would be teams of stress councillors hanging around carp venues bravely dealing with the emotional fall-out while legions of eco-warriors clubbed the nasty, furry aquatic carnivore back into extinction with environmentally-friendly, but not otter-friendly, clubs. Surreal? Take a look at what goes on now, think of a mirrored reflection of values and then ask the same question. Burglars' rights? Sensible asylum rules? The never ending attack, both financially and judiciously on the average, law-abiding motorist? The never even starting attack on joy riders and car crime? Education policy? Health service? Going to war for no reason? Anti-social behaviour? Where was the coherent, common sense policy the average person yearned for? All people wanted was a perception of justice, decency and fair play being applied equally to all members of the community. In the twenty first century it seemed society was incapable of such a relatively mundane task. Crap or what? If I ever get to run the world I'll sort it... or be corrupted by the authority, lose the humility of empowerment, get side-tracked by vociferous minorities and end up acting like all the others, feathering my own nest and basking in my own vanity.

Why this should be so – a lack of black carp anglers – to get back on tangent from the tangent's tangent, and I'm only guessing was probably due to the simple reason none of them were in the slightest bit interested in it. Perhaps carp fishing was a too physically explosive sport for them to cope with. You know, all the high-octane, quick-burn stuff that constitutes sitting on your arse waiting for a run. Just kidding.

Anyway, this lack of sleep. It had nothing to do with Amy bawling and certainly nothing to do with Sophie being bawdy – chance would be a fine thing, the poor lass was shopped out – no, it was down to the all too familiar sensation of a raging brain. I had tossed and turned on a stormy sea of self-recrimination, self-doubt and self-perceived inferior decision-making. (And there I was criticising government! Huh! At least *I* was losing sleep over it.) The peaks of the waves were thoughts of having just about muddled through, the troughs I had fucked up big-time. Although I had felt happy about taking Steve into the syndicate, and had momentarily felt at ease over my epic first judgement, it hadn't lasted. That night I had mentally beat myself up over the way I had stupidly shown him the photo and got his mind working on the ins and outs of Michael's death. Rambo, luckily enough, had played his lieutenant's part with great guile and had stepped in, sidetracked Steve quite cleverly, and led him away from our Area 51. My stupidity had only just been counterbalanced by Rambo's quick thinking.

To compound all this, the other three lads, Paul, Simon and Phil, had seemed to be fine and gave the answers I had wanted to hear and came across the way I had wanted them to. But lying in bed I'd had second thoughts triggered by my despair over my handling of Steve and the extra doubts were soon flashing across my mind like fireworks being let off from alternative ears. Had I been duped? Had it all been a charade, one in which I was eventually going to be the loser? If ever I had felt the complete desertion of the alleged psychic talent I supposedly possessed then interviewing the last three applicants, agreeing to their membership and then reviewing it six hours later – situation; stable door, bolted; horse, fucked off out of it two days earlier – had drilled it home with brutal honesty. The mind-meld mirror and the ghost's visitation might be all fine and dandy, but come the day, in hindsight, when I would like to have seen inside the head of the human being stood in front of me, I couldn't!

I had known I was thinking crap. In truth it was all about knowledge of human behaviour, not the ridiculously outlandish ability to gaze inside someone's head. It was all about understanding body language, the subtle nuances of subconscious movement, the tone of voice, the variation in speed when talking, all those very real and tangible facets of comportment. These were the clues to truth and honesty in people, not guessing stars or wavy lines on a set of cards and certainly not relating to large carp while under the influence of LSD or having the ghost of a dead woman pop in for a social while doing an overnighter.

Rambo, apart from giving me a mediocre bollocking over showing the photo of the late Michael Brown and Swansong, reckoned they were all as good as we could hope for. As far as he was concerned I hadn't made a howler and besides, they had all come with the Pup mark of approval. Even Rambo had remarked on how difficult it was to really suss someone out in such a short, contrived introduction, especially if they were up for promoting a positive image. And wasn't that what it was all about? We had done it at our interview. In fact everybody did it when they wanted to be arsed to try and impress somebody else. Okay, some were better than others, some looked natural projecting their not entirely true image but the remainder were less proficient and therefore looked inept and shifty. In the ever-downward spiralling culture of image and presentation triumphing over true substance, the ability to bullshit impressively, particularly amongst the real scum of the earth, namely politicians, was of paramount importance.

Although computer software might claim to be WYSIWYG, in many walks of life people were not what you saw and accordingly weren't what you got. Not until you saw them in their true colours. And of course, carp anglers being carp anglers, who are not exactly shy over pulling the odd stroke or two, or seven hundred (I could write a book about it. Wait! I *did* when I was in prison, I keep forgetting) would be very adept bullshitters. In the end we had both agreed how good Michael had been at his lifelong job and how hard it was going to be to emulate him. In terms of running the syndicate, not beating people to death with ballpane hammers, that is. Yet none of this made the slightest difference to my ability to sleep, I was in pursuit of purgatory.

Perhaps the real problem and cause of my self-inflicted mental maelstrom was in waiting for the dreaded run of revenge to manifest itself. Like the sword of Damocles hanging over my head by a single hair, I waited in trepidation for the seemingly inevitable mischief which either Hollywood, Rocky or Darren would conjure up for me. I had even considered the new applicants to be plants, ready to carry out the revenge of their expelled paymasters like a modern day carping equivalent of the Trojan horse, even though Pup had suggested them and had known them all for years. Yet, who was to say Pup hadn't been 'bought'? I guess the word for my condition when the mood swing takes me is 'paranoia'. On many occasions I had run through various disaster scenarios of poisoned fish, blown up functional wooden clubhouse, severe blatting with baseball bat, challenging of the Will by a Mr Furlington-inspired Hollywood, massive exposure in the angling press leading to unprecedented poaching and membership applications. Yet on the sleepless night in question it had all been intensified. The hours in bed after the interviews had created a pressure cooker environment in my head and whilst the safety valve of sleep had been blocked, all my misgivings had been magnified and I had slipped back into my original state of negativity concerning the running of the syndicate.

When I had told Sophie in the morning – which had come eventually – she had asked me why I bothered to worry so much about things I couldn't control. Why waste the energy on dreading something that may or may not happen at some undetermined point in the future, she had said. Why not store the energy and use it to fight it if and when it happened? No sooner had she said this than the phone rang and it was Rambo giving me an early morning pep talk on how well the interviews had gone and how he hoped I wasn't freaking myself out over it. Did he know me, or did he know me?

The pressure of management was there to be seen in the haunted look of all struggling men in such a position, but at least I wasn't threatened with the sack and I did own the company/club. I had kicked myself up the arse and run the 'you don't know just how lucky you are' argument past myself once again. I had made a start to running the syndicate and I mustn't go back on it now. I had to be strong. If the truth was known I was still so unsure.

On the morning of Pup's wedding, two days after Sophie's advice and three from the interview day, the post had the remaining fourteen membership renewals from existing members amongst the other junk mail. In six of those renewals were handwritten notes applauding my one sensible rule change. I immediately marked it down as sycophancy and attempted ingratiation but for once had second thoughts of a more positive nature. Rambo's words about being firm but fair and that in a month or two's time somebody *was* going to start regularly pulling out some big fish came ringing into my ears. Would they *really* care who was in charge as long as it didn't affect the reason for them being members, i.e. catching bloody great carp?

Secondly there were now only fourteen original members left, while on my side, if you want to put it in such terms, there was Rambo and myself plus my four newcomers, Steve, Paul, Simon and Phil. It was a significant shift in the balance of power, especially when added to the fact that *six* of those fourteen had taken the time to write and congratulate me on, as far as they were concerned, my first new ruling. The early morning fog lifted like it had all those years ago when I had finally twigged Watt was a complete arsehole. Rambo *was* right. When had he ever been wrong? Perhaps the six bait freezers might almost be full by summer. I *was* going to survive it and make a decent fist of it. I *would* cross the bridge of Hollywood, Rocky and Darren when I came to it. *If* I came to it. I breathed deeply and smiled. I had been so dumb, but six handwritten notes, a few succinct words from Sophie and having a mate like Rambo had made me turn another corner on my carp-obsessed road of life. By the time the taxi came I was, remarkably enough, mentally back on track, so much introspection and self-doubt had at last been squared inside my throbbing brain. My mood had swung again and I was definitely up for running the syndicate how *I* wanted. And I'd had the cheek to remark on how oddly Melissa's mind worked; pot, kettle, black and all that sort of stuff.

The taxi was waiting outside our house and it was time to leave for the wedding venue. I have to say the pair of us cut a fine dash for Pup and Melissa's big day. Myself, clean-shaven, well-groomed and dressed in a handsome morning suit hired especially for the occasion and complete with gold embossed waistcoat. Black, thin grey pencil-lined trousers with braces, white dress shirt and paisley patterned necktie. Sophie wore her new big hat, her gorgeously made, minimalist, backless designer dress with plunging neckline and her new high strappy shoes, which showed off her sexy thin ankles and shapely calves. She also had a new tiny black bag with enough room for one mobile phone, one lipstick and at a pinch, a packet of fags. As she didn't smoke it was of ample size but I knew the house keys would have to stay in my deep trouser pockets. A bulky set of keys would ruin the bag's shape, or so I was told, and I was also informed it wasn't a bag strictly designed to have anything put in it. I started to open my mouth but discretion told me to zip it, so I did.

Sophie looked ridiculously underdressed for a March wedding but nevertheless the overall package was one of stunning glamour. In spite of my concerns over her lack of warm clothing I still felt inclined to rip off what little she was wearing and make passionate love to her there and then. It had to be said, the gym was doing the business, if anything she was even more fit now than at any time prior to Amy's birth. And the dress! Even if I had mentally boggled at the seemingly inversely proportional return of material for money – less *is* more believe me – she did, it has to be reiterated, look like a film star. Her long, straight jet-black hair glistened in the soft sunlight as we halted on the doorstep and it fell poetically around her toned back and shoulders. Her body looked strong, fit and blemish free. Her eyes, her dark eyes, sparkled with life and vitality and an aura of feminine beauty, powerful feminine beauty, hung around her. I felt a vague fluttering in my loins. She was mine! This epitome of dark, sensual wonderment was my mate. She, yes she, had been impregnated by my seed and had carried my child.

As usual I captured my feelings, the very essence of them, with easy grace.

"You could do with losing the goose bumps," I told her after we had said goodbye to her mother who was doing the baby-sitting honours and were dashing down our front drive to the waiting taxi.

"If you think I'm covering up this creation after the amount of money I've paid for it, think again," she said through shivering lips.

I opened the taxi's back door and let Sophie get in. The driver clocked her in the rear view mirror, undoubtedly craning his neck to get a better look at her cleavage, and I got in. Sophie carefully took off her new hat with a manicured hand. I balked at my new observation noting my previous lack of it. She'd had a nail manicure! I hadn't spotted it before.

"Battle Abbey School, please, mate," I said to the taxi driver in my best man-of-the-people voice and snuggled up to her. Luckily the car heater was on full belt.

Now it was *my* turn to look down her cleavage and I put my hand on her bare thigh where her split dress parted on her crossed legs. My dick strained at its uncompromising – no jogging bottoms today – encasement. Fleetingly I toyed with the notion of asking her to suck it while we were speeding along in the diesel Merc. My absurd adolescent fantasy faltered, flickered, flashed and finally fell flaccid. I made do with looking down her cleavage and feeling the svelte skin on her thigh.

I ran an index finger around the inside of the second uncompromising encasement to come to my attention, namely the collar of my white dress shirt.

"Is it hot in here, or is it me?" I asked.

"It's just right, Matt. Okay?"

"Yeah," I wisely concurred.

After around a half hour or so we arrived at our destination and the taxi pulled up alongside an impressive looking old building constructed of large irregular sandstone blocks. A short driveway to a set of huge oak doors was our route to get inside the building and after I had paid the taxi driver and we had left the warmth of the car we walked quickly through them. Once inside we made our way into a large room by following the coat-tails of a couple of other guests.

The civil ceremony was to take part in a library, the library of Battle Abbey School. It had been an Abbott's house originally and had been built in the 13th century by decree of William the Conqueror, some years after his famous victory. There had been some additional construction during the 16th century and finally it had been converted into a school in 1922. (I briefly wondered if the fees compared favourably to Benenden because, apparently, the Abbey did have a lovely little lake in the grounds with you-know-what swimming in it!)

The Abbey building itself overlooks the very fields where William won his battle – the Battle of Hastings – all those years ago. The Battle of Hastings, as even the most pig-ignorant of schoolboys knows, happened in 1066, but not as you might suppose, in Hastings. The Abbey stands virtually at the very centre of the village known as Battle (if anyone asks why it's called Battle they get a rod pod up the backside, yes, locked in the 'X' position, too) and is situated some seven or so miles west of Hastings. The field where the battle occurred is called Telham Down and it's these fields that the Abbey overlooked all those years ago, after the event of course, and surprisingly enough, given our dispensation for building masses of houses on green field sites, still does to this day.

Sophie and I walked into the library where in less than half an hour Pup and Melissa would complete their vows. We found ourselves a couple of chairs to sit on amongst the smattering of guests already seated on the groom's side of the room. I sat on one of the many velvet trimmed wooden chairs and casually watched Sophie, to my left and closest to the aisle – albeit one seat in which was reserved for Rambo – out the corner of my roving eye. I absorbed the way she brushed her dress under her arse before sitting down and how she arranged the split of it on her crossed legs, like she had in the taxi. I sat fascinated at the way a small vein looped its way around the top of her outer ankle bone and remarked on how sexy her strappy shoes looked in a petite size five. Eventually, with a mental shake of the head, I moved my gaze and re-discovered the room and started to think of the history that was associated with where I was sitting.

Oh for a time bubble to go back and view the brutal clash that led to the building's construction. What prose you would be able to write after seeing history take place in front of your very eyes. Who would need the Bayeux Tapestry to know what had happened?

I tried to picture the scene, me whizzing through time and space and popping into existence alongside the battlefield on the 14th October 1066, around, let's say, lunchtime. I started thinking and imagined myself to camera, microphone in hand with a backdrop of dead and mutilated bodies strewn across green and blood-red grass… 'Harold's Saxons, fresh off the back of a fine mid-week victory three days earlier at Stamford Bridge (that bit is true, trust me!) over the Norwegians, captained by Harald III and treacherous new signing, Tostig, (Harold's brother and *also* true), found the Normans an altogether much tougher prospect. The first half started even enough, it being a dour goal-less affair until mid-way through it, Harold, who'd been having a poor game by his standards, took a heavy challenge resulting in an arrow in the eye. It was a tackle he should really have avoided and the reasons for him not doing so and his jaded, heavy-legged performance must surely lay in the previous game's exertions. At the Bridge he'd been quite magnificent, scoring a hat trick and dominating the midfield with his strong running and astute tactical play but today, it simply wasn't in him. Unlike the arrow. Obviously there was a clear case for resting the lad today but the Saxons are not keen on the squad rotational system due to their lack of depth. From the manager's point of view, with Harold being such a key player, he *had* to play but he paid the ultimate price for a bad game, one almost certainly caused by fixture congestion. With Harold down and out of the game the impact on the rest of the team was immediate and catastrophic. Heads went down, and got cut off pretty quickly I might add, and the Saxons' play slumped as they struggled to get to grips with the loss of their skipper. With a depleted side, no substitutes allowed for injuries in these days remember, the second half was all one-way traffic as the Normans piled on the pressure. The Saxons eventually went down to a couple of poorly defended set-piece goals and suffered the indignity of a late penalty given for a needless handball. Three – nil, then, to the Normans, who were over the moon and in charge of the throne! So, an unprecedented away win on the pools coupons and one eventually to be repeated when a certain Hungarian team hammered England at Wembley in the 1950's. This is Matt Williams, Telham Down fields, looking backwards *and* forwards in time. Over to the studio…'

And there you have it, as in all wars or battles lots of people died but generally speaking more died from one side than the other – and they say history is getting re-written, dumbed down and simplified. The Saxons lost, William, (he was a right bastard you know, ask his dad, Duke Robert the Devil) Will to his team mates, won, conquered even, established feudalism, wrote the Domesday book and then to add a touch of comedy to proceedings, went and fell off *his* horse in a town called Rouen and died, aged sixty, twenty-one years after the match. He probably had a delayed attack of cramp in the form of a tightening hamstring, tried to straighten out his leg and off he went! Seventeen, count them as you fall, hands straight down onto the deck. Crunch! That's gotta hurt! Ruined in Rouen. Six foot under in Caen. Why? Because that's where they buried him.

As I previously mentioned, William the C saw to the commencement of building the Abbey between winning the big match and his sudden loss of equine equilibrium. Now, nearly a thousand years later, here I sat with my arse parked on a seat in its library. I was back in my own time and I gazed up at the walls of books and then at distant trees through a large set of French windows at the end of the room. Well they would be French wouldn't they? In front of the doors was a sizeable table and either side of it, for some bizarre reason, were two huge Malaysian Palms. The sizeable table was statically fraternising with a couple of serious looking, middle-aged men who had fixed smiles aimed at nothing and no one in particular. There was also a vase of flowers on the table. It seemed to know what it was doing. I wondered if it, unlike the table – that had to be a fixture – all came as part of the kit the two men carried to every wedding they presided over.

I also reckoned that in amongst all the books were probably such illustrious tomes as 'War and Peace', 'The Female Eunuch', 'Noddy's Anal Adventures', 'Haynes Manual for the Ford Fiesta 82-86' and something by a 'celebrity' cook (don't make me fucking laugh) the sole purpose of which, was to give you something to browse through while you waited for the pizza delivery man or the microwave to go 'ting'!

I looked back yet again at a hat reinstated Sophie and checked out her décolletage. What *was* wrong with me? I had seen it enough, surely? Seen all of it, yet somehow in this new wrapping, half glimpsed, cunningly exposed and at the same time hidden, this *new* version of her, she, for want of a better word, *tantalised* me. Her heavily glossed lips glistened, they were full and pouting, and I stared at them.

She saw me from under the brim of her hat and the corner of her eye. "Stop staring at me! Look at someone else, you pervert!" she whispered, smiling and pouting her lips even more.

Ever the dutiful partner I looked at someone else. The room had filled up without me realising it because I had been lost in my little football match fantasy version of our heritage and because I had been looking lustfully at my long-term partner. Putting it that way hit home how right Sophie had been. *What* a pervert! I should have been scouring the room for other crumpet like any other normal man would have been. No! Idiot! I should have been scouring the room for *Rambo*. *Sans* camouflage Rambo! Rambo without his ever-present traditional British Army colour scheme. Would I even recognise him in civvies? How would he act? Could he cope without being clad in his usual classic ensemble? Would he be left a stumbling shadow of a man, paralysed and gauche because of the crippling awkwardness imposed by the wearing of a morning suit? I would soon find out and I mentally rubbed two hands together in anticipated glee.

I rubbernecked with fervour to see if he had tried to sneak in at the back without me seeing him, then I gawped to the side and front. I couldn't see him anywhere. In frustration I played 'spot the carp angler' and looked down at my big giveaway, the dotted pinpricks on my left thumbnail. The old hook sharpness test. I was too far away to see such conclusive evidence so, because I wasn't that fussed about playing, I labelled every male aged between sixteen and fifty on our side of the room as an angler. I made a mental note that neither Paul, Simon nor Phil was amongst those *close* friends invited to the actual wedding ceremony yet I, who hadn't seen Pup for ages, was. In spite of Pup's views I reckoned me owning the best carp fishing syndicate in Britain had something to do with it.

Just for fun I tried to guess the PBs of my supposed carp anglers. I slated all the muppets who hadn't caught a thirty and quickly chastised myself for being a carp snob now I had access to a water where a thirty was almost run-of-the-mill. Was ultimate size important? Of course. Did it give a true indication of angling ability? Possibly but not conclusively, not today, not when there seemed to be massive fish in the most unlikely of venues. How about a carp catching credibility list, putting a certain fish with a supposed higher merit above another? But who decides the merit? Don't go there! Don't think of it! The labyrinth will snare you forever!

Bored with the alleged anglers I looked at the older element in amongst the guests. In the front row of chairs on the other side I noticed the bride's mother. She looked a nice person, although the floral print dress she was wearing was big enough to prop up with a handful of curved aluminium poles and call a two man Eurodome. Provided you could get her out of it, naturally, and provided that once you got her out of it you could stand the shock of what was revealed underneath it. She was a *big* lady. Imagine having to shag that! A little shiver ran down my spine and a life of celibacy seemed less weird than it had earlier. 'If you want to see what your wife will look like in thirty-years' time, look at your mother-in-law'. It's what they say. Perhaps Pup would kill *himself* and leave his bait business to me as well, I thought cynically.

In the other front row, my front row, I spotted four boys with a woman who looked as if she had the world on her shoulders, and, for good measure, the moon tucked under one arm and six hundredweight of shopping hanging from the other. Despite heavy make-up the dark bags under her dull, tired eyes told the story of a trying life. One of the boys was older than the other three and the other three reminded me of Donald Duck's horrific nephews, Huey, Dewy and Lewy. This gaggle of males had to be Steve's attempt to overpopulate the world in a single-loined spunk-fest. The four boys were like a schizophrenic hydra, a multi-headed beast that writhed and struggled and pushed and pulled and niggled and baited and jostled and antagonised itself constantly. Trying to keep the hideous beast reined-in was clearly an arduous task and seemingly as impossible as a walk through a town centre without seeing someone leaning against a wall sending a text message on a mobile. They were continually being berated and kept in check for about, on a good attempt, ten seconds by Steve's wife before the cycle kicked in and one of them would start to tease or push one of the others.

In this formal environment Steve's wife was using all her energies to try and maintain some semblance of order and stop the boys running riot. Although hardly an expert in the field of parenting, I did know enough to realise there was no way she could keep it up all the time. I could tell she must have to give in at home and let them run amok because the effort of controlling them every waking hour would surely have sent her plummeting into a freshly dug grave years ago. To be honest, for an occasion where a certain amount of social decorum was expected, she looked vastly unprepared to my eye. The lack of a cattle prod and/or some other type of electrical stun device seemed almost negligent given her circumstances. Why the woman never even had a whip! I made a mental note to broach the subject of Sophie and I having a maximum of two children. But what if the second one is a girl as well, Matt? Well, I would put up with being the end of the Williams family line; three girls would be an attempted heir too far. I mentally kicked myself, Steve and his wife had *only* been having a second but it had turned into a third and fourth as well! Nightmare!

A little collective murmur from the guests made me turn my attention away from the four-headed monster to witness Pup and Steve walk down the aisle between the two sets of chairs. They both gave me a little nod of recognition before passing me by and going up to the table where they were pounced upon by the two men with fixed smiles. Hands were vigorously pumped all round. Steve looked a bit nervous, no doubt thinking of his big test to come during the reception when he would have to make his best man's speech. I then considered the possibility that his anxiety was not due to the speech but the thought of his four boys starting a major league argument leading to a free-for-all wrestling match on the large table and culminating in fratricide. If they did it was a dead cert the professional vase of flowers would get its nose put out of joint.

On the other hand Pup looked as if he was *really* cacking his pants. I pondered on the reason being my earlier theme, the one in which he suddenly realised his Melissa might end up in floral print dresses ten years from now with 'marquee' written on the size label. Actually I doubted if it was the getting married, or the mother-in-law's huge dress size, more like he had two hundred kilos of NRG boilies he had left to air dry on the living room carpet and he had forgotten to rotate them.

"Oh… my… *God*!" I heard Sophie exclaim.

I swivelled round to see Sophie's immaculately manicured right hand jammed up to her wide-open mouth and her eyes dangling out and yo-yoing on a couple of mini-Slinky springs. From her I diverted my attention to the large muscular man standing beside her.

"All right, boy? Sophie?" it asked. "What do you think of the outfit? All hand made, you know."

It was one of those knock-me-down-with-a-six-inch-piece-of-PVA-string moments. There before me was Rambo in a hand made British Army camouflage morning suit, British Army camouflage dress trousers, dark olive green waistcoat, white dress shirt and highly polished standard issue British Army boots. Even his fucking necktie was camo, yet in fairness it did manage to keep some form of dignity by being a static one and by resolutely refusing to revolve. Secretly I wanted it to revolve to the sound of a one-noter Delkim at around a hundred decibels complete with blinding blue, no wait, *must* colour co-ordinate, *green* LED. Life can be full of minor disappointments. Even Donald Duck's nephews plus elder brother had stopped mucking about and were staring at Rambo. In fact the whole room was staring at him; all the other blokes in their standard formal morning suits, all the ladies in their various wedding ensembles and all the kids in their uncomfortable, never-been-worn-before new clothes were looking at Rambo. Usually Rambo was about six-four but at this precise moment he seemed to be well over eight foot and totally dominating proceedings.

"Sit down, mate," I told him, "you don't want to steal the bride's thunder, do you?"

Rambo sat down and run his gaze over Sophie. "Nice dress. And what's just about inside it looks pretty good as well!"

Sophie tilted her head one way and then the other. "On the whole, I'll take that as a compliment," she said, unfazed.

Sophie was cut off by a sudden outbreak of music, the well-known piece of music, which indicates, as luck would have it, the bride has decided to turn up and there is a fairly good chance the marriage would take place. Usually the music is 'The Wedding March' by some old geezer called Mendelssohn but as *this* piece of music blared out from the hidden CD player I knew why we were all wearing formal morning suits but *weren't* sitting on church pews.

"I didn't know Pup was an aficionado of nu-metal," said Rambo, leaning across Sophie so I could hear.

The chorus kicked in. "I think it's all to do with the valued lyrical content," I informed Rambo. "I mean Mr Dirst *could* have written it specifically for Pup *himself.*"

"Let me guess," said Sophie tilting an ear to take in the chorus lyrics. "By the way they keep saying 'Keep rollin', rollin', rollin', rollin'' I expect it's called 'Rollin''? And alludes to the fact Pup does a lot of bait rolling."

"You've got it one," I said. "'Rollin'' it is. As performed by the sensational Limp Bizkit!"

"The bride!" Rambo said suddenly, turning his head back to me after it had previously been looking up the aisle. "*And* the bridesmaids!"

Melissa, escorted by her father and attended by her two sisters, Melloney and Melina, although who was who I had no idea, made their way down the aisle. Instantly I was taken aback by the triple whammy of the three girls' stunning looks. They weren't stunning in the way Sophie looked stunning, nor were they stunning in the way Hollywood's two stunning looking, lap dancing, ex-international gymnasts, who were also bisexual nymphomaniacs had been stunning. No, they were stunning in a more down to earth, openly evocative way. Hollywood's ladies had been all laser beams, dazzling lights and stun guns – much like one Steve's wife could have utilised but stupidly didn't possess. The glorious triple sisterhood was more earthy, less high-tech but equally devastating; like a piece of sawn, not prepared, four-by-two cracked across the back of your head, as wielded by hyperactive gorilla with access to a snug-fitting pair of welding gloves. My first thought was that none of them would look amiss in a photo shoot for lad magazines like 'Loaded' or 'FHM'. I was also willing to wager two out of three of them either had a pierced belly-button, a discreet tattoo, a pierced tongue or any combination of the three. Perhaps one of them had even gone so far as to have a pierced nipple. Whatever the count on hidden rings through flesh the one thing abundantly clear to the naked eye, and it was beyond conjecture, was the size of the girls' boobs. All three of them had been in the front of the queue when *they* had been dished out… or been at the back and had them surgically enhanced.

The girls looked like sisters; that was a fact as well. The family resemblance was as clear as the 36D bras they weren't wearing under each straining bodice. It was plain to see they had all come from the same mould, although you would have been bloody hard pushed to imagine the mould was the floral print Eurodome in row 'A'. They had fit, healthy-looking full figures. They were obviously women who didn't understand words like 'anorexic', 'bulimia' or 'diet' but instead radiated ones like 'buxom', 'busty', 'bouncy', 'bosomy' and 'bootylicious'. You could keep your catwalk skeletons, these were the real women who real men fancied, not mere stick-insect clotheshorses pandered to by camp fashion designers.

The girls also looked *dirty*. Not in the sense of being unclean, far from it, but in the sense of sexual nous and adventure. They emanated an atmosphere of sexual knowing, one where they recognized what they would like you to do to them but if by chance *you* didn't, then they could pretty soon put you on the right track. And it could be *anything*, by the look of them, you could be told to do *anything*. Think of a fantasy, any fantasy, and it could be the very thing they wanted. No barriers, no taboos, no holds barred. Awesome! Lucky Pup, I thought.

Despite being dressed in their bridesmaids' and bride's outfits, the traditional material of all three dresses was incapable of masking their aura of naughty, sexual magnetism. It was so hard to define the instant impact they made upon my mind, that I groped hopelessly to find thoughts to assess it. Was it simply an all-consuming powerful, raw sex appeal that engulfed the voyeur of these three sirens? I wasted a valuable second or two of glorious ogling time as I dragged my leering eyes away from the girls and onto the other males in the room. Yep! Powerful, raw sex appeal all right. I counted eight men with their tongues hanging out and four others were actually howling! Naturally, a lot of *their* other halves looked ever so slightly pissed off, although they tried to disguise their discomfort with forced smiles and whispers of, 'don't they all look so lovely'. It was a sure sign that the sisters' allure wasn't confined to male eyes alone.

I looked at Sophie, she seemed comfortable and her smile had a look of indifference. Maybe she understood her own desirability was somehow on a slightly different plane from the three sisters. Sophie looked gorgeous and like a film star, and even if I say so myself, she did look classy and sophisticated in her expensive clothes. The three 'M's didn't seem to be on the same sex appeal wavelength as Sophie, theirs was more immediate, more direct, more in-your-face. Their body shape, their hair and hair colouring, they way they wore their make-up and the shared physical features all added up to a potent mix of instant, animalistic sexual attraction. And there were three of them! I found it ridiculously paradoxical I could read so much about females I had only seen seconds earlier, admittedly on a one-tracked, highly superficial theme and yet struggle with male carp anglers. It probably had something to do with interviewing male carp anglers with my head and eyeing female bridesmaids with my cock. Animalistic sexual attraction! Certainly the three of them had reduced me down to an animal in terms of instinct at its most base level.

I returned to looking at the girls with *my* impression of the forced smile fixed in place, hiding, or trying to, the mass of assumptions their combined first impression was making on me. It was time for the next burning, vitally important question. In the short time I had seen them I would have been hard pressed to say which one of them I fancied the most because on the base level I was working on, I fancied them all. I studied all three. Maybe the bridesmaid closest to us? It was a tough call.

By now Melissa was virtually alongside our row of seats, behind her, clutching her bouquet and being the one closest to our side of the aisle, I could see either Melloney or Melina smiling at all the guests from no more than a few yards. Yeah, definitely her, she had all what the others had but more so. With the other sister now hidden by her and Melissa and her father a row or two past, I watched the bridesmaid who I fancied the most out of the three very intently. Suddenly either Melloney or Melina caught sight of Rambo in his bizarre camouflaged morning suit and her expression changed instantly and her smile vanished. Quickly her eyes widened as she looked him up and down, sucked him in, ran him around her taste buds and spat him out, like a beautiful mirror carp testing out a hookbait. Then, and only then, she winked at him! She actually fucking winked at him!!

As their sides became their rears Rambo's head swung back to me so fast I thought it might fly off.

"Did you see that?!" he exclaimed. "She winked at me! I'll tell you what, I'm in there, boy!"

I was going to say something about the possibility of it being sarcastic but one of the original Mr Fixedsmiles had started talking. I sat back and listened in a slight sulk to the commencement of the civil wedding ceremony, and all because she hadn't winked at me. I mean Sophie *was* sitting in between us; she *could* have been Rambo's partner, I could have been the available one.

I was pathetic. One minute I was lusting over my gorgeous partner, entranced by her new look and new packaging, the woman I had loved and who had loved me through thick and thin; the next getting huffy over one of the bridesmaids winking at my, let's not forget, unattached best mate. It was symptomatic of the male disease and sadly it reminded me of how shamefully I had behaved a few years ago while in France.

Chapter 5

Pup and Melissa were now boilie anorak and female with peculiar sexual attraction fetish, or if you prefer, man and wife. By virtue of the authority invested in Mr Fixedsmile, Melissa had now promised to love, honour and knock up ten kilos of Shellfish B whenever Pup asked. In return he had promised to love, honour and obey her, which possibly might include making *lurve* to her whenever she wanted it. And, to satisfy her mental kink, I imagined there would be some sort of stipulation in the small print that he had to talk dirty to her, whispering such sweet carping nothings like; 'Sliding 'D' rig, baby', 'PVA bag, you bitch! You know you want it' and 'Oh yeah! Oh yeah! Five turn grinner knot' in her ear as he did so. When Pup had kissed the bride I wondered if he could have ever dreamed such a desirable woman would have fancied him? That was a question all of its own but when you added; 'partly because of his association with carp fishing' you had to wonder what it was all coming to. Melissa, God bless her, was surely the exception that proved the rule. Never mind black carp anglers, where was the other woman in the northern hemisphere made hot by the thoughts of carp fishing? It wasn't to be one of her sisters apparently, at least not according to Steve. Maybe it was something else for them? Maybe the genetic defect would surface in some other strange and wonderful form. I could but hope, purely on the grounds of entertainment value alone.

Still, fair play to Pup and his chance meeting with Melissa in the well-known pick-up joint masquerading as a supermarket commonly known as Tesco. I reckoned, on the whole, he must be about an eighth as lucky as me, but however strange his story of love conquering rationality, it paled into insignificance compared to my blockbuster of an epic. Melissa's fatal attraction was small beer when put up against my carp fishing story. In a way it was a shame I could never tell her the whole of my tale because I was convinced she would be mightily impressed.

Once the ceremony had finished and we had all thrown our confetti – five ounce Zipp leads painted with white emulsion, two coats (just joshing) – we had all jumped into a small armada of taxis. From the Abbey we had been whisked back towards Hastings to the hotel where we were to eat a meal, listen to all the speeches and then wait for the added impetus of the evening guests arriving for the disco/reception. I have to admit I was intrigued as to whom I might see from the Lac Fumant gang, the only certainty being that Spunker wouldn't be one of them. I could deduce this on the adequately safe grounds of him being an ex-huge Rottweiler. An ex-huge Rottweiler – in the sense of him being pronounced seriously dead – after his fatal coming together with an artic full of cat chow. I bet he was getting one hell of a ribbing in doggy heaven* for that one.

*Disclaimer notice: *This does not mean I subscribe to the theological supposition of there being a separate hereafter for the animal kingdom. Also, despite having had genuine contact with a phantasm, the possibility of an abode of God specifically for humans is, as such, still only a concept rather than an actuality. Usual disappointing terms and conditions apply.*

We had arrived en masse at the rather salubrious hotel where all the wedding guests had filed past reception and were guided into a large ground floor room by various hotel staff. It was in this large room, which had its own bar and was laid out half tables and chairs, half dance floor with disco in place, where the rest of the day's proceedings would take place. A seating plan had been set out on a large sandwich-type board just outside the room's entrance showing where everyone should park their butt. Sophie and I were placed with Rambo and four other guests, two couples named Adam and Hannah and Peter and Louise, on table six. Having duly found table six the three of us had sat down and were soon joined by the other two couples. These four fellow guests all looked to be a little younger than us, being aged around the twenty-year-old mark, if indeed they were as old as that. They were gregarious and polite, and it wasn't too long before an easy dialogue ensued.

It came as no surprise to learn both Adam and Pete were keen carp anglers. It quickly transpired that despite their best efforts neither of them had caught their first thirty yet, much as I had predicted earlier in fact, and their sheepish admittance to such a loathsome crime was an eye-opener to how their carp angling minds still worked. However, they were so impressed by what Rambo and I *had* caught – we had let it slip into the conversation, only casually (yeah right), within the first thirty seconds of talking about fishing – they immediately hung on our every word. As I was posing on my carp-catching credentials I mused that maybe I really should take it all back and not be so dismissive of the credibility big carp captures still made on impressionable anglers. Size *is* important. I clearly thought so to brag about it in the first place to these younger, less experienced anglers, yet had denied it to myself. Inwardly I knew the true measure of competence was consistent catching from different venues but I had rode roughshod over my beliefs to impress a couple of lads I had known for all of five minutes.

Of course I soon went the whole mile and explained I had caught the fish, not from a commercial, overstocked puddle but from a mature gravel pit. They were obviously keen enough to put added stock on my captures, once they knew all about it, and they duly tugged their forelocks and bowed down to a superior carping acquisition. Matt Williams, professional hypocrite and part-time ghost and carp psychic. Remit; quick to deride carp fishing elitism but equally quick to blow his own trumpet and emphasise the very things he privately derided. Meeting new carp anglers certainly can bring out the worst in us all. I had listened to enough blowhards in my time and although not acting quite so blatantly I was still guilty as charged.

During further conversation it became known that although Adam swore by Trigga Ice and fluoro pop-ups as rolled by Pup, Pete preferred Pup's legendary pop-ups and his spice fishmeal bottom baits. I had told them both Rambo and I were very partial to the Pup pop-up – I had also let *that* drop into the conversation, how I had caught the big French mirror on one, on the last day of our trip – but we did *so* prefer him to roll our very own mix, rather than a leading propriety brand. I had also mentioned we had in fact been using this self-designed bait for many a year with no sign of it blowing. I had waited eagerly to see if either of them had the front to ask what the bait was but they hadn't.

Bait didn't seem to be the big secret it had been all those years ago when someone had rummaged through Rambo's rubbish for clues, but clearly Adam and Pete thought asking about it still carried the stigma of poor social decorum. I suppose their reticence could have been laid at the intimidating doorstep called Rambo. There was no suggestion of malice in the hulking great camouflaged brute but his shear size and aura of physical invincibility weren't shrouded by his outrageous outfit. In a way it emphasised it, no one would have dared wear it without some sort of physical backup to snuff out derision before it had even been lit. Who am I kidding? I reckon they were bricking it in case they said the wrong thing and it threw Rambo's brain into 'kill' mode and he ripped them apart with his bare hands. I had tried on many recent occasions to remember how I had felt about him when he had been the unknown quantity and member in Watt's SS syndicate but it was too long ago. So much water had thundered under the bridge it was impossible and also because he was now my best friend.

Both the lads had thought, or at least had said they thought, Rambo's outfit was 'neat' and 'cool', although the beads of perspiration on his brow hinted at the opposite. And before you ask I'm *not* so old to realise they didn't mean it like that. Bloody youngsters and their sixties buzz words. Life and fashion is a circle and seems to re-invent itself when nothing new is to hand, truism number thirty-four says so.

Adam and Pete were well impressed by us, I could tell, and when they had asked what I did for a living and I told them I ran a syndicate water, that was all, nothing else, just ran a syndicate water, why, I was an instant deity. When they had asked Rambo the same, he had casually muttered something about army days but then admitted those times were long gone. He had gone on to tell them he now just worked for me, helping to maintain, run and look after the syndicate water and fished. Adam and Pete stared at us both and then at each other. We were living their dream and their slack-jawed looks of incredulity and astonishment were a delight to behold. Yes, we did have it pretty good from their perspective, as good as it could possibly get, I suppose. On the other hand they didn't know about the evil baggage that went with the deal called my life, or of the disgusting deeds Rambo had carried out in the making of his very affluent new one.

A wave of something very strange washed over me, caused, in part, by their overwhelming admiration. It was something I had never felt before. As usual, being faithful to my true disposition, I analysed it. It was slight smugness! Yes! It *was* a very slight feeling of being in a very nice situation thank you very much. The very one, logically, everyone else would have had since the very first pay-off from Sophie's mum, let alone being handed the best syndicate in Britain and cash to go with it and, oh yes, a beautiful partner and a beautiful baby girl. Don't tell her I said it in that order, I'll never hear the last of it! Okay, there had been some very difficult associations with it all but my mental turning point brought on by the six letters and Sophie and Rambo's pep talk was enhanced. I felt even mentally stronger than I had earlier concerning the running of the syndicate. Yes, it was becoming even clearer, their response was a window to how I should feel. *Was* beginning to feel. I also felt like a drink and asked Rambo to come up to the bar and help me with the glasses. Adam beamed, someone who had caught a French fifty and a UK forty was going to by him a drink. The distinction between the two fish seemed important to him and was another insight all of its own.

As we walked up to the bar I took in the top table. Melloney and Melina, as the bridesmaids, were obviously seated there and were engaged in deep conversation with each other. I still didn't know who was who, but it had been the one in the lilac dress as opposed to the peach one I fancied the most and it had been she who had winked at Rambo. Succinctly I noted that they didn't appear to have any male partners to accompany them. Also sitting at the table was the floral print Eurodome. She was pegged out next to the man, her husband and Melissa's dad, who had given Melissa away. 'There you are take her, she's all yours along with the running costs', I thought might be a line from his upcoming speech. 'We've *still* got another two to get rid of', he could add, because *definitely* wasn't anyone else there who could be passed off as the remaining sisters' boyfriends. I had checked and double-checked believe me. The one remaining doubt was the possibility they were seated at another table; I guessed I would just have to keep my eyes peeled during the evening disco to know for sure. The only other people on the top table were Pup's mum and dad, Pup, Melissa, Steve and his wife. To go back to minor disappointments like Rambo's piss poor necktie effort, I was also a bit peeved that Pup's dad wasn't wearing a Nutrabaits baseball cap on back to front, coupled with a Ritchworth sweatshirt complete with egg stains and bait mix visible under his nails. Then you could say; 'Ah, *that's* where he got it from!'

The two sisters glanced up from their conversation and the one in the lilac dress appeared to glance at the two of us as we cut our way through the other tables until eventually we reached the sanctuary of the bar.

Rambo turned to face me as he had been leading the way and lent on the bar, his back to the top table.

"She keeps looking at me," he said with a minuscule backward movement of his head.

"*Every* fucker keeps looking at you," I told him in no uncertain manner. "Because you're the only person in history to ever wear a camouflage morning suit, camouflage dress trousers and a *fucking* camouflage necktie to a wedding."

"I've got camouflage boxers on as well," said Rambo, proudly.

It was a sentence I had never heard spoken before. "Got camo socks on, have you?" I said sarcastically.

Rambo's brow furrowed. "What would be the point of wearing camo socks?"

"*You've* just told *me* you're wearing camo boxers," I said slightly exasperated.

"Camo boxers make your knob look bigger, boy!"

I was just about to ask why you would possibly want your knob to look bigger in a situation where if anyone *was* happening to look at it with *that* sort of interest they would probably be finding out the true dimensions in a few minutes time. Why exaggerate and exasperate the situation? It was the same as padded bras and wearing a big hat when you couldn't fight, or something along similar lines.

Anyway, I *was* just about to ask it but one of the bar staff cut me off before I had started.

"Are you being seen to, Gents?" he politely enquired.

"Umm… no. Four pints of lager and three white wines, all medium, thanks," I said instead.

"Any particular lager, Sir?"

"Have you got Beck's on draught?" I asked. The barman nodded.

For the first time I noticed him as a person and wondered if he was old enough to serve drinks. Everyone looked so young today. To me he only looked like a spotty young man with sixteen school summer holidays in him. It was a clear sign of my rapid ageing and maturity being coupled with the hackneyed cliché about police officers looking younger than ever. I mean, I was a dad now *and* had hit thirty. "That'll do then," I informed the barboy. Now I had given it even more consideration he only looked fourteen.

Rambo looked at me again once the gawky youth had left us to start occupying himself with the not too arduous task of pouring out the beers and the glasses of wine. I expected the conversation to carry on with more remarks about the lilac-dressed bridesmaid but I was wrong.

"Something funny happened the other day, you know," he started. "Although it wasn't funny in one sense and I guess it might not be funny in the other either. That might be down to me reading things into the situation." He looked at me with a solemn intensity. I knew I didn't need to ask what had happened because it was coming next. Rambo leaned towards me, flashed his eyeballs left and then right and spoke quietly. "You remember how I told you, you were one of a few people who knew about my faked death?"

I nodded. This wasn't what I had anticipated at all.

"Well, the other few, six to be precise, were all, shall we say, implicated in the dastardly deed, whereas *you*," he touched me on my lapel with an index finger, "simply know about it. Some had a hand in helping me establish that the body, the

50

one belonging to the mug I'd paid to be my double knowing full well he was going to get murdered, was me. Some helped to get the body back from abroad and into the UK and others helped in the issuing of a UK death certificate. When it had all been done and dusted successfully it had been as slick as a magician's trick. Hey Presto! I was off the scene, officially dead and living a tax-free life of luxury and only seven living people knew about it. Six had been bribed, intimidated and cajoled as necessary and only one, you boy, knew the score. You're a unique person," Rambo said with a slight flick of the head and a wink.

"With you so far," I said, feeling slightly uneasy about my role in the matter now I had been reminded of it.

"Well, one of the other six died a few days ago in a house fire. The place was completely gutted and he, apparently, died in the bedroom. He'd been burnt alive, trapped in a raging fire from which he couldn't escape and only his charred bones and teeth, that was how he was identified, had been found, such was the intensity of the fire."

The first of the lagers turned up and Rambo gave me a discreet shrug of his massive shoulders. No mean feat I can assure you.

Rambo hypothesised. "A simple house fire with tragic consequences or something more sinister and much, much worse? Worse from my point of view that is, it could hardly be any worse for Charlie, seeing as he ended up looking like a Christmas turkey left on gas mark six until after Easter."

I nodded and felt my mouth drying so I quickly grabbed the second lager which spotty-boy had put down next to the first and took a big gulp.

"You suspect foul play, then?" I asked after swallowing it.

"I *always* suspect foul play," said Rambo. "It's why I'm still alive."

I glanced up at the top table. Lilac dress appeared to be looking at Rambo's back. I ignored it and tried to get to grips with this new revelation. "So what's the worst case scenario?" I inquired.

It was Rambo's turn to take a mouthful of lager. He wiped his mouth with the back of his massive hand. "Worse case scenario is that somehow," Rambo's voice went spiteful and emphatic despite its low volume, "and *fuck knows* how, someone from my past is onto me and they've tortured more info than I dare dream about out of Charlie before torching him and his gaff."

"Shit!" I said with feeling. "Could it really be as bad as that?"

Rambo tilted his head and gave my question consideration. "Worst case scenario... yes. On the other hand the best-case scenario is that it was a genuine house fire and now there's only five, plus you, who know all about it. You see ideally there'd be none."

I puffed out my cheeks. "I hope you're not thinking of bumping me off!" Rambo laughed and shook his head while my brain thought of me, me and me! "My second question is; did the six know anything about *me?*"

Rambo shook his head once again, much to my relief. "No. You haven't got to worry yourself over that."

"Are *you* worried about it, though?" I said.

Rambo turned phlegmatic and philosophical. He leaned even further forward and closer to me. "Not so worried about it as I am about whether I'm going to get my hand in Melina's knickers," he said in a conspiratorial manner.

"*Melina?*"

"Melina."

Here, finally, was the answer to my tiny conundrum. "So that's Melina, then? The one in the lilac dress is called Melina and the other one; the one in the peach dress is called Melloney. Melina, lilac dress, the eldest, Melissa is the middle one, Melissa in the middle who married Pup and Melloney, the one in the peach dress, is the youngest? Is that right?"

"Got it in one, boy," smiled Rambo, but not at me but to his right.

I followed Rambo's eye line to see the spotty barboy grinning at me like a Cheshire cat with acute acne. The remaining five drinks were neatly lined up.

"Fifteen pounds and sixty-pee, please, Sir," he said.

I plonked a twenty into his frail, white bony paw. "Can I have a tray?" I barked. It came out even ruder than I intended.

I carried the drinks back to our table, once again following Rambo's huge swathe of camouflaged clothing and set them down upon it. I distributed the drinks to their respective owners and then sat in my chair and supped my lager while catching the back end of a conversation between the girls. Sophie told Hannah and Louise where she had bought her 'lovely dress', as they had called it, and then went on to say what make-up she preferred, while adding that now she was a mother of five months; 'Of five months, gosh you have got your figure back quickly', the two girls had remarked, she did, on the whole, prefer Pampers nappies over Huggies. I speculated, on the unlikely chance we'd had a professional arbitrator at the table, whose conversation would be regarded as the most naff. The boys and their carp fishing or the women and their girlie chit-chat? I suspected if both conversations had been born to a pedigree cat breeder they would both have ended up at the bottom of the local lake inside a trussed Hessian sack complete with concrete block for ballast.

Within five minutes or so of my drinks distribution the waitresses started to bring around the starter course so we began to eat. As we tucked into the very passable grub our topic of conversation had moved back onto fishing while the girls' one had probably gone on to discuss such meaningful subjects as their partner's dick size. Following on in a similar theme the three of them had then most likely taken a guess at Rambo's dick size. You know, just for a laugh, wondering whether his huge physique had manifested itself proportionally in the penis department. Although obviously this assumption would had to have been made when he wasn't wearing camouflage boxers shorts because, so I'm led to believe, the distortional aspect of camo underwear can frighten even the most insatiable and willing female. Size is still important, both carp and cocks, I *had* to get that into my head. (Oh well, I had good dimensions in one out of the two, no prizes for guessing in what category though.)

Later, not wholly removed from the early topic, they had probably exchanged views on the merits and faults of their partner's lovemaking techniques. Then, moving rapidly on through their partner's disgusting habits and major personality defects, I expect they whinged about time spent fishing, money spent on fishing and time spent talking about fishing. This in all likelihood included taking the piss out of us because we were talking about fishing there and then, while they were talking about how much talking about fishing we usually did. I say 'probably' and 'I expect' and use other such vague premises because, to be frank, we were too busy talking about fishing to notice what they were talking about.

We talked about slings, shelters, spods, scales, sacks, sessions and stalking over starters. Throughout the main meal the topic of conversation was mats, the Method, Mainline Maple 8, mono versus Multi-strand or Merlin and making the most of marker floats. During pudding it was all pods, particles, pellets, PVA and presenting pop-ups. It was heady stuff, especially as I was combining the Beck's with the house red that accompanied the food. Elsewhere, on adjacent tables, I could easily imagine, given the likely amount of anglers present, an awful lot of ladies were saying pretty much what I had considered the females on our table to be saying. The chances were also heavily stacked on the men repeating our topic of conversation to some degree or other. However, it was a million to one shot that anyone in the room could cut loose on the delights and downfalls of carp fishing with the intensity I could. Despite becoming fairly well oiled by Rambo's and then Adam's subsequent rounds of lager *and* the wine, I resolutely bit my tongue. Repeat after me; I must not shout my mouth off about my syndicate (okay just to mention it in the vaguest of terms)… or mention the ghost… or the prison sentence… or Rambo's chequered past… or Rebecca at Lac Fumant although Lac Fumant itself was fine and while I was at it, if I had any sense, I must stop keep looking at the three sisters whose magnetic pull, whirled the iron filings of lust in my head around to their north aspect top table.

Was Melina looking at Rambo or was she looking at me? It was hard to tell but logic told me it had to be Rambo. I had a theory about it.

Eventually the meal was over and once all the eating paraphernalia had been cleared and glasses of cheap champagne given to each guest for the toasts it was time for the dreaded speeches. Melissa's dad's effort was short and to the point. He spoke evenly and slowly into the microphone which had been hooked up by the guy running the disco's sound system. Melissa's dad's voice magically became amplified and, slightly disconcertingly, emanated from out of the speakers ten yards to his right. He toasted the bride and groom and he even cracked the same joke I had in my head about having two more still to go. There was no stampede by the males in the room to offer marriage proposals in spite of the joking plug, most wanted to you-know-what-them *not* marry them. Besides, it would have been ungracious with your present wife/partner being… umm, present.

The floral print Eurodome's eyes welled up when he reminisced about the girls' childhood and he even wheeled out the old cliché about him not so much losing a daughter as gaining a son. Pup's mum and dad beamed and I concluded there and then, in all probability, this wedding *wouldn't* end up in a fistfight between the two families.

Pup's speech was spectacularly inept by any standards. It was basically a thank you list, took all of thirty seconds and if his bait was half as bland he would have been out of business years ago for making flavourless boilies. Pup, in due course, toasted the bridesmaids and was done, lock, stock and barrel, in less than a minute. My two lines of thought were; A, did he have a train to catch? B, if he performed similarly in bed tonight the bride was going to be distinctly unhappy.

Rambo butted into my mental picture of Pup telling a disgruntled and dissatisfied Melissa; 'I boil my baits for that amount of time and if it's good enough for them it should be good enough for you'. She didn't have time to tell him; 'Yeah, and when you do *they* don't stay hard for long enough either' because Rambo was leaning into my personal space.

"I'd like to toast them as well," Rambo confided to me, referring to Pup's mini-speech, "especially, Melina."

"Please, you're not a Premiership footballer and I'm sure you'd go solo," I answered.

It was odd listening to Rambo talk this way because apart from telling me about his unknown son, the one who had been used as a pawn by the mother to trap him into marriage – unsuccessfully – he rarely spoke about women at all. I gave him a hearty nod and abruptly, if only momentarily, became perturbed at the knowledge of Charlie becoming charcoal. The moment passed, Steve was next up to bat.

Steve stood up to a smattering of applause after being announced by Pup as the best man. Pup passed him the microphone. As he did I could sense the room was hoping for something a little more humorous and adventurous to distinguish itself from the previous dire fare. After all Steve was the best man, the best man did the jokes and the crowd were silently crying out for some. Expectations rose and the pressure increased, I felt for him. Public speaking is no easy task.

Steve's only defence against the roomful of family friends and relations was the top table, standing as it did between the VIPs and the rest of us. He glanced with trepidation at Pup and his new wife and then at his wife who, having managed to off-load her offspring onto some poor bastard who was most likely off his head, looked as if she at least, being oblivious to Steve's discomfort, was in a state of bliss.

Steve said nothing. He shuffled from one foot to the other, or at least his upper body gave the impression he shuffled from one foot to the other. The room became hushed. Steve let the microphone dip below the table and he appeared to take something from his pocket. I was just surmising the possibility of Steve surreptitiously nodding towards the guy running the sound system when the noise hit me. From out of the speakers, ten yards to the right of the top table, came the unmistakable sound of a Delkim one-noter, absolutely fucking hammering out at 'Concorde take-off' decibel level.

The reaction was catastrophic. The women screwed up their faces. Make-up cracked and would need serious re-application with the aid of brick trowel and cement mixer in the toilets later. Flat female hands jammed against ears in a vain attempt to keep out the noise. After I had recovered I realised it was exactly what I had done when the ghost had visited me on our first encounter.

But it was amongst the *men* where true pandemonium ruled. It only lasted for a few seconds, but it was magnificent. As one, all the anglers in the room lurched involuntarily as the screaming sound wave crashed against their eardrums. With a Pavlov's dog-like response we all instinctively moved for the rod to hit the run our conditioned brains were telling us was happening right there and then. In a fucking wedding reception room of all places, at six in the evening! Not a bad time to expect a take, admittedly, but the venue was a bit pants! Nevertheless, I, like my fellow anglers, had no time to consider such niceties as instinct and gut reaction kicked in at a level way, way below logical thinking. I found myself up out of my seat, right hand out, body half crouched ready to strike. I lifted up my eyes to compensate for the almost horizontal angle of my neck to see nearly all the other male guests in a similar position. My eyes locked with Rambo's. He had the striker's stoop. I looked at Pete, he had it. Adam had it. Nearly every bloke, and I'll wager *every* carp angler in the room had it. We had been duped mega big-time! Once I had realised my profound stupidity, once *everyone* had realised their profound stupidity and looked up to notice everyone *else's* profound stupidity and then the women realised the *men's* profound stupidity, the room dissolved into anarchic hilarity.

All the embarrassed blokes inched their bodies back from the prior, Neanderthal look-alike pose into one you could safely call a normal, human position and commenced laughing at each other's asininity and that of themselves. People started to wipe off beer-soaked clothing where reflex reaction had knocked over glasses, to dab fevered brows where sweat had manifested itself in the brief flurry of movement and, let's not forget, the acute adrenalin rush. We, that is to say, *all* the carp anglers, had been diminished from allegedly sentient human beings into a simple switch. Throw the switch by making a certain noise and you will get the expected response. It was sad and yet glorious. It was the sublime from ridiculous sonic suggestion. Show a man a picture of a naked, beautiful woman and his eyes widen and he gets an erection. Sound off a buzzer to a carp angler and you get the carp fishing equivalent. In our defence, our pathetic defence, I would say you could only do it *once* a day and get away with it. Maybe twice!

Sophie had got it in one, after I had sat back down once my moment of conditioning had passed. "You men, you're so predictable. What with that and all of you ogling those bridesmaids."

"*And* the bride," I reminded her.

"*You* especially," she countered.

"Hold on a minute." It was time to remind her of something else. "Only a few hours ago you were telling me to *stop* looking at you and to look at someone *else!*"

"I might have said it, but I didn't *mean* it," she retorted with feminine insight and reasoning.

"Did you mean what you *just* said?" I asked.

"You should *know* when I mean it and when I *don't*," she said smiling.

"Couldn't you put up little idiot cards to help me," I pleaded, mockingly.

"I do," she insisted. "But you don't recognise them, and if on the odd occasion you do, *then* you can't even read them."

"Run that one by me when I've had more to drink," I said, squeezing her thigh.

"Mind the dress," she warned me.

"Take it off, then!" I suggested.

"I might do later," she breathed in my ear and then kissed my cheek. I was on a promise!

It had been a brilliant stunt, the subtle nod had clearly been one to cue in the volume on the disco to max power while Steve had whizzed a piece of card over the vibration sensing device of the Delkim he had taken from his pocket. (I hoped nothing would go wrong with it because he had clearly invalidated the guarantee with such an act of wanton barbarity.) From then on, having successfully completed the ultimate warm-up act, we were putty in his hands. He cracked jokes, some good, some not so good but whatever, we laughed at all of them. He toasted both sets of parents, he toasted the groom, he toasted the bride and he toasted the bridesmaids.

"The bridesmaids!" we all cheered.

And Melina kept making eye contact with Rambo and Rambo reciprocated to Melina.

Chapter 6

There is a slack period at most weddings, a Doldrums-type situation where, with all the speeches having finished, the body of guests who were invited to the actual ceremony are becalmed with inactivity. They have little to do, other than to wait, for the even larger body of reception guests to kick-start the evening. Typically the evening guests are most likely to be casual friends, associates, acquaintances and possibly work colleagues of both the bride and groom. It is this wider social mix, rather than the close-knit family and friends alone, when combined with the less formal atmosphere, which can make the evening more boisterous, and to be honest, more fun. However, until they appear in sufficient numbers and have had enough time to get a little social lubrication inside them things remain in limbo. At *most* weddings this is usual but then *this* wedding was far from the norm in many ways. At Pup and Melissa's wedding, the three outfits the bride and two bridesmaids changed into alone were more than adequate to keep the wind blowing strongly until, to mix metaphors, the cavalry came.

The three girls, in combination with their three ensembles, gave all the men even more to gawp at, quite literally, and gave the women new topics of conversation. Firstly, for the younger ones, it gave them a chance to expand subjectively on the merits of each outfit and whether or not they would have the front, (the stomach, the legs *and* the arse) or perhaps more pertinently, the *nerve* to wear it. For the elder ones it gave them a chance to expand on themes of decency, standards and what the heck the world was coming too – like the egoistic utopia of complete and utter self-gratification coupled with the absolute abolition of personal responsibility – or something along those lines. Secondly, it allowed all the females to have underlined beneath their very noses, and therefore become fully cognizant of the second switch-like response of the male carp-angling psyche. The very same one I had thought about earlier, the one so deeply ingrained in all heterosexual men.

As I sat alongside Rambo, in a state of mild inebriation admittedly, I, for my part, became fully cognizant of something different from the females. The three girls' penchant for the frequent use of sunbeds for starters. Also leaping to my attention were the answers to some of my previous thoughts, namely; all three *did* have pierced belly-buttons while only Melissa and Melloney had *visible* tattoos. With a grinning Pup taking the lead the three girls followed him around to the tables, one at a time in order to make small talk with the guests. While they did so I furtively, not wanting to upset Sophie too much, kept a discreet eye on proceedings until it was our turn. Rambo, under no such restraints did so more blatantly. Several times in amongst my snatched glimpses I saw the two of them make eye contact yet again. It left me with the distinct feeling Rambo would be left to worry more about Charcoal Charlie in the long run than manipulating his almighty mitt onto Melina's minge by the time the evening had run its course.

For the record the bride wore skintight hipster trousers, which dipped low enough at the back to show off a pretty pair of jewelled G-back briefs and a short plunging black lace camisole. Melloney, the youngest sister, wore a minuscule pair of black velvet shorts combined with a black halter neck top. Melina, to finish off the triple attack of sexual attitude, wore knee length stiletto boots, something that wasn't quite long enough to be called a skirt, yet definitely wasn't a belt, and an even more revealing, plunging crop top.

From a male point of view it was difficult to know where to look. There were so many choices, so many fine parts of female anatomy to stare at in abject wonderment it became slightly confusing. The big fear was that while you were watching one part, another part, one you *weren't* watching, might suddenly disclose even more succulent flesh as gravity, muscular movement or a strong draft conspired to create a special window of opportunity. An equally worrying notion was that the amount of coverage would stay the same but the part itself would jiggle and wriggle in an even *more* provocative and sexually voyeuristic manner. Now, whether this happened by chance or design – who the fuck cared? – the big scare was that you would miss it! As an impartial (that's my story and I'm sticking to it) bystander I drank from all three cups, little quick sneaky sips when I stupidly thought no one was looking. But it was Rambo whose eyes remained fixed on Melina's outrageous, and highly successful, attention-seeking outfit. He was smitten and the two boyfriends, who I was half-expecting to suddenly materialise and begin pawing and touching what we were looking at, never appeared. This fuelled his enthusiasm, if possible, even further.

"They're here *alone*, boy!" he whispered, louder than he might have cared to admit too. "You know what they say about bridesmaids at weddings?"

"Aren't they meant to have an affair with the best man?" I recalled rather dimly.

"Fat chance!" laughed Rambo nodding at Steve who was holding apart two of his sons as their little legs flailed and kicked at each other. The other two, seeing their big chance for commotion, legged it off towards the door.

A distant cry of, "Come back, *now!*" wafted past my ears.

"Granted," I shrugged, "he does seem a little pre-occupied. How many are we going to have, dearest?" I said to Sophie.

Sophie, who had been quietly knocking back the wine, both red and white, gave me a massive pout. "How many what, darling?"

"Children," I told her.

I would like to think she looked at me with dreamy eyes but realistically I put it down to the alcohol. "Three," she cooed. And, even allowing for her red and white wine intake, she seemed serious.

Rambo kicked me under the table and pulled a 'fuck your luck' grimace. Perhaps I would sneak off with Steve and have a vasectomy while she wasn't looking.

At long last Pup and the girls made it to our table. While Pup introduced us I tried to control my leering at the large amounts of pristine female form to a minimum but what with *my* alcohol intake it was easier said than done. It was probably even worse for Adam and Pete because the sisters were *elder* women to them, a slight turn on in itself. But hey, I had enough problems keeping the lid on my tin of peeping Tom peppermints to start worrying over theirs.

As Pup finished the introductions Melina moved to a space on our table in between Adam and Hannah but opposite Rambo. She leaned on the edge of it, the insides of her wrists facing towards us and allowed her straight arms to form a pincer movement propelling her already remarkable breasts both together and forward. It was expertly done and with the plunging neckline dragging all eye contact into her wonderful cleavage, like a spaceship being sucked down a black hole, she had everyone's attention before she had even opened her mouth.

"Hi, Rambo," she said ignoring the rest of us, "I simply *love* your outfit."

Such was the emphasise on the 'L' of the word 'love' it was easy to see the small, bright stainless steel ball in her tongue. Quickly while we were all mesmerised by her spell, she slid fluidly around to Rambo's side. My eyes followed her. I didn't need to worry about being surreptitious now because everyone seated at the table did exactly the same. At that very moment the room's lights went out and the disco's lights came on. Music started and her diamanté studded belly-button piercing glittered in the strobe lighting as she moved. It was a poetic moment caused by chance but there was nothing random or accidental about her movements.

Now alongside the seated Rambo she ran her hand over his M25 shoulders. "Nice material," she purred.

She waited for two seconds and ran her fingers from his shoulders up to the back of his neck and the short hair at its nape. She stroked the hair. It stood on end. I was willing to wager other parts were up to the same thing. Her fingers moved around onto Rambo's face and an index finger lifted up his chin to make him look straight into her eyes.

"Shall we go?" she said. The words oozed out of her and she offered Rambo her hand.

For a nanosecond Rambo didn't quite grasp the implications of the question and his mouth hinted at the movement so similar to a carp's mouth, one having its photo taken. Then, not being a fish out of water, the penny didn't so much as drop, as got fired downwards by a howitzer. His body jolted as if someone had pumped a brief dollop of two-forty electricity through him, his eyes twinkled and two invisible elephants started to pull at the two invisible hawsers that were attached to the two invisible coat hooks placed in either corner of his mouth.

He smiled the mother of all smiles.

"Sure thing, girl," he said and he was up out of his chair in a flash.

I swear he and Melina virtually ran through the tables as they presumably headed for the room where the girls had changed from their bridesmaids' outfits into their evening wear.

"Where the hell are they going?" asked Adam with shocking naivety.

Hannah leant over to him and whispered a few words in his ear. "*Christ!* Really? What… just like that?" he said, still bemused.

"Once Mel has decided she doesn't like to waste time," explained Melloney. "She's always had a thing about soldiers and she was drooling over him the minute she set eyes on him. She likes *big* men, as well," she added.

I was about to crack the obvious joke but a glare from my beloved stopped me in my tracks. Later on in the evening I would try to convince Sophie that a soldier infatuation had been my theory, made before it had been confirmed, shortly after it had become clear Melina had been eyeing Rambo and not myself. Although I missed that bit out, obviously. Far too embarrassing on too many levels. She asked me why, by way of a tease, I hadn't written it down on a scrap of paper and presented it to her like I had the name of our only daughter.

"Because I didn't have a bloody pen!" I would explain.

"You're losing it, Matthew!" she would tease even further

"So," I said trying to maintain the impression of being an adult who could deal with what had just happened. "What's it like being married?" I asked Pup directly.

It was a crap line, even Sophie flinched, but it was all I had in the locker. You see the problem was, physically I was in the wedding reception room, but mentally I was trying to stop myself clawing at room 69's door – or whatever one it was – and attempting to shut out the image of what was undoubtedly going on there. Whereas I had sat and fantasised about what Rebecca might or might not be doing while waiting for the run from the mind-meld mirror, now I was desperately trying *not* to do the same about Rambo and Melina. Part jealousy? Part embarrassment? Part imagining Rambo's hairy arse thrusting up and down? Whatever way the coin fell I didn't want to go there, besides he was bound to tell me.

"It's all right, mate," Pup assured me and looking at Melissa I could see his point of view.

I nodded enthusiastically. Silence. Bollocks! It was my turn for another question. My mind, often not the most precise of tools and now hindered by four pints of Beck's, a few glasses of wine *and* the cheap toasting champagne grappled with itself for another one. It produced a corker.

"If Rambo ends up marrying Melina, will you roll his bait up at a discount rate because he's your brother-in-law?"

Everyone laughed because they saw it as a joke but it had been a straight question. A ridiculously moronic straight question and one I had fortuitously got away with.

"I expect so," said Pup genially. "Of course now there are two of us I'll be looking to expand the business as much as I can. We're hoping to get another property to live in and still keep my place for the bait making seeing as it's all set up. Keep, rollin', rollin', rollin', rollin', eh?" We all laughed.

"I hope you've still got my picture by the light switch in the 25mm room?" I asked.

Pup nodded. He kept on looking at me and went back to my earlier question. "Mind you, I might be charging you *double* for your bait. What with you not coming to see me and shall we say, 'acquiring' the very syndicate I gave you and Rambo the chance to get into. I couldn't *believe* it when Rambo told me what had happened. God alone knows what Rocky, Darren and Hollywood, *especially* Hollywood, were ever thinking about. It made no sense then and it still doesn't now. Still, one man's meat is another man's poison," he remarked pointedly. "And you're living on prime fillet!"

Inwardly I laughed at Pup's use of Gary's nickname, our nickname, which he had picked it up from Rambo. It had stuck in his head and clearly struck a chord. However, he *was* right, I *did* owe him and not for a skip load of boilies either.

Pup paused and put his arm around Melissa's curvaceous waist. "Actually we're thinking of starting to do a bit of fishing, just the odd short session to begin with. Mel's really keen, she gets a real buzz from it and with my baits we'll do really well on any water… even yours!"

I lifted up my head and smiled. Was that a little hint? Had Pup changed his views on syndicates? Everything else had changed for him. When we had first met him we had considered him as nerdy and sad as, let's be honest, as nerdy and sad as Rambo and I, when we had given up everything in pursuit of the TWTT. In those times his girlfriend had only recently left him and he was a complete bait anorak to the exclusion of everything else. *Now* he had his brand new deluxe sex-o-matic wife and a whole new exciting adventure in front of him. And with a woman unlikely to ever moan about the amount of fishing he did, in fact, *turned on* by the amount of fishing he did. Think about that! The only downside would be living in each other's pocket. Would you really want to go fishing with your wife all the time? As long as Melissa looked like she did and didn't metamorphose into a floral print Eurodome the answer would inevitably be yes. Not unless it was going to piss hard and you had forgotten your bivvy *and* your brolly.

"You're more than welcome to come up as guests whenever you want," I told them.

Could I make such an offer, I immediately thought having offered it? I *could*! I am the owner! I tucked it to the back of my mind. "Who's coming from the Lac Fumant gang, Pup?" I asked.

"We'll have to wait and see, Matt, because to be honest I'm not sure myself. I sent out invites to a couple of them who've become customers and friends. The ones who call in and pick up their bait and also some of the ones who get their bait by mail order who live abroad. The trouble is none of them have replied so I've no idea if they're coming or not. I actually supply Bob at Lac Fumant now, you know. I've just signed a deal with him to supply my fishmeal air-dried baits for all his customers who don't want to have the hassle of sourcing and taking their own. It's the old 'quality baits on site' crack. He's due to come and pick up the first consignment before we go away on honeymoon on Monday, so I told him to come up a couple of days earlier and come to the reception. There's a chance Japp and Wim might come. I know they're in the UK on business over this weekend as well. They've bought a hell of a lot of bait from me over the last few years, I can tell you."

"Wow! That'll be nice to see them both, and Bob of course," I said genuinely.

"Where's this Lac Fumant?" asked Adam.

I explained how Rambo and I had gone there a couple of times and went on to reminisce to my small audience about Bob's time-warp tee shirts, his catchphrases and his beautiful lake. Next I told them how the Dutch brothers' superb English was better than that spoken by most English people and how one night Wim had inadvertently slipped me an LSD tab instead of a pain-killer. I went on to explain how the mistake had led to all sorts of capers, like me being paralysed on a bedchair for over twenty-four hours for a start, and the spoof video the rest of them had made largely at my expense. If I say so myself the anecdotes went down well and everybody laughed at them, but I didn't feel it was the right time to re-tell the one about melding with the big mirror. Not surprisingly I didn't mention the one about Rebecca either. I had *never* told the one about Rebecca, not even to Rambo and Christ knows he had asked me enough times over the years.

Eventually after fifteen minutes or so Pup made his excuses to leave us. He wanted to see all the wedding guests before the music became too loud and the evening got fully under way. He and just two sisters left us, while we were also one person light. I wondered what the two of them were up to, not generally, no prizes for guessing there, but more specifically. I stopped myself as quick as I could.

"What do you think of Melina, then?" I whispered to Sophie. "Talk about up front, in-your-face and not taking no for answer! Some proposition, eh?"

"You certainly couldn't keep your eyes off her, *or* the other two come to that," Sophie said matter-of-factly.

I went to defend myself but decided better of it. When you're in a hole, stop digging.

Sophie continued seemingly unbothered by my leering. "She *wanted* him and she *got* him! And she didn't care what we thought, either." Sophie looked at me with tipsy intensity. Her head wobbled imperceptibly. "Good for her. You only live once," she said.

"Would you act like that?" I asked a little surprised at her answer.

Her answer was indicative of the 'new Sophie', the one deeply affected by the ghost and its life and death repercussions. It still took me on the hop when it manifested itself and I found it hard to quantify whether it was indeed her new life outlook or simply the wine shooting its mouth off. As Homer might say – 'Stupid loudmouth red wine.'

"*Not* with Rambo." She held out an empty glass.

"Oh! But with somebody else, then?" I probed.

Sophie pitched a couple of perfectly plucked eyebrows upwards and breathed out heavily. "Get me another white wine, will you, please."

Stupid loudmouth *white* wine.

I bought Sophie's drink from an eleven-year-old barboy, took it back to her and then went off to the toilets. On the way back I got cornered by three of my newest syndicate members who had arrived only minutes earlier, the recently interviewed Paul, Simon and Phil. They started to bombard me with questions concerning tactics and areas to fish to on Hamworthy. Although I told them I would walk them around swim by swim at the work party as I had already told them at the interview, I couldn't help but acquiesce to their demands. We all went up to the bar, they bought me another lager and time was forgotten as I built up their expectation levels to bursting point. The best part was I had no need to exaggerate one iota, it was all the truth. Hamworthy *was* the greatest water in the land. Whereas other fishery owners might exaggerate and spin the truth concerning both numbers and size of fish, I had no need to resort to such underhand deception. I revelled in the size and numbers of fish of which I spoke and *they* revelled in the size and number of fish I spoke about too. All they had to do was go out and catch them and their bliss would be permanent.

By the time Rambo re-appeared and came up to me and the three lads it had been well over an hour since he had been propositioned by Melina. During that time the evening reception had well and truly kicked off without me really realising it. I had been so engrossed in conversation with my three latest syndicate members I had failed to spot how noisy and how crowded the place had become and the host of fresh faces causing it. On looking around the seething room I spotted Sophie on the dance floor strutting her pretty funky stuff with Melloney and Melissa while in a bizarre contrast Steve's four boys were involved in a titanic – in terms of its immense fury, rather than bulk, as the bout was an under-30 kilo contest – wrestling match to the side of it. Out of the central mass of interlocked torsos, legs and arms flailed at alarming angles in their apparent desperation to beat what they were attached to, into a bloody pulp. The boys must have been duffing themselves *and* each other up because it looked utterly indiscriminate. Tiny clenched fists and small feet encased in new shoes pummelled and booted the central mass with all the demented attitude of a masochistic octopus giving itself a good seeing to.

Amazingly, or perhaps not so amazingly, depending on your viewpoint of children, no one took any notice of the mound of raging schoolboy petulance, least of all Steve and his wife, who were conspicuous by their absence. I surmised they were most probably waiting for the boys to render themselves unconscious, thus making it much easier to sort out the battered mass of junior school belligerence. As a possible alternative choice of action they may have been getting completely blasted to numb their sensibilities sufficiently before they could face up to dealing with them.

On second thoughts, the concept of the boys being kind enough to their parents to knock each other out, even though it involved desirable – from their viewpoint – rival sibling pain, was only wishful thinking. The clear assumption to be drawn for the latter case of parental action was that copious consumption aided compunction and gave them the gumption to stamp out a ruction at a wedding day function.

Apart from the squabbling boys who undoubtedly had severe fratricidal tendencies, they would probably prefer a four-way punch up even if staged in the best toy shop in the northern hemisphere, everyone else seemed to be having a great time. The disco was blasting, drinks were disappearing down necks and no one had demonstrated the disturbing potential mouth damage of the bent hook rig by jamming a size two bender into someone's bottom lip and dragging them around the room by it. Nor was anyone attempting to draw conclusions on a similar theme and by similar experimentation on the benefits, or otherwise, of using barbed or barbless hooks. Personally I was glad, and felt the evening was going all the better for it continuing not to happen.

On the subject of having a great time in general my opening line to Rambo, once I had excused myself from my three latest converts, was unsubtle.

"How'd it go?" I asked. "Wow Factor on a scale of one to ten?"

"Oh, we sat and talked. Chatted about our hopes and aspirations, had a cup of tea…"

"Of course you fucking did. I expect she had a chess board up there so you had a little game of that as well," I said acidly.

"Monopoly," Rambo corrected and changed the subject. "You'll never guess who I've just seen?"

I was a bit miffed at this distraction and could hardly hide it. "David Beckham?"

Rambo shook his head. I eyed him for signs of dishevelment, askew clothing, laddered camouflage boxer shorts.

"Bob," said Rambo. "Lac Fumant 'quality, chief', Bob. And guess who was with him?" Rambo asked again.

"Japp and Wim? Pup said they might turn up. Over here on business, Daddy's *porn* business, I expect."

Rambo shook his head, his eyes sparkling with mischief. "Rebecca!"

"No way!" I said in unadulterated disbelief.

"Here they are now. Look!" said Rambo and I turned and mimicked his direction of view.

Sure enough, there was Bob and by his side was Rebecca. It was the most peculiar sensation setting eyes on her after all this time and for all my supposed maturity and despite a reasonable intake of booze I felt strangely nervous as Bob spotted us, waved and headed towards us. Rebecca followed him, she had seen us both as well. She looked relaxed and confident as she eased her away through the throng of people to get to us. She also looked great, blonde hair, perfect white teeth plus a cracking figure. Images, ones I hadn't had much time or inclination to consider of late, shot into my head. In a state of mild panic I looked for Sophie but she had gone from the dance floor.

Rambo lowered his head down to my ear. "So, did you shag her that night after you'd caught the mind-meld mirror?" he asked gently.

For some reason, presumably the impact of seeing her coupled with the effects of a lessening of sobriety, I told him. "Yes," I admitted weakly.

Rambo seemed happy with the answer. "I *knew* you had."

"So why did you keep asking me, then?" I said, still slightly shell-shocked to have let one of my big secrets out the bag.

"Because you might not have. I have been wrong before, you know," he said earnestly.

"*I've* never known you to be," I said matching Rambo's sincerity. We lapsed into silence, the two of them were nearly upon us.

"Chiefs!" said Bob hugging Rambo and then pumping his hand before dishing out the same treatment to me. "Quality to see you both. You both look well, haven't changed a bit." Bob dusted down the lapel of Rambo's camouflage morning suit jacket. "Quality outfit, too." He peered up at Rambo as if he was looking up to the peak of a mountain. "Are you getting *bigger*, chief?"

"That's the well-known effect of camouflage clothing," I said sarcastically, "it makes things appear larger than they really are."

Everyone ignored this comment.

"Hi, Matthew. Hi, Rambo," said Rebecca and she lent forward and kissed me on both cheeks and then did the same to Rambo after he'd bent down to let her do it. *Very* French!

"Hello, Rebecca," we said in unison.

"How's Lac Fumant?" I asked. "Still as beautiful as ever?"

"Oh yes, chief, still as beautiful as ever. She's a little bit harder today than she was on your first visit, though…"

Rambo cut Bob off. "She was hard enough on our second trip! Boy, did we struggle on that one!"

"… True enough, chief. Funny, I always think of the first trip when I think of you two. Selective memory you see, remember the best times and forget the not so good. But no, she's more difficult generally than in those earlier days. It's all down to pressure isn't it? People still love going there, though. You ought to come back, some of your party still do, you know, every year."

"It's a bit more difficult now," I explained. "I've got a baby daughter and my own water now."

I glanced at Rebecca's face for any sign of reaction to this new nugget of information. God knows what I was looking for, jealousy or disappointment? A desire on her part to recapture the past, a need to rekindle the lust that had flickered between us for that one, brief encounter? Mentally I jammed the bottom of my hand against my temple. Derrh! She hadn't even been around Lac Fumant second time because she had cluttered off with her boyfriend! If she hadn't been arsed then it was hardly likely she was going to be arsed now, not now we were all even further down the line. She hadn't held a torch for me then, so she was hardly going to be holding one now. It had been a holiday romance of sorts, end of story, nothing more and nothing less. Although at the time it *had* meant more to me, I couldn't deny it, not even to myself. My life had spectacularly expanded from its compressed state in prison and the aftermath of the TWTT debacle and I guess, in retrospect, I couldn't handle the exposure to freedom and the temptation it can sometimes offer.

"Your own water, eh? When did you buy it then, chief," said Bob, keen and interested.

I flicked my eyes up at Rambo. My tongue wiped my upper lip like Steve's had when a difficult question had arisen. "I didn't buy it, it was given to me."

"*Given* to you? Quality I'd say!"

"It's a long story," I said meekly.

"Well, let me buy you two chiefs a drink and you can tell me it!" enthused Bob. Bob beckoned us to follow him to the bar.

"Oh, *God!*" I whispered to Rambo. "Will I have enough time?"

Rambo pooh-poohed me. "Yeah! They haven't even played 'Hi-Ho Silver Lining' yet, so there must be at least an hour and a half to go." He suddenly poked a vicious rock-hard index finger into my ribs that nearly brought me to my knees. "Don't mention the ghost, and, later, if you tell me what you did with Rebecca, I'll tell you what I did with Melina."

"Deal!" I groaned, wincing from the finger assault.

Bob purchased the drinks from an eight-year-old barboy and we retreated to a table furthest from the disco's speakers. Initially Bob told us how he had come to pick up four hundred kilos of Pup's quality fishmeal air-dried 20mm bottom baits and a twenty kilo sack of the legendary pop-ups. Apparently it was cost-effective for him to make the journey for such a bulk of bait rather than rely on a carrier. In any case, he explained, he could easily cover his costs plus a little extra on his mark-up of the bait when he sold it on to this year's set of punters. Bob told us how Lac Fumant was still proving to be very popular and how he was making a decent living from it. He also informed us that Rebecca still lived at home but had a full-time job working as a receptionist in the local French doctor's surgery. Consequently Bob was doing all the cooking and not one, not *one* single person had died of food poisoning, he added. He sounded proud.

I listened as intently as I could, given the amount of drink I'd had, which by my standards was now bordering on the point of losing faculties. Despite leaning over the abyss of talking bollocks and the likelihood of projectile vomiting in the next three hours, I had other problems. The overriding feeling I had as the conversation opened out was not the one of getting pissed but the need for a piss. I had reached the stage where I knew I would now be constantly in and out of the toilets emptying a bladder apparently shrunk in capacity to something akin to an egg cup. Previous experience told me this, and I had often wondered whether I would have been better off pouring the lager straight down the urinal so I could cut out the middleman. My full bladder screamed at me to go and empty it and such was my discomfort I knew I would have to before it became my turn to explain how I had acquired Hamworthy. There was no way I could even contemplate telling my tale before going to the loo, so I made my excuses and went to leave.

I got out of my seat, turned towards the room's exit in a half crouched position and bumped straight into Sophie, my face thrusting directly into her tits.

"Fancy seeing you here!" I said with a slight giggle addressing her boobs.

Sophie tottered a little on her strappy shoes. She was in a similar state of drunkenness to me.

"So *that's* where you've been hiding!" she remarked, looking at the table and the three other people sitting at it. "I know *that* big lummox," she said nodding towards Rambo. She whispered in my ear, "but not as well as *Melina* does! Who are the other two?"

I sensed a slight foreboding of danger but was too incapacitated to do anything sophisticated about it. "That's Bob," I said resoundingly. Resounding in the sense of trying to sound as if I was telling the truth but not in the sense of volume. I was whispering too. "He's the bloke who owns Lac Fumant. You remember, the French water we went to a couple of times? The one we were talking to Pup about. The one he's supplying the four hundred kilos of whatever bait he's supplying he said he was supplying?" I said getting slightly tangled in my words

Sophie waved a dismissive hand. The movement of her hand rocked her whole body. "Christ, these bloody shoes are high! Yeah, I remember. And the girl?" she asked, pleasantly enough.

She's the one I shagged after having caught the mind-meld mirror. It was *her* fault. She came onto me and I really *did* agonize for *ages* over whether it was morally right or wrong to do so. But I did and I was wrong. My cock pulled harder than my brain. You saw what all those blokes were like when that fucking Delkim went off and you saw what all those fucking blokes were like when the girls had changed into their porn star outfits. I'm one of those fucking blokes as well. I'm guilty as charged.

By the way I never said any of that. I wasn't *that* pissed.

"That's his daughter, Rebecca," I said.

"She's very pretty," Sophie remarked. "There are a lot of pretty women here."

"Yeah. Yeah, I suppose she is, I suppose there are," I said with as much casual non-commitment as I could. Inside my head I was getting in a right old pickle and a rising swell of muzzy thinking matched and then passed the aching pain of my full bladder. Now whether it was the drink or having just admitted my scandalous adultery to Rambo or the effect of being in Rebecca's company, I shall never know but I felt pressured into covering the tracks of my past.

"It's the first time I've ever met her," I lied. I wanted to run from my words because as soon as I had uttered them I regretted it. "Look, I'm bursting for a piddle. I've got to go to the toilet, I'll be back in a minute."

"Okay," said Sophie I'll be with Melloney, Melissa and Melina on the dance floor. We're going to ask for 'Hi Ho Silver Lining' soon. You can't have a wedding without 'Hi Ho Silver Lining'."

I nodded, turned and dashed for the toilets. Having blundered through the two sets of doors with an increasing fear of wetting myself, I stood as steady as I could, whipped my cock out and fired it, like a jet stream, at the white porcelain slab that had signalled my short journey's end. The relief was marvellous.

"Hello, Matthew. How are you going?"

The voice was instantly recognisable. It was Japp.

"Hi, Japp," I said.

I squeezed my stomach muscles as tight as I could to eek out the final drops of urine from my hapless bladder. I shook my dick and some droplets of urine went onto my hand. Getting those few extra drops out might buy me an extra thirty seconds until I had to come back again. I shook my hand into the urinal and made a point of washing it before I shook Japp's hand. I was shaking all over.

Japp was in his customary orange Dutch football shirt. "You have been drinking a little, I think?" he said, waving a finger at me in mock admonishment.

"Shit! Does it show?" I said sulkily.

"When you have seen as much drug abuse as I have, you very soon notice even a little indiscretion," said Japp evenly.

"Oh... right," I said with understanding. "How is Wim?"

"He is in rehab at the moment," Japp shrugged his shoulders with a Gallic air despite his Dutch nationality. "Maybe he will never learn his lesson. Maybe it is impossible for him to learn because he has to forget so much to be able to learn," Japp said without a hint of irony.

"Pup said you were over on business?" I said keen to get off the scary analysis. I didn't want bladderache in the head from any other source other than the one I was bound to get from the drink.

"Yes, that is right, Matthew. I am here in England looking for a private fishing venue that is suitable for our needs," Japp explained. "It is not easy finding what I want. Most of the waters are too crowded and too exposed, they are not suitable at all."

"My water's miles from anywhere, an estate totalling about sixty acres and with only twenty syndicate members," I bragged.

Japp's eyes narrowed. "You *own* your own water?"

"It's a long story," I sighed. "One I should be telling to Bob right now."

"Then I will come and listen to it as well if you are happy to let me, Matthew. I may well have a business proposition for you at the end of it."

"Come on then," I said pushing past him to lead the way. "I've got until 'Hi Ho Silver Lining' to tell it."

Japp grabbed me by the shoulder and pulled me round. His eyes gleamed with nationalistic pride. "'Radar Love' was *much* better."

"*You* want it, *you* ask for it," I told him.

The pair of us went and sat back down with Bob, Rebecca and Rambo. I told my story – the public version, not the dark secret version – of how Hamworthy Fisheries had fallen into my not really worthy hands and how at last I was finally coming to terms with it and the responsibility. They all listened very carefully. When I had finished Japp bought all of us another drink and cunningly cornered me when I was on my own, in the toilets having yet *another* piss – *that* was why I reckon he bought *me* a drink – and made his shocking proposal. Later, with a bolt right out of the blue – while I was trying to hang on gamely to the bar counter and being watched trying to hang on gamely to the bar counter by a six-year-old barboy – Bob made his. Going against every pre-conceived idea I had in my head concerning how *I* would run a syndicate I agreed to both.

"You're everywhere and nowhere baby, that's where you're at! Running down a bumpy hillside, in your hippy hat…" we all screamed in each other's ears.

Myself, Sophie, Rambo, Melina, Japp, Melissa, (complete with skinny roll-up superglued to her bottom lip, á la Andy Capp) Pup, Melloney, Steve, Paul, Simon, Phil, Hannah, Adam, Peter, Louis, Bob, Rebecca and some eight or so others I didn't know, were all locked together, arms over shoulders, cavorting drunkenly on the dance floor shouting our heads off. We moved in and out like computer graphic simulations of the new string theory of binding sub-atomic particles, forced by the stronger individuals who pushed and then pulled the floundering chain of human bodies. The can-can leg movements, so vigorous at the opening riff, were less demonstrative now we were getting knackered and only Melina managed to kick her legs up high enough to show off her tiny knickers. The tart.

Sticky, sweaty, laughing bodies whirled under the flashing disco lights. Sound fluctuated and distorted. Realisation tapped me on the temple with a sledgehammer. I was going to puke. I had exceeded my personal limit and it was just a matter of when and where I would be actively regurgitating the expensive liquid I had poured down my throat and previously pissed out of my prick. Up at the bar the grinning, spotty youth, no doubt ogling the scantily dressed women from a superior advantage in terms of having unimpeded sensibilities – by virtue of having *served* drinks rather than *quaffing* them – was only five-years-old and spinning. By the side of the floor a pile of four boys lay comatose and revolving on the ground. They had finally beaten themselves unconscious, or they were sleeping. To be honest I didn't give a fuck one way or the other. I had reached the high and was on the way back down. Everything was suddenly less funny than it had been a few moments earlier now the impending hangover had indicated its imminent arrival with subtle signs of nausea. It was now very clear to me why I didn't make a habit of getting drunk.

The music stopped and the lights went up. Everyone squinted as the harsh illumination revealed shiny skin and worse-for-wear appearances.

"I'll call a taxi," I said to Sophie. "I don't feel too good."

Two hours later I was still cuddling the toilet while Sophie crashed, fully dressed – if you can use such a phrase for such a garment – on the bed in her designer outfit. The only promise I got that night was one from myself, one promising myself to never, *ever* get so drunk again. Trouble was I had heard it all before.

Sophie's mum had simply tut-tutted at the pair of us and slept in the spare bedroom in case Amy needed any attention – attention the two of us were too incapacitated to give. In the cold morning light that was the bit that sickened the two of us the most.

Chapter 7

The steam rose off the kettle in small billowing clouds. Looking through it from my bedchair back in the bivvy I could see my three swinger indicators, dressed in their buzzer LED inspired, colour co-ordinated splendour, all indicating exactly the same thing. The thing they registered was nothing. Although technically speaking nothing *was* something, I guess. However, nothing was happening. Nothing *had* happened. And judging by their rather indifferent attitude the smart money said nothing *would* happen. Whatever tense you used it seemed to embrace events with alarming accuracy, but as a fully paid-up member of the non-predestinarian faith I was happy to believe the future tense was reasonably ambiguous and most issues were as yet unresolved. Mind you, I still had the *feeling* I was going to blank. Faith and reality are often at opposite ends of the spectrum, except for when they are bedfellows and completely synonymous. How's that for a bit of shite homespun philosophy?

I snorted to myself. Welcome to early season carp fishing, twenty-four hours so far and not so much as a beep. Not a single fish had crashed-out that I was aware of and to compound things even further I hadn't seen a solitary carp pop its head out of the water in a silent, flat-spot creating manoeuvre either. No carp had shown, not even the most daunting of sightings where you happen to spot a fish miles away from where you are.

The dreaded 'way yonder' sighting speaks silently to your inner soul. 'You're in the wrong spot, dummy', it tells you. 'You and your three tons of equipment should be round *this* side of the lake.'

I was grateful for small mercies. At least I could stay put and not chastise myself and slaughter myself on the alter of magazine articles compelling me, no, *telling* me, to move onto showing fish. Well, fuck that, I was staying put. In my mind, seeing as I had plenty of time to consider such niceties, I wondered how many times someone had upped sticks and ball-busted all their gear to a swim where one fish had shown, only to see another one show in the area they had just come from.

I was too experienced for such nonsense, even if I did say so myself. Maybe a number of shows, determined on the day by how keen I was to catch and whether the gut instinct said; 'Make it so, Number One', *might* make me move. Take this with the confidence factor, or the lack of it regards the already occupied swim, how long I had been in it, how long I had to go in it and the combination *could* do the trick and get me to shift my butt. Or get me to possibly *think* about it. Anyway, none of these situations came into play because the water, and I could see a fair amount of it from Rambo's favourite south-east point swim – when I could be arsed to look – was devoid of carp life and I wasn't moving anywhere. The additional proviso being; not until it was time to pack up and go home.

I knew the swim I was in pretty well. Not through firsthand experience, you understand, but from Rambo's previous efforts, subsequent results and his sharing of the information with me. He had told me of all the likely spots to get pick-ups, he had given me a pretty good knowledge of the depth and features in front of me and he had told me the most likely time of the day I would get a run. I had the facts to hand because Rambo had found out the hard way by fishing the swim many times and grinding out results from it. Consequently, because of his painstaking spadework, I did feel a twinge of confidence deep inside, as much a twinge as I could realistically hope for given the time of year. It was only early April, after all, and it was still on the cold side with a stiff northerly wind blowing almost directly in my face. The large body of water comprising Hamworthy Fisheries had not yet been warmed to any significant degree and the chances were the carp residing within the water were still in winter torpor.

The twinge of confidence didn't outweigh the feeling of an impending blank – the dot ball with nothing to trouble the scorer – so blatantly signalled by my three apathetic indicators. My Hamworthy logbook was likely to record a turned up, cast out, wound in, went home session. My one hope, given to me by my best mate, was if a carp did feed in my swim I was in with a shout because I had the right areas covered. It was why I hadn't yet packed up and gone home.

Apart from all this it was also around ten in the morning, which definitely meant it was time for a cup of tea. When *isn't* it time for a cup of tea when you're carp fishing? The kettle was now boiling and it was time for me to make it. I turned off my little gas stove and thought of Michael as I did so, because it was the one action he had decided not to do and had died because of it. Not a lot of people know that. I poured out the boiling liquid and pushed the teabag into the side of my mug with the back of a teaspoon. Teabag out and a slop of milk in. Another quick stir. Perfect.

I decided right then, just after I had made my tea, that fishing this swim was a bit like my one-way relationship with Melina. Only a bit like it and only if you subscribed to dipping your toes into the swimming pool of dodgy analogy. You see I knew nearly all of Melina's intimate secrets like I knew nearly all of my swim's intimate secrets. I knew her preferred sexual positions, I knew what colour her pubic hair was, I knew what she would do and what she wouldn't do within a bedroom, kitchen, hallway, staircase, car and *al fresco* scenario! (To reiterate, it was only early April and it was still a bit on the cold side when they had met in *March*! Outside sex! Put it down to the warming fires of love. Actually, before I close these brackets, if I was to believe what I was being led to believe there wasn't *anything* she wouldn't do, or if there was Rambo hadn't had the time or didn't possess the imagination to discover it.) I knew what noises she made when she had an orgasm (or faked it –

Oooh, bitchy, bitchy!) and what outfits she would dress up in to satisfy both her and Rambo's sense of role-play. I knew where her most intimate tattoo was positioned and what she liked to do with the ball stud on her pierced tongue.

I knew all of this because I had been told it. And the source of these revelations was exactly the same as the one for my current carp session tactics. I was indebted to Rambo for the information on Melina as I had been for the gen on the south-east point swim. I have to admit though, it would have been a tantalising prospect to have found out first hand, to have discovered every nuance, every detail and every nugget of information for myself without any help from the camouflaged one. About Melina, that is, *not* the south-east point swim. I was more than happy to fish off Rambo's back and if it transpired, pull out a carp or two by virtue of easily acquired knowledge.

The knowledge concerning Melina had been a swap, a pretty lopsided one in my opinion, in return for my informing Rambo of the sordid details of my one night of lust with Rebecca. My one night, it seemed to me, paled into insignificance compared to the shag-fest he was involved in. It had been the best part of three weeks since they had met at Pup's wedding and I had seen him and spoken to him only the once. The combination of her insatiability and his desire as he so eloquently put it; 'To get a lot of dirty water off my chest' had meant they were going at it hammer and tongs, day and night, *every* day and *every* night. Black and blue? Had to be.

Whereas Rambo had admitted to devoting little time to his CCI (Charcoal Charlie Investigation), doing little or no delicate probing into the unfortunate torching, foul or accidental, of his 'fake-a-death' associate, the opposite was true of his investigation into Melina. Here the probing was far from delicate, quite the contrary, brutal almost, extremely in-depth – up to nine inches – (show-off) and both exhaustive and exhausting. Well, it made *me* feel tired and I was only *listening* to it.

Whereas I was rendered punch-drunk by the graphic knock out account of their supercharged sexual antics, my night of passion seemed a mere slap on the cheek. Perhaps it was me. Was I comparing the incomparable? Rambo and myself for a start and then secondly, Melina and Rebecca. Rebecca had been good but faced with the all out sexual assault of Melina, who was clearly a case of what you saw being exactly what you got, it appeared to be no contest. I don't know, Rambo seemed to soak up my little adventure with sponge-like enthusiasm but it was such a tiny act of love-making set against his crashing, compelling, cataclysmic, creative, cornucopia of constant copulation I felt completely outdone.

Perhaps it was simply because Rebecca and I were total history. There had been no spark at Pup's wedding, particularly from her, and I had only felt slightly nervous due to the surprise of her being there, coupled with my fear of Sophie somehow finding out what had happened between us. Our time had been and gone whereas Rambo and Melina's time was now. It was immediate and vibrant. She was sex on legs and the bright spark that often lights many new relationships burned so brightly between them all else seemed dull. If I had a twinge of confidence relating to getting a take then sitting alongside it was a twinge of jealousy. A petty jealousy concerning my best mate having a girl as wild and as exciting as Melina. Not a very pretty thought, especially considering how great looking my Sophie was, how much shit she'd had to contend with over the years from yours truly – while still staying true to me – and how we now had a baby girl and true responsibility.

Although I thought I was getting older and more sensible and could never fall foul to the old TWTT mentality, I was still, I had to admit, a bit of a dope at times. The list went on from the nadir of the TWTT and other items such as my weakness with Rebecca, which I had been fortunate enough to get away with, to my stupidity over Rambo and Melina. I suppose to go for another analogy it was like your best mate catching a fifty while you were on the net. Sure you were pleased for him but deep down in the nasty caverns of your despicable mind you would much rather it had been the other way round. Did Rambo feel the same way about me getting Hamworthy rather than him? I had expected resentment from the other syndicate members but what about my best friend? Was he just the tiniest bit put out? How about my enduring relationship with Sophie when he'd had no one? The money I had received from Sophie's mum? Had he been jealous of all those things? Even my affair with Rebecca, surely he had fancied her and would have liked to have been the one who'd had her rather than me? Maybe it was better not to know. Who could stand the dark secrets of other people's minds, especially ones who were close? It was better we didn't know or our fundamental human nature might damage us all irreparably. Or was I the only person in the world who had such horrid thoughts? No, it had to be a general human condition, and I, despite the rumours, was human. Maybe it was a good job I wasn't psychic in the sense of reading minds, it would do *my* head in doing other people's heads. Although if I *were* a little bit psychic, say on a Wednesday, it would be an ideal day to do my future syndicate member psychological profiles.

The tea tasted nice. I cupped both my hands tightly around the mug. I looked out of my opening onto the world and for the first time noticed my left-hand indicator was at least half an inch higher than the other two. How had I ever missed such an aberration? The carping style police might be out to arrest me any minute now *and* give me a good beating with a 28mm aluminium throwing stick just for the fun of it. I would have to sort it. Perhaps it was something I could do this afternoon, provided I could shoehorn it into my heavy schedule, I did have rather a lot of things to mull over in my head and they took priority.

I finished my tea, looked at the sloppily positioned indicator, ignored it and promptly swung my legs up onto my bedchair, clasped my hands behind my head and stared at the bivvy's ceiling. No, not right. I swung my legs back off. I eased back the unzipped upper layer of my sleeping bag, pulled off my reluctant-to-be-moved thermal boots and swung my legs back onto my bedchair and whipped the sleeping bag back over myself. Much better. I wriggled my toes in a similar way to how I imagined a battery chicken might feel soon after becoming a free range one.

I snuggled and went back to my mental meanderings.

Pup's wedding had made a dramatic impact on Rambo's short term existence, what with meeting Melina and starting a sexual relationship within – let me guess – five minutes? The chance of it turning out to be a significant long-term event for the pair of them was also a distinct possibility. Not only had the waves of the wedding's gigantic splash affected them, they had also washed up onto the beach belonging to the island called my life. Not only was there the impact of Rambo and Melina being an item breaking onto my shingle but there were the other matters which had arisen directly because I had been at the wedding as well. What had also got washed up on my shoreline, as two great big chunks of unlikely flotsam and jetsam, were Japp and Bob's propositions. The very two propositions I had rather hastily agreed to, with far too little forethought, having consumed too much booze and got drunk, not only on the alcohol, but on the heady power of my running the syndicate.

As I lay, warm as toast now, in my deep, comfy sleeping bag I couldn't begin to understand why I had agreed to both men. It wasn't as if I had needed to do it and it ran against all the things I thought I would try and maintain when I so unexpectedly took over the reins. It definitely farted in the face of Rambo's firm but fair advice. Additionally it was a complete turn around in terms of my original mental state as well. If the worm had turned with the six letters supporting my one rule change and the shift in power because of the expulsions and subsequent new members, I really never imagined I could have gone so far so quickly. The truly fascinating thing was that now, stone cold sober, with a chance to reflect and to have the benefit of hindsight, I was still thrilled by what I had agreed to. Even if it did contravene everything I had believed in only a couple of months earlier, in fact it was probably even less than that. My true test would come when I had to confirm what I had allowed to go ahead this July at the upcoming work party later this month. It would be at the work party where I would have to explain what I had agreed to. And yet I felt I could pull it off with no worries. I had travelled from my pathetic attempt at trying to buy the syndicate members with four chest freezers to this. This thing – wait – these *things* I had sanctioned, things Michael would never have dared allow because of his fear and paranoia. They were in for a shock, the boys were, but I thought I could swing it because of the nature of the two events and because of the money. I would have to buy their time back with some money, but with a generous leaning I felt I could do it without a murmur of dissent. And I could still make some money and give some away to others at the same time.

When I had informed Rambo of what I had decreed was acceptable during the last time we had spoken, he had looked at me with all the incredulity of a poor caster putting a bait out sixty yards to an overhanging branch margin, spot on, first attempt.

"You've agreed to *both* of them?" he had asked.

"It'll be a crack won't it?" I had replied.

"The only crack appears to be the huge one in your brain, boy!" Rambo had declared. "No! Not a crack, more of a fissure!" he had added. His eyes had had an evil gleam to them. "If you say, 'what a carp fisher?' I might have to kill you."

"You'll pair up with me though, won't you?" I had asked, shoving the joke back down my throat as fast as I could. I didn't want it coming out through a slit one.

"Of course!" he had said. "No one will take us on *our* turf! Even if we don't know our turf all that well! I mean we haven't been walking on it for very long, have we?"

"True enough but our skill will prevail. Maybe. And it's hardly TWTT stuff is it?" I had said.

"No. And nor is Japp's escapade either!" he had said laughing.

"I'll be quite proud to have supplied the location for such a first. A unique occurrence at a unique venue!" I had stated slightly melodramatically.

It had seemed settled. Rambo, while hardly condoning my move, was going to back me up and I could tell, just tell, he was as excited as I was.

"Any news on Charcoal Charlie?" I had said changing tack.

Rambo shook his head and looked slightly annoyed. "I've been slack. Very slack, boy. Other factors have taken up my time." He narrowed his eyes at me. "You know what I'm talking about, don't you?"

I had nodded. It had been the sex. Sex had been taking up all of his time. His time had been spent, all of it, on sex. All of his time had been spent on having sex, sex with Melina. In terms of his having sex as a proportion to the amount of time at his disposal, the ratio was 1:1. You had a finite amount of time, and once you took away from that amount the value of the time he had spent having sex with Melina, you were left with fuck all, because it had been all fuck. I knew what he was talking about in the most sweeping of general terms, but I didn't know the detail.

Rambo had seemed to be thinking along a similar thread. "And as I remember you had a *third* agreement, made with my good self, to tell me all about Rebecca..."

"If *you* tell *me* all about Melina," I had interjected.

"Fair enough. You go first," said Rambo in his 'don't bother to argue with me', voice.

And I had. And Rambo had gone second.

I wondered what Melina would have thought of Rambo betraying her secrets to me like he had. For all I knew she might have been betraying Rambo's secrets to Melissa and Melloney. And now Melloney and Sophie had struck up a friendship, what was there to stop my Sophie knowing the score on Rambo's stud rating? Perhaps I ought to ask her and we could compare notes from either side of the bed as it were. We could pick up on amusing discrepancies of the 'she was moaning and screaming and going absolutely wild' counterbalanced by the 'I was having to fake it to give him back some of his self-esteem'. Then once Sophie and I had swapped notes I could tell Rambo and Sophie could tell Melloney who could then tell Melissa who could then tell Melina, or Melloney might just tell Melina straightaway, I wasn't especially *au fait* with the three sisters' lines of communication, and all hell could break lose.

I was back into the deep water of knowing deep dark thoughts, not by psychic ability but by the rather more trademark way in which they happen in gritty, tasteless real life, namely, by someone else telling you. For affairs of the heart the expression, 'always the last to know' – as Watt had been over Jennifer's adulterous liaison with Mike – normally held firm. In thousands of other different instances, where the injured party finds out the bitter thoughts of someone through a third party, perhaps people were a little less reticent, particularly the ones who enjoyed a good old gossip. But even so for the most part I believed the majority of people preferred to steer clear of such socially difficult moments for as long as they could. Why? Well, usually it had a lot do with self-protection and a desire for non-involvement as well as it being a no-win situation. Damned if you tell, like I was when I told Watt, and most likely dammed if you don't. You *knew* and you *never* told me! Call yourself a friend? The answer was to avoid all of it by pleading ignorance. What a tangled web. Think of original multi-strand, no tubing, no gel and a forty-yard cast in a big cross wind. Leave for twenty-four hours and wind in. Look at state of hooklink and become emotionally upset. Respond with despair, resolve, anger or physical violence either to equipment/adjacent carp angler/passing dog walker as befits personality.

I laughed at the bivvy's ceiling. Out loud. I could imagine the three sisters reeking havoc everywhere they went with their overt sexual appearance and all the attraction it commanded. They were one massive Shelob-made web waiting to happen. And now they were in my life in a small way, and, I checked out my bivvy opening to make sure it was still there, Hamworthy Fisheries was in it in a big one. But not in quite such a large capacity as it was in Michael's, thank God. Even wonderful things become too much if they take over completely. Even carp fishing. Even new partners! Sooner or later Rambo would become less infatuated with Melina and she less so of him. They would start to see past the lust for each other's bodies and then some semblance of normality would return. Not yet though, otherwise Rambo would have been fishing with me at this moment and the CCI would have been complete rather than untouched.

I turned over onto my side and closed my eyes. Boy was I comfy. I listened to the wind and thought of the ghost. Wind noise linked me to the ghost like the turning off of a gas stove linked me to Michael's death. I had no doubt the one sound and the one action had been permanently hard wired into my brain for the rest of my living days. And the dead ones, (if heaven* existed) (* see earlier disclaimer) or even the un-dead ones should I became a vagrant soul hovering in the twilight between life and death.

The sound of the wind's gentle noise reminded me of how I had been drawn to the old wood and seen a shimmering version of it come out and engulf me in a cacophony of sibilant sound. It seemed hard to believe it had happened less than a year ago but it had. For around an hour I went through the whole story again, the story of my return to the syndicate. It was usually when I thought about it the most, when I was fishing; it brought back all the memories in vivid Technicolor, complete with Dolby 5.1 surround sound.

I must have dozed off because when I next looked at my watch it was half past twelve, thirty minutes into the witching hour. Between twelve and one had been Rambo's most productive time in this swim during the months between October and May. In true summer it had been a very traditional early morning and evening with the banker time, a little less conventionally, smack bang in the middle of the night. As we had witnessed when Rocky had had his take as the pair of us lay under the bush by the stock pond.

I wondered if I would get one now.

I was just wondering whether wondering if I would get a take would put some sort of curse on getting one, when right out of the blue… I sneezed. Really loudly.

"That's *bound* to have scared every carp within a hundred yards of my baits right up the other end," I said to myself.

No sooner had I said those very words when I heard a single beep from my buzzer and I looked up, heart racing, to see a robin perched on the very end tip of the left-hand, sloppily-positioned swinger indicator rod. The rod tip bounced a little. I looked at the small red-breasted bird and I got the impression he looked at me. I reached for my sandwich bag in order to break off a small bit of bread to throw to him but my movement startled him and he flew off. The rod tip bounced some more and the buzzer begrudgingly let out another single beep and then, to my utter astonishment… went quiet. Stupidly, I really *had* thought it was going to carry on from the robin's original beep into another more continuous one. One caused by a carp. Ridiculous!

Now I decided I needed a piss. Blame the tea this time and not the lager.

I put on my thermal boots and stooped out the bivvy's doorway. The keen northerly made its presence felt and made me feel cold. Speedily I manipulated my cock through my two pairs of tracksuit bottoms and underpants and let it all go. More billowing steam. I had nearly finished when all of a sudden… my toes started to cramp up from being back in my boots. I pushed the ends of them hard into the ground but it made little impact, it was swimming pool toe cramp and it was getting worse. I finished peeing, tucked myself and all my layers of clothing away, hobbled back into the bivvy and took my boots off. Seated on my chair I tugged my toes back and the cramp melted away.

I looked at my watch. Five minutes past one. The take hour had passed. The thought had literally only just entered my head when… my toes started to cramp again. More pulling and rubbing eventually sorted it. The cramp had put me into a more grumpy mood than earlier on and now the left-hand swinger indicator was irritating me to the extent I could no longer ignore it. I put my boots back on, coat and hat as well and went out to deal with the offending rascal. I squatted down alongside it, and knowing full well I was the only angler on the pit, adjusted the swinger with the Delkim still at high volume. Once I was happy I went and took the Stabila spirit level out from my rucksack and checked all the swingers properly, as I should have in the first place. That's bollocks of course, but I did eye them in from several differing angles.

As I was eyeing them in from a third angle the middle one seemed to move upwards fractionally. In fascination I looked at the rod tip, a rod tip that was slowly arching down in an opposite direction. The Delkim confirmed what was happening with a couple of beeps. I rushed to the rod only to see a section of broken branch being pushed onto my line by the wind causing the false indication. I picked up my landing net, turned it around and used the handle end to prod the branch past the middle rod's line and then pushed it around the left-hand rod's line as well. I put the landing net back as I had found it.

I wandered off to the stock pond to have a look at it, seeing as I was so close. Apart from it being slightly more coloured it showed no more signs of life than its big brother. I trudged back and stared out at the main body of water, the one I was now the sole proud owner of. I walked up to my rod butts.

"Come on you, bastards! Give me a run!" I said waving a clenched fist at all three of them.

The words had hardly left my mouth when… a text came through on my mobile. It was from Sophie; she was just off to drop Amy round at her mum's before going up to the gym for her workout.

I sent her a text message back to confirm I was still alive, hadn't fallen in and drowned or bled to death by acupuncturing a major artery with a baiting needle.

"She'll be as fit as a butcher's dog what with all this gym work," I muttered totally inappropriately. "Now should I recast or not?"

I hovered over the three Ballista Slim rods. I read my name on them. It was neatly handwritten in white on the top of each butt section just above the reel fitting. What would I gain from recasting? If I cast to different spots, blind spots, I would cover more water but the track record spots were already covered. I prevaricated and procrastinated. I was very much aware of the very thin blade I was standing on that divided a successful session from a blank. One wrong move and I could go from way over there – one fish on the bank – I flung out a left hand to emphasise the point to myself, to way over there, I did the same only with my right hand – no fish on the bank. The trouble was I would never really know if I had done right or wrong because I could move three rods and blank/catch and still have had similar results if I had left the three rods. Short of being able to follow the parallel universe decision I *didn't* make, it was the classic carp fishing conundrum. Always was and always will be. All you could safely say was if you *had* done something positive or *hadn't* done something, in terms of maintaining the status quo, and either led to a carp on the bank, you had chosen the right route. You had achieved a result, end of story. You couldn't go beating yourself up over the possibility the other decision would have yielded *more* fish. It didn't work that way, it couldn't, but if they did ever make an Acme Parallel Universe Viewer, I would probably get one in order to find out.

When I thought of it in those terms it seemed so simple, the mechanics of it, but the decisions were still as difficult to make as ever. Nothing to go on during the session, no fish seen and only Rambo's info of what had happened to him on other days. Even more awkwardly there was nothing positive resulting from fishing to the info and no tangible sign of it producing before the session ended. As I stood over my three burgundy coloured rods, I wondered what the general consensus would be amongst the carping fraternity. What would be the perceived correct route of action? Re-cast all three rods; leave them, or alternatively, any combination of the two concepts within the statutory three-rod limitation? Cerebral carping, my son!

I decided I had sat on my hands long enough, nothing was happening so what had I to lose? Do something positive, was the voice in my head, and I responded to it. I wound in one rod, renewed the hookbait and cast out a single to a spot I hadn't previously covered. I did exactly the same with the second and then I brought in the third only to put a hi-viz pop-up on the hair rather than an ordinary bottom bait. If you can call our famous red boilie, as rolled by Pup and shortly, on the next batch, to be rolled by Pup and Melissa, an ordinary boilie.

This last rod I launched as far as I could. With a 3oz lead, 15lb main line, tubing, a 9" hooklength plus a dollop of tungsten putty all grabbing hold of the air, which was coming directly into my face, meant I got it out a maximum of 120 yards. Cough. Eighty more like, if it was as far as that. I had never been a big caster. I set the third rod's swinger as I had the other two, checked I had pulled out the lever on all three Emblem baitrunner converters, beeped all three Delkims and then, happy I wasn't going to get a rod pulled in or a take not registered, I retired to my bivvy.

Twenty hours later I packed up and went home, runless and obviously fishless. Nothing *had* happened. Or at least that's what I perceived *would* have happened had I been able to have viewed the decision I *didn't* make with the Acme Parallel Universe Viewer. What *actually* happened was this.

I looked at the rods and although inclined to recast them I really couldn't see the point. I was as certain as I could be I wasn't tangled, I was on the money according to the Rambo Oracle and I felt the three chances I had, although admittedly slim, were the best I was likely to get from the harsh bookmaker controlling affairs i.e. and aka the Carp Fishing Gods. I shrugged my shoulders, put my hands in my pockets and turned my back on the rods and went back into the bivvy. Eleven hours later, smack bang in the middle of the night, I had just got all toasty in the bag after having had another pee, blame the tea etc. when... the left-hand, ex-sloppily positioned swinger indicator rod went dedededededed, real slow like. A take!

With ruthless inefficiency I jammed my feet into my thermal boots. One went in the full distance, another went in about halfway and when I did eventually limp out into the darkness after making an adolescent-schoolboy-undoing-a-bras fumble of the door zip, it was akin to a ham actor playing the lurching cripple. The right thermal boot, to be precise the bit left unfilled by my right foot, slapped against the ground as I waddled towards my one-hundred-percent-cert only take of the session. On arrival – a bit late in typical British train fashion – I pushed the baitrunner conversion lever back down into the spool front, picked up the rod and leant into a heavy resistance.

Thought of the day, or rather the night? Arrange the words 'not', 'fucking', 'off', 'come' and 'do'.

The reason I leant into the fish was because my left foot had an inch and a half of solid thermal boot sole under it, while the right one had only half an inch of compressed down to a quarter of an inch, thermal boot upper under it. I tried wriggling the offending foot in further but decided I must look like a one-sided epileptic twist dancer. Not that it really mattered, of course, I was hardly in the public eye standing on a deserted gravel pit in the middle of a chilly night in early April playing an as yet unseen lunker of a carp. How *had* Rambo and Melina ever contemplated *al fresco* sex? I started pumping, but not in the same manner I presumed Rambo had, and took line.

Rod tip up and ease it back slowly but firmly. Drop it back down and wind, wind, wind, wind! Wind you fucker wind! I wound and took more line. I shuffled over and got the landing net. I turned on the small torch I had taped to the handle and put it in position on the bankside, ready for the netting process. A big fish thrashed on top, already only ten yards out. The bait the carp had picked up hadn't been far out. I guided the fish away from the lines of the other rods and to the left hand side where I wanted to net the beast. The other two rods were backleaded, as indeed the one in my hands had been, more to help in the playing of a fish by keeping the line on the bottom than for any reasons of presentation. I felt happy the hooked carp wouldn't pick up another line and complicate things any further. The fish boiled in the very edge of the soft torchlight emitted by my strapped-on light source. I held firm, the pressure told and a huge fish broke the surface for the second time, only this time I saw it. I edged out the net slightly into the marginal water and clasped the handle between crossed legs at the very end, careful not to mask the torch's output. The fish made another lunge. I moved my right hand above the reel fitting and off the handle completely to a point where my name ended. With the butt tucked into my stomach, left hand below the reel, clutch set, anti-reverse on, I imposed a little extra control on my quarry. With no little skill I manipulated her back to the surface. She gulped air. It was nearly game over. I slid my right hand back into a more conventional position on the grip, and my left hand moved purposefully onto the landing net handle. I slid the net out even further, the carp went onto its broad, *very* broad flank and then… the hook popped out. All went slack. As slack as the elastic in a ten-year-old pair of 'Y' fronts that had been subjected to a boil wash and hours of sunlight degradation whilst drying on a southern aspect washing line on a weekly basis. The leviathan melted silently away under the water and disappeared.

"Bollocks!" I said. I was raging mad.

I chucked the left-hand, ex-carp on the end, ex-sloppily positioned swinger indicator rod onto the ground as hard as I could, turned, and with a swing Jonny Wilkinson might not have sneered too much at, kicked off the right thermal boot. It sailed up into the night air. A dull thud told me it had cleared my bivvy. Three points. I stood fuming at the world, two boiling kettles lodged in each ear – but on one leg. The massive injustice that had befallen me made my very heart ache with anguish. Of all the undeserved things to have happened, after I had made the right decision as well, to have a massive fish like the one I had just lost come off right at the bloody death. I was so close to netting it, the stupid hook only had to stay in for another ten seconds and it would have been mission accomplished, but oh no, it had to come out, right when I didn't deserve it, I... I stopped my internal ranting. My right foot was starting to feel cold.

I hopped back to the bivvy, found my other small torch and then hopped around the back of it to find the missing, previously leg-lobbed thermal boot. Eventually, after a bit of ferreting, I found it, picked it up and forced my chilled right foot into it. Ruefully I remarked to myself that the boot hadn't been on properly and neither had the carp.

Nine hours after the take, during which time nothing else happened, I packed up and prepared to go home. I did one quick circuit of the pit, to see what work needed to be done at the upcoming work party, and left, tail between my legs, like a beaten dog.

I wasn't meant to catch. It must have been pre-ordained after all. Damn those Carping Gods.

Chapter 8

The door of the functional wooden clubhouse was ajar. Despite it being only seven in the morning and the pit being closed for angling purposes, someone else was already here for the day of the work party. Work began at nine. Who would be so keen? Someone who had been away too long from his number one passion in life? I already knew the answer.

"Rambo?" I called as I went to go up the few steps leading to the door. "You there, mate?"

"All right, boy?" came a familiar voice from within.

The door was pulled fully open almost immediately to reveal Rambo standing behind it dressed in his usual camouflaged attire. From his lofty perch on the threshold he towered above me by at least a couple of feet more than usual, due to me having only got to the second step. With his massive frame filling the doorframe it seemed pointless trying to go up any higher.

"Long time no see," he said, looking down on me. "I thought you might have been abducted by aliens."

"*You're* the one who's been abducted, but not by *aliens*," I said being trenchant "And while we're on the subject, *whose* fault is it that you haven't seen me for a long time?" I asked, looking up at him.

"Mine," he conceded easily. His eyebrows scrunched. "Hold on! To be fair, you're *right!* I have been abducted in a way. It's *Melina!* It's *her* bloody fault! *She's* the one who's been keeping me away from fishing!"

"Yeah, right," I said mockingly. "Locked you in the bedroom against your will, did she?"

"No!" said Rambo indignantly. "But she did handcuff me to the bed."

I couldn't stand the prospect of more graphic sex conversations so I altered the subject. Don't ask *why* I couldn't stand it, seeing as I've already covered the ground earlier.

"I lost a monster from here a couple of weeks ago, you know," I informed Rambo.

I needed to talk about it to someone. Sophie hadn't been especially interested when I had tried to relate my tale of tragedy to her on returning home from the session. And I hadn't phoned Rambo in case he was on the job, coitus interruptus and all that.

"It was when I fished a two-day session in your south-east point swim," I said explaining further. "You remember I told you I was going to have a crack at it and you gave me the low-down based on what you'd caught and seen?" Rambo nodded. "I had the one take from the left-hand spot, the thirty-yard one to the bar," Rambo nodded again, "and it happened right in the middle of the night, which was a bit of a surprise for so early in the year. I got it back ready for landing without too much fuss and I was just about to pop the old net under it, when the poxy hook came out."

"Any good?" Rambo enquired. "The fish, not the bit about the hook popping out."

I jerked my head back in disgust. "Was it! *Definitely* a *big* fish. Hard to say *how* big but I reckon it was an honest forty, maybe even a *fifty*! I was pig sick, I can tell you. The thing that really pissed me off was I'd made a good decision. I'd left the rods alone and sat it out and got the result... only I didn't, because the poxy hook came out," I added weakly. "You see, I'd thought about recasting but I'd sussed if I did, I'd blank. Blank without a run," I quickly tacked on the end, quantifying myself more fully.

Rambo's eyebrows reached for the sky. "Oh, yeah," he asked with disbelief, "and how did you suss that out, then?"

"Acme Parallel Universe Viewer," I said flatly. "Every time you make a decision it allows you to see what *would* have happened had you pursued the course of action you rejected. You hardly need one to know what happens to the course of action you choose, do you?"

"Absolutely," Rambo agreed. "And where can you get hold of an Acme Parallel Universe Viewer when it's at home?"

"The Tackle Box do them," I told him.

"How much?" he demanded.

"£9.99."

Rambo let out a puff of air. "£9.99! Fuck that! I wouldn't pay that much."

"I got mine free with a new rucksack, a Fox one, otherwise I wouldn't have got one. The one The Tackle Box does only works on fishing. If you want one for your life and one that takes into consideration everybody else's decisions you need the Universal Interactive Acme Parallel Universe Viewer. *They* cost £19.99. No wonder they're not selling."

Rambo shrugged his improbable shoulders. "The trouble with them is every non-decision ends up creating the reality of *this* universe. Namely, every fucker looking into his or her Universal Interactive Acme Parallel Universe Viewer!"

We both laughed at our little skit.

"Can I get off of this step?" I enquired. "I'm getting neck ache looking at you up there."

Rambo came down the few steps, squeezed past me as he did so and stood, both hands on hips, looking across the car park. He did this for five seconds or so before turning back to face me.

"It *seems* as if Charlie's death was an accident," Rambo informed me, all trace of his earlier levity now gone.

"Only seems?" I said, as I too walked down the steps to be on the gravel path where he was.

Rambo scratched the back of his head. "I haven't been on the case like I should have been," he said, somewhat lugubriously. "I've wasted too much time with Melina dipping my wick. What I should have done was got my arse into gear and applied myself to a little subtle investigating."

"By what you've told me I'd hardly call it 'wasting too much time'," I said truthfully.

Rambo snorted. "Okay. But you know what I mean. I've spent nearly every hour there was to have with her since we met and you know the lesson of all things in moderation better than most, don't you? Any obsession, whether it is carp fishing, drinking, gambling, work or even sex can be unhealthy. I might still go fishing one hell of a lot, it was one of the reasons why I killed myself off, but I'm not obsessed with it. Obsession was the TWTT. Now I just fish full time on my own terms and that's the big difference. I'm not obsessed to go every day, only every day I want to."

Rambo rubbed the palms of both his hands up and down over his eyes as if he was trying to clear his mind.

"We had our first row a few days ago. It was over something so mind bogglingly mundane and unimportant, I couldn't even remember what it was we were arguing over when we'd finally stopped shouting at each other." Rambo eyed me earnestly. "It brought it all back, boy. All the reasons why I've never really been happy having a 'relationship', or whatever you want to call it. I mean, don't get me wrong, the sex was great but after a month or so of it there's *got* to be something else. And to me the something else is fishing and my personal space. *Not* setting up a home or her moving in or going shopping or out for meals, none of that 'relationship' stuff. We can still do the sex if she wants but I'm not changing anything else."

Rambo paused and then snapped his fingers at his Eureka! moment. "Come to think of it, *that's* what we were arguing about! I told her I didn't want to get bogged down in all the 'relationship' stuff but was more than happy for her to come round and have sex whenever I could fit her in with my other stuff. Other stuff, as I pointed out, that I'd deprived myself of for nearly a *whole* month. I told her I hadn't been fishing, sorted out my gear, tied up any rigs or even had a walk around here to see if any fish were moving and I *needed* to start doing it. Then for some reason she went ballistic on me. The sex was great when we kissed and made up, though," Rambo added without any trace of satire.

He went on. "Between you and me all this continuous sex was cramping my life, I won't say style, and it'd stopped me, or should say, I'd *allowed* it to stop me investigating this Charcoal Charlie episode as thoroughly as I should have. *And* I'd have probably landed the fish you lost because *I* would have been fishing the south-east point swim instead of you."

Rambo came up to me and gave me a gentle left jab on the shoulder. I knew it was a gentle one because I stayed on both feet. I rubbed the spot where he had hit me.

"It's my life you see, the Army days, the mercenary stuff and the arms dealing; they were always fluid, never settled, always on the move and on the go. And harsh. Harsh and violent... but with space, loads and loads of personal space. I've always had loads of space. If you can tie a thousand cats together, tail to neck, *I* can swing them. And the one time someone tried to trap me, you remember I told you of the woman who had my son to trap me? Well, I was gone as quick as a rat down a sewer, and I use the term advisedly, I know my own shortcomings, but I'm not going to change them and have *anyone* push the walls in on *my* world. Besides it makes you susceptible and vulnerable when you've got a partner."

Rambo didn't elaborate any further on his theme of susceptibility. He stopped and went quiet while I had a little mental giggle at his apparent blindness to Melina's ballistic rage and simultaneously juggled a mental menagerie of rats and cats. I had a vision of Rambo whizzing a thousand cats around and around – above his head like a cowboy with a lasso – and the outside one, being subjected to Mach 1 and God knows what 'g' force, coming undone and fizzing out into orbit accompanied by a fading caterwaul. I bet its arse got burnt on re-entry. Charcoal *Kitty*.

"I don't know how people like you and Sophie manage it," he exclaimed.

"What the sex?" I said haplessly, wrenched from my thoughts by his unexpected statement.

"No, you *idiot*," Rambo reprimanded me. "The *relationship*. I don't know how you can be in each other's pockets and have to compromise your time and energies and still stay together after the novelty of bonking has worn off. And have kids as well!"

I wanted to say something like, 'it's called love, Rambo' but knew it would come out sounding trite and the moment had gone. Did I even understand the meaning of it? My prison sentence, my fling with Rebecca, my initial shock at Sophie's pregnancy and my lusting at the three sisters, to name but a few of my defects, were hardly conducive to making a partnership stable. After all, I could hardly be smug at the standing of my relationship although on the other hand, it had survived, mainly due to Sophie's forgiveness more than anything I had done. On the other, other hand, how many people were truly blameless and never fell foul of the myriad of human frailties? No one was perfect. Don't blame me, officer; blame my inherent piss-poor genetic make-up.

Meanwhile, Rambo was warming to his theme and pretty much mirroring mine. "How you two are still a couple, God alone knows, after what you put her through. Most women would have ditched you while you were inside, or if not, then definitely when their mum had come into a fistful of money." Rambo let out a little laugh. "I suppose your stock has risen now you own this little lot but even so. I mean, isn't there any one thing you could do that would spell disaster and finish it for good? Or is Sophie's forgiveness a bottomless well?"

"Possibly, but I can think of one." I admitted. "The trouble is I've already done it, not that *she* knows, thank Christ."

"Oh yeah, I was forgetting," said Rambo. He became pseudo-aggressive and pointed a stabbing index finger at me. "You make sure you watch yourself, boy and *don't* go upsetting me by catching a sixty out of this place, otherwise I *might* have to tell her of your infidelity."

"I'm sure you will do nothing of the kind," I said politely, "seeing as I know about your little fake death scam."

Rambo grinned. It petered out quickly. "So long as nobody *else* is aware of it. Somebody who *shouldn't* be."

Silence held centre stage as we both considered our relevant secrets. Secrets shared by both of us concerning both of us, personal secrets to go along with the secrets appertaining to the ghost and Michael's suicide. We were secret squirrels, Rambo and I, hording them, burying them underground to keep them safe and away from prying eyes. Like Michael, in fact, who had buried his big secret and a fat lot of good it had done him! Perhaps it was a salutary lesson to us all. Watch out for the diggers! Watch out for those digging with purpose and intent, watch out for those who simply happen by with a spade on their shoulder, intent only on a little recreational shovelling. Watch out for them all because it's the way secrets are exposed!

Only Rambo knew my one true grade 'A' personal secret and at the last count I think it was down to six of us knowing his. Unless unbeknown to us it was five and another helper had been burned to death. If that was the case then Rambo's 'paranoid theory' over Charcoal Charlie's death by arsonist assassin was almost certainly correct. A purposefully intent digger if ever there was one. And if the assumption was made and proved to be correct, what sort of road did it lead us down? The road of secret revelation is a rather nasty bumpy one for sure. Still, it was all conjecture and hypothesis at the moment until some other event moved it into reality.

Rambo broke the hush first. "Anyway, enough of all that old crap. Have you thought how you're going to break the news of your impetuous wedding day decisions? Is it still on, or should I say *are* they still on? Have you had any confirmation from Bob or Japp yet?"

"I have. Funny enough I spoke to Bob about three days ago and Japp gave me a ring last night to say it was all systems go with his project as well. As for telling the tribe, well I've given it some consideration but not *too* much. Basically I'm hoping for last minute inspiration in the form of last minute panic to push me through. I had thought about writing it all out but to *read* it seemed so naff. I've run it by myself a couple of times and all I can hope for is it comes out sensibly and reasonably spontaneous."

"Not *too* much consideration and only a *couple* of times," remarked Rambo, taking the piss. "I'd have thought *you* of all people would have been agonising and having sleepless nights."

I wagged a finger. "No. It's all part of my new running-the-syndicate mentality. I feel all right about it, to be honest. I know that might sound daft seeing how negative I was before, but you know what my bloody brain can be like at times. For the moment at least, it feels settled," I said.

"For the moment," echoed Rambo. "And what if they start giving you grief when you tell them?" he asked.

"Then you'll just have to wade into the hecklers and punch one of them in the face. That should calm them down a bit." Rambo let out a tiny laugh. I continued. "In all seriousness I'm hoping they get sucked into a kind of collective enthusiasm for both the projects. In any case I'm going to tell them the news before we start doing any work, I don't want it being a monkey on my back all day long."

"You won't have long to find out, boy," said Rambo looking at his wristwatch. "Give it another hour or so and I expect some of them will start to turn up."

Rambo looked a little frustrated. "Shall we get some of the gardening gear out of the lean-to and bring it around here so it's all ready to put in our vans? We can fill the mowers and strimmers up with petrol, make sure they start okay and check out the other gear. It's been sitting in the lean-to for a fair old time now and something is bound not to want to work. Besides, I can't stand hanging around doing sod-all for another ninety minutes."

I concurred, as I usually did when Rambo suggested something, and feeling only slightly piqued at Rambo moaning at the prospect of having to spend ninety minutes with me doing nothing, I followed him around the functional wooden clubhouse to the padlocked lean-to. All the gear was presumably as it had been left after its last outing and we hauled it out piece by piece and carted it around to the front.

The keeping of the estate in trim was something I had overlooked until I had eventually given it a little thought and recognition had dawned on my sloth-like brain. The one work party a year was a major event and with twenty hands available, if well organized, could make a good dent in whatever was required to keep the estate in tip-top appearance and one hundred percent fishable. It could blitz odd repair jobs to the clubhouse, do some serious swim maintenance, fence repairs, tree pruning and so on and it could also deliver a fair-sized chunk of grass cutting and weed strimming. (Bankside weeds we're talking about here, the water itself was never overly weedy for some odd reason, maybe it was all the ghostly energies within the ballpane hammer killing it off!) What it couldn't do was keep things under control all through the summer, especially from a grass and bankside vegetation viewpoint, because stuff *grows*. It was why I had always hated gardening, you could spend ages cutting the grass and pulling out weeds and in two week's time the grass needed cutting *again* and in a month the bloody weeds were back. At least when you decorated a room or painted a house externally it looked good for a number of years, with gardening you had to keep at it almost constantly to make it look good. A bit like trying to keep fit, to keep a body in good shape you needed *regular* exercise. And who had that sort of time and commitment? Sophie, apparently, on the body front but not *this* hombre when it came to things horticultural. I wanted to spend my time and commitment sitting behind three rods trying to pull out unfeasibly large carp.

Having said that, it was evident now I had thought about it, that Rambo and I would have to invest time in the dreaded gardening-type malarkey at various periods during the year to keep it all under control. Unless I took the route of pouring money into pouring thousands of tons of quick setting concrete all over the venue. I had considered the option of concreting over the lawn many a time, when faced with six-inch-high, wet grass and a crap mower with as much inclination to work as a cheap toy four days after Christmas, but at Hamworthy it was a non-starter. I wasn't a complete philistine.

I could only presume it had been Michael and Hollywood who had kept the place looking so nice all year. They must have made regular sorties down to the pit and mowed and strimmed throughout the summer months to keep it as lovely as it had always looked. Not that I had seen them during my short membership, however, I was shrewd enough to realise grass didn't cut itself, that was just wishful thinking. If I were a geneticist I would be working on self-cutting grass. Some sort of moulting or shedding gene, which made the grass fall out once it reached a certain length and then begin to grow again. What a winner, eh?

And there was another thing; my short association with Hamworthy. I was supposedly giving the three new members a swim-by-swim guided tour later on. Now *I* had fished a magnificent total of three swims in my time on the pit. Three swims! Well, you know how it is, don't you? You catch in one swim and next time you go back, if it's free, you drop in it again. Well I did, and would still do the same. Article writers would undoubtedly give me a bollocking for such a short-sighted and non-expansive viewpoint to which I would say; 'What the fuck's it got to do with you?' Except in this instance they were right. And seeing as I had been unable to remember all the info Michael had given me within half an hour of him taking me on *my* guided tour – let alone trying to recall it a year, almost to the day, later – I kind of regretted it. Rambo had followed a similar tactic to myself, so combined we had the grand sum of… wait for it… a heady *five* swims. We would have to do the tour together otherwise it would be *hugely* embarrassing instead of simple, straightforward embarrassing. Rambo's excuse had been by way of an explanation; get to know one or two swims really well, especially when they've proven to be successful and don't try to spread yourself too thin too quickly. When your first choice swims were gone, *then* it was time to venture to pastures new and increase the learning curve with, important point here, the conviction of having had a few fish tucked under your belt. A little more coherent an answer than my first reaction I guess.

The petrol engine on the rotary mower sprung into life. I wiped a beaded brow. Twenty pulls on the starting rope? At least! Still she was going now, all the engines were up and running or had been and the kit was looking in good fettle. I just hoped the members would be similarly serviceable once I had laid my plans on them. I left Rambo to tinker while I went inside filled up and switched on the large tea urn so I could greet all the members with a cuppa. Offering a cuppa to a carp angler never did anyone any harm.

By the time the big urn was boiling the members were starting to turn up. First to arrive were, coincidentally, my four new bloods, Steve, Paul, Simon and Phil. It didn't escape my notice how they had all come in separate cars and having met them and interviewed them it was evident they knew little if anything of each other. Pup must have been offering members on the basis of Michael's old stipulations. I had to remind myself once again, Rambo and I were the *first* pair. Isolationism, divide and conquer, or to put it more succinctly, divide and rule had been Michael's twin tower philosophy. I suddenly had a great idea for my little speech.

Next to arrive was, Alan, the resident artist and Ghost Contactor (failed), and then all the others including Noel, who looked especially grumpy. He *hadn't* been one of the members who had sent me a handwritten note of congratulations. He was still upset over our boat trip and antics on the island I expect.

Jim, Dean, Ron, Jez, Grant, Gordon, John, Malcolm, Todd, Keith, David and the other Steve were all present. You see I knew their names; I had made myself sit down and memorize them when I returned their membership applications but I *couldn't* put faces to them. Twelve out of twenty were faces without a name to go with them. I should have made them all wear name badges and called the work party a 'conference'. Pushing my little joke aside and getting down to brass tacks it meant as a percentage I never knew the names of sixty percent of my own syndicate membership if I met them face to face. I was going to try and blag my way through the swim tour but I daren't do the same with real people. I made the tea and started to ferry out the mugs two at a time. I told Rambo to man the sugar bowl.

"Hi, cup of tea here if you want it. Sugar? Two. There you go, mate. Sorry but I'm afraid I can't place your name. Right! *Jez.* Right! Hi, Jez, nice to see you again I'm going to do a little speech before we start, okay? See you later. Cheers."

I did that *twelve* times, more or less. I didn't make the mistake of calling them all Jez and I never gave them all two sugars because they all had *different* names, except for Steve – four lunatic boys Steve, and no boys at all Steve – but I *knew* that, and although I never knew how many sugars they might want, if indeed they wanted any sugars at all, I knew I had to ask and find out. They all got their teas, with the right amount of sugar and I got an insight into faces and their names. Faces and names I tried desperately to remember. Incidentally, without peppering Rambo with too much praise and overly buttering him up, and, with no need for the statement to be taken with a pinch of salt, it has to be said, he was absolutely mustard with the sugar bowl.

Once they were all tead-up, (hideous pun) I took out my three-wood – playing a *little* safe and keeping the driver firmly in the bag – and stood on the top step of the functional wooden clubhouse stairway and addressed the ball, which in this instance was also the gallery and the club membership. This was it. Proposal time!

"Gentlemen! Could I have your attention please!"

My voice cut through what little noise there was and silenced it. The Glorious Syndicate Leader was talking! A few brief 'Heil Williams' came from the rallied masses – okay, nothing came from the rallied masses apart from a few looks of bemusement – and off I went, nervous but possessing an inner resolve.

"Before we start today I'd like to say a few quick words to you as we're all in one place and gathered together. It mainly concerns situations within the syndicate and also to let you know a little about some ideas I have now that I'm running the syndicate and Hamworthy Fisheries belongs to me."

I looked down and out at the faces looking up and back at me. They were still quiet. That was good. They were listening intently. That was good as well. And no one had tried to harpoon me with a stainless steel bankstick. *That* was good! *Very* good! Their faces now wore lifeless expressions; the original perplexed guise now replaced with poker-player style blank looks. Whether it was affection, contempt or some other emotion that I stirred within each individual, it was hidden from me. I could deal with it, although in an ideal world I would have liked to have added to my opening few lines the proviso; 'My first idea is if any one of you should start to give me any grief – whether real or imagined, the terms of how my mind interprets it are final and not open to debate – and thus unsettle the positive charge of my brain, as it is at the moment, I shall invite Lieutenant Rambo here, to come amongst you and punch you so *fucking* hard, right on the end of your *fucking* nose, you'll require more plastic surgery to put it right than Michael Jackson's had *plus* the amount an insecure, ex-soap star actress pushing thirty whose first single had failed to chart would undertake on her *whole* body in a pathetic attempt to kick-start her fading career'.

The idea warmed me. Rambo would do it without me even having to ask if I got any gip. My self-esteem rose. No time for beating about the bush, now was the hour to tackle the questions they must all have been asking and set the record straight once and for all. And *then* the proposals.

"Now, I know many of you, those of you who have been members for a few years, will feel slightly indifferent to the circumstances of how and why Hamworthy Fisheries came to be given to me. I know some of you will have asked yourselves why Michael decided to leave his entire estate to somebody who had only been in the syndicate for such a short time." I unclasped my hands and moved them apart. "And it's a fair question. One which I've lost many hours sleep in trying to find an acceptable answer." I tried to look humble. "Finally, I believe I have. I don't want to go into a lot of detail over what has happened. What has happened is in the past and can't be changed and I want to be looking forward." I tried my first bit of levity. "Looking forward to big carp nestling in the bottom of my landing net for a start!" A few members smiled, mainly the new ones. I ploughed on. "You see the fact is, if it hadn't been for Rambo and myself discovering the terrible fish stealing which Gary, Darren and Rocky were involved in, there would have been a gradual loss in numbers of fish to catch. They were stealing Michael's fish, but they were also stealing those fish from *you*, stealing *your* chance to catch them. It would only have been a matter of time before they had removed one of the forties, if they hadn't *already* done so. Moving fish is bad enough, but *stealing* them for personal, financial gain is an odious crime and one rightly despised by all right-thinking carp anglers. When I joined this syndicate it was a pledge to pay, what is after all, a shed-load of money, to give me the chance to experience the *very best* carp fishing this country could give me. And I haven't been disappointed. What was disappointing, was that three *bastards* like Gary, Darren and Rocky thought they were above the rules and could use the place to fuel their own agendas and personal selfish motivations." I paused for a few seconds. "We *could* have turned our heads, turned a blind eye, it would have been the easy route but we decided it *wasn't* the right thing to do. I mean, how do you think we felt going to Michael to tell him his best friend had been dumping on him big-time? We knew there was a strong chance *we'd* be the ones chucked out, but we did it just the same. And when Michael could corroborate our story I know he felt grateful for what we had achieved and that we'd had the guts to tell him."

I calmed my voice down to a less strident tone. "Now, naturally Michael's accident was totally unexpected. Who can begin to answer all the questions it throws up? My own reading of the situation was he was so distraught at Gary's treachery it completely occupied his mind and he made a tragic, elementary mistake because of it. Who knows for sure? We will never know. I think he was so *deeply* upset at Gary's action he changed his Will and made me the benefactor due, firstly, to my unearthing of the scam and secondly, because he had no immediate kin or obvious alternative. Maybe he thought my commitment in unearthing the fish stealing showed a certain mettle or perhaps he thought I had shown an interest in preserving and maintaining this wonderful syndicate, something beyond being an ordinary member. I don't know. If I told you how Rambo and myself had slept in the old wood on many nights, losing valuable fishing time, I might add, having walked in from that end so we didn't give ourselves away by parking in the car park, or how we had hidden under a bush by the stock pond to be able to witness fish being moved from the pit *and* the stock pond, or tracked down incriminating evidence from the island, *all* to gain evidence against Gary and his two treacherous accomplices, you might understand how determined we were to stop it. To stop *our* fish being taken. As I've said, I cannot change history; all I can ask is that you understand it. As for the future, I can try my utmost, as far as Hamworthy Fisheries is concerned, to make it as bright as possible."

I took a swig of my tea and tried to measure the gallery's response. I caught Rambo's eye and he gave me a slight pursing of the lips and an almost imperceptible nod. I was doing all right. Conveniently bullshitting where necessary and missing out huge swathes of mine and Rambo's big secret, true enough. But *they* didn't know that.

"You all know I am not another Michael. I can't try to duplicate his style and manner." Like I'd want to be a neurotic, paranoid killer, I thought. "I *cannot* try and run the syndicate as Michael did in the past, that would be stupid. But what I can do is carry on his good work in some areas. I *will* carry on his fishery management policy because only a fool would change something so obviously successful. I *will* keep membership numbers the same and keep costs the same, relative to inflation. I promise you I won't jack up costs or flood the place with more people and I will *try*, because I think it's a very hard thing to suss out, to maintain a membership of anglers who are not time bandits or full-timers. All these things were the strengths of Michael's syndicate and I will follow his path. But some things I will *not* follow. I have made one minor, sensible rule change, which you all know about but the other thing I'm not keen on is how we all socialise and mix. It must be obvious, even to his biggest fan, that Michael was frightened of having anglers getting too friendly. He seemed to imagine plots and problems coming from it and tried to keep nearly everyone as distant from each other as he could. We're members of a syndicate and yet almost strangers. I disagree with that and with what went on before. And you could hardly say it was successful because in the end the worst possible scenario emerged, that of carp being taken, the most *serious* of crimes. So this brings me to my first radical, if you like, change to the syndicate. In order to try and cultivate a better sense of us all being together and being part of a team I have a proposal to make to you all."

I stopped and drained the last bit of my tea. I had them gripped and they waited intensely for what I was going to say next. "Just recently an old friend of mine, who owns a fantastic water in France, told me of a group of people, eight people, eight very rich anglers who are keen to sample the best fishing in the world, not just for carp, but for other freshwater and seawater species. These eight people had fished his own water after contacting him via a third party but it's their *reasons* and the *manner* of how they fish their hand-picked special venues that are unique and so exciting. They come from different parts of the world, none from the UK, they're all millionaires, they're all ultra-keen anglers and they're all dedicated to charity work having made their respective fortunes in business. Their proposal, which came via my friend once information had been exchanged, is to donate a year's fee, £1250 each, in return for them to participate in a 72-hour charity Fish-In against the membership. Whoever wins the event – it's a pairs' competition, two rods each and you share a swim – can donate the entire sum, which, if I've done my maths right is £10,000, to the charity of their choice. Now, you don't have to acquire any sponsorship, there will be no publicity in the angling press, Hamworthy will *not* be mentioned anywhere and it's *not* compulsory. If you don't want to fish, you don't have to. If you *do* want to and can sort yourself out a partner then by all means come along and enjoy the fun. I'll organise a barbeque on the middle night and hopefully over the period it can act, not only as a marvellous opportunity to raise some money for a charity, but as a strong bonding experience for us all, as a syndicate, to get to know each other. It will be the start of a more integrated, friendly atmosphere and hopefully eradicate any feeling of isolation… and the need for sour members to move fish!"

I stopped. The bonding aspect, the mirror image and exact opposite of how Michael had tried to run things, had been *my* bright idea to help sell them the *other* idea. I was on slightly thin ice seeing as I had already agreed to it and Bob had set the wheels in motion with the eight mysterious millionaires, but in my defence, pathetic an excuse as it was, I *had* been drunk.

"Has anybody got any problems with what I've just said?" I asked.

Smiling faces all turned to each other, heads were shaken, all seemed hunky-dory and then Noel put his hand up.

"Yes, Noel," I said wondering what pain-in-the-arse question he was going to come up with.

"What if *they* beat us? What if one of *their* pairs wins?" he asked with feeling.

"*They* get to choose the charity!" I explained simply, relieved at his line of enquiry.

"I'm not talking about the *money!*" he said laughing. "I'm talking about our bloody egos and our bloody carping self-esteem!"

"Well, at least there won't be any publicity. Only you, me, the rest of the syndicate and eight millionaires will know about it," I said truthfully.

"*We're* new members," shouted out Phil, who was huddled with the other three. "*We've* got *our* excuse!"

"Hardly," said Rambo butting in for the first time *and* without the need to flatten noses. "They won't have even *seen* the place until they get here."

Phil blushed at his own stupidity and some of the others laughed. It was going *really* well. Time to strike while the iron was hot.

"So. Is everyone happy with that proposal? I think it's a great chance for a pair of us to give a lot of money to a worthy cause. Although there's no publicity, I wouldn't be against any one of you, if you win, saying you had raised the money through a carp fishing event. It would be a nice bit of publicity to poke the antis in the eye with."

There were even more nods of approval. I was on a roll.

"My *second* proposal is even more unusual." I let my words sink into the clearly excited mob of carp anglers. 'How can he top the last one?' I imagined them to be asking. Here's how. "Through *another* acquaintance," I informed them, "a Dutch carp angler this time, I have the chance to put Hamworthy, although once again no one but ourselves will know it's Hamworthy, on an altogether different map. My Dutch friend has a business, started by his father, which is shall we say, 'adult orientated'. He makes, to put it in frank terms, pornographic videos, DVDs, films, whatever... umm for heterosexuals." I thought I had better clarify that point seeing as I, as I mentioned earlier, had never met a gay carp angler. I had met a lot of carp anglers who were only campers with rods, but never carp anglers with rods who were camp. I carried on. "It has long been his ambition to make a carp fishing porno film. Don't ask me why, call it a personal collision of lifestyles, an unlikely collision of lifestyles to say the least, but there we are. Anyway, he has never made a carp fishing porno film because he has been hindered by the lack of a suitable, picturesque secluded venue and the possibility of catching on film authentic large carp being caught." My mind lurched a little at all the catching going on but I stumbled onwards. "Although from my limited viewing of such material authenticity and realism usually take a back seat, my Dutch friend wants to encompass the love of his life, carp fishing, into one of his films. It's high on his list of priorities. So the top and bottom of it is I have offered him two days' filming on this pit this summer. Any of you can come along and watch, ideally you would fish at the same time and if you catch you'll most probably end up with a cameo 'carp angler' part in it. It'll be something to show your grandchildren if nothing else! When they've grown up of course!" A ripple of genuine laughter came from the all the lads. "From the money he will give me for using the venue I will be able to afford to give you all a £50 subsidy on next year's subs by way of an 'inconvenience payment'. You might not be able to fish exactly where you want on those two days and the clubhouse might be seeing something it possibly has never seen before! And you won't be able to wander in and get your boilies out the freezer when you want neither!"

Shocked faces beamed with incredulity. What had they to lose? It was written on their faces.

"Sod the cameo carp angler part, how do I get a leading role?" asked Phil.

I shrugged. "You might well do! *If* your rod's long enough and you can get your tackle out *and* put it up in front of a camera without your resolve drooping!"

Everyone laughed again. I wrapped up my little speech and went on to sort out who was doing what for the rest of the day in terms of the work party. While everyone was sorting out their tools Rambo touched my elbow and whispered a 'well done' in my ear. I felt on the crest of a wave, not even in my wildest hopes had I thought I could come across so eloquently and convincingly. It was brilliant.

The rest of the day was spent grafting under a hail of hackneyed double entendres and whispered 'do-you-want-to-be-in-my-team?' negotiations as each member assessed his strength and tried to ask a member who was ideally only a little better than them, but not so much better that it would increase the likelihood of being turned down. It was fascinating to watch it all unfurl and see individuals pair up. I had *my* partner sorted already.

Chapter 9

The galvanising effect of my groundbreaking work party speech was simply sensational. The syndicate members' hearts beat as one as they feverishly pencilled in the 10th July as the start of the 72-hour charity Fish-In and the 16th July as the first of two days' filming of the world's inaugural carp fishing porn film. My status was elevated through the stratosphere like I was strapped to the back of an Apollo moon rocket. My rise was meteoric. All the members – now here this! – *all* the members had phoned me back within a week to announce their partners with both passion and partiality and the positive pleasure permeating their very souls with the prospect of personal participation in such a pleasant, pleasing, pleasurable charity Fish-In. All eighteen members had managed to gracefully divide themselves up into nine pairs, no mean feat of achievement in itself, but the underlying implication was perhaps of greater significance. The inference was of eighteen individuals confident enough they could share a swim for 72 hours, under competition conditions, without feeling the need to bludgeon their partner to death with a rubber-headed bivvy mallet. Now, whether it would be the case *after* 72 hours was another matter altogether. Naturally I could do without another hammer-related death on the water, but it was a chance I was willing to take. Nevertheless it was a massive change of direction compared to how things had been in Michael's time. And it didn't stop there. Over the following three weeks or so my position consolidated from Supersonic Syndicate Supervisor to something approaching deity.

Now although I am happy to take credit for, if I say so myself, a pretty good sales pitch on the two proposals – God knows what came over me, maybe I was on a bio-rhythm high – the reasons for consolidation were a little more tangible. Not that it appeared so to the membership, to them – or the impression I gained from them – as they smothered me in praise, was everything that was fine and dandy in the world was down to me. When I say 'world', I mean the world of carp fishing and when I say 'the world of carp fishing', I mean in terms of a microcosm referring to the carp fishing going on at Hamworthy Fisheries. The carp fishing going on at Hamworthy Fisheries was, in a word, breathtaking, thrilling, stupendous, awesome and mind-blowing. I lied. That's four words plus a hyphenated one, and if I could be arsed to dig out a dictionary or a thesaurus I could put down a lot more. To put it into conversational vernacular Hamworthy Fisheries was fishing its nuts off. Two huge, great dangly gonads, one razor-sharp scythe and *Swish!* Off they come! Nuts *off*, and more to the point, loads of massive carp *on* the feed and then *on* the bait, *on* the hook and *in* the weigh sling. And for every fish that was caught the glory of it reflected onto me.

Rambo had been right! They had soon forgotten my inherited windfall because they were too obsessed with their own. Windfalls can manifest themselves in many shapes and forms. Mirrors, commons, fully-scaled carp, lottery wins, grand inheritances and so forth. There were a smattering of PBs all round and yours truly was left sitting looking as smug as a – let's keep it topical – porn star with a ten inch spunk cannon that could go all night *and* deliver a 100g payload. (If you think 100g isn't much, pick up a bottle of Müller 'Vitality' probiotic yogurt drink, which is of a similar viscosity – I should imagine – and pour it all over your partner's face, or if that's taboo you could chuck it on the sheets, which isn't *strictly* porn film at all, and *then* make a judgement on it.)

Everybody caught. Everybody apart from poor old 'four kids' Steve who took the trouble to phone me and tell me how he hadn't caught. He had only been able to make it down for a couple of sessions, one of those was a day when hardly anything was caught – I was fishing that day – and on the other he had been afflicted by the dreaded TTTS. Terminal tackle tangled syndrome. Fish jumping out right over one of his baits, loads of liners, thinking a run was going to come at any minute, it didn't, reel in after the fish movement had stopped, 18 hours later, only to see disaster. Been there and done it in the past and it's a complete personal downer. I felt for Steve and hoped he would catch his first fish as soon as possible.

Despite my brief pity for Steve, on the wider picture to say I felt elated was an understatement. Everything had panned out and a little good fortune in the shape of Hamworthy's carp coming onto feed right on cue had helped to keep the bandwagon well and truly rolling. It had been the icing on the cake. Experience, however, tells us the only way from the very top is down. And my down came to fruition soon after Steve's phone call. It wasn't a summit to base camp down. More a slide from an Everest peak of a few thousand feet but it was down however you looked at it. The bringer of the down, my down, not Steve's down, wasn't a tangled hooklength but Rambo and his logical brain. The brain that said if it was in the way, whether it be person or thing, and hinted at danger, then destroy it. The brain that said if ensnarement meant running away from your only son, then do it, the same brain that said it was happy to pay someone to do a job knowing full well the someone would be killed. Rambo was *good, damn good* at being clinically objective. In all the time I had known him only Melina had diverted him away from what his brain had told him he should *really* be doing. And all because of a silly little thing called amazing sex.

On the morning of the down my journey to the pit had been its usual uneventful self, save for the dark-haired individual who had been walking along one of the rural lanes two miles or so from the entrance gate to the mile long track that led down to the actual fishery gate.

"Bloody asylum seckers," I had muttered to myself, sure of the swarthy individual's foreign extraction, as I had swept past him. "I wonder what he's up to out here? Working on some farm *and* pulling in the benefits I expect."

He was gone in a flash as I had sped to the pit eager to get some – I shall refrain from using the word 'practise' – time on the bank. The car park had had three vehicles in it and one of them had belonged to Rambo. I had phoned him on his mobile to see where he was fishing and once he had told me I had driven to his swim, one which coincidentally he had never fished before, remarking on how smart everything looked thanks to the enormous amount of work done on the work party day.

I had greeted Rambo with all the usual clichés carp anglers tend to say to each other when meeting. The 'What you had, then?' and 'How big was it?' and 'Seen any fish moving?' and 'What the fuck you doing in this swim then? Getting a little practise in?' phrases reeled off my tongue and Rambo duly answered them. He had caught, but no real monsters, his best fish was only – 'only' – a low thirty fully-scaled mirror, blah-blah-blah, etcetera, etcetera and yes he had thought it prudent to get in a new swim seeing as he may get drawn in one at the Fish-In, and then again he may not. Just to go back to his fully-scaled it was a fish of a lifetime to many and yet it had been dismissed as mere matter of fact. There was the power of Hamworthy for you.

Following the fishing questions I had then progressed to the state of play *vis-à-vis* Melina and his good self. Rambo had informed me that an uneasy truce was holding at the moment and they were still 'together' in the loosest possible sense of the word. He was doing everything he wanted in terms of going fishing but was trying to make an effort to do a few extras with Melina, aside from the sex alone. I was *going* to say how magnanimous that was of him and I was *going* to ask what exactly these extras constituted, but instead I had got railroaded by Rambo starting to interrogate me on the upcoming Hamworthy jollies.

By way of an answer I had told him Bob had passed on all my details to the charity Fish-In group and that I had already received the written confirmation from the mysterious eight's solicitor telling me the ten grand would be paid out on the day by a certain Mr Brad Reeves. The solicitor's letter would act as a guarantee for the funds so all arrangements could be made and the cheque would be written out, to the charity of choice, and handed to the winning pair at the end of the Fish-In. Usually, as in past events, the charity would issue a receipt for the monies and afford the pair any publicity required, or none at all, if that was what they desired. To accompany this information I had also received a letter from the mysterious eight themselves informing me of their details and asking for a map of the surrounding area and some recommended accommodation. They had strongly emphasised their respect for my wanting to keep the venue as much under wraps as possible and assured me of their complete integrity when it came to such matters. The mysterious eight comprised two Americans – one of whom was the Brad Reeves character – two Belgians, two Austrians and two from Hong Kong. Apparently they had all made their fortunes in stocks and shares in the 80's and had retired from the money markets to pursue their greatest love, angling. They had proposed to come two days before the start of the Fish-In, hence the need for accommodation, in order to 'acclimatise' as they had put it and to view the venue. Rambo's eyebrows had risen at this and he had asked me if they had mentioned wanting to have a preliminary fish. I had answered in the negative, saying they had only asked to have a guided walk around. Seeing as how the pair of us had managed to do a reasonable job with the new members after the work party day had ended, I had suggested we could do it again. Rambo had nodded and after half an hour of similar chit-chat he had hit me with the downer.

"Have you given much thought to how you're going to oversee the competition aspect of this here Fish-In, boy?" he had asked.

I had shrugged. "Not really, I guess. It'll look after itself, won't it? Everyone can use their mobiles to phone fish in and…"

Rambo had held up his enormous hand, the one he had been using to intimately grope Melina. I don't know why I'd had that image, but rest assured I had.

"Hold on there, boy," he had interjected. "These people are paying a lot of money. They're going to be good anglers, have no doubt, but verification is a big subject. Remember how we had to go and look at each other's fish during the TWTT?"

I had remembered and my shoulders had sagged. I had seen what Rambo was driving at.

"So what do you suggest?" I had asked.

"Someone and that someone is going to have to be either me or you. Preferably you, seeing as you were the one who agreed to this whole escapade, will have to be on call 24/3, if you get my drift, to weigh-in, verify and record all captures. You'll have to make sure every pair has a mobile, they phone you after each fish, you do the business regards weighing and documentation and then everything is all above-board and runs properly. You *can't* ask the others to do it," he had said adamantly.

"But I won't be able to fish," I had whined. "I wanted to fish with you, and win… for *charity*, of course. It's all for *charity!*" I had added hopelessly trying to make a joke of it.

It had been Rambo's turn to shrug. "We could share it but then you've got a pair of rods unattended or rather unused. Besides you'll be fucked if the place is fishing like it has done recently. You'll be all over the pit like a blue-arsed fly logging fish captures. And it's three days' worth remember!"

"I suppose so," I had admitted grudgingly.

"Don't get me wrong, boy. I'd love for us to be able to slug it out toe to toe but it's got to come from *you*. If *you* want to keep things going like they have been, *you're* the one who has got to make it run right. Don't forget you said you would do a barbecue on the middle night as well, that's all got to be taken care off."

"Shit!" I had exclaimed as I came to terms with the amount of work this all entailed. "*Whose* idea was this in the first place?"

"Why don't you ask Pup and Melissa?" Rambo had suggested. "It'd be a small thank you for his original introduction and perhaps you two could share the fishing and the verifying. Melissa might help with the barbecue and I'm sure I could persuade Melina to help, she keeps on about doing things 'together' so this could be our chance. The pair of them might even rope in Melloney and come to think of it Melloney might even get Sophie to come along. Melina told me the pair of them have become good friends."

This wonderful conversation had transpired three days ago after I had caught a low thirty common and two other high twenties from a new swim, which was nice. Forty-eight hours of successful fishing had put me in the mood and although I had been bothered by the idea that Melloney could rope in Sophie if Rambo asked Melina and Melina asked Melloney as opposed to the more direct route of *me* asking Sophie, I had soon set the wheels in motion. I had no choice. I would ask Pup because it would be a nice gesture to involve him as the only non-member, apart from the paying guests, and because *I* wanted to fish in the Fish-In. Badly. Even, and this assumed he would be up for it, if it was only for half of it, which was a lot better than none of it. Grudgingly I admitted to myself that it *did* have to come from me. I had agreed to the idea, I was the host and it would show my continuing sound leadership if I could run the event successfully.

As it turned out Pup and Melissa were only too pleased to be involved. I imagined Melissa falling into orgasmic delight at the thought of being surrounded by so much fishing… stuff, both men and gear! After I had told Pup the whole story it was decided, as I had hoped, that we should share the fishing. 36 hours each and while one was on rod duty the other would verify and log captures aided and abetted by Melissa. Sound. In the meantime Rambo had 'sweet-talked' Melina – excuse me while I pick myself off the floor and try to contain my hysterical laughter – into coming along and helping at the barbeque and Melina had asked Melloney and she had agreed as well.

"Oh, that'll be *nice* for you, having three girls help to make and serve the food," Sophie said after I had just got off the phone to Rambo who had confirmed Melina and Melloney's involvement and passed on the information to her. She already knew about Pup and Melissa.

The edge in her voice didn't escape my attention. I tried to surreptitiously lift the curse of insinuation from it. "Why don't you come along as well? You could bring Amy or get either your mum, or perhaps even my mum and dad to look after her."

Sophie gave me one of her looks. "You've *got* to be joking."

I was flustered because I knew where her annoyance was coming from. It wasn't hard to suss. "I thought you and Melloney had struck up a good friendship. I would have thought you'd want to come."

"Matthew! I *am* friends with Melloney, but it still doesn't mean I want to come to a barbecue in the middle of the night to help prepare and serve food to a mob of unsightly and frankly, by then, smelly carp anglers. I've been going out with you for bloody years, had *your* child and I don't want to do it for *you*, let alone, *Melloney*!"

"Melissa thinks carp anglers are sexually attractive," I said stoically defending all smelly carp anglers everywhere, even though I'd proffered Sophie's viewpoint to Steve at his interview.

"Well, *Melissa*," Sophie tapped her temple with a finger, "has a screw loose." She put both her hands on her hips and stood fully square on to me. I knew I was in trouble. "Even *Melloney* says she's got a screw loose. Mind you, Melloney thinks *Melina* must have a screw loose to put up with that mate, Rambo, of yours. All *he* wants to do is go fishing and then graciously have sex with her whenever *he* wants it!"

She stood and stared at me, her lips clenched, daring me to say something flippant. I didn't dare.

"Hey! Don't start blaming *me* for what Rambo's like," I said defensively, on the back foot from behind a riot shield the other side of a brick wall.

Sophie was off on another tack. "Besides it'll be *pathetic*. It'll be just like it was at the wedding. All you one track-minded men mentally raping those three girls."

"Whoa! Hold on a minute," I said putting up a traffic director's flat palm. "That's a bit over the top. It's not *all* one-way traffic, you know. *Why* did they dress like they did at the wedding? Eh? Answer that. *Why* did they dress up in those skimpy clothes? I'll tell you *why*, because they *wanted* all the blokes to look at them *that's* why!"

"Why *should* women restrict themselves?" said Sophie angrily. "Why *should* women have to worry about *how* they choose to dress themselves because of how *men* might react to it? Are women really *asking* for '*it*' when they wear a short skirt?" Her eyes burned into me.

"Bloody hell!" I said. "Steady on! We're not *all* thinking like that. We're not all professional footballers for a start!"

The joke was a bad idea. Sophie raged at the floor and then ripped her head up and raged at me. "Oh! So you *weren't* thinking about having *sex* with Melina when you first clapped eyes on her?"

"Actually I was thinking of having *sex* with *you*. But *you* told *me* to stop looking at you!" I countered getting equally heated.

"You *knew* I didn't mean that. I even *told* you I didn't mean it. You *could* have made love to me but you were too bloody drunk and throwing up down the toilet," Sophie said disdainfully.

"I'll tell you what, if I *could've* managed to have done it, you wouldn't have even *noticed*! You weren't exactly sober yourself," I pointed out.

Sophie went icily cool and precise. "The reason I got drunk was because I was so pissed off being left on my own, what with you talking to everyone apart from *me*. Off with Rambo, off with your other fishing buddies and sitting talking to that ridiculous Bob bloke and his tart of a daughter."

My blood froze. As unexpected as this whole conversation was turning out to be this last comment was definitely the scariest. I tried to be nonchalant. "What on earth do you mean by that?"

Sophie was tight lipped. "I don't mean *anything* by it."

I slipped from nonchalance to incredulity. "You *never* even spoke to her! How can you possibly call her a *tart*? There were, let's see, me, Rambo, Bob, Japp and her all sitting talking. *Five* of us! And one of them was her *dad*! If anyone had walked into the room I'm sure they'd have put a few of the other women in the 'tart' category before her."

"Oh! Like *me* I suppose?"

I was dumbstruck. "Not *you*! Of course not *you*! What the *hell* has got into you?"

"I'm going to bed. And I'm *not* going to the stupid barbeque, all right. So don't waste your breath asking again."

"Fine, whatever," I sighed as Sophie turned on her heel and marched out of the room.

I felt shattered. It had been a long, long time since we'd had one of *those* conversations. I wondered what had brought it all on. Sophie had hardly been intimidated at the wedding by the three sisters yet now it seemed to be an issue despite one of them being married and the other becoming a friend. *And* calling Rebecca a tart! Scary. Very scary! I sat down at the kitchen table and tried to think it through but was equally flummoxed an hour later. The only sure thing was she *didn't* know. Only Rambo knew and he would never, ever tell Melina, I would have staked my life on it.

Ruefully I wondered if now was the time to tell Sophie about the porn film shoot. I hadn't done so yet, the idea of telling her somehow seemed tacky and sordid whereas telling all the blokes seemed to be a crack. I expected to see a lot of cracks in the final product. If she had reacted to the porn in a similar vain to how she had just a minute ago I could have perhaps understood it. I understood little at this precise moment and I laughed to myself bitterly. No. Now was *not* the right time, in fact it couldn't be more wrong. To go and tell her of the porn film would be a thing so incorrect in timing it would be like a blatant anachronism. Like a wristwatch on an Egyptian king, David Beckham kicking a brown, leather ball with a lace, the Red Baron in an F-16 or John Holmes in a nineties porn film, or John Holmes just being *alive*!

It could wait. I had other more pressing things to sort out, like where to purchase decent sausages and succulent chicken breasts for a start. Hold on! What if one of them was a vegetarian? A *vegetarian* carp angler? An unlikely crossing of lifestyles, like Japp and fishing and the adult entertainment industry, and then we were back to the theme of female, black and gay carp anglers and other unusual combinations. I shook my head to clear it of bamboozling bewilderment. Best get back to the food, I mused, before I completely wound my brain up into the state of a cheap nylon carpet attacked by a high-revving speed bit in a cordless drill. There were the jacket potatoes, the drink, the crusty rolls, the sauces, the sweets as well as the meat to think of and I still had to get a barbecue to cook it on in the first place. And the charcoal. Not Charcoal Charlie, but charcoal bricks and to be on the safe side, a flame-thrower to make sure I could get the bloody thing alight. My mind flicked back to Charlie and I wondered if something similar had been used on him. A sobering thought, especially for Rambo.

Over the next few days I grafted on getting the mundane jobs associated with the Fish-In well and truly sorted. It was a dull, niggling, time-consuming chore and one at the complete opposite end of the spectrum compared to the excitement of the event itself. Unfortunately there was a moral to what I was doing and it told me in no uncertain terms how important this boring groundwork was to the success of the whole event. If the accommodation I sourced was nice, if the food was good, if the competition aspect, in terms of efficiency, honesty and impartiality, were dealt with in a manner beyond reproach, all else would follow. I made a snap decision on the food and decided to get in outside caterers. It would be too much to expect me and the two sisters to deal with it, especially as I might be needed elsewhere to weigh and verify fish. By word of mouth I found out about a couple of youngish lads who specialised in outside catering, who could supply and do everything for me at a reasonable cost. I chose a menu, gave them all the necessary details, paid a deposit and it was done. It was one less thing to worry about. The two other sisters could still attend the barbecue and now they wouldn't have to concern themselves over the grub, just like me! It was a much better idea and I was pleased to have made it.

One other little idea, which I thought would be appreciated, was to purchase a national flag for each pair. I bought fourteen of them. Ten St George Crosses to represent the ten English pairs; one Stars and Stripes – 'Old Glory' – to represent the two Americans; one Austrian flag – a horizontal triband red, white, red – for the pair of Austrians; a Belgium one – vertically divided black, yellow, red – for the Lowland Europeans and one Hong Kong flag with an unusual swirling five-leafed flower with a red star on each petal, set on an all-red background. Despite the warning of patriotism being the last refuge of a scoundrel, I felt the large 5' x 3' flags, when set up in each swim, would add a fetching and colourful personal touch for each pair. I left a flag for each syndicate pair in the functional wooden clubhouse, to pick up at their leisure, and with it I left a little note suggesting they could write their team's name on it if they so desired. I took our flag home and in black indelible pen stencilled our team name across the horizontal red band of the St George Cross flag. I made an executive decision and named us 'Team Rambo'. I thought it had a nice ring to it!

I had little fear in Hamworthy itself not coming up with the goods, whether in aesthetic appeal or fish caught. Sure the pit would be under a brief bombardment of relatively intense pressure, the like of which it had almost certainly never witnessed before. Yet with only fourteen of the larger swims in use on twenty-nine acres worth of prime carp pit it was hardly your local day ticket venue on a weekend in mid-summer. There a margin bait put ten yards down to your left meant going over the top of eight lines and putting side-strain on a fish would see the bloke in the next swim with a mouthful of carbon. All he had to do was pluck your main line, as the fish pulled hard you would get a higher note and vice versa, and it would be something like playing a Jew's harp. As Rambo had said, it was all about space. All over the world space was at a premium, in both a personal and physical form.

On the fishing front I was convinced many cracking carp would be taken over the three days. The combination of local knowledge and expertise plus the added possibility of a fresh approach, from what I presumed were highly experienced anglers – though maybe not necessarily experienced *carp* anglers – seemed a recipe for fish on the bank. The prospect, however remote, of everyone blanking didn't bear thinking about. Besides, it wouldn't happen, *couldn't* happen. If by any chance it did happen, even though it couldn't – but just suppose and to be hypothetical for a second it did – I could always fall back on the perennial fishery owner's response by telling our guests they should have been here earlier in the year when the place was fishing its nuts off. I wondered how you said 'fishing its nuts off' in Flemish, German, Chinese or even flipping American come to think of it. Forget it! They would all speak perfect English. Even Japp's porn stars would probably speak perfect English. 'Ja! Das pit war fishing die nutz ab'. I passed German 'A' level, you know – cough – and was therefore pretty fluent in all things Austrian; Kitzbühel, Frans Klammer, Wolfgang Amadeus Mozart, Vienna – my God, the Austrian duo will be impressed!

Although the chores were mundane I made a point of doing them well and got everything detailed right down to the small print. The reason for my conscientiousness was pride. This was my water, my competition, not *strictly* true but I had agreed to it, and I wanted it to go off perfectly. The creeping satisfaction of owning something as prestigious as Hamworthy was fully realised at last and I looked back at my early negativity with increasing derision. It was like looking back on a particularly embarrassing photograph, where for some reason, whether due to pose, fashion or surroundings, you appeared as a complete arsehole and as a virtual stranger to your present day self. But not dead like Michael had been. Brain dead, maybe! As I walked around the pit deciding on the fourteen swims to be used, I scoffed at my previous mindset. The run of revenge still hadn't materialised and I began to doubt if it ever would. If Hollywood was going to try something, surely his burning anger would have made him chance his arm by now. On the other hand perhaps he had managed to move on and come to terms with his self-inflicted loss and had decided against attempted revenge. At a stretch he may even have admitted, to himself at least, his guilt and realised his own shocking culpability.

As I soaked in the ambience of the pit a large carp crashed out fifty yards away. This *was* the best carp water in Britain. I had no doubts in my mind and *I* owned it. And I had taken refuge in it and thrown all my efforts into making things right for the two forthcoming attractions. To be candid the reasons for my refuge were partly down to the state of things at home. Sophie's fury had abated from when she had attacked me over the three sisters' barbecue participation, but there was still a slight lingering coolness to our relationship where previously there had been none. It wasn't serious, we talked, we got by, we cuddled Amy together but there was enough of an atmosphere for me to back away from her and give her a little more space than usual. I did so, partly because I genuinely did think it might be for the best and secondly because it gave me the chance to get off and do my errands. It was all rather convenient really and she let me get on with it without questioning me.

The only other thing to add to the brew was my admitting to rather savouring the idea of spending some time with the three sisters. Melissa was likely to be there for the duration and Melloney and Melina would be around for the barbecue night. Strangely, or, I suppose being logical, not very strangely at all, now I come to think of it, it reminded me of a Lac Fumant and Rebecca type situation. Me on my own, in the sense of Sophie not being there, *three*, as opposed to one stupendously attractive women and loads of fresh air and fishing paraphernalia. Still, I wasn't about to make the same mistake again, if 'mistake' is the right word to use for having sex with a beautiful woman. No, I had matured past that sort of thing and the old adage of not shitting on your own doorstep was crude, succinct, profound and poignant.

Mind you, a *little* flirting would hardly go amiss, not necessarily from myself, but from any of the males present. The girls would lap it up – the attention that is – and I was certain they would add an 'extra dimension' to proceedings. I was willing to wager our eight guests were very unlikely to have experienced such wonderful eye candy to accompany such wonderful fishing.

In the dark recesses of my mind a lustful monster stirred. I prodded it back into its dank cave with a sharp stick while it screamed; 'You don't fool me! I know you from old! You like the one beginning with 'M', don't you?' I tried my best to ignore it but when I couldn't I rammed the rock of alleged maturity and responsibility over the cave's entrance. 'Don't fuck with me!' I told it. Save *that* expression for the girls, I thought. Chance would be a fine thing.

Having circumnavigated the pit and decided on the fourteen swims to be used, I went back to the clubhouse and picked up the swim number boards I had painted up the day before. With these 10mm external ply squares screwed to Hammer Horror 'kill the vampire' wooden stakes and a club hammer tucked inside an old rucksack, I began to make my way to the first chosen swim and thumped the board marked '1' into the ground. The marker was positioned directly in front of the opening to the swim through the bushes and was on the inner side, the driver's side, of the car track. *If* you had a right-hand drive car and was going clockwise. I made a meticulous, pedantic mental point to ask the eight guests if they were coming in left-hand drive vehicles. If they were they could go get their passenger to look out for the swim boards.

When I got to swim '2' my mobile rang. It was Rambo enquiring if everything was going all right. I told him it was. He asked if I had sorted the fourteen swims and had pegged them out yet. I told him I *had* sorted the swims and in fact the pegging was the very thing I was doing at this precise moment. In fact, I informed him, if I hadn't stopped to answer *his* phone call asking if I had done the pegging out

I would have probably thumped in another swim marker by now and been another step closer to accomplishing it. After he had told me to 'eff off', he went on to ask, purely out of rampant curiosity, which ones they were. I told him the ones I had deemed, as Supreme Syndicate Supervisor, were the most suitable. Rambo congratulated me on my choice, it was more or less exactly as he would have picked if he had been Supreme Syndicate Supervisor rather than a mere Syndicate Lieutenant. We had an animated chat concerning the various chosen swims' prospects for producing the goods and what ones we would like to fish given the opportunity to pick. This was an academic discussion because I had decided to do a straightforward swim draw rather than a watercraft one. I felt a watercraft draw would give the members an unfair advantage, albeit a minimal one. It would be left to fate alone to decide who was to fish where. The results of our hypothetical talk were that all of the fourteen swims were good but ideally we would be happiest given a swim we had previously fished lots of times and were therefore fully conversant with it.

"Can't we rig the draw?" Rambo asked. "One thing might lead to another and you know how they say history repeats itself."

I took the mobile away from my ear and pulled a face at it then quickly clamped it back. "Oh yeah, of *course* we can! I could do with another eighteen-month spell in the gulag. I *don't* think!"

I heard Rambo guffaw into the phone. "Only joking, boy. Are you staying for a session after you've finished the pegging?"

"Yeah, I might do a night. I've got all my gear with me," I said. "How's Melina?" I added.

"Not *too* bad. We've come to a truce about where we're going as a 'couple', whatever the fuck she means by that. Anyway she's not going to ask any more and I've promised to give it some serious thought and get back to her when I've thought it through. That's what I've told *her* anyway, it appears to have done the trick, I can't get on with her crawling all over me – except for when we're shagging!"

I verbally congratulated Rambo on his shrewdness while not necessarily agreeing with his course of action, a thought I kept securely encased within the confines of my skull. We passed a few more pleasantries and he rung off. Melina was flogging the proverbial stiff nag if she thought she could turn Rambo around to her way of thinking. Rather tastelessly I thought she would be better off sticking to flogging a stiff dick, as that seemed the limitations of Rambo's commitment to her. What did I care? I didn't care to answer that question for a kick off.

I managed to get two more markers thrashed into the deck before the phone was off again. It was Noel, asking if there was still plenty of room left in the new bait freezers for his stash. I informed him that as far as I was aware there was at the moment, but I had moved all the boilies from the one closest the door into the other three. This was done to leave our guests a freezer all to themselves. Noel thanked me and said how much he was looking forward to the Fish-In and that he was desperately keen to win. His wife had survived breast cancer and a ten grand donation would be a wonderful thank you to the hospital staff that had treated her – *and* he wanted to kick everyone else's arse at carp fishing. Perhaps it had been this personal trauma that had led to Noel being so unexpectedly unopposed to the Fish-In. I'd had him marked down as the most likely candidate to kick up trouble but it hadn't materialised. His wife's awful luck had fallen the opposite way in my fortune stakes, and made my path a little less difficult. How strange that such an unrelated occurrence should work the way it had.

I eyed in the swim nine board for level and the mobile rang again. Four kids Steve was the cause and his angst at suffering TTTS had been surpassed by his latest dash of ill-fortune.

"You'll never guess what?" he started.

"What?" I asked.

"Do you remember me telling you at my interview how I was going in for the snip? A vasectomy?"

My mind leapt straight to the image of his constantly fighting sons, the eldest one and the triplets. He was *years* too late in my opinion.

"Now you mention it, I do. Good idea!" I said with feeling.

"Because I'm a strapped for cash, having joined Hamworthy, I've gone for a National Health Service appointment and it's just come through and it's the day *before* the Fish-In!" said Steve clearly agitated.

I choked back laughter. "You'll be all right! Christ, it's only a couple of little snips!"

"Don't you believe it," Steve said in a huff. "I've heard some real horror stories. Blokes ending up with balls the size and colour of an eight ball!"

Steve's terms of reference needed confirming. "Is that the black one? I've never played much pool."

"It's the black one," confirmed Steve sounding worried.

"Steve?" I asked.

"Yeah?"

"*Why* are you telling me all this? Because there isn't much, well, there isn't *anything*, I can actually do about it. I suppose Rambo could do you the eunuch version with his big bowie knife if you asked him nicely but…"

Steve cut me off, which was funny because I had thoughts of Rambo cutting his you-know-whats off.

"I know, sorry. I had to tell someone," he said pitifully. "Promise you won't laugh if I'm walking a bit funny," Steve pleaded.

"I promise," I lied.

Chapter 10

Confidence can come in many forms. The confidence I had in me was the one of knowing I was thoroughly, and I do mean *thoroughly*, prepared. I suppose there were a few eventualities not catered for, like a nuclear bomb landing on my bivvy during the Fish-In or the fires of hell breaking out from the depths of the earth's core and boiling the pit dry – poached carp for tea, Vicar? – but generally speaking I was happy I had covered the *main* ones. Good food, good organisation, good fishing, good weather – according to the forecast and, yes, I was happy to claim the glory for it – and good company. I was so happy with my preparation it led me to think that if I was a kid about to sit an exam I would be the swotty little geek who got bullied, wore glasses, was crap at sport but had revised big-time. The examination room held no fear. The playground, on the other hand, could sometimes be a bit tricky, but break time was hours away, hours of exams away. Let the other kids quake in their scruffy trainers, I knew *I* was going to pass with flying colours because of the work I had put in.

Secretly I hoped my confidence would also transpose itself into carp on the bank during the upcoming competition. Fishing with confidence equates to fish on the bank. I knew this was said to be true because I had read it in a magazine. Lots of times. I had read lots of things lots of times in carp magazines, fundamentally because there *are* a limited number of options when it comes to skinning a cat. I hadn't ever read about skinning cats, that was a statement of fact but could my confidence in one department of my life really affect how I would fair in something as – groping for a word here – 'variable' as fishing? Well, it certainly wasn't going to do me any harm. Only time would tell if I was to have all my confidence unceremoniously knocked out of me by a mob of non-feeding, belligerent carp wearing steel-capped tail boots and fin dusters. (Knuckle dusters – fin dusters – fins being the nearest anatomical fish equivalent to a hand. Come on, keep with it!)

All my preparation for the first of Hamworthy's two major events had been done and dusted – not knuckle dusted or fin dusted – for some time now. In fact all was completely sorted for the second, less conventional, event as well. I had used my time wisely and hadn't scrimped on anything however trivial it might seem. There was absolutely nothing left to get ready for the Fish-In, it only had to happen. And it was happening *today*. Today was the 10th July and my whole body bubbled with expectation and excitement.

I had been at the functional wooden clubhouse since six this morning and had left the upper gate open in readiness to receive all the anglers who were coming on this most special of days. Apart from the entire membership plus the newly-weds, Pup and Melissa, there were eight additional anglers due to pass through the gate. The eight others were the Fish-In's sponsors, the people whose ten thousand in honest British Sterling – you can poke the Euro where the sun doesn't shine – we were all aiming to win. For charity; pronounced *charedee*. The very significant factor I was heavily relying on to lift any bad vibes of a competitive nature that might be swirling around in the atmosphere. Everyone wanted to win, don't get me wrong, everyone wanted to come out as the top contestant and convince a small cache of carpers of their class and calibre, culminating in a clear case of quintessential carping kudos. And get the ten grand to donate to a *charadee* of their choice, thus basking in being the bountiful benevolent benefactor. There was no argument over that, but the aspect of all the winnings being given away to a deserving cause hopefully lifted the curse of how human nature *might* react to trying to win ten thousand quid for personal gain. Competitive but friendly, was my vision of mindset, not competitive and win at all cost – like the TWTT. No hand grenades, no bitter infighting, no prison sentence and no social and domestic upheaval.

I had already met our eight guests a few days earlier when Rambo and myself had shown them around the pit. There were the two Americans, Brad and Tom, the two Austrians, Horst and Helmut, (I have to admit my initial thought on being introduced to them, after quelling the desire to titter like a schoolboy at Helmut's name, was to phone Japp *immediately* and tell him I had a couple of *gay* porn stars for him, sporting as they both did, thick moustaches and mullet haircuts! Gay carp anglers, was this my first encounter? No. They seemed heterosexual enough and the odds were stacked against it, besides they were probably married. Like that meant anything.) the two Belgians, Leo and Mark, and finally the pair from Honk Kong, both from refugee families who had fled the Chinese revolution to live there in the fifties, Li and Hu. They had all been impressed with the pit and when I had produced the latest version of Alan's paintings of all the known forties the nods of approval had been vigorous and plentiful.

If I felt confident today because of all my preparation then it was obvious this same quality was brimming in our guests. The satisfaction of having made sufficient money by your late twenties/early thirties, by your own efforts, so you need never worry financially again had given them great self-belief. I recognised that I too was in a similar boat, although in the scale of things it was only the lifeboat getting pulled behind the luxury cruiser. These blokes owned the cruiser and navigated wherever they desired. The world and all its water had become an enormous fishing venue to them and their novel approach to opening the less known and hidden venues had enthralled them.

"You see, Matt," Brad had told me as we circumnavigated my particular patch of prime venue, "we love meeting you guys. Everywhere we go and fish we met guys. Guys like you, guys like the members of your, whaddaya call it? Syndicate?" I had nodded. "Yeah. Guys like that. We don't want no tourist crap! We've been there and done it! We want the more *exclusive*, less well-known but highly prestigious clubs, the private venues, the *syndicates*, and the occasional, exceptional commercial venue like our buddy Bob's place. That way we *meet* and then fish *against* the people who know the place. Yep! We've got in on the scene and the grapevine keeps popping up some real neat surprises." He put both clenched fists on his hips and surveyed the view. "Like here, Matt. Like here." Hamworthy *had* looked pretty damned neat and it did again today.

Over the few hours I had spent with the guests they had told me how they were going to fish regarding pairings. It came as a relief to learn they would be fishing in twos of like nationality. (And there I was thinking I had covered *every* angle! The flags I had later given them would have been of little use if they hadn't paired up as so.) As an interesting aside they were quite candid in admitting to the large side-wager they always had between them. Over the ten years or so they had been doing the charity Fish-Ins it was the Austrians, Horst and Helmut who had won the side-wager more times than any of the other three pairs. I had asked them how many times one of them had won the whole event, been the top pair out of all the entrants rather than amongst themselves. I had been astounded to hear that of the thirty or so Fish-In events they had taken part in, one of them had been the top pair on no less than twenty-five occasions. They were going to be serious competition, unless they were coming the big 'I am' and were full of bullshit. Somehow I doubted it. They were good anglers, I could tell by the questions they had asked, all in pretty respectable English thankfully, although with the associated accent as you would have expected. The interesting thing was they weren't solely carp anglers. They had fished for many varied species with many varied techniques; boat fishing, lure fishing, fly fishing and static bankside fishing like our event was going to be. I had been left with an impression of them being very competent anglers and decent people who were used to getting the best by way of having a big wad in the back pocket.

Brad and Tom had come across as the most brash, possibly because of their almost stereotypical open, in-your-face personalities backed up by their American accents and language which seemed to emphasise and enlarge their personalities. Against my Sussex 'old young'un' rustic vernacular their words seemed to gain an extra swagger and boldness when uttering even the most simple of statements. They were physically striking as well, both had a shock of blond hair, both had perma-tan Californian complexions and Brad in particular had a set of teeth that only Americans seem to possess. They were flawless and were the reason why, as Tom had the 'premium set' to Brad's 'ultimate set', the Yanks forever take the piss out of the Brit's orthodontic omissions.

They reeked of affluence, well-being and the confidence – that word again – of knowing they came from the most powerful democracy on earth and not knowing, they were probably blissfully unaware, of how much of the rest of the world hated them. Not them personally, but America as a whole and what it represented. America's detractors pointed to the reasons for the hate; its package of trying to be the world's policeman, attempted Western globalisation, dubious foreign policy, insular population and bloody McDonalds and Disney and Nike and Reebok and Pepsi and Coca Cola and Michael Jackson and Hollywood and its brain dead movies and all the wearing 'can do' and 'have a nice day' crud. Add to the sins the birthplace of political correctness, compensation culture, litigation, gun culture, Billy Ray Cyrus, bible-belt preachers *and* rap music and you could easily see where they were coming from, or, alternatively, you could see what made it so vibrant and successful. Poor old America, she was like any entrant on the list of 'favourite artists' and 'most loathed artists', when you were the biggest artist, you always appeared at the top of both!

Horst and Helmut, the gay porn stars who in fact *did* turn out to be both married and heterosexuals – or so they said – were, allegedly, the couple to beat on the fishing front. They had spoken in heavy German accents but were far less outgoing than the two Yanks. They had actually made little notes as Rambo and I had taken them around the pit and had talked quietly yet intensely to each other in German. I had sensed in them, let's get even more stereotypical once again, Teutonic application. I had imagined their kit to be perfect, well laid out, structured and organised. I could see them fishing well as a pair, I couldn't see them making many mistakes and I was sure they would grind out a result from whatever swim they happened to draw. The only departments where I could see they would come up short would be flair; in the sense of trying something off the cuff, spontaneous and away from the original game plan and – even more importantly – hairstyles! M and Ms were right out now we had hit the twenty-first century! They were right out for a good part of the twentieth come to that! (Mullets and Moustaches! How many times have I got to tell you to keep up?!)

The Belgians, Leo and Mark, were very friendly and obviously Europhiles. Mark looked as if he had eaten a few too many Belgian chocolate truffles and his short frame struggled to cope with the two to three stone of excess fat deposited on it. Leo looked the youngest of all the eight, said very little and spent much of the time texting on his mobile. Mark chatted more to Li and Hu than any of the others and the two diminutive Chinese men, dwarfed by the tall Americans, Germans and Rambo beamed constantly in what appeared to be a state of high happiness. Their English was almost faultless and their grasp of technical carping terms such as 'buzzer', 'bivvy', 'snowman rig', 'spodding', 'parallelogram baiting pattern' and 'single hookbait stealth attack' was equally exemplary. Of course they said 'oh, velly big carp', which kind of made it hard to take them too seriously until you had the presence of mind to ask yourself if could say any technical phrase in *French*, let alone *Chinese*.

And that was yesterday. It was a superficial encounter in many ways, everyone was very polite to each other and the necessary exchange of information took part regarding swims, the draw and weighing procedures etc. Everyone appeared to be fine with the 'rules' as such and all were in agreement as to how much they were looking forward to the event. Rambo and I, in an undoubtedly reciprocated state of affairs, were left with first impressions, clouded by pre-conceived notions of national mentality, physical appearance and the fact all these blokes were awash with moolah. We had got to meet them but not to know them, as is always the case. Apart from our mixing at the barbecue on the middle night for a few hours, the layout of Hamworthy dictated we would hardly get to know them any more. Whatever. It didn't matter, from my point of view if it bonded the membership against trying to beat the guests that was good enough for me. Let the contest begin!

A voice jolted me out of my reminiscing. "Hello, boy!" said Rambo. "No sign of the aliens yet, then?"

"No. I've abandoned any aspirations of abduction on the grounds of you being unable to cope without me," I said grinning.

Rambo gave me a short left to the top of the shoulder that jarred my whole body. "How very true," he said munificently. "Where *would* I be without you?" Rambo jerked a thumb over his shoulder. "Steve's just arrived. I wonder if he went through with his couple of little snips?"

I shrugged; I had passed on this little nugget of trivial information during one of our earlier phone calls. "There's only one way to find out, let's go and ask him. If he is suffering I did promise I wouldn't laugh, but it's okay to take the piss because I *was* lying when I said it!"

"Nice one!" said Rambo.

"Oh, a couple of things before we go and have a look. Here's the list of the fourteen pairs in the order they'll be allocated their swim. Keep it on you until I call you up for the grand draw. And the flare gun, have you got the flare gun?"

"All safe in my rucksack," Rambo assured me and cast his eye over the list. "We're on the bottom!" he proclaimed.

I pulled a face of complete indifference. "That's the way it's got be. I can't be seen to give my pair the slightest whiff of help, real or imagined."

Rambo nodded. "Yeah. I get where you're coming from."

We made our way out of the functional wooden clubhouse to see Steve walking very gingerly around to the back of his car. His gait was unusual to say the least; try to think John Wayne strutting his stuff with an iron bar bolted horizontally across both kneecaps and a full bottle of Coke up his arse. Steve's gait was so bandy there was no way he could have stopped a pig in an alley, an exceptionally *fat* pig in an alley, an exceptionally fat pig in an alley where the pig farmer had strapped pannier bags to it. *Bulging* pannier bags, pannier bags *so* stuffed with wadding, that when strapped to the obese pig gave it a width comparable to the wingspan of an albatross that had recently been tortured on a medieval stretching rack. The *full* Coke bottle? Well, no one would want to drink the stuff… even *before* it was put up his arsehole!

I choked back laughter. "How'd the vasectomy go, Steve? All right?"

Steve turned his neck and faced us. "What's it bloody look like?"

I chanced my arm. "Mild discomfort?"

Steve snorted. "Pah! *Mild* discomfort. It feels as if Jonny Wilkinson has gone for a fifty-yarder and kicked my bollocks instead of the ball!"

I was just going to tell Steve I had used a similar analogy when I had kicked off a thermal boot when the hook had popped out of my night-time leviathan but didn't.

"Still, small price to pay for not having any more kids," I said instead. 'Especially the way your four little bastards behave,' I also didn't say.

"Mmmm," said Steve amazingly unconvinced. His brow furrowed. "How long have you got to get to a run before you're deemed to have left your rods unattended? I can't remember what the ruling is."

I was feeling magnanimous. "How long do you want?" I said tongue-in-cheek. "A fortnight?"

Steve ignored my sarcasm. "Seriously though, for me to get off a bedchair and waddle down to a take in the state I'm in..."

"How about a bike?" said Rambo butting in unhelpfully. "I've got one with one of those nice racing saddles that's like an upturned axe. You could ride it down to your rods."

Steve's face twitched and showed traces of extra pain as he thought of the ordeal of hitting a take by bike. "Four stretcher bearers on round-the-clock call, one for each corner of my bedchair, would be better."

"I'll see what I can do," I said. "Failing that, you just get down to them in whatever time it takes. But be careful where you stick your butt end, *rod* butt end, when you catch one. Don't go jobbing it in your groin or you'll wake the neighbours in the nearest village."

"How far's the nearest village," Rambo quietly asked.

I waved a vague hand. "Four miles."

"I *still* haven't caught one yet," said Steve.

Rambo and I went silent. There etched on Steve's face was true pain. The type that *really* hurts.

"You'll get one in the comp," I said reassuringly. "And it'll be a *monster!*"

"As long as I don't get a monster erection," said Steve. "That really would kill me off, getting a stiffy and a tightening nut sack."

"I thought that was how it was supposed to work," I teased.

"If it is then you'd better not look at what's in the next car," Rambo pointed out. "Here come Pup and Melissa and *she* won't be wearing much, *that's* for sure!"

All three of us watched Pup and Melissa get out of their boiliemobil, as I liked to think of it. Pup looked keen and eager while Melissa looked flushed and excited. Now whether I looked keen and eager or flushed and excited I shall never know. I expect the truth was I *had* been keen and eager to see Melissa. Once I had clapped eyes on her and the ridiculously short pair of denim cut-offs, and the midriff-revealing top she was wearing, it was then I had moved swiftly onto the flushed and excited stage.

I turned to Rambo who had simultaneously turned to me. "I wonder if there are any more like her at home?" I asked.

"It's the mother you want to meet," he said winking. "She's the looker."

"Pup! Melissa!" I said lording it up and moving down the steps from my very own functional wooden clubhouse. "Good to see you again. And *still* together, I see. And they said it wouldn't last!"

Pup and Melissa laughed. "We're old campaigners," said Pup. "*Three* months now."

"Is it really? Doesn't time *fly!*" I said with heavy exaggeration. "You know, I'd have sworn it was only *two!*"

"Melina not with you then, Rambo?" Melissa asked.

Rambo shook his head. "She'll be at the barbecue. I think she's coming with Melloney, that's what she said she'd do anyway."

"Sophie not coming, Matt?" Melissa enquired of me.

"No, no. Not really her kind of thing and what with Amy being so young," I answered trying to be as casual as possible.

In truth Sophie and I had yet to return to our normal relationship balance. In fact if I hadn't been so wrapped up in sorting out all the arrangements for the two Hamworthy events I guess I would have been quite put out at the way things were. Especially over the last week, she had become more introverted than before and although her initial anger over the original argument had long faded something was still not right. A little selfishly I had used the tiff to abscond, rather than be abducted, and channelled all my energies into the Hamworthy stuff and getting some fishing practise in the swims I hadn't ever fished before. Once this and the porn movie had been put to bed – I still hadn't told her – I would have to get the domestic side of my life up to speed. Melissa's far from innocent question had jangled my head and made me defensive. Perhaps Sophie had mentioned something of how we weren't getting on so well to Melloney and she had passed it on to Melissa. If she had it was a little galling because the three sisters were a part of the original problem in the first place.

Melissa pouted and flicked her dyed hair. "Oh dear, you'll be *all* on your *own*. Don't worry, *I'll* look after you!" Her immaculately plucked eyebrows hinted at levitation and then the moment was gone.

I looked away from her tanned face to see if Pup had heard but he was too busy rummaging in the back of the boiliemobil for some piece of kit he had imagined he had left behind. Melissa turned with a smile and walked back to her husband. Her arse was only a little short of sensational and she proceeded to park it against their car and made it her business to roll a fag. I eyed her as her tongue licked along the edge of the Rizla paper and watched fascinated as she took her first long drag on the roll-up and blew out a cloud of white smoke. It was quite erotic, if you could quickly discount the likelihood of increased lung cancer, heart attack, along with hideous phlegm and coughing in the mornings. And the permanent smell of nicotine, of course.

Rambo surreptitiously sidled up to me and whispered in my ear. "You have *her* and I'll have *Melloney!*"

"What about *Melina*?" I hissed.

"She can have Melloney as well." I looked up at Rambo in puzzlement. "At the same time as I'm having her," he explained.

I snorted. "You wish! You're not Hollywood and those two stunning looking, lap dancing, ex-international gymnasts, who were also bisexual nymphomaniacs, you know."

Rambo put out his lower lip and angled his head. "I don't mind another girl having my girl, just so long as I'm there as well," he said philosophically.

"What about another *bloke*?" I said.

Rambo drew a finger across his throat. "At *any* time," he growled.

Sensibly I decided not to let Rambo in on the fact I found *Melina* the most attractive of the three sisters. Or how I had hoped it was *me* she had been winking at rather than him, when all three of them had walked down the aisle and into both of our lives. I easily foresaw the impact they might have on the anglers at the barbecue would be akin to being tapped on the cranium with a sledgehammer as manipulated by a blacksmith on LSD who was convinced he was David Grohl, your head was a snare drum and the sledgehammer a drumstick. 'Chemistry' they would call it, searching for gas leaks with a naked flame I would call it.

Over the next forty-five minutes all the remaining syndicate members drove down the long track to the car park. Alan had arrived last, a good fifteen minutes later than everybody else, looking a little harassed and dishevelled. Sandwiched in between the membership our eight illustrious guests also made their appearance. They had arrived in four top quality Range Rovers crammed full with tackle. The combined effect of the four expensive vehicles and the burning curiosity of the syndicate members to clap eyes on the Fish-In sponsors meant they had created one hell of a stir and everyone rubbernecked to get their first glimpse of them.

Once I was sure everyone was present and reasonably correct I asked them to come inside the functional wooden clubhouse and informed them that after we had all greeted each other I would make the draw for the fourteen swims. Dutifully I made a point of introducing the eight guests to every single one of the syndicate members. It was all; 'Horst, this is Steve. He's just had his nuts severely tampered with, so please excuse his bizarre perambulations and the falsetto voice. Steve, this is Horst. He's a self-made, Austrian millionaire who, despite his rather ludicrous M and M, (mullet and moustache, that's the last time I'm going to remind you) isn't a homosexual porn star, but *is* one hell of an angler. Helmut, this is Steve. He's just had his bollocks butchered, so please excuse his ridiculous perambulations and the high-pitched voice. Steve, this is Helmut. Fucking stupid name, then pretty much the same as the other geezer with the mullet'. That *type* of stuff, only without quite so much candour.

It was mundane yet at the same time it was important, and from my point of view, essential it should be done properly. There was a lot of pressing of flesh in the palm department, lots of vacuous platitudes like 'hello', 'nice to meet you', 'if you're a millionaire and that rich there shouldn't be a reason why you can't lend me a couple of grand' and everyone wished everyone else the best of luck. Some *may* have been lying on this last point, but hey, lest we forget, we are talking about carp anglers.

The last introduction I made was when I presented the two Americans to Pup and Melissa. "Okay Brad and Tom, finally, this is our newly-wed couple, Pup and Melissa. Pup, we call him Pup," I elucidated, "because it's short for pop-up Pete, runs a boilie-making business and he's the bloke who's going to be sharing my partnership with Rambo. Rambo's the big bloke in the camo jacket? You remember him I'm sure? He'll fish with Rambo to make up a pair for thirty-six hours while I document all captures and once he's put me into a winning position, I'll fish out the remaining thirty-six hours while he does his bit on the refereeing front! Melissa, here, will be coming round with both of us to help weigh the fish in."

It was at this stage when I needed to quickly put on my sunglasses to avoid retina burn out as Brad unleashed his 'ultimate set' teeth onto a slightly flushed Melissa. His handshake seemed to linger longer than it had with everyone else and his gaze lowered for a brief take on her bronzed, flat stomach complemented by her pierced belly-button. I could hardly sneer. Man's lust was international after all.

"Gee! What a great incentive to catch a carp!" said Brad turning to Tom who nodded enthusiastically. "Pleased to meet ya, Melissa. I hope you're around plenty! And pleased to meet you too, Pup."

"So, where do you make all your boilies, Pup? You gotta small factory or something?" asked Tom.

Pup waved his head. "No. I make them all at home at the moment. You see I've got a 25mm room, a…"

"I'll see you all later," I said softly. "A few things to sort out for the swim draw."

I left them to it, unable to listen to Pup's description of his 'cottage industry' and unable to watch the Americans' response to the idea of a couple living in a boilie-making factory that doubled as a home, even if Pup *was* hoping to expand the business and move out from his flavour impregnated three-bedroom shrine to all things round and stinky.

As I pushed my way through the small crowd of anglers I accidentally bumped into Alan, the syndicate artist and second most psychic angler to ever be a member of Hamworthy Fisheries. Second to me, of course, although it might be sage to point out my apparent waning in the psychic ability stakes of late.

"All right, Alan?" I asked. I still felt a tiny bit guilty for snubbing him over recent months in case he had started harping on about the ghost. "Looking forward to it?"

Alan stroked his neatly trimmed grey beard. "Very much so, Matthew. Very much so. It *should* be thoroughly enjoyable, I just hope…" he paused and gave a shake of his head with closed eyes, "…I just hope it doesn't turnout disappointing in any way, like things have gone so far today," he said sounding flustered.

"Oh?" I said sounding concerned but actually wondering what the old fool was wittering on about. "What happened?"

Alan gave a little laugh. "It was nothing at all really, only a stupid flat tyre. But it made me late and I had to unload nearly all my tackle to get at the spare."

"I wondered why you were so late," I said. "And when I saw you I thought you looked a little hot and bothered."

"Yes. It could have been even more inconvenient if this nice chap hadn't helped undo the wheel nuts. I simply didn't have the strength to do them myself. They were extremely tight and I am getting old, you see," Alan explained.

"Blimey!" I exclaimed. "You were lucky to have someone around to do that. I'd have been less inclined to be surprised if you'd said he smashed you over the head and stole your wallet! Was he driving by in his car?"

"No! *Walking!*" Alan said. "To tell you the truth I thought that was exactly what he *was* going to do, hit me over the head and rob me, when he approached me. Quite an intimidating chap he was, swarthy, dark hair, obviously not, um, how can I put it, *local!*"

My mind pictured the bloke I had imagined to be a benefit claiming, farm working asylum seeker. The one I had seen early one morning walking off to his workplace.

"I'm sure I've seen him! It sounds exactly like the bloke I spotted walking near here one morning a month or so back. Bloody asylum seeker I expect. We're riddled with them being so close to the ferry ports!"

"He told *me*," said Alan clearly with the intent of putting me straight on the matter, "in very poor English, he was a Kosovan refugee working on a local farm so he could send money back for the rest of his family."

I wanted to tell Alan the explanation was almost certainly a load of old bollocks. I wanted to tell him this man was a freeloading, bogus asylum seeking piece of scum. One using up resources *I* had paid into all *my* life and those other people had paid into all *their* life because we were a pathetic, soft touch country riddled with old imperialistic guilt, political correctness and trendy liberal bullshit. But once again I didn't.

"Well, I don't know about *that*," I said.

"He *helped* me," Alan stated. "I wonder how many of *our* young men would have stopped and helped me? Perhaps *they* would have been more likely to have beaten me up and robbed me."

He had a point. We had white trash by the skip-load. Maybe we could throw them into a massive container, along with the bogus asylum seekers, and let them punch fuck out of each other, last one standing gets State Benefit for life, and put it out on Channel 4 prime time. 'I'm a Complete Bit of Lowlife – Don't Get Me Out of Here!' (If any television executives are out there, *don't* steal my idea or I'll set Rambo on you. You *have* been warned!)

"You're here now, though. And *raring* to go!" I said before getting sucked into something I had no interest in discussing further.

"Oh yes! I think Keith and I might do rather well," said Alan.

I slapped Alan on the shoulder. 'Stick to painting, mate,' I thought a little cruelly. "I do too!" Were the words that emanated from my deceitful lips.

I left Alan in his delirious state. If he and Keith won I would shove a couple of four ounce Zipp leads up each nostril, wrap an unhooking mat over my head, pinch the ends under my chin to form a bonnet and sing 'Mary had a little lamb' – the Monty Python version, where it was always gruntin' and got tied to a five bar gate and Mary kicked its little... – in a nasal whine and drop dead of lead poisoning – or an unrelated disease, say 'old age' – fifty years later. The news of my death would provoke a storm in carp magazines over the dangers of not discarding leads. Subsequently all anglers would use a system where they would discard a lead on every sneeze, line bite and take. Due to this, leads would be left en masse in every venue, water levels would rise, lead scrap prices would go through the roof and shares in Korda, Zipp etc. would quadruple. Features on waters would begin to comprise entirely of lead. Lead bars, lead plateaux, lead lined gullies and lead mountains. Lead recovery firms would spring up, diversifying from the golf ball reclamation industry and eventually bring all the old leads back into circulation. Markets would start to stabilise. Eventually some rogue, bright spark would say; 'This is complete and utter bollocks. All you need to do is shove a bit of silicon over the inline lead's central section of tube or through the pendant lead's swivel, then push the hooklength's swivel into the other end of the bit of silicon and the initial take will pull it out around eighty percent of the time. A *snagged* lead will pull it out *every* time and effectively, once it does, you're now fishing a sliding lead and not a lost lead. *If* you get snapped up, *then* the lead will come off the line and be discarded'. This would seem to make sense. In a matter of months Korda and Zipp would go bankrupt due to the flooding of the market with second hand leads and decreasing demand. Everyone would look back and wonder why the fuck they had been so stupid over it in the first place. And then go and follow the *next* fashion fad like a herd of sheep.

I left the large room of anglers and went to my secret stash of fourteen numbered ping-pong balls and one large bag. I grinned. What a delicious irony. This was how it had all started, that night, all those millions of years ago at the 'Black Horse', when Rambo had accused Watt of rigging the draw. He had been proved right and it had all gone on from there. Weird! And now, as a direct consequence of those actions, I was the owner of the best carp fishery in Britain. Via a rather convoluted route, granted, but nevertheless it *was* the reality.

Armed with my implements I returned to the scrum of anglers and stood on one of the chairs to make myself apparent.

"Lady... and gentlemen," I called. Most of them turned to look at Melissa, which wasn't what I had in mind. "If I can have your *attention*, please!" I waited for the room to become quiet and for all the faces to turn and look at me. I wasn't on an ego trip but I wanted all present to be sure that *my* draw was scrupulously fair and above board. "Firstly, welcome to Hamworthy Fisheries' inaugural charity Fish-In and especially to the sponsors of the event, Brad, Tom, Horst, Helmut, Leo, Mark, Li and Hu! I hope you all have a great time and catch some good fish. I'm sure you will." My eyes fell on Steve and I gave him a little nod of encouragement. "The format for the Fish-In is as follows; firstly it will be a seventy-two-hour event, starting at ten this morning and finishing at ten on Monday. The start, finish and the half-time breaks of this event will be marked by a single shot from a flare gun, which will be fired from the swim that my team occupy. The half-time break, as it were, will be when we will have the barbecue. The first flare will mark the start of the competition, the second the half-time break when you will all make your way to the clubhouse for food and drinks, the third flare will be the recommencement of the second half and the final flare will be the end of the competition. The barbecue will start at half eight tomorrow evening and will take place, as I've said, at the clubhouse. We will restart fishing at half eleven and it's up to you, as individuals, to make sure you are back in your swim for that time. The barbecue is strictly a non-fishing time and although this is a seventy-two hour event the non-fishing time is inclusive within those hours so you will be able to fish for sixty-nine hours only. Now, the teams consist of fourteen pairs with each individual angler fishing two rods. The pair with the heaviest overall weight shall be declared the winners and it will be the winning pair's choice of charity which will benefit to the tune of ten thousand pounds. I think we all agree it's a marvellous opportunity for a deserving cause to gain from our little bit of enjoyable fun." A ripple of applause went round the functional wooden clubhouse's biggest room. I continued my speech. "The only rules to apply other than the fishery rules are that you must phone either myself or Pup, whoever is on duty, to have each individual fish weighed and verified. I will hand out sheets with the relevant contact number shortly. I shall be verifying for the first thirty-six hours and Pup will do the second shift. I presume, as I asked you all previously, you all have mobiles with you and they're all fully charged?" The room nodded as one. "As you know I have already marked out the fourteen swims and I hope you agree that they are the most suitable ones on the pit to accommodate a pair with two rods each and that they will give all of you as equal a chance as is possible." There were a few more murmurs of agreement. "I expect a few of you are hoping to get one of your favourite swims in the draw, one you've done well from in the past, because I know I am! Of course, for our eight guests there is no such luxury of past experience, it's all new to them, although I have passed on a little local information when I first showed them round. Mind you, all of it was false!" I held up a hand. "Just joking! Actually to let you guests in on a secret, fishing with no bait has really produced on this water over the last few years!" I held up the bag with the table tennis balls in it. "Inside this bag are fourteen balls, numbered from one to fourteen and I shall ask Melissa to draw out the balls to correspond with the pairs that are on the list Rambo has with him. Rambo if you could come up here, Melissa as well, please."

I watched Rambo ease his powerful body through the throng of anglers and turned my attention quickly to Melissa as she snaked her taut, buxom body to my chair. There was no doubt about it; she was a real saucepot. I didn't need to be psychic to read the minds of the men in the room. Nobody did.

"Rambo, could I have the names on the list as they will receive their swim allocation."

Rambo read out the pairs. "Right. Pair one, Leo and Mark. Pair two, Li and Hu. Pair three, Horst and Helmut. Pair four Brad and Tom. Pair five, Alan and Keith. Pair six, Grant and David. Pair seven, Steve and Paul, that's Steve Arnold our new member. Pair eight, Simon and Phil. Pair nine, Noel and Jim. Pair ten, Ron and John. Pair eleven, Jez and Malcolm. Pair twelve, Steve and Dean. Pair thirteen, unlucky for some, Gordon and Todd and finally, pair fourteen, myself and Pup for the first thirty-six hours and myself and Matt for the last thirty-six hours."

"Cheers, Rambo. So if Melissa would like to take out the balls one at a time and call out each number as she does so, we can find out who's fishing where!"

I squatted down on the chair and held the bag out to Melissa who pulled out the first ball.

"Number four," she said.

"Right, that means Leo and Mark will fish in swim four," I clarified.

Rambo wrote a '4' on the list next to the first pair. Melissa went on to pull out the next ball and the next until she had completed the task of removing all fourteen balls and the draw had been finalised.

The last ball left in the bag had been number nine. Swim nine was the swim where I had fished when the ghost had visited me, the very first swim I had ever fished on Hamworthy. I wasn't unhappy. The island wasn't a long chuck and hopefully Pup might be able to reach it with his tackle, because one rod of the two wanted to be on its margin. If he couldn't make it then adjustments would have to be made to let him fish closer in. The south-east point went to Horst and Helmut, which would have been my probable number one choice; certainly it would have been Rambo's.

"Ok, folks. That's it!" I called to the group. "If you'd like to go and get ensconced in your swims and get ready that'd be great. Make sure at least one of your pair gets the mobile number sheet for Pup and myself. I'll hand them out at the door. Remember all cars must be returned to the car park before fishing starts, and if you pull over tight while you're unloading, everyone else will be able to get by."

I moved over to the door and handed out the bits of paper with the mobile numbers on them. Melissa held out her hand for one as she sauntered through the door. I gave her it.

"Oh! *Now* I've got your mobile number!" she said suggestively.

I smiled and heard a lustful monster snigger in the depths of my mind.

Chapter 11

"What's the time?" asked Pup.

"Ten minutes later than when you *last* asked," Rambo replied, rolling his eyes at me.

"What time was it ten minutes ago? I... I can't remember." Pup's eyes widened in consternation. The tone of his voice raised a couple of octaves. "How long have we got until the off?"

"*Twenty* minutes! You've *still* got *twenty* minutes!" Rambo reiterated. "Don't panic, boy, just chill out and don't panic, Uncle Rambo will tell you *where* to cast and *when* it's time to cast out!"

Rambo walked over to where I was fiddling with my bivvy and where I was also not trying to laugh.

"Fucking hell!" Rambo hissed in my ear. "Can I kill him now or do I have to wait a couple of minutes?"

I stifled another snigger. Swim nine was, shall we say, a *little* strained. Although Pup was undoubtedly a boiliemeister, his precision regarding all things flavoured and round hadn't readily transposed itself upon the rather less controlled environment of a carp swim. Basically, when it came to the actual fishing, Pup was a tad rusty. Years of devotion, time and effort to the pagan god Bait had meant the skills required to organise a fishing session had been sadly lost, sacrificed upon the alter table offering only consecration to Bait, and a useful surface on which to roll it. Whereas Pup was an expert on mixing mixes, rolling mixes and a demon at boiling mixes, deciding the location of his four single banksticks was another altogether far more tricky proposition.

Pup could concoct brilliant recipes for blinding baits, he could invent stunning formulae for superb pop-ups, he could roll baits with tiny indentations, like a golf ball, so you could – with practise – draw and fade boilies with a throwing stick. He could crank out thousands of baits all accurate, in terms of their constituency, ingredients and their diameter, to one percent. He *was* a bait guru, an authority, a specialist, a consultant of the highest esteem, yet as an angler he was a bit of a Noddy. Perhaps not a Noddy with the little yellow car charging sixpence a ride, not a fully-blown Noddy with the hat and bell on top, just an ex-carp angler who was out of practise. Call it Noddyish! And rusty! He *was* rusty. In fact he was *so* rusty, he was as rusty as an old Datsun doorsill that had been left outside underneath, for some strange reason, a constantly running saltwater shower.

His tackle didn't inspire confidence either, the bulk of it having terminated its evolution in the mid-eighties. Maybe that was the problem. Looking the part can be half the battle to gaining a positive mindset, which is a good job, otherwise there would be even more tackle shops going belly-up. Resting on the eventually, finally, at last, I-suppose-this-is-the-right-spot positioned four individual banksticks sat two chocolate brown glass fibre rods; with full cork handles and each with two sliding rings for reel fixings. Estimated length? Something a shade under twelve foot. On the butt was the name of carp rod legend, Terry Eustace. The rods *had* been state of the art in the late seventies/very early eighties, but time and technology had marched on and now they were only *has* been.

When Rambo had first seen them he had looked at them and then cast a dour eye out to the island margin, a full seventy to eighty-odd yards away and into the slight breeze. The island margin was the very margin we had gone out to in our wetsuits along with the inflatable full of ghost bone locating equipment. Despite Rambo being able to cast a dour eye out to the island margin, he had known Pup was unlikely to be able to follow suit, especially as the reels were Abu Cardinal 5s. Abu Cardinal 5s, *not* – unfortunately – the classic 55s, so points had to be deducted on the vintage tackle front. The Cardinal 5s' specification; no baitrunner, not much line capacity, fading bail arm springs but a fair chance of a decent clutch. Due to his concern Rambo had earlier suggested to Pup that he should cover the near margin and other assorted close-in spots, which he would point out in due course. Pup, well aware of his limitations but not Rambo's imposing way of suggesting ideas, had agreed.

To indicate the runs he might get Pup had set his faith in a pair of monkey climbers and an original pair of Delkim Optonic conversions; the ones with the GPO speaker on the front and the incredibly tiny volume and tone controls. To be fair they looked sound and sounded as good as they looked. It was all rather fascinating; Pup was in a carp tackle time-warp bubble. However, Rambo and I had noticed the new modern line and new rig bits Pup had already tied to his two rods and had at his disposal, all stored in an ancient rucksack. The really important bits were up to date and the rest was simply dated, dated from the time Pup had forked off the fishing trail and headed down the bumpy road of supplying fellow anglers with catching baits.

"He'll be all right," I told Rambo. "He's just nervous because he's fishing with you and he's got right out of the swing of it from not going. It'll be interesting to see how he does. It'll be the classic argument about whether flash gear is really necessary to put carp on the bank. I've seen his rigs, simple but effective, he obviously read up on those, his line is good and you *know* his bait will be superb. You can tell him where to put the hookbait and because he can't reach the island he'll have to drop in on the other short spots like you said. That might be a good tactic, for him to cover the margin and short stuff while you go two to the island. And we'll see what happens. Give him time to get into it and you might be surprised how well he'll do." I paused and reflected. "Okay, so we can all laugh at his unfashionable monkey climbers and they might not be so good as your tensioned swingers, but practically speaking, in the 'real' world, will it make the slightest bit of difference? It's all new product development aspiring to increase commerciality and a Tackle Tart mentality." I gave Rambo a serious look. "Think how many carp fishing rules were set in stone only to be completely reversed in years to come." I started to count off my fingers. "The hook buried in the bait. No weight on the line. The hair and bolt rig kill all that. Supple hairs and hooklengths. Very short stiff links and the knotless knot, where you make the hair from the same material as the hooklength, all go against previous wisdom but are equally if not more successful." I halted. I was fast running out of ideas what with talking myself into the topic at such short notice. I went for bluff and bluster. "Your British Army camouflage is well out of style now," I added, "and you don't even camo-up your bait bucket with the appropriate duct tape. Your bivvy is plain green, so's your sleeping bag, you don't wear sunglasses on cloudy days, you've got no power pack to run your TV or laptop, you *haven't* even *got* a TV or laptop, you haven't changed your rig design for ages, you keep to tried and trusted Big Game Line rather than changing to something which is twice as expensive and therefore twice as good and you stick to our old boilie recipe and fail to get seduced by the latest 'killer boilie' from the big bait companies while refusing to shove one of their beanie hats on your head even though it's the middle of summer." I stopped and stared Rambo in the eye, my voice going flat and monotone. "Frankly speaking, I'm surprised you ever catch anything."

Rambo looked unimpressed and ignored my pseudo-diatribe completely. "It's not so much his *gear*, or that he's been out the scene, it's all the flapping around like a shot bird that's not quite dead that gets me. He *will* be dead if it keeps it up, I don't mind telling you." Rambo seemed exasperated. "He must have farted around over where to put his banksticks for *ten* minutes, and you should have seen the fuss he made putting up the bivvy. He's got no marker float rod, no spod rod *and* he keeps asking the sodding time all the time." Rambo paused. "What *is* the time?"

"Ten to."

"Christ! Ten minutes left! I'd better put my hookbaits on!"

Rambo scampered off to his rods and I was left alone to run my eye over the scene in swim nine. Pup had invested in a new two man bivvy, or to be precise a one man plus one woman bivvy, or to be even *more* precise, a man and wife bivvy for him and Melissa. He had set it up, after having quite a battle with it, at the extreme left edge of the swim. My bivvy was located a little further back and more central than theirs, while Rambo's was situated in what tradition would have decreed as the 'proper' place to bivvy-up should you be fishing the swim. Rambo had placed the flag I had bought and stencilled with 'Team Rambo' in between a couple of old bivvy storm poles. He had tied it to the poles with Big Game Line and tensioned it by placing the poles the correct distance apart. In spite of this, due to the largeness of the flag, it bowed ever so slightly whenever enough wind could fill it and the storm poles moved fractionally with it. I thought it looked neat.

Although the other two members of my 'team' were, on the face of it, all prepared and ready to start fishing, my rods were still tucked away inside their rod holdall. At some stage during the half-time break I would swap respective duties with Pup and would push my buzz bars into terra firma, somewhere near where his banksticks were, and get the rods out. I could hardly wait.

Due to this shift pattern of fishing the competition I was torn between wanting Hamworthy to fish very well initially and it proving to be a bit miserly. The first instance for obvious reasons, the second so I wouldn't be completely shot away from being up all night weighing and verifying fish captures. I knew I wouldn't feel tired then, not with Melissa being with me all the time to keep my adrenalin going, but once I had started fishing it would hit me. The first rush would keep me going but once the waiting game had started I could imagine beginning to feel totally knackered. If the pit did fish well I would just have to fight tiredness if I wanted to fish on top of my game and catch. And I *wanted* to catch, believe me. Of course if the pit went mad and then switched off that could be somewhat embarrassing, the owner blanking and not even troubling the scorebook. Everyone would soon conveniently forget I only had half the allotted time, however, if it turned out the other way round I would be fresh and I could cover myself in glory as Rambo and I sprinted to the winning line via a glut of high twenties, thirties and possibly even bigger fish.

Naturally I wasn't alone in wanting to catch, all the others did and I was convinced an awful lot of determined effort was going to be spent in trying to do so. Certainly there were going to be some very tired anglers after the event.

At that moment Melissa came out of the new his'n'her's bivvy. As she stooped to come through the door I got an eyeful of bosom as gravity pulled her large boobs downward and her top with it. She suddenly looked at me and caught me staring. I moved my head away instantly but I wasn't fooling anyone, least of all her. She had probably even stage-managed it for either my benefit, Rambo's, or at a pinch, her husband's. Years of being attention-grabbing eye candy had made her a master of the trade and most men were her subordinate slaves, to some extent or other. I wondered to what extent my extent was.

Melissa was a flirt; there was no doubt about it. And so were her two other sisters. Flirting and hawking their lust-inducing bodies whenever and wherever they could, only too aware of the impact they were making on the men being subjected to the onslaught. However, flirting and doing were two different things and Melissa *was* now married and Melina *was* going out with Rambo. Sort of. Melloney was going to the gym with Sophie and by all accounts was single and unclaimed but she would be at the barbecue whereas Sophie wouldn't be. I felt a twinge of both excitement and disappointment at the prospect of Sophie not being present. Mind you, the way we had been getting on lately perhaps it was better she wasn't turning up. The twinge of disappointment faded.

They would be there though! The three sisters. The Witches of Eastwick, as I decided to christen them, weaving their bedazzling spell of blatant sexual promise and cackling over a cauldron of bubbling, female sexuality and enticement. How would the twenty-nine red-blooded carp anglers cope, given that only two – to my knowledge anyway – had had hanky-panky with only two of them? I would find out later. I had called it 'chemistry' earlier, the relationship between the three witches and the rest of the blokes; maybe 'carnage' would be a more apt word. Carnal carnage? I asked myself. God alone might know what their true morals were, I didn't. I had seen Melina virtually throw Rambo over her shoulder and carry him off so they could have it away, and all within minutes of meeting him. Melissa was clearly mentally unstable, what with her lustful leanings towards anglers and her supermarket made-in-heaven meeting and marriage to Pup. I mean, *per-leeze*! Maid-in-maelstrom more like. And finally Melloney, the youngest of the bunch, friends with my Sophie, equally as outrageous and revealing in dress as her two elder sisters, yet an unknown quantity to me. Sophie had said too little of her to me to glean any answers. So, individually intriguing with a whiff of madness but in combination, all three of them together, their lines of communication criss-crossing between each other, discussing lovers, who they fancied, who they didn't and you had brain meltdown. Well, I did. Watch this space was my advice to myself.

I looked at my watch; it was three minutes to ten.

"It's almost time, Rambo. Can you get out the flare gun and load it up for me?"

"Sure thing, boy," said Rambo and he went into his bivvy and reappeared a few seconds later with the flare gun.

Rambo expertly manipulated the gun and gave it to me. "Point it straight up in the air and pull this thing back towards you. That's called a 'trigger', and it's what makes it go 'bang'!"

"What happens if I fire it into your bivvy?" I asked a little upset by Rambo's sarcasm. Making me look small in front of Melissa wasn't on. I could manage that all by myself, thank you very much!

Rambo wobbled a horizontally placed palm. "Eighteen months and no time off for good behaviour?" he offered.

I tried not to smile but couldn't quite manage it. "Straight up in the air it is, then!"

I looked at my watch again. "One minute left," I said to no one in particular.

"Can I cast out now?" Rambo enquired in a little-boy-asking-his-teacher-if-he-could-be-excused voice.

"Certainly not!" I said indignantly. I aimed the flare gun up at the cloudy sky and pulled the trigger. The flare zoomed up into the air, reached its final height and hung in the sky, shining brightly and drifting slowly on the slight south-westerly breeze.

"Close enough!" I volunteered, heady with the power of starting everything off a good forty-five seconds early. "Go on, then. Away you go!"

Rambo immediately ripped his marker float out to the island and it fell in the perfect position a few yards out from the island's edge. The hookbait and lead followed shortly landing within feet of the marker float. Rambo tightened down, set his indicators and alarm and then spodded out some hemp with great accuracy and fifty or so boilies whizzed out from his throwing stick a few minutes later. A single bedsheet sized for a single bed would have covered the lot.

"He's a mean, lean fishing machine," I told Melissa who was looking on in awe, her pupils wide and black.

"Where shall I put my first one?" whined Pup who was dithering, rod in hand and also watching Rambo with the slack jaw of admiration.

"Flick it underarm as far down to the left as you can. Put it a rod length out," came Rambo's command.

Pup nodded. He gave a quick lick of his lips and went for the underarm flick but crucially forgot to undo the bail arm and his lead and boilie looped back and wrapped around his rod tip.

"Shit!" he exclaimed.

Melissa gave me a straight look. "Come on, let's go and see some of the others before I have to divorce him on the grounds of unconsummated casting."

"Nice joke," I said earnestly, taken aback by Melissa's wit. Perhaps there was more to her than met the eye. Okay, so who gave a toss if there wasn't? The body was more than enough.

"If you like," I said to her. I went and fetched my set of Reuben scales from my rucksack and the clipboard with the catch-logging sheet and pen attached. "We're off now," I called to Pup and Rambo. "We're going to have a wander round and look at the others. Make sure you phone up soon with that first thirty! Start catching and keep ahead of the others," I warned them, "I don't want have to pull it all back and come from behind to win!"

Rambo gave a distracted wave and Pup only nodded due to him trying to untangle his line from his rod tip, apparently while wearing invisible boxing gloves.

Melissa tucked several strands of her dyed blonde hair behind one of her ears and made eye contact with me. "I *like* it when men have to come from behind," she said to me.

My mouth dried in an instant. Several alarms of different pitch and oscillation went off in my head. I gave a pathetic smile. I felt like a non-swimmer unceremoniously dumped in the deep end. Would I ever be suave and sophisticated with women and be able to take this sort of banter/proposition(?) in my stride without buckling at the knees? Seeing as I was already well over a third of the way through my life expectancy it looked like mission impossible. Give it a few more years and I would be bum-hole lucky to even get any.

With a pleased-with-herself look on her face, Melissa turned and walked up to the grass track that ran around the pit's perimeter, gyrating her arse more than was strictly necessary. The top of the legs of her shorts cut up into her buttocks but there was no hint of a suntan line. She probably went on the sunbed naked. It was the Rebecca thing all over again; attractive woman, me on my own – in terms of a female partner – in a fishing environment. How odd!

I felt a bit of dick after my non-response and was wondering how I could kick-start conversation when my mobile chirruped and saved me the bother. I answered it and listened to the strong accent on the end.

"Right, we'll be straight round. Congratulations! First carp of the contest," I said to the phone. "Bloody hell!" I said to Melissa. "The M and Ms have had one!"

"M and Ms?" she said confused.

"The Mullets and Moustaches! The gay Austrian porn stars! *Horst* and *Helmut!*" I explained. "Helmut's had a fish already… The *bastard*! Let's get in the van and go see how big it is."

"They're *not* gay porn stars are they?" Melissa asked giving me an agitated look.

"Nah!" I admitted. "We've got some *real* ones coming to shoot a film in a few day's time, not gay ones, though. Ordinary porn stars. If there's such a thing as an *ordinary* porn star!" I babbled.

Melissa gave me a look similar to one you might give a person while trying to guess how much they weighed. "Are you on drugs, Matt?" she said slowly.

"No!" I said with umbrage.

She gave it a moment's thought. "Maybe you should be," she suggested with no hint of irony or humour.

"Any particular one you might like to suggest," I said sounding more annoyed than I was.

"Viagra?" she said sullenly.

I went to the human equivalent state of a pinball table going to 'tilt'. Come-on or put-down? Put-down or come-on? Put on or come down? Or was she messing with my mind? If she was, she was doing a good job.

My lack of reply and neural shut down meant Melissa answered her own question. "Let's get in the van and go and weigh the fish, shall we?"

We both got in. That's twice – my brain reminded me – *twice* she's rendered you speechless. I told my brain to quit bugging me about it; after all, it was the thing that was supposed to come up with the answers, not *me*!

I drove the van around from the northerly swim nine following the track clockwise back down to the south-east point swim where Horst and Helmut were fishing. My earlier astute preparation had suggested the need for a vehicle because to have hopped from swim to swim on foot would have been a ludicrous task. As it was the first capture had taken us from one end of the pit to the other and who knows, perhaps Rambo might catch the next one and we would be on our way back. I had full tank of diesel to be on the safe side, in case the pit went completely bonkers.

I glanced over at Melissa who had miraculously produced some Rizla papers and a pouch of tobacco from somewhere and was rolling one up. How she had ever managed to conceal something as bulky as a packet of Rizla papers in her tight shorts, and then prise them out was amazing. The tobacco pouch was an even greater mystery – one that defied all laws of physical displacement – and we still awaited the lighter.

"That Rambo's quite a guy, isn't he?" she remarked unexpectedly between drags. The lighter had been, gone, done the business and I had never even clapped eyes on it.

"Yeah," I concurred. "I guess he is."

"Melina says he's a bit of an animal in bed," she said offering me a sideways glance.

"That, I *can't* vouch for," I admitted.

Melissa pushed air down her nose, made a noise in the back of her throat and smiled. "Melina says it's a pity he's such a jerk when he's out of it. The bed that is, *Rambo* doesn't need any drugs. I don't know how much longer she'll put up with it. Melloney absolutely *detests* him because of the way he treats Melina."

"Rambo's Rambo. I don't think he'll ever change," I said truthfully, ignoring her little dig at me, even if it had annoyed me. In spite of my spite my curiosity was piqued and I had to solicit the question. "Is Melina getting fed up with him?"

"Why do you ask?" Melissa said, her eyes boring two neat holes in me. She made the same noise as she had a few seconds earlier. "You *fancy* Melina, don't you?" Melissa gave me a knowing smile. "You fancy me as well, but not as much as Melina."

Three strikes and you're *out*, buster! Not a word came from my paralysed lips. I had the uneasy feeling of being totally and utterly transparent. The feeling of every secret I had in my head being written and subsequently lit up on a great big advertising hording – with Melissa in front of it reading every single word. I stopped the van. We had reached the M and Ms' swim.

Melissa let out a proper laugh. "Men! *Soooo* predictable! So easily read!"

I was getting a little hacked off and tried to bite back. "You three certainly show off plenty for us to get predictable about. I reckon you must thrive on the predictability of our responses because you certainly try and provoke it enough," I said, as I undone the door and started to get out, pleased I had come up with a semblance of adult dialogue.

Melissa got out as well and spoke to me over the top of the van's roof. "It's the mayhem, Matt," she said smugly. "We thrive on the mayhem. And the sex that usually goes with it," she added casually.

"So why did you marry, Pup?" I asked. "I wouldn't have thought marriage was the ideal carriage for promoting mayhem and sex, especially amongst lots of *different* men."

It was Melissa's turn to struggle with what I had said rather than the other way around. "It did seem like a good idea at the time," she admitted. "We've all got to mature at some point or another and I'd thought I'd reached that point."

"But not now?" I said sharply. This was one fishy question I didn't want to slip the hook.

"The house does smell more than I'd hoped for," she conceded, "and rolling baits all day can be a monotonous task and being tied to one man only... it'll take some getting used to." She let the words drift as if I could make up my own interpretation of them.

I chose to overlook the latter comment and focused on what it must be like being married to a one-man boilie factory.

"What, rolling baits is boring? Surely not! Despite all the different flavours, all the different colours and all the different sizes?" I said laughing.

Melissa nodded. "Despite all the different colours and flavours and sizes. They're all boilies at the end of the day!"

I nodded in recognition. "I know this is an odd question but have you *really* got a thing about anglers?" I said, quizzing her now I appeared to have the upper hand. "I don't want to be intrusive but it's very unusual. You're giving us all hope, you know! If it is true."

She took a deep drag on her roll-up and shrugged. Her two wonderful bosoms heaved and she flicked away her dog end onto the grass and blew out the last cloud of smoke from her tar-lined lungs. I made a mental note to pick it up later when she wasn't looking. The litter lout.

"Sort of. I don't really know why, I think it started as a teenage backlash against traditional sporting icons and went on from there. I *do* find fishermen sexy, although I'd be hard pushed to explain why. There's something there, I guess I'm just not your average woman that's all. It's not completely indiscriminate, you know," she pointed out, "I haven't got the hots for *everyone* who picks up a fishing rod." She paused. "Only *some* of them."

I knew I would never make a good poker player because my face must have betrayed me.

"It's not *you*, Matt!" she suddenly informed me. "You don't have to agonise over whether it's *you*, because it *isn't*! I *might* be attracted to you if I was drunk *and* you had spoken to me really nicely, bought me a few drinks, and the time and the place made me feel like some fun… But otherwise you've no chance."

"Thanks a lot," I said sarcastically. "Care for a glass of vodka?"

"I *never* drink when I'm weighing in fish," she replied.

I'll be doing the weighing, I thought vindictively. You can fucking write it down, madam! My mind raced. Maybe she fancied *Rambo*! *That's* who it was! She had just been prick-teasing me! Having said that, I could still see it all ending in tears and us having to find someone else to roll our bait. Why on earth would Rambo bed someone else's attractive wife when it meant ruining our bait rolling source? What *was* he thinking of? Talk about lack of priorities.

I was getting rather ahead of myself, deliriously so, and the sight of Helmut's thirty-four pound, six ounce mirror stopped me in my tracks, slapped me around the chops and poured a bucket of iced water over my head. I was all the better for it as well.

"Yes. I had only just been setting ser indicator ven ser line started going," Helmut explained in his heavily accented Germanic English. "I vasn't expecting a bite so soon, but is gutte! Very gutte!"

I tweaked Helmut's mullet like an eight-year-old schoolboy might pull the ponytail of the little girl in front of him, informed him that, *that* was a matter of opinion, snapped at Melissa to get the weight down correctly onto the catch-logging sheet and left the south-east point swim in a huff. Only I didn't of course – I don't do the things I would like to do or say enough I'm afraid – I did tell Melissa to get the weight details down and we did leave rather quickly, but only because Noel had caught one from swim two.

From swim two we went directly to swim three leaving a stunned Noel to come to terms with the fact his thirty-pound common hadn't been the first fish of the competition. We were an hour in, that was all, and there had been two thirties caught. Take it away Hamworthy Fisheries; the *best* carp water in Britain! The reason why I went to swim three was not because there had been a fish caught but because Steve – four kids and provided his *vas deferens* hadn't healed back together definitely *no* more kids, Steve – and Paul, his fertile and still sperm-ridden partner – I assumed – were fishing it.

"How's it hanging, guys?" I asked as I walked into their swim. The double entendre went unnoticed or was ignored.

Steve, who was sitting rather delicately on a bedchair with the back section at ninety degrees to the rest of the chair, gave me a little wave and Paul gave me a thumbs up.

"We've had a few fish boshing out in front of us," said Paul enthusiastically and Steve's had a couple of liners, "but no takes yet. Anyone else had anything?"

"The Austrian pair have had a fish, in the first five minutes that was. Noel, he's been a member for yonks, has also had one in the swim next to yours and they were *both* thirties." I motioned my head back southwards to indicate where Noel was fishing. By now, Melissa had stopped by my side.

"How's hubby doing?" asked Steve, craning his neck towards Melissa. It was an odd compensatory movement, one the observant Melissa quickly spotted.

"Are you all right, Steve?" she asked with true concern.

"Not really," he admitted. "I shouldn't be here, not in my condition, but I'm buggered if I'm going home." Steve's eyes misted over. "*Three* whole days' fishing! You know I can't remember the last time I went fishing for three whole days. It *must* have been before the eldest one was born. That's over eight years ago! Christ! How time flies when you're up to the gunwales with muck, bullets, nappies and bottled milk." Steve folded his arms defiantly across his chest. "No! I'm staying here for the duration even if they *both* drop off!" he said emphatically.

"It's only pain, Steve, after all," I said. "Anyone can take physical pain, it's a breeze."

Melissa looked confused and then she managed to put two and two together and her memory kicked in. "Of course! Your little op! I'd forgotten! Hurts does it?"

Steve pulled a grimace and shifted his weight slightly. It reminded me of someone trying to let out a sneaky fart. "You could say that," he confirmed. "The physical pain though pales into insignificance compared to the mental one caused by not having caught from here." Steve waved his arm around in a vague area defining gesture. "Especially seeing as how light in the wallet it has left me. Not that it's all about money, it's more to do with a carp angler's self-worth. Every carp angler needs to catch from a new venue before he can relax, it's a kind of self-inflicted pressure we all put on ourselves. Bit silly really, but saying it's silly doesn't make it any less real." Paul and I nodded; we both knew *exactly* where he was coming from. Steve continued. "The additional torment of not really being sure both of my hooklengths aren't tangled is pretty gruesome and something I could do without as well. You see, it's the same as the last time I was here," Steve explained. "Fish jumping over my baits, getting liners but *no* takes. Last time it happened I reeled in and I was all tangled up. Twenty hours later. *Twenty* sodding hours! What a killer! D'you know I cast out on the flare earlier and because it looked as if it tangled through the air I wound back in to check. It wasn't tangled. Second cast I thought the same so I pulled that one back in and that wasn't tangled either. I left the third one out because it looked okay and now because of what occurred last time and because of the fish movement, the liners and *still* no takes, my confidence is being eaten away by the second. *And* my nuts are throbbing like a couple of Bull Mastiffs are attached to each one while a sadist is cranking their jaws even tighter by winching down a couple of 'G' clamps fitted to each dog's muzzle!"

I laughed out loud. "Nice image, mate! Don't worry, they'll be all right in a few days' time!" I told Steve.

Like I knew anything about it. Maybe they *would* both drop off. If they did, I wasn't going to pick them up. Melissa's dog ends – yes – Steve's bollocks? No, sir!

I started speaking to Steve again. "But on to more important matters. You don't normally get tangles do you?"

"Not as a rule," admitted Steve.

"And it's not as if you haven't had a take from here, you were simply unlucky and lost one. Shit happens. *I* lost a monster a few weeks earlier; it's been magnified as far as you're concerned because it was your *first* take. Magnified beyond proportion. You haven't dropped lots of fish in the past, have you?"

"No. No, pretty good on that front usually," said Steve.

"There you are. Like I said, no worries," I said trying to convince him. I carried on like a Dutch uncle. "I've known of carp anglers disappearing up their own backsides to the point of neurosis and they usually do so over the perennial favourites, bait and rigs. They get so preoccupied with searching for the 'wonder bait' and 'wonder rig' that's going to let them haul out carp left, right and centre, they don't concentrate on the fishing. The greatest bait and rig in the world won't catch in the wrong spot but an average rig and bait with good bait application put in the right one often will. Chopping and changing, trying to find the 'wonderstuff' leaves them with no confidence in anything because they haven't given it long enough to work. I know. I know because I was one of those carp anglers. You'll be fine, mate. You'll get one and then you'll look back and laugh at how daft you were."

"Even so, I might re-cast in a minute to make sure everything's okay," said Steve.

"Are you mad?" I screamed. "If you pull in and it's not tangled you've got to cast out and go through the whole episode again. You won't gain a thing; all you'll do is possibly disturb the feeding carp you have in your swim. You've *had* the liners; you've *seen* the fish. Leave it! You've *got* to have faith in what you've done before and what's worked before."

Steve squirmed like a worm. A worm that had a couple of Bull Mastiffs attached to each one of its nuts while a sadist cranked the dogs' jaws shut even tighter by winching down a couple of 'G' clamps fitted to each dog's muzzle. Granted all the worms I was aware of didn't have gonads but then, who actually *owned* a *pair* of 'G' clamps? Not I! Or, if push came to shove, a couple of testicle unfriendly Bull Mastiffs?

"All right, for God's sake! I'll leave the sodding thing!" Steve relented, finally cajoled into defeat.

"You won't regret it!" I said whole-heartedly.

If he did pull in later and was tangled I would be for the high jump. Although to be fair I wasn't bricking it, Steve would never catch me in his state of swollen nuttery.

As if to underline the point, in one of those absurd moments of miraculous coincidence usually confined to the unreal world of films, novels and carp articles, Steve's buzzer went beep! Another liner? Then it went beep beep! Then it went beep beep beep! Then, having finally made its mind up and decided it *was* worth the battery discharge, went dedededededededededede, which is the correct grammatical interpretation for lots of beeps coming very quickly one after the other. Steve had a run, on the same buzzer he had used to dupe us during his wedding speech – like a true anorak I had remembered the LED colour! It was his second Hamworthy run. The alarm carried on dedededededeing.

I turned and looked smugly at Melissa. As smugly as a cat who had eaten all the double cream and then worked out how to manipulate a can opener and had successfully opened the last tin of evaporated milk, which, by fate, had been hiding the key to the freshly cooked chicken cupboard. And what are a mere lock and key when you can manipulate a can opener? "See?" I said as the alarm shouted its continued warning. "What did I say?"

"What did you...?" asked Melissa. "I didn't... you because... the alarm."

I didn't quite catch what Melissa had said because of the alarm. I turned away from the riveting non-conversation we weren't having and watched the tragic Steve, who by now, some ten seconds after the original indication, had at last struggled to his feet.

Over the years I had seen some awful cases of sloth when it came to hitting takes. Amongst the reasons were deep sleep, sleeping bag entrapment, bivvy zip quandary and general disorientation due to being asleep, drunk or spliffed-out. Then there had been tardiness due to incorrect angler location i.e. around the other side of the lake talking to your mate, in the pub, fish spotting on another water and being in the car with the engine running, the radio and heater on to avoid the crap weather. Then there were the more specific yet random events; losing a thermal boot, falling over, falling in, caught having a piddle – or even worse – and while on the subject, stepping in dog shit as laid down by cunning Rottweilers, and – my favourite – becoming entangled in bivvy guy ropes, so comprehensively entangled a bailiff had to cut the person free two days later – I had only *heard* of that one – but what a great image, one you could only hope was true! What I had *never* seen, *or* heard of, was delay by vasectomy.

Steve's painful, bulging, black and blue bollocks were clearly not conducive to speedy movement. In fact it looked as if they weren't conducive to any movement whatsoever. The shambling John Wayne, full-Coke-bottle-up-the-arse, never-stop-a-pig-in-an-alley gait from earlier was all too apparent. The pain etched on Steve's face was apparent. The fact he should have been resting in bed rather than being involved in a seventy-two hour carp fishing competition was desperately apparent. But there was also something *else* apparent. It was determination. Grim determination was written on Steve's face in equal measure with the pain. Each contrived step, each forced, distressing step, each small step for Steve – which was an infinitely smaller and far, far less consequential one for mankind – was absolutely *killing* him. But he was determined, *utterly* determined it would not halt him in his quest to catch an inaugural Hamworthy carp.

Pain, agony, acute discomfort and suffering were all there to be seen and easily recognisable to the naked eye. Steve moved like a frail, wizened old man on a zebra crossing who, although nearly moribund, had enough dignity left to try and not hold up the waiting motorist any longer than was necessary. Like Steve, he was physically incapable of faster movement, yet the human spirit still burned brightly inside him and willed him to damn well try. It was truly noble to see the man who had fathered four children – and definitely didn't want to father any more – struggle against the hideous impairment of incredibly bruised and swollen bollocks and force his butchered body down to his rods. Steve had mentioned self-worth and it was this along with his pride, his determination, his desire and his willpower that drove him on and allowed him to play down the excruciating pain of his debilitating condition.

So heroic was Steve's crawl to his rods, so uplifting and gracious, so reminiscent of all the most appealing human endeavours in the face of crushing adversity, that it brought a tear to my eye. I was so moved I was crying. Crying with laughter. In most comedies someone suffers and in this instant it was Steve. And my God was it funny. It reminded me a little of how Rambo and I had laughed at the Cowboy coming out to draw at Lac Fumant 1st time. There it had been the pretentious and preposterous posing of the Cowboy, slowly being undone by the weather and a carp that had been so funny. Now it was the sheer pain and suffering counterbalanced by the desire to overcome it that was so amusing.

I held my sides, literally, and laughed hysterically at Steve's grotesquely agonising slow motion run of pain to his second Hamworthy run. At last he covered the ground between his bedchair and rods and like a tormented, exceptionally bandy chimpanzee – with crippling arthritis – picked up the rod and struck.

"Arrgghhh!" Steve cried as the butt touched his terrifically, tender testicles. "Owww!" he moaned as a nervous spasm caused the contraction of the cremasteric muscle thus pulling his inflamed nuts against his pelvic bone.

Now Steve had a rod in his hand, his posture looked even more deformed. One half of his body – the top half – was attempting to control a big carp, while the other – the damaged bottom half – was trying to stop any contact, however slight, of anything, including air, touching his ballooning ballbag. So sore was his scrotum – his undoubtedly, slick, shaved sore scrotum – that the slightest waft of a molecule brushing against it was instant torture. The more the carp fought, the more it hurt Steve. Every thump of the rod tip transferred itself into odious pain. Every response to the carp's struggle for escape caused a non-proportional correlation – being multiplied many times – to the excruciating two-veg pain Steve was receiving. Man's Achilles' heel isn't a tendon, the true weak spot is hanging underneath – if the general male response to the three witches was anything to go by – his main centre of thought.

Steve screamed in agony. "Arrgh! My *God*! What a powerful fish! *Christ*, that hurts! There it goes again! Ohhhh! Another run. *Jesus*! It's great… but it's fucking killing me! Arrgh! The pain! The pain! Come on! In you come, I'm not losing you, you bastard!"

As I stood next to Melissa, who had summoned up another roll-up from thin air and was dragging on it with delicious enthusiasm, with tears of mirth blurring my eyes, I pondered on the masochistic element of carp fishing. We had all forced ourselves to go, at some time or another – the phrase 'I'll be glad when I've had enough of this' rung so very true – especially at times of inclement weather. The odd accident with a knife, hook or baiting needle had been endured, perhaps a twisted ankle, or even worse a pillow which had gone a little lumpy or a poor TV reception had occurred. These were all things that conspired to put a session on a downer, yet the response from the hardy was to grin and bear it. In fact not only that but to *enjoy* it *because* of the macho element of toughing out the difficulties. But I had *never* seen it – the masochistic side – manifest itself in such bleak terms of discomfort, and nor had I seen the discomfort be revelled in quite like Steve was revelling in his torture.

"Come to daddy, you big lunker! Owww! You're putting me in agony but I'm going to land you!" Steve shouted through clenched teeth and I would chance, through clenched buttocks.

A huge common rolled on the surface. Paul was poised with the net. All Steve had to do was back up a few feet and pull the lunker over the net and the job was done.

Like a two-legged crab in reverse that had lost its sideways gear he backed up, one bowleg back very gingerly, then the other bowleg. A passer-by, unaware of Steve's perilous predicament, might have assumed that here was an angler who was not so much cacking his pants over losing a big fish, but an angler who had already done so. There was an artificial stiffness, bordering on the robotic, to Steve's legs as he tried to protect his testicles and walk backwards with what looked like forty-pounds' worth of carp attached to his hook. Somehow it seemed even *more* ungainly and even *more* hilarious in reverse motion than when he had done it going forward. And it had been side-splitting then! Duly I collapsed onto the floor, axed by amusement, helpless with hilarity and light-headed from laughter.

Paul netted the fish while I tried to get control of myself.

Melissa looked down at me with contempt. "You complete sicko!" she sneered.

"What?" I exclaimed, easing myself up from my knees. "You *can't* say that wasn't funny!" I said defiantly.

Melissa narrowed her eyes and pursed her lips, but it was unnatural to her and it quickly turned into a pout. "All right, I suppose it was funny and he *does* look very happy despite the pain it put him in."

We both turned to look at Steve punching the air and slapping Paul on the back. He had a smile a mile wide, and his knees, bless him, were a mile wide apart. Where *was* his horse?

"You see," I said triumphantly. "This will be one of the greatest day's of his life and all because *I* allowed him to join my syndicate and gave him the chance to catch what's now inside his landing net."

Melissa gave an unaffected air. "Okay, Mr Bigshot, but *I* still don't fancy *you*." She said forcefully. Melissa smiled and gave me a sly look. "But perhaps that's a self-defence mechanism because I know you fancy Melina more than me!"

"What makes you so sure I fancy *any* of you, *including* Melloney?" I asked. I was getting a bit miffed at her presumptuous stance on who I found attractive; mainly on the grounds she was always right.

"You're not gay are you?" she asked self-confidently, as if an affirmative answer would be the only possible case where I wouldn't fancy any of them.

"They don't *do* gay carp anglers!" I said as convincingly as I could. You never could be sure what Tesco might come up with next, what with their matchmaking aisles and whatnot. And if The Tackle Box could sell Acme Parallel Universe Viewers...?

"Melina!" she stated assuredly, pointing an index finger at me. "You like Melina the best. I could tell by the way you were trying not to look at her at the wedding!"

"Don't be daft!" I said somewhat embarrassed and taken aback by Melissa's keen observational cuteness once again. "Anyway, she's Rambo's girl. Like I'd want to fall out with my best mate over a girl!" I said trying to justify my denial. "And besides," I shockingly suddenly remembered, "I'm with Sophie and my daughter Amy."

Melissa's expression changed and she moved her gaze to look at the ground. After a second or two she looked back up at me and seemed about to speak when a yelp went up from in front of us. Not a yelp of pain, but one of delight. We both turned to see Paul hoisting up the common, all safely tucked up in a weigh sling, on a set of scales. Steve was craning his neck to check the dial. As it transpired and as it was later registered on the catch-logging sheet, Steve had just caught his first ever forty and by virtue of this carp-fishing milestone, he and Paul were in the lead.

"You can name that carp," I informed Steve. "Syndicate policy says all new forty-pound fish can be named by the angler who captures it. Obviously I'd have to confirm by analysing the photos whether or not your common *is* a previously uncaught forty but to me, going from memory of the latest chart painting Alan has done, I think it is. It's got a very distinctive tail shape and I'm sure I would have remembered it."

Steve gave another smile. I was convinced his head was going to horizontally split asunder.

"Wow! *Really*? Excellent! I'll be a part of Hamworthy history if it is a first time forty." Steve shook his head as if he couldn't believe it. "What to call it, though?" he said in quiet introspection.

"It's up to you, mate," I told him. "Anything you want."

Steve mused for a while. "Something classical, I think," he said eventually. "I'm thinking my condition, I'm thinking Tchaikovsky and I'm thinking ballet..." He shot me a glance to see if I could get what he was thinking of. I gave him a completely blank look. This wasn't my field of excellence.

"No?" said Steve starting to laugh. "Why it's 'The Nutcracker'!"

"And that's a ballet by Tchaikovsky, is it?" Melissa asked.

Thank God she was as ignorant as me.

"Last time I looked it was!" Steve confirmed.

"And are your nuts well and truly cracked?" I asked.

Steve eased out the waistband of his jogging bottoms and peered down the gap. "It's hard to tell with all the bruising but they sure feel as if they are!" Steve confirmed.

"Good choice!" I said crinkling up my nose. "And excellent anecdotal material for the children and any future grandchildren."

Chapter 12

Over the next nine or so hours Melissa and I criss-crossed the pit with the haphazard abandon similar to that of a blowfly stuck in a downstairs cloakroom, but not as frequently – not even Hamworthy could produce *that* many takes! Of course we weren't the ones making the annoying buzzing noise, it was all the catching carp anglers' alarms that were the culprits. We, as befitted our position of mobile adjudicators, were limited to opening and slamming shut the van's doors and bringing a noisy diesel engine to life. And answering the trickle of mobile phone calls in the style of a carp angling Dom Jolly – 'Hello, I'm at the pit! What? You caught another one? Okay! Be there in a minute! Ciao!' – all at top volume! I had often flinched at a mobile call coming in while fishing – another reminder of my conditioned response – but now the two were inextricably linked. A ring on my mobile meant a run on someone's alarm somewhere; it only needed verbal confirmation to ascertain the important bit, namely, whose run it was.

As we approached the passing of the first twelve hours of the Fish-In I had a chance to reminisce now I was alone in my bivvy getting ready for some shut-eye. A clear pattern had emerged over the period so far and it had led to us returning back to four swims more often than any of the others, and two in particular. It was as if we had been attached to a large piece of powerful elastic and after a period of time the build up of stored energy in the elastic overcame our inertia and pinged us back, tumbling head over heels, to the fixed end. The primary fixed end had been the M and Ms' swim, the secondary, the two Americans' and the two lesser ones, Noel and Jim's and Rambo and Pup's. Of the fourteen swims only three had failed to be worth a visit during the opening half day, and guests occupied two of those three. It had been Leo and Mark and Li and Hu who were struggling, along with new members Simon and Phil, their common thread being a severe lack of local knowledge and possibly a swim bereft of carp. Of the remaining others? Well, they had all scored a single fish to each pair.

Steve's huge common, which was still the biggest fish, had put them ahead of the pack for the best part of two hours until Brad and Tom had had simultaneous takes. The two takes, both successfully converted, had been a brace of mid-thirty mirrors. Brad's teeth had been incandescent in the now emerged, bright afternoon sun, as he had beamed, literally, at the capture of the two magnificent carp. When he had smiled I really did feel inclined to put on my shades, or a welding mask, to protect my eyes from the reflection of light off his splendid teeth. I'm being facetious and had done no such thing as usual, but with his mass of blond-white hair and 'ultimate set' teeth framed against a skin colour of golden brown he had been dazzling. There was no need for the past tense, he still was dazzling, too dazzling. Certainly too dazzling for Melissa, who had wound up the flirtometer to somewhere near maximum – or I supposed it was somewhere near maximum – as I was a little unsure of how far she could actually wind it. Eleven on the amplifier is the old guitarist's joke.

"Hey, man! Awesome!" Brad had said as he sucked me into giving him a high-five.

For all I knew he could have been talking about Melissa's tits, and if he had been, who was I to argue? Melissa had stood with her hands on her hips, her shoulders a little further back than normal and projected her two weapons of mass destruction into our psyche. Coquettishly she had written down both carp weights and had involved herself in conversation rife with subtle suggestion and hints of sexual promise. She had been a real pro and a complete mistress of the art of philandering. She had been full-on, up-for-it and in-your-face with the two Yanks and not a man was safe from her when she was in such form. Amazingly she had made a point of bending down to pick up a dropped pen and had provocatively displayed her toned arse to all and sundry with the skill of a preening peacock. Then, thankfully, before she could start pole dancing around one of Brad's banksticks, Rambo had phoned to say *Pup* had caught one and we had to go.

As we had left Brad and Tom's swim to head back to the man she had married, Melissa had turned to me and said. "Those two are nice aren't they? Very pleasant. They come over a bit loud and full of themselves but it's only because of the way they speak rather than anything else."

"Do you fancy either of them, then?" I had asked.

"Not really," she had said. "I could understand why lots of women would find them attractive but no, not especially so."

I had been about to point out her rather contradictory actions when I wondered whether that was the very point of her flirting. She had mentioned the mayhem and it seemed that as along as she was the centre of male attraction it mattered little to her whether or not it was reciprocated, as far as she was personally concerned. After all, she had flirted with me only to tell me I was an angler she never fancied. She had then backtracked with a proviso of possibilities under exceptional conditions, designed – I could only imagine – to maintain my interest in her. What did I know? Secretly I reckoned she liked them.

Now it was dark and I put my weary head onto my pillow. Peace and quiet but for how long, I wondered? How long before the dreaded mobile squawked again? Thankfully – now I was isolated in my little bit of private space – the Williams' bivvy in swim nine, I could fully relax until it did ring. Were the others relaxing as well? I didn't know but I imagined Horst and Helmut could happily stroke their moustaches and run their fingers through their long-at-the-back hair with few worries.

Undoubtedly, at this precise moment, they were performing some sort of celebratory Tyrolean dance in their swim, one where they smacked each other's arses while wearing tight fitting lederhosen. Not that they were gay or anything. The reason for their joy was the pair of them led the way having caught six fish, Brad and Tom had four, while the other swim nine occupants had a brace to share equal third with Noel and Jim. Let them dance, I thought, there was a long way to go.

Lying on my bedchair I had to chuckle to myself as I remembered how Melissa's presence at each weight and capture verification had given the relatively innocuous event an added edge. It had certainly made all the blokes much more self-conscious and their gawping – while trying to appear not-to-look – at her buxom, curvaceous body was a delight to behold. Hair had been quickly smoothed and faces slicked with water in an attempt to take some of the grime away, as all of a sudden personal appearance actually entered into the carp fishing equation. It was hardly natural. The anglers had even attempted to re-arrange their scruffy clothing and all because of Melissa's presence. And it had all been done without trying to appear as if it was being done! What a hoot!

As Melissa had seen desire in me regards Melina at Pup's wedding, so I saw it manifest itself in the Fish-In competitors. As I had become slightly – only slightly – familiar with her tiny tight shorts, skimpy top and bare, belly-button pierced midriff, I had directed a little more of my sensory observations to the anglers' reaction. It was quite compelling to objectively watch the hold she had over all the men, in between me doing my own slightly – only slightly – curtailed version of the popular looking but-not-looking scam.

To quantify, *all* the men except Rambo, Horst and Helmut and ironically, or maybe not, her husband, definitely changed their mannerisms to ingratiate the newly appeared sex-bomb in their swim. Even old codgers like Alan, who surely wouldn't have approved of her sense of dress, reacted to her. If only he could remember what it was he was supposed to be reacting to! The *dirty*, old man! The M and Ms, on the face of it, seemed the least affected of all the other pairs and behaved pretty much as they had, as far as I could discern and remember, when she hadn't been present. They were concentrating too heavily on the fishing to be distracted by her and I labelled it as a Teutonic trait even though they were Austrian rather than German. I gave myself a little laugh. What was going to happen when all three of them turned up? Pandemonium at the very least. Mayhem with a capital 'M', inscribed in Copperplate Gothic Bold.

I quickly stopped laughing. *Melina* would be there. I would have been less surprised at alien abduction than Melissa not informing her elder sister of her viewpoint on my fancying *her* the most out of the three sisters. So, armed with this nugget of socially awkward information – to me at least – how would Melina wield it? The endless situations of what she might or might not do either in Rambo's presence or behind his back – both seemed equally awful – were dead scary. I rapidly moved on to the concept of whether Rambo would actually kill me for just fancying his 'bird', for want of a better word – somehow 'fiancée' or 'girlfriend' didn't seem apt – or just give me a damn good thrashing with some sort of blunt instrument – like a 28mm aluminium Cobra throwing stick or a sock full of 4 ounce Stonze ledger weights. On the up side, perhaps he might laugh and take it as a backhanded compliment to the attractiveness of his girl. The sleeping Lust Monster inside me sniggered and muttered something about not looking at her in the first place. This was unfair because she hadn't even been Rambo's girlfriend at that stage and besides it had been *Sophie* who had told me to look at someone *else* when I had originally been looking at *her*! It was her fault, Your Honour, all *her* fault!

Moving on rapidly I remembered that I had never crossed Rambo in all the time I had known him. We had always been on the same side right the way down the line. I had seen or heard of people who *had* and they had tended to wind up either dead or not particularly alive. Or so severely pummelled you would have been hard pushed to have noticed the difference from the other two states, which, if you looked closely enough, were in fact only *one* state. I was getting ahead of myself as I often did in this sort of mood. My brain's apparently endless capacity for grinding out what-ifs and maybes and pontificating on ridiculous scenarios could be a bane at times. It was a legacy from having too much time to think over too many subjects. I could blame carp fishing for that. I tried to think more about the carp fishing.

Rambo and Pup had taken a fish apiece with Pup's one being the opener and his excitement had been nice to witness after we had left the two Yanks. His self-esteem had flooded back on capturing the first carp for our team and although he wasn't in Rambo's league of fishing dexterity, the change from his earlier underarm fuck up was considerable. His old skills were slowly returning.

"Come on, son. Keep your end up, I don't want to be too far behind the M and Ms!" I had chided Rambo as we had weighed in Pup's high twenty.

"Here! Hold on, boy. I'm claiming an assist on that fish. I told him where to cast it!" Rambo had proclaimed with a grin.

Underneath the grin he had been desperate to catch one. It was no different a situation to any of the other hundreds and hundreds of carpers who fish together socially as a pair. Your mate gets one and you want to get one too. For lots of reasons. Some nice, some not so nice. It's the way of the world and forever will be. Rambo had had his desires granted a further three hours later when he had caught our second fish around tea-time.

Melissa had congratulated her hubby while flaunting a little with Rambo, a trick she managed with frightening alacrity. I had asked myself how long would it be before she cheated on Pup and tried not be harsh in my judgement. I could hardly talk. Melissa could have as many blokes as she liked, it was likely she could get accosted every day if she wanted. How would I cope with such a bombardment of proposition? I tried to ignore the ultimate answer I had come up with, despite all the prior agonising I had done, I could remember what had happened at Lac Fumant and I would never forget. I had been weak and temptation had done me good and proper, me old china!

"She fancies you," I had hissed to Rambo as we had waited for Gordon to come up from swim eight to independently verify Pup's fish.

Rambo had looked puzzled. "What makes you say that, boy?"

"Oh, just things she's said to me," I had replied.

"Are you mad?" Rambo had asked.

His reply had thrown me. "What do you mean?" I had said.

"Why on earth would I want to get involved with Melissa?" he had said.

"Why on earth *wouldn't* you want to get involved with Melissa? Look at her!" I had countered.

"She's *Pup's* wife!" he had told me.

"Okay, so she's married. I wouldn't have thought *that* would have bothered you," I had said a bit offhand.

Rambo had looked frustrated. "You're missing the emphasis on what I said, boy! She's *Pup's* wife. *Pup's*! I hardly think he'd be likely to carry on rolling our bait if I'm fucking around with his wife, do you? *Then* we'd have to find someone *else* who we could trust to do the job. Use *some* common sense for Christ's sake!"

I had shrunk back into my shell like a snail being poked with a twig. "I did think that… but I'd forgotten," I had lamely clarified, lying at the same time.

I nuzzled my pillow. I needed to get some sleep. If I knew Hamworthy there was likely to be a mini-glut of phone calls in a few hours' time. Midnight was the witching hour. I fell asleep thinking of the three witches, which one in particular I cannot divulge!

My mobile stirred me from my slumber. I groped in the blackness to find it, my eyes stuck together with sleep.

"Hello," I croaked having at last grabbed hold of the blessed thing.

"Come on, boy! Shake a leg, I've just caught a massive mirror for us!" said Rambo.

On hearing the news I stumbled out of my bivvy and my head had barely passed through the opening when Rambo shouted loudly right in my right ear.

"*That* was quick! *Much* faster than last time!" he hollered.

"I was in the vicinity," I explained staggering upright and rubbing a flat hand against the earlobe that had borne the brunt of Rambo's shouting.

I glanced up at the night sky. It was clear and stars sparkled back at me. For the umpteenth time in my life I stared in fascination at the bright dots and was briefly mesmerised by their beauty. So wonderful, so far away, so breathtaking; they were incredible.

"Look at them," I said to Rambo. "Don't they look great?"

Rambo gave the night sky a cursory glance. "If they ever come to get you, you'll get a closer look," he said.

I eased my already aching neck back to look at him in the darkness. I could make out a grin.

I caught his drift. "Oh, I scc! The alien abduction joke!"

"Like I've said, boy. It's all you've got to do to have the full set of contacts. You've mind-melded with fish, spoken to the dead, spoken to the unborn via the dead and all that's left is a cosy chat on an intergalactic spaceship's settee with an alien life force," Rambo explained.

"If it ever did happen," I said to him. "They'd be intellectually vastly superior to us, what with having the ability to come all the way to our planet, so what would be the one question you'd want me to ask them?"

I saw Rambo's massive camouflaged shoulders move in the dark. "I don't know. Just get them to make me a mono that acts like 15lb Big Game Line but is only a sixth of the diameter. That'll do me. And maybe a laser gun that can shoot round corners and a personal time machine… and some ever lasting batteries for my buzzers."

"Anything else?"

"Nope. I could always nip to the future corner shop for anything else I might want," said Rambo.

"Shall we go and weigh it?" I suggested.

Rambo nodded. "I'll wake Melissa up." He walked over to the new his'n'her's bivvy and screamed into the opening. "Oi! You two! Stop all that malarkey and get your butts out here! I've caught a kipper!"

As long as Pup's fingers don't smell like one, I thought. That would be embarrassing.

Melissa was first out looking slightly dishevelled, but only from sleep, not passionate love-making, and she was only a little less attractive than normal because of it. Mind you, it was quite dark.

"Calm down, Rambo," she said while pushing her fingers through her dyed hair. "We're married. You don't have to worry about us getting up to anything like *that*! Of course if I was sleeping in *your* bivvy…"

"Jesus!" I said getting slightly fed-up with Melissa's constant stream of advances. "Don't you ever turn it off?"

"Jealous, darling?" she quipped.

"No," I said wearily. "I just thought a change of CD might do us all some good," I suggested, updating the old saying. Melissa might not have heard of vinyl.

"What've you had, mate?" asked Pup, who had only just dragged himself out into the night.

"Come and have a look," Rambo suggested, and as is the norm when Rambo suggests something, we all did what he said.

Rambo walked down to the pit's edge, got down on his knees and pulled in the chord belonging to the sack plus carp he had placed around a bankstick. He lifted the sack and its contents from the water and I could tell from the bulk it was a good fish. Rambo carefully placed the black mass onto an unhooking mat, squeezed the chord's toggle and slid it up the two strands and started to peel back the sack. Pup, who was shining his torch onto proceedings, gasped at the size of the revealed carp.

"Wow!" I said. "Definite forty!"

"Nice one, partner," said Pup. "I'll go get the scales and weigh sling." And with the enthusiasm of a schoolboy running to buy a chocolate bar, and have a sly look at the top shelf, he disappeared back into his bivvy to find the required implements.

"Gosh!" cooed Melissa. "What a huge carp!" She was impressed, I could tell.

"I'll give Gordon a ring and get him to come up," I said trying to stay oblivious to Melissa's gushing. Rather crudely, I wondered if Melissa was gushing somewhere else, then I would know if her flirting with Rambo had an ulterior motive and was for real.

I phoned Gordon and told him the news. No doubt he was as pleased as I had been to be woken up on the account of somebody else catching a carp. It was bad enough hearing other people's buzzers when you were asleep, but at least you could turn over and ignore it *and* you didn't have to get up to have your nose rubbed in it! Having said that, I did have a vested interest in Rambo's capture, seeing as he was on my team, although I was hard pushed to think of it in such clear-cut terms. I knew I wouldn't get truly involved in the competition aspect until I had cast my rods out. My role was too peripheral at the moment. Sure I kept a weather eye on the weights and catches, but until I was right in the fray, slugging it out boilie to boilie, I was happy to see Rambo and Pup hang onto the M and Ms' coat-tails – actually they could hang onto their hair – and then I could kick in with my input and help overtake them later.

Rambo's carp was a corker, 42lbs and 6ozs of pure delight, an almost perfect linear. A stonking, mahoosive kipper of a lunking leviathan lump if ever there was one. And it was *fucking* big as well!

"Name it!" I told him once the others, including Gordon, had gone back to their bivvies and all the necessary paperwork had been sorted. "I'm sure it's another new forty. Once again it's far too distinctive for me not to remember it."

Rambo sucked on his teeth and tasted a remnant of something he had eaten. "Hmm! I was eating a Twix when it ripped off! So let's call it, 'Twix'. Not overly original but it'll do, I can't bend my brain any more, I'm too knackered."

"Why weren't you asleep?" I asked wondering why Rambo had indulged in a midnight, torch-under-the-bed-sheet feast when he should have been kipping.

Rambo pulled at his ear. "You know," he said ruefully, "I was thinking of Charlie. I couldn't sleep because I was thinking about him and because of my being awake I felt a bit peckish."

Blimey! A little insecurity from the big man, I thought.

"Melissa's a girl, isn't she? I have to put up with all that double entendre chit-chat all the time, you know," I said changing the subject. "Between you and me, I'll be glad to get on with the fishing and leave her and hubby to do the verification."

"I'll be glad, too," said Rambo sincerely. "He's getting his act together slowly but I'm sure the pair of us would catch more. I don't *especially* want to lose to someone called Horst and Helmut! As good a pair of anglers as they both might be." Rambo paused and then asked. "How far are we behind them at the moment?"

Melissa had left me with the catch-logging sheet, so by torchlight I quickly totted up the weights for their fish into approximate poundage.

"They've had six fish for around one hundred and seventy pounds of carp, the two Yanks have had four for one-thirty and we've had three fish for a gnat's nudger under the ton. Realistically, even though you've had a forty, we're still two or three fish behind." I let out a low whistle. "The average weights are *so* good, it's nigh on thirty pounds for those thirteen fish!"

Rambo cocked his head in approval. "Michael might have been a suicidal, neurotic embezzling murderer but he knew how to manage a fishery."

"One man's tragic ending is another man's joyous inheritance," I said.

My mobile rang. I recognised the number, it was the one that kept occurring with the most frequency.

"Shit! The M and Ms, *again*! Hopefully they only need some dubbin for their lederhosen." I shone my torch straight into Rambo's eyes. "Maybe all the smacking has dried their shorts out and made them start to crack."

"Eh?" said Rambo pushing the torch away, his face screwed up against the light. "Are you on drugs?"

"No!" I said with as much indignant denial as I had to Melissa. "You're the *second* person who's asked me that."

"I reckon you might want to try some, boy," he suggested cheekily. "It might help!"

"That's what *they* said!" I told him.

I pulled a face and answered my nagging phone and heard the voice of Helmut. It was always bloody Helmut who rang. As it turned out they *weren't* after dubbin and I said I would get to them straight away to weigh yet another carp. *More* tonnage to pull back!

"That Helmut..." I started to tell Rambo and then paused. I groped for an expression. "Is a *right* helmet!" I said and viciously warmed to my theme. "Helmut the Helmet-head! Happy Helmut the Headless Helmet-head!"

"The *headless* helmet-head?" Rambo queried.

"You've got it in one!" I assured him. I wagged a finger in the gloom. "If it's a forty I might have to cut off his mullet right there and then. Don't you *see*? That's where he gets all his fishing powers! The *mullet*! Sampson was strong because he'd never had his hair cut and Happy Helmut the Headless Helmet-head is a carp-catching machine because *his* is cut in the style of the mullet. Horst as well! I'll have to get one of the strimmers out of the lean-to and attack them with it! The strimmer will make short work of them; both the mullets will be history! *History*, I tell you! They'll be the severed strands of hair on the barbershop floor of life and the pair of them won't catch a single carp for as long as they both live!"

Rambo put an arm around my shoulder, turned me about and started to walk me back towards my van.

"I can get you something. Ritalin if you like, the old methylphenidate, or some kind of sedative, it could help. Until then try and get some rest for now. You see, I shall want you to catch loads of carp when it comes to your stint." He held up a pacifying hand. "No pressure, mind. You've just got to catch loads and loads of thirties when it comes to your turn to cast out. Then together, you and me, we can *metaphorically* trim the power of the mullet and render it a crew cut. In any case the strimmers are both out of petrol."

I stopped and raised a fist. "To the trimming of the mullet!" I said.

Rambo touched my knuckles with his. "To the trimming of the mullet!" he reiterated.

"Matt and Rambo!" I cried. "Mullet trimmers extraordinaire! Mullet trimmers by Royal Appointment! Official World-Record-Holding mullet trimmers!"

Rambo turned sober. "Okay, we don't want to labour the point. Better get down to their swim and see what they've caught, eh?"

"Yep," I concurred. "Suppose so." I let out a sigh. "Better get the sex-bomb up, not that she'll get much change out of those two. They're about the only two, apart from you and Pup, who treat her with indifference. They've both got their fishing heads on too tight to worry over her."

"What?" said Rambo surprised. "Even Happy Helmut the Headless Helmet-head."

"Yeah, he's got his fishing head on over the top of his severed helmet-head," I said.

Melissa was a grumpy bunny in the van as we drove around to the south-east point swim where the two Austrian carp-catching machines were embedded. She was tired. *I* was bloody tired as well and I was praying Hamworthy would do me a favour and switch off for half a day and let me get some serious kip. There was no conversation between us and Melissa sucked silently on a roll-up, blowing the smoke out of a half opened window. She had put on a pair of long trousers and jumper to keep out the slight chill of the night. Silently I wondered if she was grumpy because she knew the two men we were about to visit would be unimpressed by her charms. Perhaps that was another reason why she had elected to cover up.

To emphasise the point Melissa had taken off her baggy jumper shortly after we had weighed in Helmut's tiddler – 27lb 3ozs, I don't know why he even bothered – and were on our way, having been summoned by phone, to Brad and Tom's swim. Tom had caught their fifth carp, a high thirty leather which by autumn would be yet another Hamworthy forty. Michael had truly known his stuff; the strain of the carp in Hamworthy was simply awesome. During the process of weighing in the scaleless beauty, Melissa had knocked the flirt gearbox out of neutral and put it straight into overdrive and she had been all over Brad like the proverbial rash. The baggy jumper, however, had been all over the van's passenger seat while her buxom boobs had been a bouncing and very much on view. The M and Ms had got knitwear; the Yanks got the skimpy top.

Of course her assets were only as visible as the meagre lighting qualities the night had allowed them to be. To counteract this lack of light, Brad, who was wearing a strap-on head torch, had kept flicking the beam of light on her cleavage more than a statistical analyst would have considered to have been deemed as average. It was a bit of a giveaway to say the least but it fairly thrilled Melissa to get such an illuminating response from him. Brad's teeth had glinted in the light of Tom's head torch and Melissa's bosom had heaved in the light of Brad's. Although I looked at them – I mean how could I not look at them? – I had gone past the point of being interested. Honestly. No, I *had*!

Once the formalities had been completed I went to get in the van.

"All fit, Melissa?" I asked.

She sidled over to me and and lit another roll-up. So *that* was where she had kept the lighter! "I'm going to take a walk back," she said. "The fresh air will do me good."

"Well what are you doing sucking on that thing for?" I said nodding in the dark at the red glowing tip held between her two lips. "And what about if someone else gets a take when you're not with me?"

Melissa exhaled heavily. "Give me a ring," she said dismissively, the red tip wafting vaguely in the air from in between her two fingers. "You can always pick me up. Here, you look after this." She shoved the catch-logging sheet and clipboard at me after she had scribbled her mobile number on the top of the sheet.

I was annoyed but felt disinclined to make a scene. "All right. I'll catch you later. Watch out when you come back, there are a lot of strange men about tonight."

"Not as strange as you, darling," she said.

On the whole she was probably right.

I drove back on my own to swim nine, my only company a knitted baggy jumper. I was hoping against hope my mobile wouldn't ring and was wondering with a lot less intensity why Melissa had wanted to walk back. More likely she wanted to stay and talk to the two sun-soaked, handsome millionaire Americans. When I put it so succinctly it hardly came as an eye-opener.

I parked over to the old wood side of the track and got out the van. This was where it had happened, the spot where the ghost had whooshed out from deep inside the wood and battered me senseless on contact. I looked down at the grass, half expecting to see the pile of vomit I had heaved up after my senses had been so devastatingly overrun and overloaded. It still was hard to take in, for all the times I had thought about it, all the times I had talked to Sophie about it, all the times I had looked at Amy and talked to *her* about it! For the thousandth time I was left with a feeling of disbelief and that the whole episode had been a figment of my deluded imagination.

My thoughts turned away from the most bizarre event to have ever happened in my life – it *did* happen, my life isn't an episode of Dallas – to the two best things that had happened in it. Sophie and Amy. My stomach stirred slightly. Sophie and I were not having the best of times of late. It was hard to put a finger on why, especially this late at night when all I wanted to do was go to sleep and I made a mental note to sort it out once the Fish-In – and better make it the porn video as well – were over. Once again, with the gift of hindsight, I could see I had let mine and Sophie's spat go unresolved for too long because it had suited my carp fishing preparations. I had used our ugly silence and row as an excuse to invest more time in getting everything ready for the event we were now sixteen hours into. And, if I was brutally honest, because I had been swayed by the possibilities of the three witches being here with me while Sophie wasn't. Although the thrill of Melissa was wearing thin – her constant flirting with other men while cooling towards myself might have had some bearing on it – Melina and Melloney were arriving tomorrow – no wait! *Today!* – and that still got the adrenalin going a bit.

What *are* you hoping for? I asked myself. The monster inside my deep, dank cave started to laugh. I told it, it was only a *superficial* craving. A dream fantasy, as unlikely as a Jonathan Creek episode – and believe me that is *fucking* unlikely – one invented to titillate my mental wanderings. The monster laughed a bit louder, an edge of disbelief to its chuckling. It was waiting for its time, biding and waiting its time.

Swim nine was deserted. All its carp anglers were in the land of Nod. It was where I needed to be. I climbed into my sleeping bag and started to worry over how big the M and Ms lead was over my team. I should have attacked Horst and Helmut with a pair of unhooking forceps and plucked out their stupid bloody mullets and been done with it. And their bushy moustaches. That would have taught them a lesson, catching more carp than us and giving poor old Melissa the cold shoulder. By the workings of her self-defence mechanism, the same one used by men who accuse non-consenting women of lesbianism, she probably thought they were gay. I would beg to differ until I actually saw the lederhosen, but a tin of dubbin casually left on the top of a bedchair or on a bivvy floor would give the girl a strong case. Whatever way they lent, the bastards could catch carp.

Chapter 13

Mercifully, from the viewpoint of me getting some sleep, Hamworthy's carp had gone AWOL since I had drifted off into the desired land of Nod and were still unavailable to produce calls – rather than take them – by the time of my morning cuppa. My mobile had stayed mute all night and not for the first time in my carping life I rejoiced in the simple fact everybody on the venue had caught bugger all!

The morning felt warm, even if it was still only a little after seven, as I sat on the middle of my bedchair, legs over the edge at right angles to it, drinking my cup of nectar and looking down at Pup and Rambo's rods. Unexpectedly, I saw Melissa appear into view and then disappear into the new his'n'her's bivvy. She hadn't come out from the bivvy in the time I had been awake so perhaps, giving her the benefit of doubt, she had just returned from the clubhouse after completing exhausting renovation work on her lip-gloss. I began to formulate a clutch of suppositions in keeping with the possibility she hadn't come back from the clubhouse, but for once managed to stop the process in its tracks. The overriding one before I managed to curtail my mental meanderings was now I wasn't so sure it was Rambo who she fancied!

To further disengage myself from bothering to work out her most feasible night-time itinerary, I perused the catch-logging sheet. Although I had scoffed at Helmut's last carp and bestowed upon it the status of 'tiddler' – by the stunning set of Hamworthy parameters – it had created even more daylight between themselves and the chasing pairs.

"We need a fish!" I said to myself in between mouthfuls of tea.

I was reasonably content to be lingering a *little* down the field, basically so the impact of my carping talents would be clearly emphasised when – I hopefully surmised – I hauled our team up by its bootlaces and into the lead. What I didn't need and what I didn't want was for us to be too far back. I was under no illusion as to how much better I would fare compared to Pup, but I was confidant I would catch as least as many as he would have done, if not the odd fish or two more. Obviously this would have required an Acme Parallel Universe Viewer – the £9.99 version – to confirm such a statement but if one was not to hand, as was the case at this juncture, then I would have to take my own word for it. What I couldn't see me doing was catching enough carp to overhaul the hauling M and Ms if we dropped more than four or five fish back. We were at least four fish back as things stood at the moment. Even the Yanks were still ahead of us. If the pit turned off big-style it could already be over apart from the collecting of the ten grand cheque for charity – pronounced *charedee*, remember?

What we could do with I reckoned, mentally clutching at straws, was a strong southerly wind blowing up from where the M and Ms were in the south-east point swim to where we were at the north end of the pit adjacent to the old wood. This might make a few fish follow the wind up to our area of the pit and, equally important, might entice a few more to move out from the area where they were. This sounded good and the behavioural pattern was accepted logic, yet I had to admit it was all conjecture to some extent or another. I hadn't fished the pit enough under differing weather conditions to say for sure it would help greatly on this particular venue. And it was highly doubtful if enough copies of Carpworld had been lobbed into the pit so adequate numbers of fish had had the opportunity to read up on what they should do, given certain conditions. After all, following the wind, a warm southerly wind, was what all, decent, self-respecting carp were expected to do. But what if they hadn't read what they were supposed to do? Did carp follow a warm wind because some carp somewhere at sometime had done so once, and it had been written in stone and the word had got round? Or alternatively and more pertinently, did they *not* follow a warm wind on some venues because word *hadn't* got round?

I smiled to myself. I was being highly facetious, carp were wild creatures – more or less – and their behaviour, although being open to sweeping generalisations at times, was venue specific. 'Being in touch with a water', as the phrase goes, usually meant an in-depth knowledge of varying circumstances leading to other important varying circumstances. For instance, a certain wind and temperature leading to carp feeding in a certain area – most times. *Nothing* is truly set in stone. The in-depth knowledge was gained the hard way, through time on the bank and the 'interpretation of personal experiences'. A knack for doing the interpreting correctly was at the very epicentre of carp fishing and was the basis for a good deal of the thought process in angling. A beep on a buzzer, for instance. Rationalise it, sort it out and uncloak its hidden meaning, if indeed there was one. So – tentatively – a line bite, perhaps? Okay, so fish on the bait or brushing the line fifty yards away from it under the rod tips? If not, was it a hookbait investigation by a carp or by other unwanted, nuisance species? Was it an aborted take, or a pick up where the carp has 'got away with it'? Could it be a hooked carp, one cunningly staying put, still attempting to eject? More mundanely was it the wind? Undertow? An unseen bird landing on a rod tip? A wonky buzzer? A herd of mischievous ants tugging your line to get you going? All were theories, and all were theories that needed to be evaluated correctly in order to put carp on the bank. The difficulty lay in either proving or refuting each one when you never had an Acme Parallel Universe Viewer to aid you. Especially when someone was relating what had happened four days later to a fellow angler in the pub, or even months later, in a magazine article, to people who weren't there. Still, it made for conversation and lively debate.

If a crowd watched a football match, it saw the same game and yet, even with slow-motion replays at endless different angles, some instances or decisions would still be unresolved and cause dispute. In carp fishing – to draw a parallel – most of us are at different matches, on different days and the pitch is in varying states of invisibility due to very thick fog. We hear a ball being kicked, a crunching tackle, an appeal for offside and sometimes the fog clears for a split second and we see a goal in the shape of a fish on the bank. Interpretation. It revolved around interpretation, and the good translators are the best anglers because they understand it correctly more than the others and adjust their actions accordingly. Either that or they're born with golden balls, can bend it like Beckham, catch fish in a puddle or pull out the big one first or second attempt. This phenomenon we call instinct or natural ability. If it happens too much we call it luck, or stroke pulling, and the angler concerned something much worse. Which is as it should be. Nobody likes a smart arse, especially if they're a lucky, stroke pulling, smart-arsed, motherfucking, son of a bitch!

With a flick of my mug I chucked the dregs of my tea out of the bivvy's opening. I looked at my watch. Half past seven. Someone would get a run soon or my name wasn't Matthew Williams. In less than ten hours' time the two caterers would arrive with the food for the barbecue. If I was thankful for a good night's kip I was also very pleased to have decided upon outside catering. Originally I had toyed with the idea of cooking it all myself with the help of the three witches, but I'd had the forethought to realise it would have been too much to cope with, what with having to keep score *and* control my ogling of their flesh. I had also sussed that I would need some time to shower before the barbecue and sort my rods and gear out in order to be prepared for my second half input into Team Rambo.

The barbecue was going to be a strange affair what with the witches being flung into the company of a large group of males who were carp anglers. Christ knows what Melina and Melloney would think of it all. Christ knows what all the blokes would make of them. Christ knows what sort of a tangle I would get in, and I'm not talking about underarm fuck-ups (Pup) or imagined Terminal Tackle Tangled Syndrome (Steve, 'my-nuts-are-killing-me-but-at-least-I-won't-add-to-my-horrifically-behaved-brood', and now, 'I've-caught-a-forty', Steve). Terminal Tackle Tangled *Trauma* sounded better. Perhaps I would write a thesis on it. It should be good for a year's worth of articles.

All of a sudden, as things usually do in carp fishing, I was snapped into a time warp as Pup's original Delkim Optonic conversion, the reed switch having moved sufficiently to turn it on – I know about these things – stuttered into life. Bemused I watched as the monkey climber yo-yoed up and down the stick and his Abu C5 reel churned. Nostalgia welled up inside me. His reel was *churning*; bless its little worm gearing.

Inside my head I went 'David Attenborough', his quiet voice saying my thoughts as they came into my head.

'Here, at last, the ancient carp tackle is to be put to the test. The rod itself harks back to the latter end of the Fibreglasseous Period and the reel, as the clockwise spinning handle shows, is old enough to be dated BB – Before Baitrunner. The angler who owns this equipment, you can see him scurrying down to his tackle like a cockroach on amphetamines, is from the virtually extinct Rollshisownbaits tribe. Widely scattered and now mainly isolated, this tribe has dramatically shrunk in numbers over the last fifteen years, while the Readymade and the Freezerbait tribe have amalgamated and grown in strength and numbers. However, what this run demonstrates and bears testament to, is his innate, highly developed boilie-making skills. Now we must see whether his tackle can be as effective as his bait, for if he is to land his prize fish, it will surely have to be. His alarm, though, with its distinctive screeching cry, has been heard by another hunter's ears and the large, aggressive, camouflaged Alpha male has been attracted out of his primitive home and is coming to help'.

I wandered out of my bivvy with a dumb smile plastered on my face, pleased with my personal piece of pastiche. For all my mucking around this was a fish that needed to be landed for the sake of all onboard the Team Rambo ship. I walked to within ten yards of my team-mates and watched Pup's face with fascination, contorted as it was, with concentration, excitement and fear. It was amazing what hooking a carp could do to a grown man, one who wasn't necessarily grown-up all the time, one which regressed as soon as it got anywhere near a fishing rod. Pup had probably regressed to an eight-year-old boy on Christmas Eve, an eight-year-old boy with a heart rate of one hundred and forty and enough adrenalin kicking around his system to jump-start the dead. I hoped, on several levels, he would land it.

Melissa had managed to drag herself into the open by now and she came and stood next to me as we both watched Pup attempt to land his second carp of the competition. Melissa looked a bit shot away; her previous late night had taken its toll.

"What have you been up to, you look *shagged* out?" I said to her quietly, I didn't want to put my team-mates off. I laughed inwardly, now it was *my* turn to bring out the hackneyed double entendres.

"I didn't get much sleep last night," she proclaimed, not rising to the bait but speaking as softly as I had.

"I don't know, you newly-wed girls, you can't get enough of it can you?" I said with only the tiniest smidgen of sarcasm.

Melissa gave me a sideways look and folded her arms indignantly across her was-bare-an-instant-ago midriff. "Look you, idiot," she whispered pugnaciously, her quick temper taking me by surprise. "Just because I decided to walk back last night rather than come with you, like I'd *want* to do *that*! Don't start giving me a load of mouth and pathetic, sarcastic insinuations. If you want to know the reason why I didn't get much sleep it was because I had a long chat with Brad and Tom last night. And *very* interesting it was too, not like talking to *some* people I could mention. They both lead a fantastic lifestyle and it was fascinating hearing about how they made all their money and how they choose to spend it. Just because I'm married doesn't mean I can't talk to other men, you know, and just because I *do* talk to other men doesn't mean I'd do anything else with them."

"I never said it did," I said making my voice go even softer so Rambo and Pup couldn't overhear.

"I know what you're hinting at. What you're *implying*," she said scathingly at the same volume.

"No you don't," I lied. She *did* have a pretty good idea what I was thinking but I wasn't going to give her the satisfaction of letting her know she was right. She'd had enough success as far as I was concerned with all the Melina crap. Besides, her ultra defensive stance made her guilty, as guilty as I thought she was likely to be.

"I don't like it! It's not nice and it's not fair," she hissed, ignoring my previous comment.

"Whoa! Calm down," I told her. "You're getting all het up over what you *think* I'm implying rather than what I *actually* said!"

"All right! What *are* you thinking? What do you *really* think I did last night after you'd gone?" Melissa demanded, the strident tone of her voice at direct odds to the level it was spoken.

"What do *you* care what *I* think?" I countered.

"Lame answer! Come on! Tell me!" and she moved up to me and prodded a finger under my nose. But not before she had checked to see the remaining members of Team Rambo were completely engrossed in landing a carp.

I lost my rag a little. "Right! If you *want* to know," I said forcefully, but in a hushed voice. "I reckon you were up half the night having a bit of hanky-panky with Brad. Not Tom. Just Brad. There you are! So now you do know what I think!"

Melissa's eyes narrowed in anger. "So what if I *did*? Who are *you* to judge *me*? What if I *did* have sex with Brad, not that I'm saying I did, but what if I *did*? What gives *you*, of all people, the right to make moral judgements over *my* actions?" She stopped for a second and became more composed. "You think you're *so* clever don't you? Having all this..." she looked around and groped for a word, "... *given* to you. You're not so bloody clever! You're not so bloody clever by a long chalk! Moral hypocrite!"

"What on *earth* do you mean by that?" I said completely flummoxed.

"You'll see! You can see it one way but the other way you're blind!" And with that she walked down to where Rambo and Pup had landed a carp.

Bloody hell! Not only was she a witch, she spoke in the riddles of a twenty-five-quid-a-go clairvoyant. I had no idea what she had meant but I put it down to complete and utter bullshit and bluster because I had sussed her. Poor old Pup, there he was, happy as a sand boy having caught another carp, and the poor sod was married to a cow like her. Albeit an extremely *attractive* cow like her. Maybe it would be enough for him, dividing up the booty, perhaps he would put up with getting a share even if it wasn't the exclusive deal he had signed up for. I bloody wouldn't, she would be out the door and down the road before her cute arse could touch the ground. Mind you, I mentally pulled in the reins of my convictions; I *could* have been wrong about her and Brad. In a court of law my hunch would hardly have pulled up any trees. Uncorroborated evidence and unsubstantiated facts they would have labelled it. To get the true facts I could always pop round to Brad, ask him where he bought his teeth and subtly drop it into the conversation. 'Really, Wal-Mart? That's surprising. Say, while we're chatting, that Melissa, did you goose her the other night? You know, slip her one in the bivvy, if you'll pardon the phrase. I know it's not any of my business but I *do* need to know for the sake of my own personal sanity'.

I watched Melissa kiss Pup on the cheek as a reward for landing the fish and we locked eyes for a second. Defiantly she stared me down, our conversation was off limits as regards to Pup's ears. She didn't have to fret over it; I was back onto my earlier theme of secrets. Our little chat was another tiny one to add to the pile, one that could go in the sack along with the other bigger ones. Whether it transpired to be a topic picked from a freshly opened sack – at a suitable later date with Rambo – well that was a distinct possibility. Whatever. In any case I could hardly say anything to Pup seeing as I had not a single iota of evidence to substantiate my theory. Ha! They had all laughed at the mind-meld mirror and me, but I had been spot-on then.

I gave myself a rueful grin; perhaps my psychic powers were going to wax rather than continue waning. Maybe it was a type of moon phase thing, only over a much longer period. It had been nigh on a year ago since they were at their zenith and then there had been a ghost afoot! Talking of time scales, the next nine hours or so were going to drag what with me having to put up with Melissa now we had apparently fallen out. The only good thing was it was reciprocal and she would feel as uncomfortable as me.

Pup's carp was a mid-thirty and Melissa made the point of swarming all over him as she congratulated him again and again. Duly and dutifully she wrote down his accomplishment on the catch-logging sheet once Gordon had done his expert witness bit for us. Amusingly, Pup seemed a little flustered by Melissa's fuss and was so keen to get his rod back fishing again he actually asked her to leave him alone and told her to stop pawing him.

"Well done, mate," I said genuinely. "That's helped close the gap between us and the M and Ms. If we could only get a string of fish under our belts without them picking any up, we'll be well in the hunt."

"Christ, boy! Do you think so?" said Rambo. "So if we can land a few while they don't, that'll help us catch up will it? Bugger me! I'd never have thought of that!"

I squirmed at Melissa's enjoyment of Rambo's piss-take. "Fine. I know. Stating the bleedin' obvious as someone once said. Mr Fawlty, I presume. But you know what I mean?" I went for a bit of rhetoric. "The pride of England is in our destiny and ours alone, for we fight the heathen foe hand to hand in front of our glorious flag of England!" I gestured towards the Team Rambo inscribed St George Cross. "We cannot, must not, *dare* not let the M and Ms prevail!"

"According to this sheet, Brad and Tom are *still* ahead of you," chirped Melissa. "What about them?"

"No worries," I said. "They'll fade faster than a cheap tee shirt put on a hot wash." I looked Melissa in the eye. "Those Yanks, they won't be able to keep it up for long! They're not stayers!" I said with a cheeky glint in my eye.

"You might be in for a surprise," came her reply. "They seem very good carp anglers to me," she eventually added with a smirk.

And then she winked at me! Just like Melina hadn't winked at me because she had been winking at Rambo and I had got the hump over it. I quickly checked to see if the same thing was happening again. No, she had definitely winked at me!

"Time for some tea, I think," I said. It was a reflex reaction. In the quicksand, up to the hilt, struggling to make sense of anything, so, what's the answer...? Make a cup of tea! Bleedin' obvious, innit?

"Can I have one?" Melissa asked.

"Yeah, of course you can. I'll put the kettle on," I said still in a mildly confused state.

I began walking back up to my bivvy and Melissa fell in alongside me. "I don't have to *like* people to want to sleep with them!" she told me. "You ought to get me drunk later and ask me for a favour and see what I say!" she pouted.

The old Melissa was back.

I felt strangely punch drunk. She was *one* witch, on her own, and she was doing my head in! Right there and then I realised how dangerous she was, how dangerous *they* were, all bloody three of them, and how seriously I had underestimated their potential. All this talk of mayhem had been a joke but now I saw how the joke could cut across real people, real lives, real emotions and leave people scarred forever. Ask any man who a *femme fatale* had tempted – there were enough of them! The sisters were a catalyst to complete catastrophe. They could rip asunder the strongest bonds imaginable with their magnetism, a magnetism weak men could no more deny or resist than an iron filing could resist the pull of an electromagnetic scrap yard crane. The three sisters were trouble. Never mind the mayhem with a capital 'M' in a high-faluting font, they were trouble! Triple trouble. Triple, titillating, tempestuous temptresses who were terrifying, tormenting, tantalising trouble! Typically a tad tawdry, but undeniably sensual, sensational sex-sorority sirens! And they would all be together with a group of twenty-nine carp anglers, conditioned carp anglers, later on today.

My mind raced. Were we men all so one-dimensional? Had society provided us with so much we had become so self-absorbed, *sex*-absorbed to the point of considering only self-satisfaction? Were there no bonds strong enough, no commitments worthy enough that they stopped us indulging our self-centred selves in the heat of the moment when faced by an attractive, female sexual predator? The morning might bring regret and guilt but it was too late then. I knew all about regret and guilt after the event because I had fallen short at the crunch time at *my* moment of truth. At my moment of truth I *could* have walked away from Rebecca's bedroom door and gone back to my bivvy. The simple fact was I hadn't.

Perhaps I was being too harsh. For those who were uncommitted we were ships in the night, one chance as we passed – and we all had to live a little before we died. Even those with long-term partners could think along similar lines. Maybe it was why I *hadn't* gone back to my bivvy, that and the crucial thought I could get away with it and have my cake and eat it!

Get away with it! Suddenly I wondered if that was what Melissa had meant when she had said I had no right to morally judge her and called me a moral hypocrite. Shit! My head went kaleidoscope. Get a grip, I told myself, how could she possibly know? Only Rambo knew the truth and he would *never* have told Melina, who definitely *would* have told Melissa *and* Melloney if he had. But he hadn't, *had* he? I felt a rush of panic. I gave Melissa her tea I had made on autopilot and made an excuse to go and see Rambo.

Rambo was squatting on his haunches outside his bivvy staring at his indicators. He looked up as I came down to see him. I must have had a worried look on my face – I had one on the inside, which I was all to well aware of – because he stood up and spoke.

"All right, boy? The M and Ms haven't caught another one have they?"

I waved a distracted hand. "No. Nothing like that."

"You look a bit put out. What's up?" he asked.

"It's something dumb, that's all." I felt a bit awkward confronting him but it had to be done. "You've never mentioned me and Rebecca to Melina, have you? By mistake or anything?"

Rambo laughed. "No *way*, mate! That particular secret will go with me to the grave. You don't have to worry over that!"

I felt a rush of relief and tension oozed out of me like a lanced boil. Studiously I mopped up the pus. "You've already been to the grave," I reminded him.

"Not my proper one. And I'm not planning to go yet, either!" Rambo replied.

"Great!" I said my fear dispatched in a jiffy. "Now catch some more carp!"

Rambo smiled. "I'm trying, boy. I'm trying!"

Although I relaxed over the diminished-to-zero possibility of my adultery at Lac Fumant 1st time being uncovered, I was still on edge; only it was a different edge. In fact as the day wore on I became more and more edgy on several edges. The edginess worked itself onto so many edges I felt like a large cut diamond, a large cut diamond in a state of high nervousness.

Firstly, I hoped the witches would behave themselves and add the chemistry I had envisaged rather than rip up relationships in the carnage I had also envisaged. Secondly, my mobile, after its slack period, recovered, got second wind and started to ring like the phone of a very popular person – who had a large close-knit family – on his or her birthday. Melissa and I were back in blowfly mode once again and

155

the close proximity of the two of us – coupled with the notion she was just as likely to make a pass at me as crack me alongside the head with a rusty iron bar she had kept concealed in her shorts with her lighter – only added to my stress.

Then there were the caterers. I phoned them and they assured me, Mr Williams, that everything was in hand and they would be on site as required. Good. They had better be. Then there was my gear. It wasn't as if I had anything to sort out specifically, but it niggled away at me when I couldn't spend a little time preparing. And I couldn't do it because of the runs all the other bastards who were fishing kept on getting. And there was the crux of it. I was getting the DTs through fishing withdrawal. Everyone else was getting their fix and I wasn't.

Then there were the Yanks. They had started to catch a little too regularly for my liking but probably not regularly enough for Melissa's. Using my intuition, it was hardly psychic ability – or something similar to it that I couldn't really explain or in any way understand – I could tell something had gone on between Melissa and Brad. Now it may have been a very long polite, interesting conversation or it might have involved Brad putting his bedchair under more duress than it had ever been under before. I could picture the ad. 'JRC. *The* bedchair for bivvy-bound bonking. It'll *never* let you down. Is *all* your equipment as reliable?'. The very thought of it, the two of them at it and what it might do to Pup if he found out – i.e. mentally unhinge him so much he would never be able to face a rolling table or a bait gun again – made me edgy. As Rambo had said, who *would* we trust to roll our baits?

Then there were the M and Ms. The lederhosen clad lads whose utter indifference to Melissa's physical charms implied superior Teutonic application and clarity of purpose – winning the competition – which was both fearsome and impressive. Either that or they were a couple of screaming gay boys with superior Teutonic application and clarity of purpose – winning the competition – which was both fearsome and impressive. I didn't think of myself as overtly homophobic, although I probably was, but they made me edgy. Edgy because they were good enough to win and double edgy because they were good enough to win and didn't bat an eyelid at Melissa's bum, boobs or body.

"They're *gay*," she said with an off-hand air after we had weighed in yet another beautiful thirty-pound plus mirror that Horst had caught and were off to our next swim destination. "They don't look at me like the others do."

"Surely you must have come across *some* blokes who didn't give you the eye at *some* time in your life," I said, a little peeved at her conceit.

Melissa gave this some consideration. "Not since I was fourteen," she said. "They all try the not looking trick but I've become wise to that. I see what they would like to see however clandestine they try to be. And those two *aren't* interested. *Ipso facto*, gay boys!"

"Ipso what so?" I said.

"*Ipso facto*. It's Latin," said Melissa.

As much as she was a serious witch who was making me seriously edgy, I had to laugh. "What's it like," I asked, "being constantly lusted after?"

"You mean you don't know?" she teased.

"Hardly," I said.

"Not even with Horst and Helmut? *They* were looking at *you!*"

"Fuck off, were they!" I said.

I probably *was* homophobic now I thought about it. I could remember how I had felt when Rambo had asked me to come in on bait with him outside the 'Black Horse' all those moons ago. More immediately, because the idea brought tears to my eyes, I didn't care for the idea of a mullet and moustachioed Austrian shoving his you-know-what up my you-know-where.

Melissa raised her plucked eyebrows heavenwards and walked off to my van.

"Hey! Come back! You're having me on aren't you?" I called.

Melissa started to run and cackled to herself as she did. She cackled just like a witch, a sexy, sassy saucepot of a witch. I ran after her and caught her by the shoulder and pulled her back.

"You *were* joking?" I said, slightly breathless from the sudden exertion.

Melissa shrugged. "They're not interested in *me*, *that's* for sure!"

"But that doesn't make them a pair of iron hoofs does it?" I said.

"It does in my book," she said.

Double shit! Just when I was getting really edgy over them catching so many bloody carp, now I had to get another edge out and start getting edgy over them being a pair of AAs, as well as being M and Ms. Austrian Arsebandits – Mullets and Moustaches. You should have been able to work it out on your own.

I sat in swim nine staring at the catch-logging sheet. My excellent preparation had foreseen the need for a calculator, and it was on this ubiquitous instrument – but not when fishing, that was why my preparation was so excellent – that I punched the buttons, which represented the numbers, which represented the weights, which represented the carp that had been caught so far. The sum totals told their conclusive story and we were third. Team Rambo was in the bronze medal position now, but we were going for gold. Brad and Tom were second, having caught right up on the M and Ms who were slightly in the lederhosen, I mean, in the lead.

Everyone had now caught at least two carp and the point to note about the catches from early this morning was their more even distribution. Fish had come, literally, from all over the pit and although the M and Ms still held the advantage, they hadn't increased their lead from the time when I had considered us, Team Rambo, to be three fish light. It was as good as I could have possibly hoped for. Brad and Tom had done the best during the daylight hours and they stood only a touch over twenty pounds behind the tonsorially tortured 'tache twins.

Other statistics pointed to the fact that Steve's nuts were now larger by a factor of 0.432635987 than they had been at the start. Roughly speaking. I had got him to check them with the micrometer Pup kept in his rucksack. The micrometer Pup kept so he could check the accuracy of his pop-ups and, if necessary, give himself a good bollocking if they happened to come up more than a millimetre out. Steve, on the other hand, was giving himself a good bollocking of a different nature throughout the whole period of the competition. It was doubtful if his participation was good for him – from a testicular health point of view – but he seemed more than content now he had caught three carp and his partner Paul had had a brace. They were doing well, even if the bit about him measuring his testicles was complete fabrication. Believe it or not, Pup *did* have a micrometer in his rucksack and would utter oaths under his breath if he chanced upon a disproportionate boilie.

I looked at my watch. Only ten minutes to go until the break. It had come at last and soon I could hand over the whole verification package to Mr and Mrs Pup. Thank God! I was bursting to get my rods into action and let myself loose into the fray. I massaged my face with my two hands. So far things were going to plan; the caterers were in the clubhouse preparing the food, Melloney and Melina had phoned to say they had arrived, we were close enough to be in with a shout of winning, I had managed to squeeze in a quick shower and felt all the better for it, Melissa and I hadn't got on each others' nerves too much and Hamworthy had produced the goods as becoming of the best carp fishery in England. All that remained for me to do was to double up with buddy-boy Rambo, kick arse, catch carp and win, provided the barbecue didn't turn into something akin to what was going to be filmed in a few days' time. Would I find it an erotic experience? Actually being present during the proceedings with both the men and the women physically engaging each other? The barbecue that is, not the porn shoot!

Five minutes to go. I decided I had better get the flare gun ready to indicate to all and sundry it was time to eat.

"Rambo!" I called. "Can you get the flare gun out for me?"

Rambo was sitting on his chair outside his bivvy tying up some rigs. He gave me a frowning look.

"What did your last servant die of, boy?" he asked.

I shrugged. "Being overworked?"

"I don't doubt it. It's in my large rucksack, you fetch it and a flare, the flares are in a side pocket, I can't remember which one, and I'll load it up for you," he informed me.

"Okay, bwana," I said with a tinge of acrimony and a smile.

I went into Rambo's bivvy and then delved into his rucksack. The bulky flare gun was nestling in amongst a host of tackle items and I unzipped a large side pocket and thrust my hand inside it. What my hand felt was not the cylindrical shape of a flare but of another type of gun, and then another! Two guns! Curiosity got the better of me and, hoping I had no particular feline traits which could spell ultimate doom, I took both weapons out. They were a pair of identical hand guns made in black/grey metal and reminded me of the gun James Bond used to kill the fifteen other blokes who were firing at him with sub-machine guns, rocket launchers and small tactical nuclear bombs. I then unzipped the other pocket and found the flares, so I took out one of those as well.

I went back outside and gave the flare gun and flare to Rambo and put the other two guns on his bedchair.

"What are those two?" I asked.

Rambo looked at the two guns, looked at me, back at the guns and then back at me again. After a second or two he turned his attention on the guns and picked one up and started to examine it like one of the crusty old gits from the Antiques Roadshow.

"Ah! Now, these *are* interesting," said Rambo in a pseudo-posh voice. "This is a 9mm calibre pistol, made in Austria, and is known as the Glock 17, due to it having a seventeen round magazine capacity. Approximate weight… around 656 grams, with an overall length of 185mm. The bullet will leave the muzzle at a velocity of 360 metres per second, so, generally speaking, the person whom it is aimed at is unlikely to outrun it." Rambo looked up and I rolled my eyes on cue. "This particular weapon was first used by the SAS in 1991, and it is set to supersede the Belgian made Browning as the standard issue gun to all Army soldiers. The reasons for this are the Glock carries four more bullets than the Browning and is accurate to *forty* metres, a good ten more than the Browning. However, perhaps most crucially, the Glock is inherently safer and far quicker to fire than the Browning due to it having a built-in safety catch, which is released only when the trigger is pulled as opposed to the Browning's cumbersome manually engaged one. The Browning has had problems both in jamming, when needed in quick use and in accidental firing, and this is why the Glock is a more modern and superior weapon." Rambo changed his voice back to normal. "And it's why I've got *two* of the fuckers in my rucksack rather than two of the Brownings."

Ignoring the question of why Rambo even needed two *Brownings* in his rucksack I had to comment.

"Those Austrians," I said. "So *damn* clever! Do you have to have a mullet and a moustache to shoot one straight?"

Rambo sneaked an eye down the sight of the short barrel. "Not that I'm aware of," he admitted.

"What the fuck have you got two for? If it's *so* reliable?" I asked.

Rambo pulled down both corners of his mouth. "Seventeen extra bullets?" he offered.

"Or can you shoot yourself up in the air like Yosemite Sam with two guns?" I said.

"You know, I've never tried," said Rambo stroking his chin.

"Can I have one?" I blurted. I don't know why I asked but I did.

Rambo gave me a cold hard stare. "All right, boy," he said eventually, and threw me the gun he had in his hand. I caught it and eyed it with fascination. "Pull the trigger when you want to shoot it. It's all you have to do. After seventeen goes if what you're trying to kill is still coming after you, try throwing the gun at it. If it's still moving after you've chucked the gun… it's probably best to run away." He gave me another long biting stare. "*Don't* do anything stupid with it."

Chapter 14

The functional wooden clubhouse was heaving with an excitable group of cosmopolitan carp anglers plus three of England's finest luscious lovelies – a teasing little trio from the Professional Man-Mesmerising Union – of which they were fully paid-up lifelong members. (Provided their looks held up and they didn't all suddenly expand into a triplicate doppelganger of their mother.) The three beauties were also surreptitiously moonlighting as the Witches of Eastwick, but I was the only male present who was party to this exclusive information. This was because I had coined the phrase in my head and had not told a single soul, which kind of explained it.

To my mind, the scene inside the functional wooden clubhouse was like a bait-box full of maggots left in the warm sun, what with all the animated wriggling and writhing that was taking place. The animated wriggling and writhing was usually done to get a glimpse of one of the girls, to fabricate an introduction to them or to describe an earlier battle with a lump of carp. The introductions came primarily from the known Melissa, who would acquaint the anglers with the unfamiliar Melina and Melloney, who in return would say something like; 'Gosh! You're *sisters*!'. Occasionally, someone would chance their arm with an opening chat-up line straight to one of the two girls they hadn't seen before and interestingly I noticed not a single one of them was rebuffed.

All the anglers were extremely keen to take their turn and to have their desired time slot in the sisters' company. Joyously for all concerned, all *males* concerned, the girls didn't deny any of them. It was an incredible effect, as it had been at Pup's wedding, how they effortlessly dominated male attention, except that is, for Horst and Helmut. The M and Ms stoically talked only fishing to fishermen, as perhaps they tried to glean some priceless nugget of information from one of the 'locals' to help in their quest to win the Fish-In. If this wasn't the case and they ignored the girls on other quite separate grounds, then Melissa's warning of homosexuality certainly gained substantial credibility.

The maggot/bait box thought, I had to admit, was iffy. The human bodies didn't look at all like maggots – although to be unfair, to him that is, Jez did have a larvae-like air about him – the spaces between the bodies were much greater than those usually associated with a pint of mixed and the functional wooden clubhouse was hardly a functional plastic bait-box. To stretch things further, it was in the evening and the sun was now *behind* the trees, thus putting the clubhouse in the shade. Yet in spite of the host of weaknesses in my simile, the scene inside the functional wooden clubhouse still reminded me of a bait-box full of maggots left in the etcetera, etcetera. Objectively inaccurate? So go on, sue me.

An atmosphere of heady carping 'joie de vivre' (Hamworthy, you are so fine!) was turbo charged into something akin to rocket fuel and a pilot with a light – a pilot light – by female oestrogen, male testosterone, competitive rivalry, sexual tension and the prospect of hot, wholesome food and cold, quenching drink. The very air we breathed seemed charged with energy and was intermittently punctuated by the tantalising waft of inexpensive perfume, deodorant 'pour homme', body odour, (not guilty, I had showered) carp slime and barbecued chicken. And someone out there was definitely on Monster Crab, or if not, had a major personal hygiene problem.

If I had the gun with me, I suddenly mused, which seventeen would I shoot? Which of the lousy maggots would I put away? Or would I pump the lot into one body, leaving it riddled with bullet holes and looking like a cadaver colander? It was an insane question. Logically, I thought, trying to rectify my hastily conceived question, simply because I had a gun with seventeen bullets at its disposal, didn't necessarily mean I *had* to shoot anyone. I didn't *have* to use a single bullet, if I didn't want to. Anyway, it was academic, the gun was in my rucksack and even if it hadn't been, I still wouldn't have wanted to shoot anyone. Well, not so early on in the evening, I said to myself in jocular fashion, it might put a bit of a damper on affairs. The question that begged to be asked was, if I didn't want to shoot anyone, why had I asked for the gun in the first place? I truthfully didn't know the answer; the request had been a knee-jerk reaction. Why the *hell* had I asked? I had no idea; apart from thinking I was the jerk rather than my knee, the one reliable fact to come out of the situation. I mean, what had I been thinking off?

I went outside the functional wooden clubhouse, or more accurately on this occasion, the wooden clubhouse with the function going on within it. I descended the steps to where the two caterers were barbecuing the grub, not the grubs, which weren't maggots, or any other type of insect larva for that matter. There appeared to be enough food to feed considerably more people than were present.

"Christ!" I said light-heartedly, nodding at all the food. "Have you got some mates coming over as well? A couple of football teams, or something?"

One of them, the proprietor, if that's the correct word, whose name was Mick, wiped the sweat from his forehead and answered.

"That lot in there'll eat all this lot out here, no probs, Mr Williams. They look a hungry-gutted bunch of whelps to me. Especially that big geezer in the army outfit, he looks as if he could eat for England!" He gave me a conspiratorial wink. "I wouldn't mind eating one of those three girls!" he confided. "Eh? *Jesus*! All three of them are hotter than anything we've got cooking on here *and* we're doing a spicy chicken! Eh? Hahaha! I'm not letting Danny, here, go to the bog, he'd be in there all night beating his meat rather than doing his job out here cooking it. Eh? Hahahaha!"

Danny gave a sickly smile, he was seventeen and spotty. He did look as if he was

161

prone to a little, possibly even a lot, of sexual self-abuse.

"One of them is the 'big geezer's' girlfriend," I told the pair of them. "And woe betide you, if you so much as talk to her!" I dragged an index finger across my throat like Rambo had when I had asked him what he would do to someone who mucked around with his 'bird'. "Don't upset him, it's not a pretty sight. The person who upsets him, after he's finished with them, that is," I warned the two non-celebrity cooks. I watched with satisfaction as two Adam's apples bobbed in their respective throats. One doesn't want the caterers getting overly familiar with one's guests, I thought rather haughtily. "I'm going to do a quick speech and then we'll start on the food, okay?" I pointed out.

"No probs, Mr Williams. It'll be ready," said Mick.

I gave him a nod and went back inside and, as chance would have it, bumped straight into Melina. She looked *fantastic*. Melissa was right. I *did* fancy her the most out of the three sisters. I quickly soaked up the vision of enticement before me. Melina had made an effort to look stunning by the careful application of make-up and the careful omission of unnecessary clothing. Impractical as they undoubtedly were, she had opted for high, wedge-soled sandals to set off her tanned, shapely legs. This pair of legs had mercifully been left uncovered until viewing of her svelte thighs was interrupted by a miniscule skirt, which was a mere incidental strip, until more bronzed skin returned to the agenda in the form of her flat, toned stomach complete with belly-button piercing. Moving higher still, her curvaceous waste and ample bust were accentuated alarmingly by the top she wore. I call it a top, it was more of a bikini top than anything else, and everything was coaxed into perfect shape by two tiny little straps each secured with neat, symmetrical bows; one at the nape of her neck and one in the middle of her back. One gentle pull on any loose tag and… the thought had to be doused in cold water!

The monster inside me roared with delight, as he too became party to the delightful vision flooding down my optic nerve. From its cave it nipped out, put its left hand flat over its green, reptilian-like right bicep and whipped that arm up with gusto while forming a tight fist. 'Phwooar!!' it said. I couldn't argue with it on any level. Pleased with itself, the monster hung around doing a little dance, one with lots of hip gyrations, only marginally in my sub-conscious.

Melina looked a little different facially. She had recently had her hair dyed as it was certainly more blonde than I remembered from Pup's wedding, and was now a very similar colour to Brad's. Melina's skin tone was as dark as Brad's as well, and while hers may have been originally grounded in artificial light the overall effect was no less powerful because of it. Melina's teeth could never hope to match the set Brad had plugged into his gums but her full, red lips were more than adequate compensation. Searching for the imperfect form of a verb, I came up with 'smouldering'. Her hair was longer as well as more blonde, it was dead straight, parted slightly off-centre and down to her shoulder blades. She could have walked out of the centre of the Sunday Sport only moments earlier; apart from the fact she had never needed, would never need, implants. She was a vision of the new style ladette; bold, sexually self-confident to the point of being predatory, hugely attractive with the slightest hint of tartiness and a willing participant in high-octane love-making at anytime, anywhere. And she was Rambo's girlfriend, I informed myself, in case I had forgotten.

"Hi, Melina," I said as casually as I could, trying to mask my secret from her. The one she undoubtedly already knew about because her middle sister had told her, or because she had seen my interest for herself.

"Hi, Matt," she answered.

I looked for clues in her reply. I couldn't see any. "The food will be ready to eat in a few moments. I'm going to announce the catches so far and let everyone tuck in afterwards."

"Fine. I'm ever so hungry. I've been saving myself all day… for the food," she said smiling.

I smiled back, slightly rocked by her little pause. Here we go again, more manipulation of the Matt Williams' libido. "Let's hope it's nice. It smells pretty good," I said.

It was small talk, real small, so small you needed an electron microscope and 20/20 vision to see it. It was all I had in the locker. "I'll catch up with you a bit later on."

"I *hope* so," she simpered.

Witches! They were all *witches*!

I wandered off into the throng and found Rambo chatting to Melloney. She didn't look like a girl who detested the man she was talking to, the two-faced trollop, but as long as she was getting attention perhaps it was all that mattered.

"Excuse me," I said butting into their conversation. "I'm just going to announce the catches so far," I said directly to Rambo, "and then I'm going to let everyone loose on the food."

"*Hello*, to you *too*, Matthew!" Melloney said a touch crossly.

"Hi, Melloney. Sorry. How are you? How's the gym stuff going with Sophie?" I asked, guilty of my rudeness.

Melloney flicked her eyes at Rambo. "Yeah! Fine thanks. How's the competition going? Are you three going to win?"

I looked at Rambo. "I don't know. Are we going to win?" I asked him.

"If you get your finger out and fish half-decent, I don't see why not, boy!" He turned to Melloney. "We've got *vast* experience when it comes to carp fishing competitions, not only in getting good results but in entertainment value as well, you see there's usually an explosive ending to finish it off coupled with a good old punch-up!"

I cringed while Melloney frowned.

"I'll explain it all later," I said, lying. I had no intention of telling her of *that* rather grim day in my life.

Melloney put a hand on my arm. "That'd be interesting and fun," she said warmly.

I gave them both a little wave and pulled out the totals I had checked, then checked, and double checked, and got Pup to check once again, from my jogging bottoms.

Happy I had all the facts to hand and they were correct, I jumped up on one of the tables, called for attention and read out the results once it was quiet. In many ways what I was doing was superfluous as nearly all the initial conversation between the anglers had been over who had caught what. Obviously that was *before* Melina and Melloney had arrived. At least they now knew the score *officially*, and the score was the M and Ms had a total weight of 302lb 6ozs, the Yanks were a close second weighing in 282lb 14ozs and Team Rambo was third with 201lb 9ozs. The other pairs staggered down to a bottom weight of 58lb 11ozs where new boys Simon and Phil held the wooden spoon. Once I had reminded them that the competition would restart, on my flare, at eleven thirty, it was time to eat, drink and be merry. But not gay, I should have added.

Everyone formed an orderly queue and within a quarter of an hour had a plateful of excellent food. Mick and Darren were a dubious couple of jokers but they *could* cook and the barbecued meat was succulent and lean, much like Melina, and the jacket potatoes were hot and tasty with perfectly browned skins. Also like Melina. I took a swig of my chilled beer, I was only having two, *maximum*. I had two baits to get out in a couple of hours time and the last thing I needed to be was pissed. I didn't think Rambo would be too impressed if I got hammered either. He wanted to win; he wanted to trim the Mullets as much as I did. And not lose to the Yanks. To leave the Mullets untrimmed and to go down to the two Americans on home turf would be a disastrous result. Talking of disaster, of the imploding team kind, I wondered how impressed he would be with my fixation on his girlfriend. It was a good job I was the psychic one. Perhaps I should quantify that – the *supposed* psychic one who had pulled two rabbits out the hat in three or so years. Mind you, they were fucking big rabbits, the mind-meld mirror and the ghost. I *was* on a hat trick, I mused, what *would* my next big psychic achievement be? Would it ever come? I doubted it.

In truth, to go back to Melina, I hadn't realised quite how attracted to her I would become. It was just that seeing her again, looking even better than she had at the wedding, *and* knowing what she had got up to with Rambo meant I simply couldn't deal with it. Ridiculous as it was, with Sophie, Amy and Rambo all in the frame, my monster trampled around in my *conscious* now, virtually unimpeded and unrestricted. I had known I would still look at her and fancy her but hadn't comprehended how much she would get under my skin. Still, I thought philosophically, unreciprocated lust was hardly a new concept; it had been around since mankind and womankind had begun. All in all, especially as my stark warning to the caterers surely also applied to me, it was probably, no absolutely and categorically for the best that it remained unreciprocated!

As host and Supreme Syndicate Leader, I felt it was up to me to mingle and spend some time with all the pairs. I proposed to have a little chat, swap a few clichés, discuss absurdly complicated 'bullshit rigs' and generally make them feel as valued and relaxed as possible. It was a little needless in a way as the universal language of carp fishing and sexual attraction appeared to have broken all barriers of creed and background, but nevertheless it was something I felt duty-bound to do. Even so, without my input the room easily maintained its frenetic energy as pairs amalgamated into larger groups and tales of daring carp-trickery were related in both graphic and physical terms. Invisible rods were wielded, unseen catapults fired and transparent landing nets scooped up large 'no-see-um' carp. Syndicate members, new syndicate members and the overseas guests became enmeshed in groups of four, six and eight as they tucked into the tasty food and discussed the Fish-In in elaborate detail. Every now and then a pair would move off to another little group and start to chat to them. Invariably they were greeted with warm handshakes and a slap on the back as they passed on their derring-do escapades in blow-by-blow fashion. And during all the carp-talk they only had to look up, spin their heads around and be greeted by the sight of pristine female form, in three versions. The fishing could then be put on hold as they discussed the girl's finer merits and, as their turn came, they could get an even closer look and talk to the object of their infatuation first hand. If they could have you-know-what-them I could have laid claim to creating a near heaven on earth. If such a thing existed. (See earlier disclaimer)

Pleasingly there were no cliques, no 'us and them' divisions to be viewed anywhere, pairs even split up to talk to others and, as I had hoped, despite the strong desire of all involved to win their seemed not a shred of animosity anywhere. The girls were clearly operating along similar lines of complete integration because I noticed how they too hopped from group to group, like exotic hummingbirds flitting from flower to flower, drinking the nectar of male regard. They usually performed their flights alone but every so often they crossed each other's paths, linked arms and seamlessly carried on socialising, bedazzling the men with their abundant charms. Wherever they alighted they dominated proceedings and halted the carp fishing talk in its tracks. Except when they alighted on a group containing Horst and Helmut.

It wouldn't have been apparent to any social observer that either Melissa or Melina were romantically involved with anyone else in the room, let alone Melissa being *married* to Pup. Romantic Rambo was never likely to be a nickname levelled at my long term fishing buddy but if either of the two men involved were put out by their partners fraternising with the other anglers, they never let it show. Rambo chatted happily to the other anglers and the other sisters and so did Pup. It was to Pup's group I moved in on first.

"How are your balls, Steve?" I whispered with genuine interest as I joined in the group comprising Vasectomyman, Melloney, Paul, Noel, Jim and Pup.

"Killing me," he whispered back. "But who cares? This is *great*! Hamworthy is *fantastic*! It's all and more I ever wanted in terms of carp angling. If I never catch another fish this year I'll be happy!" he grinned. His face was pale and drawn from discomfort but his eyes sparkled with pure elation.

"Whoa there! Don't sell yourself short!" I said trying to talk with a chunk of chicken in my mouth. "There are loads more carp to be had this year, mate! Loads more in this comp, come to that. You're doing all right, you and Paul." I playfully punched him on the arm. "You *see*! *What* did I tell you?" I gently chided him. "If I hadn't told you to leave your bait out you might not have caught the forty at all! I'm claiming an assist!" I laughed.

Steve cocked his head. "Fair play. You *were* right!"

"I'm sorry I laughed at you when you had the forty," I told him with a tinge of sincerity. Only a tinge, though.

Steve looked puzzled. "*When* was that?"

"When you were getting down to your rods and when you were playing the fish," I explained, surprised at his inability not to have registered my mirth.

Steve shook his head. "I never noticed. You could have been attacking an opera diva with a meat cleaver and I wouldn't have noticed. I was in the zone, focused in the 'now'. Oblivious."

"An *opera diva* with a meat cleaver?" I asked. It was my turn for bewilderment.

"Someone with a strong voice, someone who could scream really loud... but I still wouldn't have noticed."

"Right! Get you! Anyway, sorry, but it was funny. Even Melissa said it was funny, although she did moan at me for laughing in the first place."

"Good old, Melissa!" said Steve mischievously.

"So!" I said to the group en masse ready to move on. "How's it going? Is everyone enjoying it so far?"

Everyone nodded enthusiastically, even Melloney.

"Food's good," said Paul and everyone nodded again.

"There's plenty more if you want it. I think I'm going to take some for later, the chicken will keep and it's all got to be used up," I said.

I sneaked a look at my watch. Bloody hell, it was half past nine already. I wanted to be back at my bivvy well before eleven to sort out my rods and kit. The time I had chanced on having a shower before the break meant I had all my fishing prep still to do. Thankfully I had remembered to get my baits out of the freezer – the very-much-in-use-freezers, I might add. My popularity was soaring I tell you! Soaring! – and they were thawing back in my bivvy, steeling themselves for the battle ahead.

"Shall we swap over phones now?" I said to Pup. "And I'll give you the keys to my van as well."

"Yeah, might as well," he answered.

Pup eased his way over to me and I noticed Paul engage Melloney in conversation while having a quick, sly look down at her cleavage.

The reason for our swapping of phones was the logical one of continuity. The anglers would still ring the same number to get weight verification, only from now until the end of the competition it would be Pup and his wife rather than Melissa and I who would do the verifying. With Pup's phone I was independently able to alert him to Team Rambo's catches should the team's sponsor either lose his mobile, drop it in the drink, run its battery flat or attack it with a bivvy mallet in a fit of exasperation caused by his latest partner's inability to catch carp – or if *he* was abducted by aliens and his phone happened to be in his camo jacket's pocket. My van would give Pup and Melissa the necessary transport to flit back and forth around the pit. This was provided he could keep it on the track and not careen off it and mow down a couple of unsuspecting, snoozing carp anglers tucked up in their bivvy. You suddenly awake; 'What was that? My Buzzer? Oh no, it's a mad boilie-maker and his witch of a gorgeous wife cutting me down in my prime with a diesel Escort van'.

Going back to Melissa this time – rather than Melina – now she would have to spend time with her hubby I wondered if she would spend another night 'chatting', for want of a better euphemism, with Brad now Pup wasn't otherwise engaged by being embedded behind his chocolate coloured rods in swim nine. It was all supposition on my part, chatting may mean chatting, or it may mean sordid hanky-panky. What did I know? The Psychic Minnow, that's what I was, the two-trick pony, although the Psychic Stickleback had a much nicer alliterative ring to it.

I gave Pup my mobile and van keys and he gave me his phone. "What was it like, fishing again?" I asked him.

Pup gave me a circled thumb and index finger. "Brilliant! I've really enjoyed it. I'm so glad you asked me. I was well nervous to begin with, what with fishing with Rambo and not wanting to let him, and you, down. But it gradually came back and my baits did me proud." He nodded as if he was thinking in his mind. "If we do start to go a bit more, me and her, I'll have to invest in some new gear. Mine looked shite compared to everyone else's."

There's one born every minute, I thought. A Tackle Tart, that is. In a few years time I could envisage Pup neo-camoed up to the gills, his white bait bucket mummified in camo gaffer tape, colour co-ordinated everything, with a pile of kit heavy enough to sink a small frigate and a collapsible aluminium ladder – for fuck's sake – to see over the top of it.

"I don't know, you've proved it isn't necessary to have every gadget advertised. Good bait, decent line and sensible rigs, sharp hooks, they're the important bits. Okay, so you were restricted by your rods and reels as to how far you could cast, but you still out-fished a lot of blokes who could put a bait out sixty yards further than you," I reasoned.

"Yeah," said Pup unconvinced. "But I still think I'll invest in some new gear."

I laughed. His arse had been bitten and he had got the bug. All over the world men had their arses bitten by different bugs and the disease they caught from it made them siphon money from other areas of their lives – savings, pensions, mortgage repayments, wives' birthday presents, food – to buy kit for their new leisure pursuit. It was a good job, manufacturing jobs depended on it; capitalism, to an extent, depended on it. Trading in for this year's all-singing, all-dancing model was the very nub of financial survival for many companies and it made life *so* worth living!

I made my excuses to Pup and his group and dropped in on some of the others. I spent twenty minutes talking to Li, Hu, Leo, Mark, Jez and Malcolm on the delights of Hamworthy and its magnificent carp, another fifteen with Alan, Keith, Ron and John who button-holed me as the five of us went for second helpings and then I waltzed into a group containing the M and Ms, Brad and Tom plus two thirds of the witches, in the pleasing form of Melissa and Melina. Scanning for the missing sister I spotted Melloney talking to Rambo with Gordon and Todd.

Brad's smile exploded with the ferocity of a star going supernova.

"Hey, buddy. How'ya doing?" he asked genially.

"Good," I told him. "Even better when I can start fishing against you guys."

"Ah! The secret weapon is about to be let loose!" he said. "Hey! But what a swell place this water is. What a venue! You must be mighty proud of it?" Brad gushed with honest enthusiasm.

I nodded. "I am. This is the first time anything like this has happened at Hamworthy and it's nice to hear anglers like you, who have fished all over the world, are so impressed with it."

"Sure, like we're impressed one heck of a lot. I was only saying to Horst and Helmut a few minutes ago, this is the best carp venue we've ever been to."

"Better than Lac Fumant?" I asked.

Brad shrugged. "I kinda think so. But don't you go tellin', Bob, we don't want to upset him unnecessarily. You see, Bob never had *three* beautiful women at any of his barbecues! And he sure didn't have a carp fishing adult entertainment film shot on-site! No way, did he! Man, is *that* true?" asked Brad laughing and slapping his leg. "Your other members say it's true, but *no* way!"

"It's true!" I confirmed. "Funnily enough, the bloke whose company makes the films is a Dutch carp angler who I met at Lac Fumant on my very first visit. He propositioned me, if you'll pardon the expression, at Pup and Melissa's wedding when he found out I now owned a water. He said it was something he had always wanted to do and asked if I'd mind it happening here at Hamworthy. It hasn't happened yet, though," I pointed out, "it's due to start in a few days' time. Basically, I said as long as I could have a little look here and there, I was more than happy to let him go for it and use the facilities here at Hamworthy."

"A *look*!" cried Brad. "Man, you should have asked for a starring part! You too, Rambo. You could be the Ron Jeremy of the carp fishing world!"

"I haven't got the moustache for it," said Rambo levelly, his group now standing adjacent to us and listening in. Those who had heard and knew who the hell Ron Jeremy was and what he looked like laughed.

"That's the first time I've ever heard it put like that!" I said to even greater laughter. "Horst and Helmut have *definitely* got the moustaches for it," I heard myself say before I could shut my big, fat gob. This was after only *two* bottles of cold beer. Thank God I had stuck to my game plan on the alcohol front and hadn't drunk any more.

Horst almost blushed and looked at Helmut with embarrassment. He wagged a finger and shook his head.

"No. Ve vill stay vitt ser fishing, I sink. Our vives vould not be happy if ve vere fucking vitt ser porn stars."

And everyone, because everyone in the room had now homed in on our conversation, disintegrated into laughter. Except Melissa, who looked as if she had lost ten kilos of Mainline Maple-8 and found a bag of pellets, *and* been smacked in the face with a stocking full of hot shit. Her nose, the joint in it, way out! Unless the pair of Austrians were barefaced liars, here at last, were two heterosexual men unimpressed by the Witches of Eastwick. Or they *were* gay and their wives were only a cover, a presentable face to show to a world that didn't really like queers despite its burgeoning political correctness. At least not in the prim business circles where Horst and Helmut had made their filthy lucre.

"Hey, man," said Brad continuing. "You know how you get your porn star name, don't you?"

"What?" I said dumbly.

Brad explained. The whole room hung on his words. "Imagine you were a guy who performed in a porno movie, you wouldn't wanna use your real name, right? So you would use your *porn star* name. Your *porn star* name is the name of the first pet you had as a kid added to the surname of your mother before she was married." He gave me an f22 aperture smile. "So what's yours, Matt?"

I had already worked it out while he had been telling me the parameters. I had pictured the black kitten from years ago and I knew all too well what mum's maiden name was.

"Tiddles Tugwell," I admitted somewhat crestfallen. Howls of laughter burnt skin off my rosy cheeks.

"That works!" Rambo shouted sarcastically.

"What's *yours*, then?" I asked indignantly.

"Oscar Rodgers. Not *too* bad," Rambo replied grinning.

"Guess what mine is?" said Steve.

"Big Bollocks McBride?" I said. *Again* before I could stop myself.

Steve held up an 'Oi! Stop that!' finger. "No. It's Rover Spinks. Good, eh?" he said without umbrage.

"'Bivvy Gangbang from Behind', starring Rover Spinks, Oscar Rodgers and Tiddles Tugwell! In the Garden of England, a rod is twitching!" Rambo said, amid much hilarity.

"Debbie Does Yatley Car Park Lake," chipped in Dean.

"Hey!" I suddenly thought. "What about you lovely ladies? You'd all have the *same* name wouldn't you? Same first pet, same mother… so come on, let's hear it."

For once the three girls looked unsure of themselves.

"*You're* the eldest, *Melina. You* tell them," Melloney said.

Melissa, the Rizla Queen, who had rolled a fag in double-quick time and was dragging in smoke, quickly expelled it.

"Yeah, Melina. *You're* the eldest. And it was *you* who named the flipping hamster, in fact it was *you* who wanted it in the first place."

Melina's luscious boobs heaved with resignation. It didn't go unnoticed.

"*Never* be the eldest," she stated. Like you've got control over *that*, I thought to myself. "Not only do you have to break the parents in so that *they*," she glared at her two sisters, "can have an easy time of it, getting their bodies pierced, tattooed and staying out late at night but then they try to steal your boyfriends *and* you have to do crap like this. *And* get the blame for it. My... our... porn star name is Cuddles Buntin."

I choked on laughter. "Get the flags out, here comes Cuddles Buntin!"

"Very witty," sneered Melina trying to look cross but I could see she was fighting back a smile.

The room quickly echoed to hubbub as lots of mini conversations started up due to everyone discovering their porn star name and telling it to the person adjacent to them. My mind turned to Ian, the owner of the infamous Spunker, the Rottweiler who had lost the epic fistfight to Rambo in the storm at Lac Fumant. I had no idea what Ian's mother's maiden name was, but with a first name like Spunker, it hardly mattered.

I looked at my watch and was taken aback at the time. It was twenty to eleven. I needed to be somewhere else, swim nine to be precise, and although part of me wanted to hang around with the lads, and obviously the lassies, the desire to get ready for the next vital thirty-four and a half hours came out on top. My Lust Monster must have dozed off. I quickly said my goodbyes to all the anglers, thanked Melloney and Melina for coming and for being so honest over their unusual porn star name and went outside to where Mick and Danny were clearing up. Nearly all the food had gone. Everyone had eaten well.

I picked up four chicken legs and wrapped them in a serviette. "Great food, lads! Excellent stuff! Thanks very much."

"No probs, Mr Williams. Pleasure cooking it for you," said Mick.

"When you go, can you make sure you chain the gates up and tumble the combination padlocks after you've snapped them shut?" I reminded them.

"Will do, Mr Williams. Will do," Mick assured me.

I gave them my customary thumbs up and started to hurry around the perimeter track. The walk would take me roughly fifteen minutes seeing as we were right up the north end and I still had to get my rods out, bait them up and do all the last minute adjusting of buzz bars, alarms and indicators. My heart pounded with excitement. Would we catch the Yanks and the M and Ms? Well, we would have a bloody good go, Rambo and I. It was almost like old times and the TWTT, not that that was a good thing but it did get the adrenalin pumping.

The evening had gone well – apart from the Tiddles Tugwell incident – there *must* have been worse but instinctively I knew there wasn't – I thought to myself, as I walked quickly in the dark, my footfalls and breathing my only company. It had passed rapidly, a sure sign of it being good, and the two and a bit hours I had been in the functional wooden clubhouse had flown by. I'd had to spread myself pretty thin in the time available but I had managed, as I had intended earlier, to speak to virtually everyone. In any case, the atmosphere had been terrific and it certainly hadn't needed me to boost it. The combination of the fishing experienced, the prospects of the fishing to come, the hope of winning, the added flair our guests gave to proceedings and the girls' flirtatious energy were more than adequate. A few words with the Supreme Syndicate Leader were hardly the high point on the agenda, whereas catching an eyeful of bronzed, youthful flesh, talking to the owner of it and making carp-talk to decent anglers *was* high-ranking stuff!

Thinking of the girls I was a little surprised at how easily I had dragged myself away from them, considering how I had visually eaten Melina alive earlier on. Maybe realisation of having a partner, even one I wasn't getting on with too well, and a baby had sunk in. Also Rambo had been in the same room, a factor which could be slightly persuasive, to put it mildly, and put any fantasy involving his girlfriend well into the shade. In truth when I analysed it critically, what had I *actually* been expecting to happen? The Lust Monster could be such a daydreamer at times.

It was a bit like when I had been single. There was all the expectation of going out on the pull and when it didn't pan out, as, let's be honest, it often didn't, it was only then that the reality distortion pills wore off. And what were you left with? Hindsight, true reality and a touch more experience. Having said all of that, *my* reality was a heck of a lot more distorted than most. Unbelievably more distorted! I chuckled to myself, maybe my reality distortion pills worked in reverse. If it was the case, now they had worn off, something bizarre should happen pretty soon. I glanced up into the sky for signs of an alien ship and impending abduction. There was no ship, but I stopped dead in my tracks and peered up at the glittering pin-pricks representing stars unimaginable distances away as I had on umpteen previous occasions. I was looking back in time. The light from them took so long to reach my retinae; I was, in effect, looking back tens, hundreds, thousands and even millions of years if I could have found Andromeda. 186,000 miles per second and it took years, let alone tens, hundreds, thousands and even *millions* of years for the light to get from the star or galaxy to the back of my eyeballs. It was truly mind-boggling and humbling in a spacious kind of way. I was a speck, an infinitesimally insignificant atom on the universe's arse.

If I didn't get *my* arse into gear, I reminded myself, even *those* distances would seem small beer compared to the M and Ms' lead of a hundred pound's worth in weight of carp. The hundred pound's worth in weight I had to help Rambo claw back if we were to win the cheque for *charadee*. Bugger a time machine, or an Acme

171

Parallel Universe Viewer for that matter, I needed a carp-catching machine. I straightened myself, pulled my shoulders back and puffed out my chest. Perhaps, just perhaps, I was that very thing. Completely free and unfettered by any abduction, either terrestrial or extraterrestrial, I walked on to swim nine and set about my business of loading two carp rods so they could deliver their weapon of mass attraction, the 'B' bomb payload – 'B' is for boilie, all stinky and round, 'C' is for catapult in whose pouch it is found – on time, with accuracy, and hopefully with devastating effects.

I had been working on the project for only five minutes or so when I heard the movements of another human, or an ALF from Alpha Centauri, who had popped over for tea, it being a meagre 4.3 light-years away. It was a bit late for tea, I decided, so it must be Rambo.

"Matt! Matt! Are you there?" said a softly spoken female voice.

It sounded like *Melina*! My heart rate upped to around one-eighty.

"Hello?" I answered shining my torch in the voice's direction. The Mag-lite found its target. It *was* Melina.

"Rambo's not here yet," I informed her as she walked up to me, gradually getting more and more illuminated as she came closer.

"Who says I want to see *him*?" she asked, as she came right up to me. "You can stop shining the torch in my eyes now," she said.

I lowered the torch. "Sorry," I said, a little on the croaky side for my liking.

Melina unexpectedly flung her arms around my neck and started kissing me, her tongue feverishly exploring my mouth. My switch flicked and I put my hands around her bum and squeezed it, pressing my mouth back hard on hers. Air was pushed down both our noses as our passions lit.

Melina pulled back and ran her hand over my crotch. "Is that a torch in your pocket, or are you just pleased to see me?" she panted.

I lifted up the torch to show her. "No," I enlightened her. "That's my cock."

She started rubbing it with her hand. "I want you *now!*" she said aggressively. "Fuck me *now!*"

Frantically I guessed she really did mean it. This wasn't alien abduction; it was alien *seduction*, alien to me anyway. No woman had ever demanded it from me like she just had. Fuelled by depraved lust, my mind fogged as to consequences or repercussions, we staggered to my bivvy and ripped off each other's clothes.

"How?" she asked huskily

"Doggy," I yapped.

She knelt on all fours, then gripped my bedchair frame with both hands, opened up her knees nearly as far apart as Steve's were when he had waddled to his forty and I plunged into her from behind. My knee knocked over a box of Pedigree Mixer I had brought with me in case they started feeding on top. There was a poetic irony to that but I was beyond it. My Lust Monster roared and it filled my head; 'Go on my son!' he bellowed and in recognition I pulled Melina's hips back hard as I thrust forward into her nubile body. She gave a moan of pleasure. I shifted one leg up off of its knee and planted my foot down next to her knee for increased penetration and started to pump madly. The Lust Monster howled his approval. Sweat beaded on my forehead and Melina's long straight hair swung in rhythm to my pounding thrusts as my thighs smacked into her buttocks.

I wasn't *quite* Rover Spinks… but then I definitely wasn't Tiddles Tugwell either.

Chapter 15

It was nearly half past. Life has its ups and downs, less than half an hour ago I was up – and when I was up I was well and truly up – and now I *was* down, I was down. And I'm not talking nursery rhymes. I was a spent force, my driving urges having dissipated into the cool night air leaving me bereft of urgency and ardour. My legs were a bit wobbly too, and my knees, the left one especially seeing as it had been in contact with the ground all the time, still bore the imprints of mixer pieces. Melina had also gone. She too having dissipated into the night air, riding her broomstick back to the car park where I imagined she met her two sisters, already huddled around the cauldron to relate the tale of her latest sexual conquest. The conquest had been me, one suitor who *hadn't* been turned into a frog but something more rodent-like instead. Once she had departed – like a zombie in a dream – I had loaded my two rods, set my buzz bars, alarms and indicators and was now sitting in the dark, on my bedchair, contemplating the likely outcome of my recent exploits.

My head was cupped in my hands. What *had* I done? That was an easy one – had sex with Melina. What was the motivation for such an act? Rather inconveniently, if I were searching for an answer to the question – now I had shot my bolt – my Lust Monster had done a runner. *He* knew the answer, only he wasn't bloody there! Instead he had been replaced by my Guilt Monster, who, apparently, could only get into my head when aided by the Hindsight Nanny and the True Perspective Doctor *combined* with the Lust Monster having left, fully sated. Therefore all the reasons to my motivation were gone, and all the reasons why I *shouldn't* have been motivated to perform the dirty deed in the first place were in the ascendancy. It was a bit late now for introspection, the damage had been done, but me being me, I still put it all under the microscope.

On the whole, taking all things into account, my prognosis was, basically speaking, that I was in deep doggy-doo. What I had done, I concluded, was to sign a rather nasty contract giving certain people the right to deal with me as they saw fit. If Rambo didn't apply his particular, specialised type of hideous punishment then Sophie would surely apply hers. I would probably cop both. The chances of my second adultery going undiscovered by either of those two were similar to, say – a relative winning the lottery or the psychic meeting of a genuine ghost. I knew all the probability/fate crap wouldn't wash, this was Melloney, Melissa and Melina we were talking about, and what possible hope had I of *them* keeping secrets as jealously as I did. Even if they didn't tell Sophie and Rambo directly I was convinced it would only be a matter of time before the awful news fell on their ears. What a terrible curse to have hanging over me. It would be like waiting for Hollywood's run of revenge all over again, although admittedly I had stopped worrying over that one too much of late. The fact still remained, by having a quickie with Melina, not only had I managed to cheat on Sophie, but in an incredible double bird shoot-down with a solitary stone, I had also done the same to my best mate, Rambo.

This was history repeating itself. For Tom Watt read Rambo and for Mike read me. Both sets were on the same side in a fishing competition and when I had finally revealed what Mike had done, all those years ago, Watt had attacked me. When I revealed what *I* had done, I presumed Rambo would once again attack the same bearer of bad tidings. I was the perennial bringer of bad news, but this time *I* had been the individual who had made it. Consequently I was standing on thin ice in red-hot, furnace-heated, metal diving boots, in the margins, but right above the well-know 14ft drop-off. My lust, my overpowering lust, was well and truly gone and all I had to fill its void was deep regret, impinging guilt and a tiny redeeming glow of egotism. Melina *had* wanted to have me after all was said and done, and had gone out of her way to make it happen. There was also a certain satisfaction in my almost, but not quite, Rover Spinks sexual performance. I could think kindly of these Lilliputian compensations as Rambo ripped me limb from limb and Sophie dipped my stumps in salt.

Talking of my best mate – the one whose doorstep I had well and truly dumped on, just outside his bivvy, Spunker-style – where the hell was he? If he had as much desire as he said he had to trim the Mullets he ought to have got his arse back here over ten minutes ago. Something *must* have delayed him. I cringed at the most likely reason. As I was thinking this I heard footfalls. Running footfalls. This would be the camo-clad bloke who was soon to knock me into October, maybe early November and certainly straight to A & E. Resigned to my fate, like a convicted man, I went out into the night to meet my executioner. Another summer was soon to flash by. Carp angler in a coma, I know I know – it's serious. (Williams, Morrissey and Marr)

Rambo came pounding down into swim nine. I could picture it all. Melina had clearly told him of our sex-in-the-bivvy romp – she must have bumped into him on the way back to the cauldron while flying low to keep under radar – he had confronted her on what she had been up to and she had told him. *That* was why he was late. Retribution was on its way in the shape of a huge fist on the end of a steam-hammer arm. If I was lucky! I did have the gun, I suddenly realised, but it wasn't a realistic option, not now I had only just thought of it and it was buried in the bottom of my rucksack in a pitch-black bivvy ten yards away. Besides, I couldn't shoot Rambo, it would ruin his camo jacket and it would only serve to make him even angrier.

"All right, boy?" he asked, as he jogged up to me, only a smidgen out of breath. "Sorry I'm late, but you'll *never* guess what I've just done?"

His opener took me so off balance, I almost laughed and said; 'You ought to try and guess what *I've* just done?' Sagely I didn't.

"What've you done?" I said intrigued and happy to go with my mini stay of execution.

"You'll never believe it, but I've just had a right old knee-trembler with *Melloney* round the back of the clubhouse!" Rambo said quite proudly. "Two out of three ain't bad! Bring on Melissa! Only I wouldn't," he quickly corrected, quelling his enthusiasm, "because then we'd have to get someone else to roll our bait."

I think I physically staggered back on my heels. It was akin to standing at the point in the sea where the big waves break and getting a watery wall slam across your legs and gut, forcing you backwards. (While – as a minor incidental – your whippy ice cream gets knocked out of your hand straight onto the huge cleavage of the fat girl you spotted earlier doing the beached whale impersonation. Sometimes your knotted hanky can get washed off as well. And don't forget to re-apply the sunscreen, that ozone layer isn't getting any thicker. Ask the fat girl – she'll be up for it.)

"You're *joking!*" I said incredulously. "*Melissa* told *me* that *Melloney* had told *her* that *she* thought *you* were an utter bastard because of the way you treated *Melina!*"

Rambo considered this. "Maybe Melloney was milking my mismanagement of Melina, mouthing off to Melissa to maximise the surprise, when she came and prised off my pants, put her hand on my dick, then gave it a lick and slipped it inside her."

I gave Rambo my best cold stare, although it was probably wasted due to the lack of light. "The flare gun, Mr Poet Laureate?" I stated bluntly.

"I'll get it," Rambo replied.

This soap-style circus of roundabout sex was good news, I reasoned, as it took a little of the edge off my indiscretion. Well, I hoped it took a little of the edge off my indiscretion – only as far as Rambo was concerned of course. It had no relevance whatsoever on how things fared with Sophie. I'd had loads of edges of late and to lose a little bit off one, however slight, was fine by me.

Rambo came back with the flare gun. "Fire it off, mate," I told him, "It's well gone half past!"

We both watched the flare zoom up into the night sky.

"Let's go trim mullet, boy!" Rambo said in a gravely sounding voice-over similar to a Hollywood war film where America (yawn) kicks butt and saves the planet from all those *nasty* people. "This time… it's tonsorial!"

I held out my hand so Rambo could give me five. He slapped his bunch of bananas across it. It was more like five hundred.

"Let's do it!" I said enthusiastically.

Thirty-four and a half hours left to pull back the deficit, I said to myself, mentally rubbing my hands together – one of them was still stinging – could we do it? Perhaps I would leave the Melina moment to a more appropriate time – when either Rambo or I were dead for instance – or at least until we had discovered whether we could out fish the Yanks and the M and Ms. But what if he found out from another mouth during the competition I asked, wouldn't it have been better to have told him myself? To have personally confessed and to have owned up, man to man, to my wicked deed? I pondered on the dilemma. Get the fucking baits in the water, I told myself. First things first, eh?

My buzzer didn't blast me out of my sleep because I hadn't been asleep. I had been lying in my sleeping bag wide-awake – a sleeping bag I was thinking of suing under the Trade Descriptions Act – agonising over my second betrayal of Sophie and my first of Rambo. *Why* had I done it? It was obvious. Because she had flicked my sex switch, that was why, and I had no protection overload system to flick it back off. Not while the Lust Monster was on the prowl, not until it was too late and the damage had been done and my circuits had been temporarily drained of juice, if you get my drift. Now my *second* auxiliary switch had been thrown, the one on the carp angler circuit wired in my head, and another base instinct had kicked in. The first switch gave me a stiff member, raised pulse rate and a slug of adrenalin, the other gave me exactly the same except for the rigid appendage. Thank God for small mercies. It wouldn't look nice would it? Charging out of your bivvy with a hard-on, what would the neighbours think? Cue endless jokes on rods, wedding tackle and storm-poles.

I was out of my bivvy and down to my rods, not like a frog, like a *rat* down a drainpipe. A love-rat down a drainpipe. I hit the take on the left-hand rod I had positioned out on the very tip of the island's margin, the margin Pup couldn't reach or had been unwilling to try. I pumped a hefty fish back as forcefully as I dared. As I did so, Rambo appeared and prepared the landing net. No words were said. No words needed to be said. We both knew our respective roles – we had been here before – twice now under competitive circumstances, most times purely as fishing friends. I valued our friendship immensely – although obviously not enough to turn down a jump with his luscious girlfriend – and wondered if it would survive the inevitable showdown. I decided now was not the opportune time to tell him of my Melina moment as it also hadn't been after we had originally cast out after the flare had gone up.

The mirror weighed over forty pounds. I was ecstatic. No sooner had I called Pup on my mobile, no, no sooner had I called Pup on *his* mobile which he answered on *my* mobile, than Rambo's right-hand rod rattled off. Rambo converted his chance with a debonair demeanour and all of a sudden, within the space of half an hour, we had slashed the M and Ms' lead to around thirty pounds.

"No one's had anything else," Pup told me as Rambo weighed his fish in front of Gordon.

"Some of us have had a *lot* more than others!" Melissa said to me when Pup drifted out of earshot to where Rambo and Gordon were. "You *naughty*, boy!"

"Eh?" I said in an all-time world's-worst bluff.

"She's *told* me!" Melissa informed me with glee. "You don't have to try and deny it, my older sister *always* tells me. And there you were having a go at *me* because of what you *thought* I *might* have done with Brad!" I could feel her smugness even if I couldn't see it properly. "She said you were *almost* as good as Rambo! *That* surprised me, I didn't think you'd be *anywhere near* as good!"

I felt like a cornered beast, trapped and with nowhere to go. I lashed out.

"Do you know about *Melloney* and Rambo? The pair of them at it like stray dogs round the back of the clubhouse? Were you aware of *that*?" I hissed.

Melissa paused. I had fought fire with fire. "No," she admitted. "I didn't know. I should have guessed, though, Melloney's *always* after Melina's boyfriends. It's the younger sister/elder sister's boyfriend infatuation thing, the trouble is she can't wait until Melina's finished with them!"

"Beat you to it did she?" I said carrying on slugging.

"Hardly," Melissa scoffed and turned to more immediate matters. "The sneaky cow!" she said to herself as much as to me. "Not the *first* time those two have shared boyfriends by a long way, I have to confess," she admitted candidly. "But as I think I told you before, we rather like all the mayhem we cause."

"Mmm," I said dolefully.

"You men can't resist it can you? You're so weak-willed, so eager, so keen and yet so full of remorse *after*. It's always after. The men who are in good relationships are always so full of remorse when it's too late. Men like you," she added pointedly. "Men like Rambo are different, they're in it for what they get out of it but you, you already love someone and should know better."

"Don't you love someone?" I asked.

"I thought I did," Melissa said. "But maybe I was wrong."

It sounded to me as if Pup would be rolling boilies on his own again in the not too distant future.

"Will any of you tell Rambo and Sophie what I did with Melina?" I asked.

Melissa sighed. "If past history is anything to go by Melloney and Melina will have a huge row when they find out and then it'll all be forgotten in a few days. I expect you and Rambo might have to go through a similar process. It's bound to come out sooner rather than later but I'm sure Melloney won't tell Sophie."

"Will you make sure you ask her not to?" I begged.

"Not yet," said Melissa. "I'll wait until it becomes common knowledge between all us girls as to what's gone on. I won't let on to the others that I know about Melloney and Rambo just yet, best to let Melloney come out with it, but when she does and when she finds out about you and Melina, I'll ask Melloney to be discrete and not tell Sophie. She's not a gossip, you know, otherwise she might have said something to *you* about Sophie already."

"What?" I said.

"She told me," Melissa explained forthrightly. "I *nearly* told you, and Melloney had definitely *thought* about telling you but she didn't. Apparently there's this bloke at the gym who has been trying to chat her up, chat Sophie up, and Melloney thinks she was starting to warm to him a little. Now there *is* a reason why she might warm

178

to him," Melissa explained cryptically. "Do you remember when I called you a moral hypocrite when you accused me of sleeping with Brad?" Melissa asked.

"Yes," I managed to utter. Now I was completely in a tangle. Line twist? Bird's nest, more like!

Melissa continued. "Sophie might have reason to think something happened between you and that French girl. Rebecca? The blonde-haired one who was at the wedding with her oddly dressed dad. And if she thinks something might have happened it might push her even closer to this bloke who's been paying her all the attention."

A small bomb went off in my head. Frantically I scraped the smatterings of brain residue from the inside of my skull and pushed it back together, like trying to mould a snowball with very dry, cold powdery snow.

"Rambo swore he would never mentioned me and Rebecca to Melina at all!" I blurted.

"Oh! So you *did* sleep with her?" said Melissa.

Fuck! Fuck, fuck, fuck, fuck, fuck! This was going horrendously wrong. My life was falling apart, stitch by rotten stitch.

"But Rambo never said *anything*! Would *never* say anything!" I pleaded. "And you've just told me Melloney *isn't* a gossip!"

"No! It wasn't anything blatant or one hundred percent certain," Melissa said calmly. "Now what was it? That's right. Rambo must have told Melina that Rebecca was in France all the time you were there on your first visit. Melina happened to pass this on to Melloney and she happened to tell Sophie during the course of some conversation. According to Melloney when she mentioned it in passing, they were talking about the wedding, Sophie exploded and said something like; 'That's *not* what *I* was told!'. It was something along those lines. If I'd been Sophie I'd have started to wonder why someone was telling me porkies and have drawn my own conclusions. I can only think of *one* person who would have told her a pork pie over Rebecca," Melissa said regretfully, "and it *wasn't* any of us. What goes around comes around, Matt."

Bollocks! Double bollocks! Steve's big double bollocks! You *fucking* idiot! I chastised myself. It was *me*! At the wedding I had made that stupid lie; '*It's the first time I've ever met her*', I had said when she had asked me who Rebecca was.

My mind went to go into fifth, jumped out, and over-revved with valve-float. "Who's this bloke who's been chatting her up?" I said, hysteria in my voice.

"Some *bloke*!" Melissa exclaimed. "I don't know! Some *bloke* who wants to get what *you* had a few hours ago!"

"Melina came on to me, not the other way round," I whined pitifully.

"Matt! Even I could see you fancied her terribly," said Melissa.

"But I didn't pursue her," I said pathetically.

"Did you pursue, Rebecca?" Melissa asked softly.

"No. It was a similar sort of thing, she came onto me and once she did, I couldn't resist," I confessed.

179

"Well, well! Perhaps you needn't be so critical of us in future. We have men come onto us *all* the time. If I took them up on it at your hit rate I'd never get off my back! Or if it was with you, off all fours!" And Melissa gave me a kiss on the cheek and giggled in my ear.

Vaguely I heard my mobile ring and went to answer it. Only Pup had already done so.

"The M and Ms have got one!" he said brightly. "Come on, Melissa. To the Batmobile!"

"If he says that *once* more," Melissa whispered, "I'll stab him in the eye with a stringer needle!"

The M and Ms had got one. Talk about kicking a man when he was down.

When the menagerie of fish weight verifiers had gone and all of Team Rambo's four rods were precisely placed and back in action, I walked over to Rambo.

"There's something I've got to tell you, mate." I told him. "And believe me, it's not pretty." Now was the Melina moment, now or never, as the saying goes.

I invited him into my bivvy, I turned on my light, we both sat on my bedchair and I told him *everything*. Everything about Melina and everything Melissa had told me concerning Melina, Melloney, Sophie and Pup. Rambo never said a word, he simply sat and listened as I poured it all out until eventually, with no rock unturned, I was finished.

"Blimey, boy," said Rambo, his face eerily lit by my bivvy lantern. "That's a tidy old tangle."

"That's what I thought," I said. "I'm sorry about Melina, all the blood went from my brain into my dick."

Rambo waved his huge hand dismissively. "Not a problem, boy. Been there, done that."

"Really! Do you really mean it?" I said, my spirits lifting slightly. You know, like a twitchy little movement on a light hanger.

"I wouldn't say it if I didn't mean it, especially as she thought I was better than you! If it had been the other way around I might have been a little pissed off!" he laughed. "Seriously, she didn't mean much to me, apart from being any exciting screw. In a way it's a bit of a relief, she was making me feel a bit claustrophobic and she was getting a bit too close for my liking. Now after going with you, possibly to get back at me, I *know* she won't be asking me to say the 'C' word to her."

"Commitment?" I said, choosing to ignore the concept of me being a revenge-lay. Thoughts like that could hurt my delicate feelings.

"No. Cock. I haven't mentioned this before but she wanted me to say things like; 'I'm going to put my cock in your, whatever, I'm going to get my cock out and give you a good seeing to…' It all became a bit contrived. I'm all for dirty sex talk, except when it's *me* who's got to say it. I'm more of an action man than a words man."

Rambo was right. He was a real life Action Man.

Rambo became distracted. "Having said that, I wonder if I could convince her *and*

Melloney to a three-in-a-bivvy sex romp?" Rambo looked me in the eye. "I would ask Melissa as well," he explained, "but it's the old boilie rolling problem again. Perhaps I should wait until she leaves Pup, it sounds as if she will, and *then* ask all *three* of them! We wouldn't need Japp and his entourage, we could do our *own* version of 'Bivvy Gangbang from Behind'!"

"By the time Melissa leaves Pup the other two, hopefully, will be on their broomsticks and be long gone from our circles. And good riddance! I can't cope with the temptation," I said fitfully.

"You see," Rambo said seriously. "*You've* got something to lose. Sophie and all those years together, surviving the outcome of the TWTT, her money, your money and all of Hamworthy Fisheries, Amy, little Amy, there's her as well and the grandparents. You've got a family life and foundations, Melissa was spot on there, you *do* love someone. I haven't, never have had, not since I was much younger when mum and dad were both alive. I've walked away from it all, always walked away and the things I've done have always been done for *me*. Nobody else. Sometimes I look at you and wish I had something similar… but it makes you *too* vulnerable for my liking and it's too restricting. Too many considerations to account for, too many responsibilities other than the ones I need to make for me. I can carry on being self-centred Timothy Eugene Ramsbottom, or whatever alias I want to call myself, shagging whoever I want, doing whatever I want, without the fear of hurt." Rambo paused. "I don't mean the physical pain but the pain of hurting someone I cared for or the hurt of something precious being taken away from me because of my selfish antics. The only thing I have to care about is my own life. That's the *only* thing I've got. I've done some *terrible* things to other people, where I've actually, knowingly, callously caused their death, and *not* in a war situation either."

"What, like when you used that bloke to impersonate you, knowing full-well he was going to get killed?" I interjected.

Rambo nodded. "All done for *me* and for *my* agenda. There are a lot of people who would like me dead but they don't know where I am or who I am, because I've got no roots. No family. No foundations. No way of getting to me." Rambo paused again. "Not unless someone *did* get to Charlie and got something out of him before he died." Rambo punched his fist into the flat of his other hand. "Enough! You're the closest thing I've got to family, boy and if you had a moment of desire with a woman then you're on a par with me, because I had one with Melloney!" He playfully jabbed me on the arm. I fought back a grimace. "Say! Do you want me to go down the gym and beat up this arsehole who's been sniffing around Sophie?" Rambo suddenly looked a little sheepish. "I guess we're fifty-fifty on the Rebecca thing, *I* shouldn't have said anything and *you* shouldn't have lied."

I nodded my concurrence but only at the last part of the sentence. "Don't worry about it, it's not *your* fault, it was totally *mine*. I panicked under the influence of alcohol and opened my big fat gob once to often. As a less violent alternative to beating this bloke up I *could* phone her and try and set things straight," I said. "I

181

knew there was something else upsetting her but I thought it was just the three witches, and I was so involved in sorting out the Fish-In I let it all slide. Now it *is* about the three witches, or at least having sex with one of them, and as it now turns out, it *was* about bloody Rebecca! You know, I wondered when you lot were all taking my photo with the mind-meld mirror, whether I'd ever live to regret what had happened in her bedroom." I looked wistfully at Rambo. "Sometimes I wish I had a bit of your life, uncluttered, no ties, no responsibility… I guess the grass is always greener until you get to walk on it."

Rambo wiped his nose. "We want all things, but only *some* of the time," he said wisely and then he stared at me in the artificial light. "The three *witches*?" he said questioningly.

"It's what I call them in my head," I told him. "Not a good analogy physically but they sure can cast a spell."

Rambo lifted up his head. "Now I get the broomstick reference. Look, why don't we concentrate on winning the Fish-In?" Rambo suggested leaving all else aside. "Another thirty or so hours, or whatever's left isn't going to make any difference. Let's concentrate on giving this our best shot and then, when it's over I'll help you sort it. Don't phone her up, it'll be much harder over the phone, wait until you see her face to face. Whatever comes back to Sophie's ears, if in fact anything does concerning the witches, I can always say it wasn't true. We can concoct a story to put you in the clear. If we stick together, we can ride out the storm on a horse named denial. As for Rebecca, you can always plead memory loss, being drunk, any old shit like that and I can always vouch for your impeccable behaviour."

"Okay," I agreed feeling better. "Cheers, mate. You're the best. A true top man and a gent."

"Good," said Rambo.

This was turning out to be beyond my wildest hopes. No beating up from Rambo over my Melina moment *and* he was going to help me dupe Sophie if it happened to get back to her. Like a true male friend he was willing to lie to her over Rebecca and the Lac Fumant 1st time trip. What a star he was! On the other hand I might be a complete arsehole, but I might also be a complete arsehole who could get away with it! *Again!*

"It *is* our word against no substantiated evidence," I said. What a conniving little sod I was.

Okay, I told myself, I would lie this time, just this once, and promise never, ever to be unfaithful again. Briefly I wondered how many times I had actually lied to Sophie. Usually it was to go fishing, or catch ghosts or hide my infidelity that's all, nothing too heavy! I had a quick tot-up. Fucking hundreds. It would serve me right if she did have a fling with this gym bloke, but I knew she wouldn't. She was too decent, as I had recognised time and time again.

Thinking aloud I asked. "Who do you think the bloke is?"

Rambo shrugged. "How the hell would I know? He's just some fucking bloke chancing his luck to get a leg over. It happens all the time, Sophie's very attractive, she must get loads of come-ons, perhaps not as many as the witches because she doesn't walk around advertising it, but the difference this time is she's a bit vulnerable because she thinks you *might* have played away. *Might*. She won't do *anything*, you mark my words, she's always stood by you before. A bit of flirting won't harm her, or you, and I'm one hundred percent certain that's the extent of all she's done. Probably the difference is, in Melloney's eyes, if it had been her, it would lead to an affair. Melloney *isn't* Sophie," Rambo added emphatically.

I nodded, my feelings exactly. Sophie *had* stuck by me before and I felt both better and then worse when I thought of it. I didn't deserve her and she didn't deserve me at times. I would make it up to her, if I could get away with my infidelity on two counts. If she found out, well then I might not have the opportunity, but as I reminded myself, she might never know. Not for certain. I perked up. Good old Rambo, he would help me out of this torrid mess. Again. Like he had helped me in all the others I had got myself into. I would have to try and repay him by winning this Fish-In with him. As he had rightly said, another day and a bit wouldn't make any odds so I had better put all my energies as best I could into the fishing. It was the least I could do.

Once Rambo had gone back to his bivvy I tucked myself up in my bag and thought what a lucky boy I was. My despair, so deep and total shortly after Melina had gone had lifted, and the flicker of egotism burned a little brighter now I could see I might get away with my act of betrayal. The boot was hovering somewhere near the other foot – what with this bloke trying to pull Sophie – and I tried to imagine how gutted I would have been if Sophie had done to me what I had done to her. Twice! *And* she had stuck by me after I had 'Al Qaedaed' Watt's bivvy! Quite rightly my egotism was snuffed out with this thought. Matt Williams, I told myself, you are a complete shit at times. I was so lucky to have a partner who stuck to the proper rules, even if I occasionally didn't. 'Occasionally', I mean, how many times does it take? Once is bad enough!

Fortunately my Melina moment from the Rambo angle had been completely put to bed. Now all we had to do was win the Fish-In, trim the M and Ms in the process, beat the Yanks, pick up the cheque, deny *everything* in terms of other women and if push came to shove *I* could go down the gym and empty the Glock into Mr Motivator and Sophie could stick by me once more as I wiled away a life sentence in prison. There wouldn't be much sexual temptation in there, not unless I went on the turn. I reached into my rucksack and felt the cool metal of the gun's handle. Perhaps I could shoot the M and Ms if we were losing with a few minutes to go? Not very sporting, although animal activists might be impressed with two cowhide-clad anglers being gunned down. Nah! They were so on the case I expect their lederhosen were bulletproof!

At 10:45am, right on the very last knockings of prime time feeding, I had another low thirty mirror effectively cancelling out the M and Ms last fish. Their lead was back to the thirty-pound range, which by Hamworthy Fisheries standards meant one fish. One fish to claw back and then we would be level. Rambo jutted out his jaw a little further to prove, as if I didn't know already, how serious he was over winning. The large St George's Cross he had pegged out across two old storm-poles rippled in the slight breeze. 'We're fishing for England {In-ger-land}. We're playing the fish. We're singing for England {In-ger-land}. Team Rambo is gonna be number one'. (To the tune of 'World in Motion'.) Not that we were jingoistic or xenophobic, just pretending to represent our country, like you do!

Pup and Melissa decided to stay in swim nine after they had verified the Fish-In's latest carp – the one I had caught at the end of the feeding spell. A couple of hours later and it was time for *us* to have a little feed, so the four of us sat outside our own respective bivvy homes, drinking tea, eating the last of the chicken from the barbecue and munching biscuits. At least three of us tried, despite being engaged in refreshment, to will the four rods representing Team Rambo into life. Melissa merely sunbathed, and who knew what she was thinking, but I would have wagered a fair sum it wasn't rattling indicators. She did hitch up her skirt so the sun's rays could reach the parts my eyes hadn't seen, but had now, and I looked on in force of habit rather than lust. May God be my expert witness – if he ever did stuff like that, or jury service, or reality TV. 'Okay, God, we want you to eat the bush tucker right now!'

'Eat it? I fucking made it, you stupid cunt!'

That Rotten God, always out for sensationalism, cheap headlines and maximum exposure. Everyone knows it was all down to Evolution. Nice language though, the type us couch potato deadheads can relate to.

My mobile, the one sitting in Pup's pocket stayed mute – that was cool – but so did our alarms, which wasn't. The day became much hotter as it moved into the afternoon – that wasn't cool either – I moved into the shade – a little cooler – the St George's Cross stopped rippling altogether and Melissa's skin started to glisten with sweat – same as before on the looking front. Her sunbathing *was* stopping her smoking but what she saved on the lung cancer roundabout she was losing on the melanoma swings. That's the trouble with living, it kills you.

The day was turning into a bit of a scorcher. With little or no conviction I fired out some of my dog mixers. I knew until the day I keeled over and pegged out a box of dog mixer would be synonymous with doggy-style fornication with Melina – eldest of the Witches of Eastwick. They were bastards to kneel on, another interesting fact brought to my attention, and also, on this occasion, uninspiring in terms of making carp come on the feed. For some reason the carp in Hamworthy never seemed prone to taking mixers off the top, although one of the first forties, the aptly named Lassie *had* been caught off the top on one. Ever heard that one before? One of the many, legendary all-embracing generalisms associated with the fine art of carp fishing. But in this instance partially true. If you're ever rich enough or lucky enough to secure a place in Hamworthy you'll have a go at finding out, until then you'll have to take the word of the Supreme Syndicate Leader.

I watched the mixers gradually float down to my right on an invisible, gentle underwater tow. The water was dead calm, not even a ripple disturbed its mirror-like surface. After ten minutes a small group of mallards came in and gobbled up most of the mixers.

"Did they forecast this heat?" I asked Rambo who had stripped down to his waist. "I can remember them saying it would be fine but I don't recall them saying it was going to be this hot."

"To be honest I didn't check the weather before I left home and I haven't had the radio on much," he replied.

I barely listened to Rambo's reply as I was distracted by his superb, powerful physique and how his tattoos rippled as he moved. I don't know about October or early November, he would have thrashed me straight into Boxing Day. Ha-ha. I turned away before Melissa started to think *I* was a gay carp angler like she had so incorrectly assumed Horst and Helmut to be. I sneaked a look at her out the corner of my eye and caught her sneaking a look at Rambo out the corner of *her* eye. If he could sort out a new bait roller we could trust to make our baits he might have the opportunity to get the full set even yet. Then he could nip back a generation and do the floral print Eurodome, if he felt so inclined. I couldn't see it happening to be honest.

Chapter 16

Evening came, and dusk with it, at the end of a very sticky, anti-climatic day. Now this might sound like a contradiction in terms but I can assure you it was true, you're just thinking of the wrong bodily fluid. Our initial burst of captures, from the time when I had figuratively stepped into Pup's bivvy slippers, were consigned to ancient history as the long, hot day wore on with no action and seemingly no prospect of action. Frustration reigned. In truth it was our own suspense and anxiety that contributed to the situation as much as the heat and fishing conditions, after all, my last fish had not even been more than twelve hours ago. In carp angling terms this was a time span so modest, a break in takes so small, it shouldn't have unduly fazed a couple of experienced 'old hands' like ourselves. But it had, due to the pressure. Up and down England there were umpteen carp anglers fishing large, sparse, low-density-of-fish-stock, headbanger waters, where to them, twelve hours equated to eight minutes and thirty-four seconds – I worked it out – in their fishing time. The difference being they had until they went completely round the twist or died of boredom, where we had until ten o'clock tomorrow. Time was not a plentiful commodity as far as Team Rambo was concerned, hence the pressure, hence the suspense and anxiety, hence more pressure. These things are called vicious circles, our circle was armed with an obscene looking hunting knife and a motorbike chain, and its name was Sid. (Sid *Vicious*! How many times must I tell you! Oh, and by the way, while we're on the subject of Sex Pistol members, did you get the 'Rotten God' reference? Good! Pleased to hear it.)

Due to this pressure, anxiety, whatever you would like to term it, we had the first signs of a desperate aura in swim nine. The desperate aura was lurking and skulking in between our bivvies, poking its tongue out at us and making childish farting noises every time one of us bent over. The aura hung in the hot air with no brisk south-westerly to disperse it and it threatened to severely disrupt our campaign to bag the *charedee* cheque. We *needed* another fish. And we needed it soon. Our only consolation was that the stalled bus in which we found ourselves trapped also had every other participating angler on board as well. Pup and Melissa's continued presence in swim nine proved the very point. My silent mobile, the one nestling in Pup's pocket, underlined it.

During the afternoon, to stave off our lurking desperation and to ease our angst, we had tried to buy a bite. After much discussion we had decided on a change of emphasis, which might tease us out a carp. Consequently we had fished *two* rods on a Zig Rig rather than one, the idea being two rods gave us the best in probability terms and the most suitable balance. One rod on the Zig didn't seem bold enough or capable of giving the tactic a fair crack of the whip, whereas *three* on the Zig would have compromised our safety net in what had worked so well up until now. Three on the Zig, we concluded, was simply *too* bold and four was instantly dismissed as being right out and away with the fairies in cloud-cuckoo desperation land. However, to have fished on the same, with four *bottom* baits, appeared the indolent, easy option. To have sat back and let the rods fish themselves, without trying *anything* would have bordered irresponsible. So we hadn't. What we *had* done was to agonize, bounce ideas and for-instances back and forth at each other and eventually formulate our cunning plan. The cunning plan that hadn't worked!

By evening I had reckoned that if I'd had access to an Acme Parallel Universe Viewer and it had told the soul-destroying tale of us choosing the wrong option, I would have considered shooting myself with the Glock. Considered, and then rejected out of hand – much like the carp had our baits of late. As it turned out all our worry and high-level strategic discussions were rendered utterly pointless. For, as Pup and Melissa's presence in swim nine etcetera, etcetera, had proved, *nothing* would have worked any better than anything else because *nothing* worked at all. Every idea was reduced to failure because something had switched off the Hamworthy carp and not *one* angler, in any swim, received the slightest hint of action. I shouldn't have complained, not with how it had fished so far, yet nevertheless I was a grumpy little bunny muttering morose incantations under my breath as I prepared for sleep.

The last big decision we had taken before the light went and it was time to get our heads down, was how much bait to put in before we had recast all four rods, with bottom baits, to set the night-time traps. We knew this decision was likely to prove even more important than the earlier attempt to fluke out a carp on a scratching tactic. In fact it was likely to be the conclusive decision for the whole event. I imagined the M and Ms deliberating in a similar fashion, twisting their moustaches between thumbs and forefingers, running their hands over their mullets and buffing their lederhosen with top quality imported Dutch dubbin as a nervous reaction to their almighty carping conundrum. Undoubtedly they had asked themselves pretty much the same as we had. How much bait was already sitting out on the four spots? How much should we top up? How much were the carp likely to feed? How much *had* the carp fed? Was it time to open up another spot? Would they be our last four casts if we had no action? When was the time to make the decision that they were/weren't to be the last four casts? How much wood could a wood chuck chuck, if a wood chuck could chuck wood? And other such dilemmas.

The suspense – in waiting for the answers – was killing me, not *had been* killing me, *was* continuing to kill me. As I lay in the dark I hoped and prayed we had got the balance somewhere right. If a carp or two did feed on our spots, I thought to myself, let's just hope we had a baiting situation conducive to getting the one pick up we needed to haul in the M and Ms. I listened for my buzzers wondering if one would go in the next five seconds. And when that five-seconds had passed I wondered if it would go in the next five seconds. And then the same again. And again. I was living a life in five-second increments – plus the time in between the five seconds when the cassette in my head looped to the beginning, if you want to be pedantic – and it wasn't necessarily a healthy thing to be doing. In an attempt to forget this – as when you inexplicably become aware of having to breathe in bed at night – I tried to think of something else. My recent sexual misdemeanours, plural, recent – as in the last few years – coming to the fore were hardly any better, and the thought of Sophie even *thinking* about getting up to something similar made my stomach knot.

I sat up on my bedchair. As soon as the Fish-In was over, I told myself, I would zoom home, lavish her with unctuous charm, and try to sort out the recent deterioration in our relationship. And never look at another woman. Okay, let's be sensible; never touch another woman. All right, let's be practical; never *touch* another woman with sexual intent or in a manner *construed* to be promoting the intention of sexual intent (a bit more ambiguous). And even if I *did*, accidentally, when I was drunk or something, never, *ever* to take up on it. I put my head back on the pillow and closed my eyes.

That buzzer's going to go in a second. One thousand and one, one thousand and two, one thousand and three, one thousand and four, one thousand and five.

That buzzer's going to go in a second. One thousand and one, one thousand and two, one thousand and three, one thousand and four, one thousand and five.

That buzzer's going to go in a second. One thousand and one, one thousand and two, one thousand and three, one thousand and four, one thousand and five.

That buzzer's going to go in a second. One thousand and one, one thousand and two, one thousand and three, one thousand and four, one thousand and five.

That buzzer's going to go in a second. One thousand and one, one thousand and two, one thousand and three, one thousand and four, one thousand and five.

I sat up. *Fucking hell!* This was mental, or I would be in a few more minutes. I stormed out of my bivvy and down to Rambo's.

"Are you awake?" I asked urgently.

"I am *now*," said the voice from deep within. "Let me guess. You can't sleep because…" Rambo's voice tailed away in sleep-driven weariness, "… There's too many reasons why, I can picture that. Why don't you come back in the morning for a full consultation?"

It went quiet. I knew a brush off when I heard one. I slowly turned away from Rambo's bivvy door and a glowing red tip caught my eye. Melissa, as befitting her title of Rizla Queen, was having a fag outside her bivvy. I couldn't have noticed her as I had rushed down to Rambo, all stressed and hyper. Maybe I needed one, but then I remembered I didn't smoke. I walked over and could see she was sitting down, the insides of her elbows resting on her pulled up knees. I sat down beside her and mimicked her body position.

"I was gasping," she explained.

"Well, you didn't have one *all* afternoon," I said trying to make it sound as if I wasn't being sarcastic because I wasn't. "What with catching all those rays," I explained.

She cocked her head back and blew out some smoke. I looked through it to the stars.

"I love looking at the stars when I'm fishing," I said. "Hamworthy is great for seeing them, there's so little light spillage around here because we're miles from anywhere."

Melissa looked up and stared at them. It was a perfectly clear moonless night and the stars glittered in magical splendour. That Big Bang was some big bang and was also known as – as I had read in a cartoon some years back, about a kid who was miffed at the dull phrase for the most amazing event of all time – The Horrendous Space Kablooie!

"What is it they say?" Melissa asked herself. "Even when you're lying on your back in the gutter, you can still look at the stars."

"Something like that," I agreed. "Oscar Wilde? If it wasn't him who said it, it definitely wasn't the well-known porn star, Oscar Rodgers, either!" I said chuckling. "They *do* symbolise aspiration. Only sometimes," I added, thinking as I had earlier of the huge distances to them, "it's unobtainable aspiration."

"Do you know what I aspire to?" Melissa surprisingly asked.

"No," I admitted.

"A better life," she said.

"I suppose we all would like that," I said.

Melissa expanded. "Yes, but *completely* better. A life *far* removed from one I'm ever capable of making for myself." She turned and looked at me as she stubbed out her roll-up into the ground. I never had gone and picked up the dog end she had chucked on the grass. "Would you ever condemn anyone for taking a chance on getting that life?" she asked me.

"I guess not," I said, a bit unsure of what she was driving at.

"Don't judge me harshly when I take my chance," she said. "And don't worry too much over my sisters. I'll keep them in check and make sure they don't divulge your little secret. As long as you keep what I tell you to yourself for a bit longer," she said smiling. "Deal?"

I nodded. She held out her hand for me to shake it. I shook it. She was going to do something, I could tell. What it was I didn't know, but I had the feeling Pup was going to be a lot more lonely at some vaguely undetermined point in the future. My psychic powers were crud.

"What are you thinking of doing?" I asked her.

Melissa shook her head and lowered her face to the ground. "I won't tell you yet but I expect you've already guessed... I'm going back to sleep," Melissa told me, her voice shaky and distressed. "Goodnight, Matt."

"Yeah, goodnight, Melissa," I said softly.

In spite of the darkness, I felt as if I could see her eyes welling with tears. I never knew witches could cry, even ones who were married, even ones who might end up divorced. I wondered who the third party might be, the third party who could offer her this wonderful life. Rambo? Hardly. Brad? Yeah, Brad was the favourite. He had the money and lifestyle she could aspire to all right. I expect in a few months' time he would come back, they would get in contact and then she would be gone. I could have been right all along over the two of them and they might well have got intimate the night she stayed and 'chatted'. Whatever. It wasn't going to affect me catching or not catching another bloody carp but if she was true to her word with keeping her sisters in check then that was fine and dandy by me.

Alone once more with my thoughts I wandered down to my rods and gazed out over the water to the island where we had dug up the ghost's bones. Where was her spirit now she had finally been laid to rest? Yet again I pondered on the rank improbability of my life as created by carp fishing. How could a hobby, a pastime, a pursuit, whatever you wanted to call it, have such a profound effect on an individual? And I didn't mean from the stereotypical obsessive angle – the angle where it had all started out for me – but from a much wider, weirder perspective. For example, the unusual people I had met, the wide range of men, the handful of women, and how could I forget the fucking dog as well? I felt a sharp pang of remorse for the huge ex-Rottweiler. Would I ever witness anything so vivid as the Rambo/Spunker fist fight in the storm again in my life? Then there were the adventures it had created; the tight squeezes, the arguments, the laughs, the tensions, the excitements, the adulteries, the psychic phenomena, the wealth, the sex *and* the violence. To name but a few! Where would it end? What was round the corner? What was the next bombshell to fall into my life, my carp fishing life? Short-term it was the bastard – in the nicest context of affectionate vernacular – M and Ms catching another fish. Long-term? Who could dare guess? For all I knew Melina had been on the phone to Sophie – in spite of Melissa's reassurances – and told her of our little 'adventure' and Sophie was preparing the separation papers even as I thought. Could you split a gravel pit in half? Or would she make me sell up and give her half in hard cash? I couldn't sell for five-years! I think that was detailed in the small print Mr Furlington had pointed out concerning the restrictions of my inheritance. Shit! The financial repercussions of my flings hadn't figured greatly in my soul-searching. Perhaps – hold on – definitely they most unequivocally should have! I could lose the fucking lot! All for a couple of rub outs – worst case scenario.

It *couldn't* come to that. I had to believe it wouldn't go that far, it wouldn't have been fair. So when did impartiality ever enter into the equation of existence, I asked myself? Misfortune dumped on the good and wicked in equal measure. But come on, to lose so much over so little? I mean it wasn't as if I had *killed* anyone. I had killed Michael, I reminded myself, without Rambo's efforts and mine he would still be alive today. That didn't count, I argued, he *deserved* to die. We administered justice not murder.

I looked round the dark Hamworthy Fisheries. I looked at the pit and the old wood behind me and realised I could, in theory, forfeit it all. All because my switch had been flicked by the wrong woman a couple of times. Why didn't I have a Greed Monster who was strong enough to quell the ambitions of my Lust Monster? It wouldn't have done any good, I told myself, greed comes in many forms, not solely financial. What I needed, apart from a carp on the bank, was a High Ethic Laser Gun to zap any Monster who materialised in my head, and *not* a poxy Glock 17. If I used the more traditional firearm my brains really would be plastered to the inside of my skull. Where my skull would be was another matter entirely.

I had better *try* and get some sleep, I thought.

The short night did pass, even if it had seemed interminably long, and I awoke – so I must have fallen asleep – in early morning daylight. It was now 4:30am and still, despite fifty-six traps being set, nothing else had been caught. (*Were* there any bloody carp in this place or had it been netted out, with amazing stealth, right under our very noses?) Rambo and I were both up and searching for clues to their whereabouts. There were no discussions over the causes of my insomnia, no talk of Government education policy, world hunger, the fight against terrorism and absolutely no swapping of notes on the slightly touchy subject of Melina's sexual performance! Actually comparing Rambo's sexual performance and mine was the touchy subject, touchy for me that is! I wasn't *too* bothered, I could live with being marked a close second to the big man. Anyway *none* of those subjects were broached because more important matters were pressing. Let the Earth grind to a halt on its axis, let the Sun fall from the sky, let some 'A' list celebrity break a false nail – it mattered not a jot – this was fishing-head-on time. *Big-time!* We scanned the pit for evidence of carp. Rambo used his binoculars and in a subtle indication of the seriousness of the situation, didn't crack a solitary joke revolving around Panther tanks being on the horizon. One rolling fish within range was what we sought, not WWII tanks, one single fish that could be the pointer on which we could act. As hard as we looked we couldn't see one, neither carp nor Panther tank.

"What are we going to do?" I asked him. "Sit it out or do something desperate?"

Rambo gave me a thin-lipped smile. "I think we've got to sit it out in a desperate style, boy," he answered. "Not unless something crops up that we feel is worth taking a crack at. You see, it's a totally different situation from yesterday afternoon. We *are* coming up to a prime feeding time and I think we've got the balance of bait somewhere about right. I can't see any advantage in moving spots or changing tactics at this moment so we'll have to tough it out and hope for the best."

"You're the boss, boss," I told him.

Rambo winked. "We'll pull it out the fire, boy. We always do!"

I gave him a wan smile and never bothered to ask whether he was trying to kid himself, kid myself, or kid any carp that might have been listening. (They *do* listen you know, they bug your main line and can pick up conversation as easy as anything.) The conditions still looked cack to me; no wind, no cloud and it felt as if it would be another hot summer's day. Takes were going to continue to be a rare occurrence and we were still one fish behind the M and Ms. Physically there was nothing left for us to do other than to sit it out and hope we had set our traps correctly. Here, in a nutshell, we had the very essence of carp fishing; the waiting game. All that could possibly be done had been done and only time would tell if it had been enough. The time – the remaining time until Judgement Hour, unusually for a carp angler as I had mentioned earlier – was dictated not by the need to return to work, or home life, or to replenish food/bait stocks, or have a wash, or by rota restrictions, or by mental illness, or by tedium induced mortality, but by the competition rules. Ten o'clock this morning was the time when we would be judged. I looked at my watch, five hours to go. If I knew time it would seem more like two, not unless we caught one and leap-frogged into the lead, then if there were, say, three hours left, it would seem like six. Alfred E was right; time was relative, relative to what you were doing with it.

"Morning, lads. Anything happening?"

It was Pup, boiliemeister supreme, time warp kitted carp angler, newly-wed and official fish weight verifier for the second half of the inaugural Hamworthy Fish-In. The same Pup who was likely to become another divorce statistic within his first year of marriage – if Melissa reached for the stars like she said she would.

"Fuck all, mate," I said sulkily, swigging the cup of tea I had in my hand. "The pit's switched off big-style. No one phoned you up in the night did they?" I asked, looking for confirmation.

"No." Pup looked down at his clipboard. "Do you want to know the *exact* state of play, so far?"

Rambo and I both turned to him and said 'yes' in stereo.

"Horst and Helmut are in the lead by exactly thirty-two pounds and nine ounces," Pup informed us, "and you lead Brad and Tom by the massive, insurmountable weight of around eighty, 18mm boilies."

"So how much is that?" I asked.

"Have a guess," said Pup.

"Round or pellet shaped boilies?" I queried.

"Round," Pup replied.

"What sort of mix?" Rambo enquired.

"Birdseed," Pup told him.

"With or *without* the golf ball-like indentations allowing you to draw or fade them with a throwing stick should you possess the required technique to do such a thing?" I said.

"With," said Pup.

I looked at Rambo and pulled a corner of my mouth trainer-ward. "A pound?"

Pup snorted in derision.

"Ten ounces?" Rambo guessed.

"Miles out!" said Pup.

"Well come on then, tell us!" I said.

"Eleven. Eleven ounces," Pup said.

"Christ! I was only an ounce out!" said Rambo indignantly. "A few boilies out! That's all, how can that be 'miles out'?"

"Even one boilie's a boilie," said Pup, standing his ground.

"One 18mm boilie's *nothing*," challenged Rambo.

"*You*," said Pup pointing a finger at Rambo, "wouldn't want it on the end of your nose for a wart!"

I burst into laughter. "A nose *stud*, maybe! The new must-have trendy accessory for all hip carp anglers! You'd have to hair rig it onto your pierced nose! It'd be a bit of a palaver when you had to change it, what with baiting needles and eyes being in such close proximity but you *would* have to change it though. Especially when it got a bit tatty because some mouse had been nibbling at it while you were asleep in your bivvy!" I was in full flight now. "You'd have to have a colour co-ordinated boilie stop or else it'd look a bit naff, and one of those ones that embeds in, not the old-fashioned dumb-bell type, *and* you'd have to pick a fruity flavour! You wouldn't want to go round with something like Secret Agent wafting up your nose all day! A fluoro would look good, nice and bright, and if you could get one to glow in the dark that might look cool. If you could ever look cool with a boilie hanging off your hooter, that is! Of course, if you had a nose ring you could hang *stringers* off of that! PVA wouldn't been any good, you'd have to use mono or braid or you'd be grovelling on the floor picking up your carp bait jewellery every time it rained or you sneezed!" I said snorting with laughter.

"Have you finished?" Rambo asked.

"I think so," I said, wiping the tears of mirth from my eyes.

Rambo puffed out his cheeks. "Thank God for that…"

Pup's mobile, no! *My* mobile that was in *Pup's* pocket – I keep forgetting – burst into life. Rambo and I froze, our expressions locked in horror at who might be making the call.

Pup answered. "Hello, Horst," he flicked his eyes up to us and widened them. "Helmut's just had one, has he? Okay, we'll be right down. Bye."

Pup put my phone in his pocket. "Bad news I'm afraid, lads. Let's hope it's not too big!"

By the time Pup and a subdued Melissa had returned with the news of Happy Helmut the Headless Helmet-Head's scraper thirty common there were only four and a quarter hours left. Sixty-three pounds five ounces was now the significant deficit but perhaps even more importantly it was now *two* fish we needed.

"I like those two," Pup admitted to Rambo and I, "even though they're winning and giving us a bit of a carp fishing lesson on our own water."

"It's *not* over yet!" said Rambo, his arms folded defensively across his chest, the muscles in his forearms clearly bulging now he was down to his camo tee shirt. "I pulled it off in the TWTT, Matt caught the mind-meld mirror, last gasp, at Lac Fumant, and we discovered the… er… fish knickers on here just in time."

Pup looked bemused. "You're talking English but *I* can't understand a word of it."

Rambo ignored Pup who decided it was time to go and see what his wife was up to. "What do the tea leaves say, boy?" he said as Pup wandered off.

I looked into my mug of tea that I was drinking. "Sod all! There aren't any, I use tea bags!"

"Some psychic you are!" Rambo scoffed. "Even *I* knew the M and Ms were going to get another one."

"Well I knew that as *well*!" I said. "That's just natural pessimism and the fear of what you *don't* want to happen, happening. Sometimes it do, and sometimes it don't, matey and there ain't no clairvoyance involved, I can assure you!" I said stupidly.

"It's funny not being able to see them, isn't it?" said Rambo on another tack.

"Who? The M and Ms?" I said.

Rambo nodded. I laughed. "In the TWTT I could actually *see* Watt sitting by his rods, the shithouse! It's *so* different this time. I want to win just as much but it's driven by self-esteem, the charity money would be nice, and a little by the desire to avoid embarrassment. I don't want to lose on my own water to someone who's never even seen it before, let alone fished it before. Imagine what it's like for the other members who have been here for much longer, I mean, it is only our second year." I tilted my head in admission. "What I'm *not* driven by this time is pure hatred of the people we're fishing against. This time there's been no stroke pulling and everyone has behaved impeccably, carp fishing has united us rather than ripped us apart. No little cliques, no petty jealousies, no hidden agendas, only twenty-nine blokes from all over the world enjoying their favourite way of spending time. Pup's right, they are top anglers, you know, respect where it's due. Anyone who can beat us on our own patch is a *top* angler! I added jokingly.

"Very profound, boy," said Rambo. "Even you screwing my girlfriend didn't ruin the party!"

I reddened a little. "You were screwing her *sister*!"

"Ah!" Rambo pointed out. "But *you* didn't know that!"

My head lowered. "Fair point. You know I thought you might beat me to a pulp when you found out."

Rambo gave me a considered look. "Anyone else and I would have! I haven't beaten anyone up since… Rocky! I must be mellowing in my old age! Anyone else but you, boy, would have got a right old pasting! Disregarding Melloney and what I was up to with her, believe me. Like I said to you earlier, when you don't care it doesn't hurt, there's no vulnerability, that aside anyone else would have copped it on principle. I shouldn't really tell you this but I'd let you get away with most things, you know."

"*Really?*" I said, genuinely humbled by what Rambo was saying.

"Yeah! You're a good mate, the only true friend I've ever made outside of my army/mercenary/arms dealing life, if I stop and think. We do share a bond, the one that started outside that pub all those years ago, a bond that is the love of carp fishing and the crack that has gone hand in hand with it. And *what* a crack! Have you ever sat and thought how amazing the things are that have happened to us?" I raised my eyebrows up my forehead. Rambo understood their meaning. "Yeah, okay. Of course you have, probably every single day, every single *hour* of every single day! That's your penchant, worrying and analysing. But, no, it is *amazing*! You'd need to write a book…"

"I *did*! *Remember*! In the gulag!"

"… Oh, yeah!" said Rambo remembering now I'd jogged his memory. "But that was the *first* bit! You'd need to write, what? *Three* more to get up to now?"

"Three more is about right," I agreed.

"How d'you think the latest one will end?" Rambo asked.

"I haven't the foggiest," I admitted.

"Some psychic you are," said Rambo.

"And I haven't been abducted," I added.

"Maybe that'll be the big finish," Rambo ruminated. "The big finale, right at the end, before the reader hits the inside back cover!"

Possibly, I thought, but I wouldn't be holding my breath on it.

There was a little over an hour to go, my watch confirmed the remarkable statistic. Whoosh! Thirty-four and a half hours gone in a flash! The big finale, as far as the Fish-In was concerned, was not far away. The big finale for Team Rambo, in terms of us busting out a couple of quick carp and winning, was light-years away. Having said that, I had just had a little liner knock on the rod that had produced our last fish – the one I had caught twenty years ago – on the last knockings of prime feeding time yesterday. If a run came at the same time it would be too late. 10:00am and it would be curtains for us.

Both of us had flinched at the double beep and both of us had looked at each other and smiled and had said; 'Pup's wedding!'. Pup had looked up from his bait catalogue and Melissa, who had hardly said a word all day, carried on sunbathing. It wasn't quite so nice for sunbathing as it had been yesterday because the odd cloud had started to drift very slowly in from the south-west. Melissa stoically ignored the sun going in and I noticed she was smoking *and* sunbathing today. She must have needed her nicotine input to calm her nerves prior to her voyage to the stars, and I wondered if she had any concept of when the lift-off was due to take place. The capricious zephyr that gently nudged the few small puffs of cloud over our heads was hardly the big south-westerly I had hoped for. Although I did feel a little more confident of catching one more fish, it went without saying – but I will – the M and Ms must have felt similarly. However, I certainly wasn't confident of catching *two* more than whatever they caught.

Unfortunately it was more or less a dead cert we were going to lose and be the runners-up in a winner-takes-all competition. If either of us had any fishing rabbits in the hat – as opposed to the psychic hat trick I was on – now was the hour to hoick one out by its long, fluffy ears with an extravagant theatrical flourish and a jubilant cry of 'Hey Presto!'

Bum! The one piece of kit I had left out of my rucksack appeared to be my top hat!

Ten minutes later, with me in a mindset of having handed the Fish-In and all its spoils to the M and Ms, the same rod that had had the liner went off on a slow deliberate take. Consider my auxiliary switch, *switched*! I lent into the fish, the fish that was eighty odd yards away from me, and felt a heavy resistance transmit itself down my burgundy-dipped (tart!) $2^3/4$lb test curve Harrison Ballista Slim.

"Good one?" Rambo questioned.

Carp on long lines are notoriously hard to put a weight on, but it was no scamp of a common knock-knock-knocking on my door. It did *feel* a good fish.

"It's the winner," I said winking.

"Good," said Rambo. "Let's hope it is."

All those in swim nine, namely Pup, Melissa and Rambo formed an audience behind me as I played the carp. In spite of my little joke to Rambo about the fish being the winner, I didn't feel overly nervous because it obviously wasn't. There was no huge amount of weed to cause undue concern and as long as the hook stayed put and if nothing calamitous occurred, I should land it fairly comfortably. 'Ifs' and 'ands', I know, but I had a feeling I would be all right. Fifteen minutes later I was starting to wonder. I was still leaning into the fish; the fish that was *forty* odd yards away from me, and still feeling a heavy resistance transmit itself down my burgundy-dipped (tart!) $2^3/4$lb test curve Harrison Ballista Slim.

"Any time today, boy!" said Rambo gently.

The heavy resistance continued to plod up and down in a slow unhurried, yet powerful manner. This was a lump – it had to be! Rambo had dipped all three other rods as a precaution to the aforementioned lump picking up another line and it was a good job he had. My unseen adversary stomped right over the top of Rambo's lines and I had to exert the maximum pressure possible to turn it back and then try to gain some line. Even Melissa, who wasn't herself at all but an introspective, introverted version, perked up and took enough interest to drag her thoughts away from pre-blast off contemplation.

"Go on, Matt," she said excitedly, jumping up and down on the spot. "Land the bugger!"

"I'm doing my best," I said coolly, my eyes never leaving where my line hit the water.

"I wonder if it's foul-hooked?" I heard Rambo say.

"Don't start all that nonsense again!" I said. "In any case, I'm fresh out of hand grenades!"

"What does he mean by that?" Melissa asked Rambo.

"Well, a long time ago me and the boy got, how shall I say, *involved* in a rather long-winded, extremely bitter, carp angling competition. Now…"

I closed my ears and concentrated on the lump on the end of my line. On the spur of the moment I wondered if Melissa thought *I* was the route to the stars, what with all my wealth, and she was going to offer her body and soul to me in return for it. Only, *dipshit*, I wouldn't have much wealth if I left Sophie for her, might not have it in any case if her sisters shouted their gobs off. I don't know – get a smart rod in your hand with a big bend in it from a lump of a carp and all of a sudden a headful of delusions of grandeur! Mind you, not the first *or* the last carp angler to suffer from that one!

The lump was much closer now, much, much closer. It was so close I caught a fleeting glimpse of it through the clear water. Now as we all know, the old adage of fish looking bigger in water due to the supposed magnifying properties of said water, is complete, and may I add, utter bollocks. Fish look *smaller* in water, end of argument. They just do. However, the lump on the end of my line, with full recognition of the statement earlier, looked – searching for a suitable adjective – *fucking* enormous. I blinked my eyes. A trick of the light? My imagination running riot? An unusual, unearthly patch of proportion-distorting water? Perhaps I had been bitten in the night by a rabied bat or mosquito or earthworm and impending hydrophobia was ruining my sense of fish-size judgement. The lump rolled on the surface. Three gasps wafted against the slight south-westerly, came to my shoulders, hovered, and then drifted into my ears, turned on every available alarm in my head, jangled my optic nerves, started a small fire in my cerebral cortex, nipped down to my stomach, put my intestines through a rusty old mangle, hitched up my scrotum to give me an insight into Steve's agony, connected my heart to a small, portable compressor, whizzed the gauge up to within three PSI of its bursting point, stripped the bones out of both my legs, instantly wasted away seventy percent of my muscle bulk and increased phlegm production in the bronchial tubes within my lungs by a similar amount. For the first time in the fight I thought I was going to lose the fish. Now why *was* that? Answers on the back of a signed, blank cheque.

"Look at the size of that!" screeched Pup. "It's a submarine!"

Frantically my mind popped up photos of previous carp captures. Nope, bigger than that one! Bigger than *that* one! Bigger than that one as well! *No* contest with that one! The mind-meld mirror? I swallowed, bigger than *that* one as well!

The fish rolled on the surface again and then got its head down and powered away stripping line off my clutch.

Melissa screamed. "Don't lose it, Matt! Don't lose it!"

Her piercing voice – she probably used it on her belly-button – cut me in half but in a strange way helped snap me out of my oh-my-God-it's-going-on-a-run-and-I-don't-want-the-hook-to-pull-out state of ephemeral paralysis. This was my match point at Wimbledon, my penalty at 1-1 in the World Cup Final, my two-foot putt for the British Open and boy did I know it! We've all been through it – probably many times – every time it *really* means something. Luckily I controlled the carp's plunge for freedom – I was going to give it to it once I had its weight and photo, why didn't it just give up now and save us both a lot of trouble? – and after a few more heart-stopping minutes of to and fro, eventually, with Rambo on the net, the huge mirror was mine!

I felt a little bit like I had after I had 'finished', for want of a better euphemism, with Melina.

Rambo laid the beast on my large – fortunately – unhooking mat. It wasn't an especially aesthetically pleasing fish as it had an absolutely huge stomach that was disproportionate to the rest of its body. Its body was still that of a massive carp it was just that its stomach was *mahoosiver*! My eyes boggled at it. I could remember an uncle from my childhood who'd had a stomach of similar proportion but unfortunately he had died years ago. He had suffered a heart attack and the chain had snapped when the crane had tried to lift him into the ambulance – which was a pick-up truck in disguise – or something like that. It was belly-related whatever it was. Christ knows what *he* had weighed. Christ knows what this *fish* was *going* to weigh.

"God! Look at the size of it!" trilled Melissa.

"I bet you've never heard her say those words before, Pup?" Rambo said, tongue in cheek.

Pup gave him a double take and then the penny dropped. "Oh, I *see*! *Very* funny!" Pup gazed at the carp in astonishment. "God!" he said. "Look at the size of it!"

Rambo was kneeling down by the side of the carp as he unhooked it. Carefully he lifted up the carp's head and pulled away the terminal tackle and put my rod back in its rest for me. All I could do was gawp; I *was* the proverbial 'spent force'.

"You sure know how to pull it out at the end, boy," Rambo said shaking his head.

"That's not what Melina said!" Melissa giggled.

"What?" said Pup looking puzzled.

"Nothing," said Melissa, her face over-written with blind panic. "Just being silly."

I gave her a subtle shake of my head and mouthed the words 'Rambo knows'. Her relief was all too apparent. 'Sorry', she mouthed back. It was a touch unnerving and I thought, rather sarcastically, that my secret was *really* safe with her, I could *just* tell!

"I've seen this fish before," said Rambo. "On the first time forties list that Alan paints. And I seem to remember Hollywood saying it was the biggest one in Hamworthy when we had our interview. It's called Gut Bucket," Rambo stated, pleased with his recollection. "It was on the list as a first time out forty at forty-three something and Hollywood said it had been out at nigh-on fifty at a later date, and that it was stacking on weight. It isn't spawn-bound, more like boilie-bound!"

Now Rambo had said it I could bring it back to mind as well. For some reason I looked at my watch, it was five to ten.

"It's nearly over!" I said in a daze.

Rambo looked at his watch. "Right," he said taking charge. "Let's sack her up. I'll put up the flare in a few minutes time, we'll get everyone up here to see the fish, I'm sure they'll all want to, and then in front of all and sundry we can weigh her and see if you've done enough for Team Rambo to scrape home and win."

I looked at Gut Bucket. "Do you think there's a chance? How much are we behind?"

"Sixty-three pounds five ounces," Pup confirmed.

"What do you think, Rambo?" I said.

Rambo heaved *his* massive shoulders. "It's beyond my range of experience, I've *never* seen a fish that big." He looked me in the eye. "Let alone *caught* one, you jammy bastard!" He gave me a wink. "I reckon it'll be very close. Remember if it goes over sixty I'm duty bound to kill you! You can't say I didn't warn you!" Rambo scratched the stubble on his chin. "I'll tell you what, if it wins the comp, I'll let you off. Can't say fairer than that!"

"Cheers!" I said.

We all stood and looked at the remarkable fish in front of us.

"I'll get her sacked," said Rambo.

Chapter 17

It was over, all over bar the shouting. The shouting of the weight of the descriptively named Gut Bucket, and with it, the final scores on the doors of Hamworthy Fisheries' inaugural Fish-In. Every angler involved in the event was now congregated in swim nine, like a big shoal of carp, awaiting the final result and a glimpse of the 'special' fish I had caught. Twenty-nine men there were in swim nine, one woman and tucked up in the margin was one brute of a carp, which, despite having the intellect of a below par chicken, dominated most people's thoughts. (Just as an aside, what idiot dreamt up 'below par' as an expression to signify a lack of standards? Below par is good, it's when you get 'above par' you're doing badly – in golfing terms that is – and who thinks of the word 'par' in any other context? So why did I use it? I must be below par, no, above par… forget I ever mentioned it.)

Previously the anglers had reeled in once the flare had gone up and had made their way to where Team Rambo had been fishing for the last three days. The reasons why they had all homed in on swim nine were firstly, because Pup had driven round and told everyone I had caught something extremely special and that they ought to come and witness it, and secondly that the final Fish-In weights would be announced. What was so special about my capture, Pup hadn't revealed. Once they had all arrived, had settled down and I had straight batted and stonewalled all questions regarding the carp, Rambo had lifted the enigmatic black bundle out of the deep margin. Even his powerful arms had hinted at the effort required to elevate the combination of carp, sack and water from its previous resting place and it hadn't gone unnoticed by the savvy group of carp anglers. Water had poured from the sack's punched holes as Rambo had walked it back up the bank, yet despite the water stopping fairly soon, the vast bulk within the sack was still there to be seen. Rambo had carefully placed the monster onto the unhooking mat and slowly unveiled the secret of her to the gallery by peeling back the folds of thin, black material that comprised the sack.

Gasps of astonishment, cries of exclamation in forceful Anglo-Saxon, one 'Gott in Himmel' and general synchronised jaw dropping had been the unrehearsed response. Many of the more established members, having moved in closer for a better look, had recognised the fish and confirmed Rambo's continued avoidance of Alzheimer's disease. It was Gut Bucket, all right, the physically enhanced, Fatboy Not-Slim-At-All version of the fish they had known before.

Once the hubbub had died down and everyone had taken a good look at her on the mat I had held the fish for photos, showing both flanks to camera, with a permanent trying-not-to-strain smile. It hadn't been easy I can assure you, to cradle the large slippery bulk of Gut Bucket, and I was paranoid of making a hideous faux pas with her in front of such an audience. To drop her would have been a sin, number eight on the carp angler's list of commandments, the one that clearly states; Thou shalt not let thy carp plummet to earth, especially when thou poseth for photos. Consequently the carp's stomach, literally, was held only inches above the ground, but even on such a low flying mission her dorsal fin was flying high in style! Her depth was astounding. Once I had successfully negotiated holding what I reckoned was over half a hundredweight of carp whilst smiling at the same time, Gut Bucket was prepared for weighing.

I had asked Rambo to do the honours of holding the scales because he was definitely the most suitable candidate to avoid the dreaded muscle tremor, the one so prone to giving the pointer on the scales a touch of St Vitas Dance. And I had asked Horst and Helmut to shout the weight.

Rambo had transferred Gut Bucket to an already zeroed in weigh-sling and hoisted up the scales, my Reuben Heaton scales, only for me and the M and Ms to see the pointer go round once, and then once again, and then more so. My scales were sixty pound scales, once round the dial equalling thirty pounds, and they were marked in one ounce increments. Gut Bucket, local leviathan, mid-Kent monster, Hamworthy hulk and genuine lard-arse could now safely be pronounced as being something or other *over* sixty. An *English* sixty! I had caught an *English* sixty! The nationality was superfluous in a way, I hadn't caught a French sixty, a Romanian sixty or an Outer Mongolian sixty for that matter, but now I *had* caught an English one! In an instant I had been catapulted into a very elite band of world anglers with this fish and as far as I was aware it was only the second ever sixty from our green and pleasant land. Those matters aside, it had been abundantly clear the Reuben scales weren't up to the job so Rambo had put Gut Bucket back down gently onto the mat and someone had legged it for some bigger scales.

"I know what to get you for Christmas now," Rambo said, big grin on his face.

Very quickly someone handed Rambo a set of Nash Nitelites that went up to seventy pounds in two ounce increments. If these scales didn't go heavy enough I would have to put Gut Bucket in the back of the car and nip down to the local scrap metal dealer. 'How much for carp, mate?'

'Depends how big a lump it comes in, pal.'

'I've got this lump,'

'Hmm. Looks about thirty. Three pound a pound for that size.'

It wouldn't do, you could never trust a scrap metal dealer on a fair weight. If the Nitelite scales bottomed out I would call it a round seventy, not around seventy, and be done with it.

Rambo tried again. He took Gut Bucket out of the weigh-sling, zeroed the new set of scales, put her back in the weigh-sling and lifted smoothly. The pointer walloped round to sixty-three something – it was clearly under the eight ounce mark – and I simply couldn't believe it as it fluttered between the sixty-three two and sixty-three six markings. Gut Bucket was taking the piss. Just so long as she didn't *take* one and lose a couple of ounces!

Horst and Helmut perused the scales for twenty or so seconds, looked at each other and spoke quietly in German. With my vast knowledge of German I picked out a 'ja!'.

Helmut turned and smiled at me with a nodding head and slightly pursed lips. "Ve make ser veight, sixty-sree pounds and ser six ounces! You vin, my friend! You vin!" he said warmly.

The pair of them shook my hand strongly and once Rambo had put Gut Bucket back down on the unhooking mat they shook his. The pair of them made a point of signalling Pup over and shaking him by the hand as well. Once all the handshaking and congratulations were over, Helmut shouted out the weight and the result in his heavily accented voice to the gathered multitude.

"Ser fish veighs sixty-sree pounds and ser six ounces! Team Rambo are ser vinners!" he proclaimed. "By ser one ounce, only!"

The two Austrians started clapping and the others followed suit, heads shaking in stupefaction at the ridiculous closeness of the result. I have to admit I was emotionally moved, not only because of what I had caught, or because we had won, that all seemed secondary, but by Horst and Helmut's civility, decorum and generosity. They had known how much they were in the lead, yet, almost perversely; they had *wanted* me to win with that fish. If they had split the difference on the weight and called it sixty-three four, which was how I saw it, they would have won. But they hadn't. They were true gents, mulleted and moustachioed gents, mulleted and moustachioed gents rumoured to be gay, if you were to believe the middle one of the Witches of Eastwick, but true gents nonetheless.

The rest of the anglers all came down to the water's edge to watch me put Gut Bucket back to fight, *and* eat a shed-load of boilies, another day. The huge fish waddled off; unaware of the fuss it had created in the alien world in which it had played a fleeting part. The fuss could grow considerably greater in the coming weeks should I want it to, I mused. However, I was determined not to go down that route of engaging the angling press and seeking extra publicity. There was also the commercial aspect of catching such a fish where I could, if I wanted, suddenly become an instant 'consultant' for manufacturer XYZ, or a 'field-tester' for a self-styled 'Bait Baron'. Equally I could have become a 'rig guru' – the one who nailed the sixty, bottom lip, with the awesome 'hook of my choice', fished whistles and bells, with sliding doodad and rotating whatchamacallit – whatever the fuck a rig guru was meant to mean. Probably someone who could dream up five thousand words a month on the subject for the next five years. I think not, I thought, which although paradoxical, made sense to me.

In spite of the carrot of undoubted freebies national press exposure would bring, it was a magnifying glass myself and Hamworthy could do without being under. Naturally a part of my carp fishing ego wanted to cry it from the rooftops, who wouldn't? But I knew I couldn't and I knew I would have to settle for reminding Rambo of the day I caught the sixty to get my ego kicks. Constantly. By mouth, letter, text and email until we were doddering coffin dodgers. Today's events could become my epitaph. 'Here lies Matt Williams, a man who didn't amount to much but did catch an English sixty. R.I.P. You jammy git!'. Maybe I would buy some consecrated ground and get myself buried alongside Gut Bucket, the carp with the harp. Or the other way round, get Gut Bucket buried next to me, if the alien abductor's anal probing went hideously wrong and they dumped me back on Earth, unwilling to take their trash home with them. Some aliens and anglers have shared bad habits unfortunately.

"There goes England's first seventy pound carp in the not-too-distant future," said Noel, his eyes gleaming as Gut Bucket swam strongly off into the depths of his watery home. He looked up and over to me. "I might have to enter into a pact with the Devil and sell my soul so I can catch it!" he said.

"That's what I did!" I said jokingly. "The trouble was I had to sell Rambo's and Pup's at the same time! I didn't bother to ask them if it was okay because it *was* a team event!"

"We could be in trouble, boy," Rambo chipped in. "I've already flogged mine, years ago! When he sees the soul duplication in his books, it'll be a bit of a revelation for him! I think my soul is number six hundred and sixty-six!"

We all laughed.

"Well, gents," I said to the horde by the margins. "I guess that's it. I suppose it's been what you might call a grandstand finish! Fantastically improbable, which seems to be a trait of my life, incredibly enjoyable and…" I ran out of words and shrugged "… just *utterly* amazing, really! I don't know what to say. Reality *can* be stranger than fiction. I think I've said that before as well." I stopped and in the fervour of the moment went a bit 'film star' after receiving an Oscar. "What I must say, now I have the opportunity, is to thank you, thank you *all*, *immensely*, for coming, and for your support of this Fish-In. Especially in terms of the manner and the way everyone has conducted themselves. *All* of you have been a credit to the name of carp fishing and *all* of you have been superb sportsmen. We sometimes get bad press, carp anglers in particular, when our obsession drives us beyond the realms of decency and fair play. I know to my own cost how badly that can turn out, but it hasn't been the case here at all. We've competed against each other and against the fish without a hint of animosity or bad feeling, in fact quite the opposite. The camaraderie and overriding feeling of affinity has been truly superb and I genuinely thank you for it! A special thanks has to go to our eight guests. I hope you've enjoyed yourselves and perhaps one day we can do something similar again." I paused and contemplated. "I think all that's left, before I become too over-indulgent, is for me to wish you, our guests, a safe journey home and to say to the rest of my syndicate members… see you at the video shoot in a few days, time! I think that's going to be an altogether different experience!"

"Oh, I don't know!" Rambo whispered very quietly in my ear.

There were a few 'cheers, Matt', wolf whistles and a couple of 'way-hays!'.

Brad, feeling he had to say something on behalf of the guests, stepped forward from the throng and unleashed his teeth in a grin of perfect symmetry and spacing.

"Guys! What can I say!" he said turning to address all present. "*What* a three days' fishing! Wow! *Totally* mind-blowing! And what a grand finale! Why I'd have paid the entrance money just to *see* a carp like that, let alone have the chance to fish for it! It's been great! All of us guests have had a seriously great time, isn't that right guys? Great fishing, great company," – Did his eyes stray to Melissa? Not sure. Keep listening – "and great surroundings. Thank *you* very much! All I have to do now is to keep up our end of the deal and give Matt, here, the cheque for charity and we're done. What's the charity, Matt?"

"The local hospice we said, didn't we?" I said checking with Pup and Rambo. "St Michael's Hospice?" They both nodded confirmation. "Yeah. St Michael's Hospice."

Brad pulled out a pen and cheque-book and wrote out the cheque, there and then, resting it on his thigh as he scribbled away.

"There you go, buddy," he said offering me the single sheet of paper. "Let's hope it does some good, huh?"

"Thanks, Brad. Thanks a lot," I said shaking Brad's hand.

Brad gave me the cheque and I took it and quickly glanced at it. Ten grand! Would they put up a statue of Team Rambo in the hospice's lobby, or a carving of Gut Bucket?

"My pleasure." Brad turned away from me. "Gee, Tom," Brad said to his fishing partner, "I guess it's time for us to go and pack up our stuff now and head for home. We've got a plane to catch!"

Tom nodded. "Yep! Sure is, sure have! Not that I wanna go!"

There was a moment's hesitancy as the huddle of carp anglers waited for someone to make the first initial move. It was as if no one wanted to be the one who started off the true end of the event.

"Goodbye, Rambo," said Tom and the spell was broken.

Gradually, amongst a plethora of handshakes, goodbyes and mumbled conversations, the group slowly bid its members goodbye and after a good ten minutes finally began to shuffle off towards the main track to divide and go their separate clockwise and anti-clockwise routes back to their swims and tackle. Having said goodbye to all of them individually – a lot of handshaking but immensely pleasurable – I had a strange overwhelming compulsion wash over me and in panic I sought out Horst and Helmut again. The pair were walking and talking together in German and had only got as far as my bivvy.

I chased after them and put my hand on Horst's shoulder. He looked round in mild surprise. "Lads, before you go. Can I ask you a personal question?"

"Yes. Of course, if you vish," said Horst, sliding a glance at Helmut.

I touched my temple with my right hand. Shit! I hadn't thought this through but I couldn't pull back now. "This might sound really strange but," I was really grasping for the right phrase. "You know at the barbecue when the three girls were there? Well, you were, God this is dumb, what I'm trying to say is, that, you, you two, weren't interested in them at all. You wanted to talk fishing and you didn't pay them any real attention... I mean you spoke to them and were polite to them but not interested in them in another way. You know, they *are* very attractive, sexy looking girls. Also you never paid Melissa that sort of male/female attention when she and I came to weigh any fish. It was like she was another bloke, not this sexy young woman... *why?* For some reason I really need to know why that was? Why was that? Everyone else was enthralled by them..." My voice tailed away although I should have said 'especially me'. "... Except you two," I added softly.

"Do you think it is because ve are gay?" Helmut asked, rather too directly for my liking.

I hastily back-peddled. "No. No." I lied. "It's more a matter of temptation. You did say you were married, remember?"

"Many times ven ve are not in Austria, people sink ve are gay, a gay couple," said Horst laughing. "But I am not in love vitt, Helmut, only my vife!"

Helmut nodded, smiling. "Me too! *My* vife! Not, Horst's!"

"But aren't you tempted?" I asked. "By other women," I hastily added in case they thought I was referring to quite the opposite.

"Ven Horst and I made all ov our money, ve vere both single. Because ve had ser money, ve had ser lifestyle unt many vomen vanted to be vitt us," Helmut explained. "Unt ve said yes! Of course ve said yes, ve had our fun, but now ve love only our vives. Ozzer vomen do not interest us now."

"Helmut is lying," said Horst flatly. "Ve *are* gay!"

"Horst is now telling ser truth, ve *are* gay," said Helmut. "Ve have ser leazzer trousers to prove it!"

Holy dubbin impregnated lederhosen, Batman! Those mullet and moustachioed monsters are a pair of shirt-lifting, shit-stabbing uphill workers! Now I *was* totally flummoxed. "I'm sorry, I've lost the plot and I'm totally confused!"

"I vas *very* confused ven I vas a young man," said Helmut gravely, but his eyes glinted mischievously.

"Does it make any difference to you?" asked Horst. "Vether ve are gay or not?"

I pulled a face. "I suppose not," I said, not really sure if I did suppose it made any difference. On second thoughts, I supposed it *did*.

"Come on, Helmut, ve must go and pack up," said Horst. "Our vives vill be expecting us soon!"

The pair of them turned and went to go, leaving me floundering in my own excruciating embarrassment and befuddlement. They had gone only a few yards and they burst out laughing and came back to me. Tears of laughter were in their eyes.

"Sorry, Matthew! Our little joke!" said Helmut. "Look at sis!"

Horst and Helmut took out their wallets and they both showed me photos of their respective beautiful Austrian wives and children, two in Helmut's case, and three in Horst's.

Helmut wagged a warning finger. "Vomen like, Melloney, Melissa and Melina are trouble! To ser rong man. To ser right von, sey might be fun. But not for us, not now!" said Helmut. "Ten years ago, yes! Not now!"

Now you fucking tell me! Why couldn't you have rammed it home to me earlier and saved me from my stupid self? Why couldn't you have taught me how to control my switch, to make me envisage the hindsight and transform it into foresight? Who was I kidding? I knew the score but didn't have it in me to resist.

I gave them a weak laugh. Rambo and I had just about trimmed their mullets and moustaches on the fishing front but when it came to relationship maturity we were trailing in their wake by miles. I had cheated on Sophie *and* Rambo, Rambo had cheated on Melina, Melloney had cheated on Melina, her *sister*, and Melissa was going to cheat on Pup in the not-too-distant-future. They were trouble, all right, but lest we forget, it always needs two to tango!

The M and Ms, the Teutonic twins, whatever you wanted to call them, were part of a nuclear family and the bonds between it were too strong and couldn't be broken. I was part of a nuclear family as well, the trouble was every now and then when an attractive electron came by I went completely out of family orbit and 'bonded' with the rogue party. The others weren't much better. Rambo orbited around himself and the three sisters were like supercharged electrons fizzing all over the place in search of positrons regardless of where they came from. It was mayhem all right. A chaotic chaos theory with families ripped asunder and children deprived of their biological parents as bonds were broken and re-forged, but usually much more weakly, in different nuclear families. I had always thought it wouldn't happen to me but if my secret got out and Rambo and I couldn't successfully deny it, who knew what might happen? It didn't bear thinking about.

An hour later we were nearly packed up, the other anglers were long gone and only Team Rambo plus Melissa remained in swim nine. I was carrying my rucksack to my van, wondering what both Sophie and Gut Bucket were doing, when Melissa furtively approached me. She stuffed an envelope into my hand.

"I'm going," she said quickly. "Give this to Pup."

"What *now*? *Where*? Who with?" I said completely flabbergasted.

Melissa avoided my stare. "With Brad, to America, to take my chance on a life of true possibilities. To reach for the stars, if you like. You were right," she stated. "We *did* have an affair on the night I came back late, he asked me to come with him then. He told me about his fantastic home, his boats, how he travelled the world fishing and how he wanted me to come with him. How can I not take the chance of a lifetime? He *is* the angler I've been waiting for all my life. We hit it off straight away, in more ways than one, and there *was* an immediate affinity and chemistry between us. I've always liked anglers but he is *the* dream ticket angler. I know it's a shitty thing to do to Pup but a life making boilies isn't what I want to do!"

"You shouldn't have married him in the first place if that was the case," I said.

"We all do things we know we shouldn't, but at the time I did think I was ready, and I *did* love him," Melissa told me.

"But fifty kilos of Grange and fifty kilos of Active-8 down the line you were having second thoughts?" I said smiling.

"I suppose so." Melissa squeezed my hand. "I must go, he'll be waiting. Sorry to leave you as the harbinger of bad news."

"Oh, I'm *used* to it!" I assured her, giving my head a jerk and looking my eyes up into my skull. "I hope it works out, that's all. Pray *Brad* doesn't do a 'Melissa' on you!" I warned her.

Melissa shrugged. "It's a chance I'm willing to take." She looked at her shoes and then into my eyes. "Don't fret over Melina and Melloney, I *will* see to it they're discrete."

"Like *you* were earlier?" I said sceptically.

"It was the excitement of that big carp," she admitted. A look of concern drifted across her face. "Are you and Rambo really okay about it? You're not going to fall out and ruin your friendship are you?"

I shook my head. "No, we're not," I assured her. "Amazingly it wasn't an issue, not after what he had done with Melloney. He could have got the hump, a lot of blokes would've, despite the obvious hypocrisy, but to be honest I think Melina wanted more than Rambo would ever dare commit himself to. He's an out and out loner, you know."

Melissa glanced over to Rambo. "One day, one woman will change him."

"Isn't that what all women think they can do?" I asked. I was sure I had read it in one of Sophie's magazines.

"Possibly." Melissa's eyes were brimming with tears. "I can't stay any longer, I've got to go, I can't face seeing him now. I've got to go and not look back."

"Okay. Good luck," I said. I meant it.

Melissa gave me a peck on the cheek. "Give me as long as you can before you give him the note. Goodbye, Matt."

Melissa turned and ran off to the track avoiding both Rambo and Pup's eyes. She didn't look back. I stared at the 'Dear John' letter in my hand. This message will self-destruct... the person who has to read it, most likely. Poor old Pup, he was in for a momentous jolt, one not particularly useful when it came to promoting self-esteem and enhancing confidence. Still, there was nothing I could do about it, only to carry out Melissa's bidding and hang on to the bombshell as long as possible. In any case it would help avoid a 'scene' if she was off and away. A Pup/Brad confrontation would most likely be really ugly – a real cringe behind the sofa job – and it was not something I would like to have to witness out of choice. I put the letter safely in my pocket and carried on with the chores at hand.

By the time I had finished loading my tackle into my van, a half hour later, the tremendous euphoria of the Fish-In and the momentous capture of Gut Bucket began to recede a smidgen and be replaced by other less salubrious emotions. Sophie. Sophie and our deteriorating relationship were next up on the agenda before, in a few short days' time, the carp fishing porn video adventure hove into view. A case of oil and water if ever there was one. I decided there and then not to tell her about it at all. I would say I was going fishing instead, which in a way I was, I would simply forget to mention it would be a session punctuated with pockets of prime porn perusal of an in the flesh, live-as-it-happens, bonking-in-the-bivvy kind. I could offer some helpful pointers to the cast, I thought to myself wryly; like don't do it doggy-style while kneeling on a spilt box of dog mixer, for a start.

"Here's your mobile back, Matt."

Pup's voice made me jump. "Cheers, mate," I said as perkily as I could. This was not going to be pretty.

"A strange text message came in on it a few minutes ago," said Pup, his face a picture of concern. "You have a look."

I took the mobile off him and went through the menu to get to my inbox. The number was not one the phone or I recognised. The message said; 'hope u r enjoying the fishing. u wd need to be. sucker'.

I was stumped. "*No* idea what that's meant to mean. It might be a joke from one of the syndicate members, but I think I've got all of their numbers in the phone and it's not from one of them." I shook my head. "Nope! Don't know. Someone mucking about I expect."

"Where's Melissa?" Pup asked. "Hey, what *are* you doing, Rambo?" he said as his eyes, like mine, had caught Rambo taking his tackle back out of his car.

"Call me mad but I've just heard on the radio there's some rain on the way and I said to myself, sod it! I'm going to stay for another day and see if there's *another* sixty in this place! If golden bollocks can catch one there's no reason why I can't!"

Pup rolled his eyes and tutted. "I don't know. All right for some. We've got a load of orders to catch up on, we'll be rolling for a couple of days solid I expect."

His use of the royal 'we' cracked me up and my heart bled for him. "I'm sorry, mate," I said, giving him the envelope. "You'd better read this. It's from Melissa."

Pup took the envelope from me, his face a mixture of non-comprehension and trepidation. His hands shook as he ripped it open and took out the letter and started to digest its chilling message, his eyes growing wider in disbelief at every sentence he read.

Poor, poor Pup I thought. Years of being a bait anorak saddo and then, majestically – from out of the aisles at Tesco – comes his queen, his Rizla Queen, a woman of great beauty – steady on, let's say 'physical allurement' – come on, once more from the top, okay, go! Poor, poor Pup I thought. Years of being a bait anorak saddo and then, majestically – from out of the aisles at Tesco – comes his queen, his

Rizla Queen, a woman of great physical allurement and sexual excitement to lift his life from its shabby, monotonous, flavour-enveloped, humdrum mix-a-thon. She is a woman – amazingly – who loves anglers and – double-amazingly – from all the anglers there are to choose from, elects Pup as the man and boiliemeister to marry her. And now, less than half a year down the line, she had committed adultery and literally fucked off with a handsome, blond-haired, ultimate-set-toothed American globetrotting millionaire angler.

My heart wept for him. Life can be cruel. Never mind all the 'it's better to have loved and lost than never to have loved at all' crap, or the 'there's always someone worse off than you' defeatist resignation. There's always someone *better* off than you and it's better to have loved and had it whole-heartedly reciprocated. *That's* how it should be. Not summarily dismissed as Pup was finding out, his love not being reciprocated because his wife had run off with someone better. Better off, better looking, better fun, better meal ticket and better teeth. *Much* better teeth.

Pup looked up at me in complete astonishment. He looked back at the letter in mute horror, his bottom lip quivering like that of a child who had lost a favourite toy. His body deflated with a massive puncture – a massive puncture of the heart – and his shoulders sagged as the weight of the message on the paper in his hand crushed down on his very soul and squeezed out of him the very will to live. He pulled in air deeply through his nose, in short jerky intakes, a prelude I imagined, to him baring his emotions to me in floods of tears.

"She's… she's *left* me!" he said quietly, his head hanging towards the ground, his back rounded as if gravity was pulling with all its might upon his cranium.

Again he breathed in deeply but this time, heroically, he straightened his body and stiffened his sinews, halted his wobbling lower lip and steeled his upper one. Mentally I applauded his tragic resolve in reining in his utter desolation, of managing to keep a lid on the boiling pot that was the tatters of his life.

"The fucking *cow!*" he exploded. "*Shit!* She must have found out about me and Melloney!"

A large wrecking ball on a chain had just crashed into my left temple. "*What?*" I said.

"Me and Melloney! I've been screwing around with Melloney for the last month!" Pup admitted.

"What's he been doing?" said Rambo who had materialised, as if by magic or Star Trek transporter, at Pup's shoulder.

"Screwing around with *Melloney!*" I said gobsmacked.

"Jesus Christ!" Rambo exclaimed. "Is there *anyone* here who hasn't had sex with at least one of those bloody girls?"

"At least it was *only* one!" I blurted before I could stop myself. I was worse than Melissa.

Pup eyed me with increased interest. A smile of incredulity slowly spread across his face. "*No!* Which one?"

"Melina," I said grudgingly. "But it was only *once!*" I pointed out. "*Once* with *one* of them."

"I've been doing it with Melloney once a *week*," said Pup matter-of-factly, bordering on slight swagger. "And with Melissa about four times a week, on average that is, when we haven't been rolling bait in the evenings."

"Too much information," said Rambo dryly. "I didn't need to know it all."

"Don't you dare tell *anyone* what *I've* just told *you*, or *he'll* kill you," I said to Pup whilst pointing at Rambo.

"Have I ever let you down on your bait secrets? The bait secrets on which, if I remember correctly, you issued a similar sort of threat?" Pup asked a touch peevishly.

I shook my head. "No, you haven't," I agreed lowering my voice. "I'm only *reminding* you, *okay*? My wife finding out about my one night kneel is more important than anyone finding out what's in our base mix."

"Two questions," said Rambo holding up a 'V' for victory sign. "One: Are you sure? Two: *Kneel*?"

"Doggy style!" I said as if it was self-explanatory. "It was in a bloody *bivvy*, I'd hardly be standing! Not like *some* of us," I explained raising my eyebrows at Rambo.

"Very drool," said Rambo.

I tried to clear my head. Melissa *hadn't* known about Pup's infidelity, that statement had to be true. I was certain she would have told me because it would have given her a ready-made excuse – even though she had been rolling freezer baits – it was a ready-made excuse and one to paint her in a better light. She would never have passed on it, and her awareness of the callous nature of her deed seemed total and undiluted by Pup's wrong doing. Best I didn't tell him, I decided, let him wallow in the guilt and stupidity of his sexual misdemeanours and be minimally consoled by the 'Jack-the-lad' aspect. It was much better than having to wallow in utter rejection.

"I can't cope with all this, I'm afraid," I confessed flatly, "and I'm going *home!*" I eyeballed the two others. "Any objections?" None were forthcoming. "Excellent!" I said with an air of finality. "See you later, lads. Good luck and well done for winning. I'll be in touch and perhaps all three of us can go round to the hospice and present them with the cheque. I'll ring you soon, Rambo, and arrange a time for meeting when I hear from Japp about the video shoot."

Pup and Rambo nodded, returned my congratulations and set about their business. I left Rambo setting up his gear he had only minutes ago completely packed up. Pup I left considering the state of play of his sex life, availability regards bait rolling hands, if he should sell, set fire to or start wearing Melissa's underwear – if she had ever worn any – and whether he ought to propose to Melloney once his divorce from Melissa came through.

I had to get home and sort out *my* relationship, my proper one, let alone try to unravel who exactly stood where regarding Team Rambo *vis-à-vis* the Witches of Eastwick. The social slights and infidelities were racking up like a pinball machine gone haywire. Sister cheating on sister, fellow team angler cheating on another team member – sometimes aware they were doing so, sometimes not – then there was Brad – my God what a horrific maze of tangled connections. I could spend years trying to fathom it out and be none the wiser. What I could see though, was the moral, the applicable moral, of what had happened to Pup, and it wasn't lost on me. It was time to go.

Rapidly I checked I had all my stuff with me by walking my swim, even though Rambo was staying on fishing it and would have picked up any items of tackle left. Old habits die hard! I left him and Pup chewing the cud, the cud being Melloney, Melissa and Melina most likely, and drove back around the grass track, checked the clubhouse was locked and went out the two gates, unlocking and relocking them both.

Who had sent the funny text message? It was the uppermost question in my mind as I drove home. How odd. Not as odd as the Witches of Eastwick. Mayhem? Shit! That didn't *begin* to describe it. The whole seething mass of events whirlpooled in my mind and the text message question got sucked into the maelstrom alongside the witches, the M and Ms, Brad, Steve's nuts, Gut Bucket, Team Rambo, the host of sexual liaisons committed in the name of lust – I couldn't think of any in the name of love – the deceit and the lies, all in the pursuit of sex, and yet for once – in contrast – the decency and sportsmanship that had arisen due to the common bond of carp fishing.

It was a hell of tale. I tried to grapple with all the facets of the Fish-In and the time back to when I had interviewed for new members. I tried to evaluate all what had happened, the characters, their interaction but it was too much, too much to cope with as I had realised earlier.

I wiped all but the glowing satisfaction of the capture of Gut Bucket and the success of Team Rambo from my mind and focused on setting things straight with Sophie. I had learnt my lesson. I loved her and Amy and I vowed to myself that should I manage to come through my indiscretions unscathed and undiscovered I would never be as stupid again. (Was I lying? The jury was still out on that one.) Maturity. That's what I needed to discover, maturity as possessed by the M and Ms… and who the hell sent the text message. And what the hell had it meant.

I parked the van on the driveway to our house and went straight inside before unloading it. In the kitchen Sophie was feeding Amy who was sitting in her highchair. Amy gave me a smile and waved her little arms excitedly. Sophie gave me what I construed as a rather strained smile, a little like the one I had pulled while holding Gut Bucket.

"Hello everyone," I said as brightly as I could. "Guess what? We won! Ten thousand pounds for a local charity! Not bad for three days' work, eh?"

Amy gurgled in delight while her mother appeared less convinced. She looked *very* strained it had to be said.

"Gosh! That's great," said Sophie, although the way she said it, it didn't sound as if she thought it was *that* great.

"You'll never guess what again," I said trying to be as chipper as I could. "I caught a sixty pounder! Biggest fish ever from the pit and the second largest on the all-time UK list! It was absolutely huge…" The doorbell rang and halted my gushing. "I'll get it," I said.

I walked back down the hallway and opened the front door. There, in front of me, to my utter, complete, total, outright and comprehensive disbelief stood, of all people, Hollywood.

"Hello, sucker," he said, his handsome face leering at me. "I've been sitting outside waiting for you to come home." He flicked his head backwards to where a car, his car, the one I clearly hadn't noticed when I had driven up my drive, was parked on the opposite side of the road. In the car I could see the silhouette of another figure. It looked like Rocky. "Get my text message did you?"

Words collided in my throat and blocked it quicker than a bucket of tealeaves down a sink. My heart hammered at my ribcage and my knees were knocking like a bad domino player.

"Rrrghh!" I said masterfully.

"Hey, Sophie!" Hollywood called at the top of his voice. "It's me, Gary!"

I heard Sophie come running down the hallway behind me and turned back to see her cup both hands up to her face as she recognised the person calling her. Her eyes had a look of such dread and horror it was as if they were witnessing the murder of her only daughter. All in all, being a sharp tool – tool being the operative word – I recognised this not to be a good sign.

"She's pretty good in bed, you know," Hollywood sneered, before any thought process of mine could kick-in, let alone any action. "Once I'd fucked her, she sucked me off and swallowed the whole lot. Didn't you, darling?"

I was frozen rigid unable to move, every emotion I had ever had, plus a few I hadn't, surged and hacked their way around my nervous system, a nervous system rapidly deteriorating into freefall. Out of the corner of my eye I caught sight of Sophie's body jack-knifing in two, like an articulated lorry in an accident and she started to cry.

Hollywood's face distorted into handsome, aesthetically pleasing anger. If only it was a film and he an actor, if only this wasn't really happening.

"You don't think I was ever *interested* in you, do you? You stupid *slut!*" he raged at the cowering Sophie. "I only *fucked* you like you've never been fucked before to get back at this *cunt!*" Hollywood jabbed his finger at me. His eyes were incandescent and spittle came from his mouth as he spat out his vile, bilious, odious bitter hatred – literally – all over me.

"*He* took my pit away from *me!*" he screamed. "And *fucked* up my life! And now, hopefully," Hollywood's voice calmed and became sinister and sure, "I've fucked up yours!" He eyed us both with malicious delight, satisfied at the destruction and carnage that lay before him. "Goodbye, suckers!"

And he turned, walked down my driveway, out of my gate and into the waiting car. Rocky drove off giving me a sarcastic double toot on the car's horn. Hollywood had, at some as yet undetermined point in the past, presumably over the period of the Fish-In, screwed Sophie and me with it. Actually he had only truly screwed me a few seconds ago, when I had found out. Unlike most others, he couldn't wait to tell his big secret.

Hollywood's run of revenge, the one I had initially fretted over and then forgot, had rattled off, and the banshee scream of it would haunt me until I died. How typical – a run right out of the blue when you least expect it. With the gift of hindsight the text message and Melissa's story of the 'guy at the gym', Sophie's unusual behaviour were all liners I should have interpreted better and made me realise Hollywood's trap had been set. My 'interpretation of personal experiences' had been poor. I wasn't the carp angler I thought I was despite having caught an English sixty. Even so, it was a dubious notion to have assumed I could have prevented it. Hollywood had planned his trap with cold malice and cunning, and my input into our relationship had made Sophie vulnerable enough to become susceptible to it. That and the profound effect the ghost had had on her.

I had wondered whether I would ever live to regret the events in Rebecca's room and now I was. Only it was more likely my stupid offhand remark about not having met her, Rambo's gainsaying of this fact to Melina that had found its way to Sophie's ears via Melloney, which was the true regret. These were the set of circumstances that had led to me being, if not exactly caught in the act, then intimating the possibility of it. I had lied over the presence of a woman and not unreasonably, not unreasonably at all given what had actually happened, Sophie had been aggrieved at it. It was this, the impact of the woman who'd had her life grimly snatched from her, her annoyance at my gawping at the witches plus our relationship deterioration that had allowed Hollywood's plan to track and trace and meet and shag my partner to come to fruition. What a sorry, sorry mess.

I turned away from the view out my front door and looked the other way, back inside and down onto Sophie. Previously my mind had been clear-cut when I had imagined – when thinking of Melissa – how if I had found my wife to be cheating on me, she would have been shown the door straight away, with no compunction. Now, given the circumstances it didn't seem clear-cut at all. Sophie was a huddled mass on the hallway floor, knees together, feet apart, sitting on her behind, her face covered completely by both arms her hands resting on the top of her head. She was sobbing incessantly. I looked at her and the pathetic, broken figure she cut. And the first thing I considered out of all the trauma available was the particular sexual act Hollywood had mentioned, had been one she had never performed on me. How that hurt. How that cut me to the bone and sliced my flesh apart in a wide, gaping, gruesome open wound that might never heal in this world or (as previous disclaimer) the next. If by chance it ever did, the scar would be repulsive and to see it every day, as I surely would, would forever make me wince.

Here was irony, forget Pup. Here was so much iron it could make a solid club hammer and an anvil to put either side of me and pulp me to a bloody, gore-ridden puree. Here was I, twice the adulterer, in the very situation I had dreaded, with infidelity revealed and a relationship shot to bits, able to take the moral high ground all because Sophie had been exposed first. She was but a mere pawn, a pawn in a plan of great Machiavellian wickedness aimed solely at destroying one person. Me. She was expendable. I was the king, and I had been put into check. I was well and truly in check, mate.

I pulled her up off the floor. Now was the time for me to show I was a true man, to stand by her as she had stood by me when I was in the gulag. Now was the time to realise she had committed only half the number of affairs that I had committed and to see the rampant sanctimony of my actions if I didn't forgive her. Now *was* the time but could I actually do it? I was raw emotion. I had been hung, drawn and quartered mentally, it might fade, the rawness of it, but could I face a life of making love to Sophie? Wouldn't I be forever thinking of what she had done with Hollywood, closing my eyes in moments of orgasmic pleasure only to have a mental image picturing him fucking her? And her enjoying it and responding with an act she had felt unable to do for me. This was the price of lust, of sex outside a bond, and a heavy price at that. I had to pay the price because I *knew*. I had been told, maliciously so. But should Sophie ever have to pay the price for my lust? I had been determined to never have her pay it, prepared to lie and to get Rambo to lie for me and yet in a horrid, bitter tangled way would it now be *better* for her to know? Would our collective weaknesses help even out the bill and save our relationship? Did I *want* to save our relationship?

"Come on," I said. "Let's put the kettle on." It was the carp angler in me speaking.

I started to go through the familiar motions of making the tea in utter silence – neither of us knew any words to say – only for the phone to ring. The sound jarred my body and my numb brain. My eyes met Sophie's bloodshot orbs. What *now*? With trepidation I answered it.

"Hello?" I said dully.

The voice on the other end of the phone sparked into life. "Ahh! Hello, Matthew. Alan, from the syndicate here! Thought I'd phone to congratulate you on your wonderful fish and the event as a whole. Marvellous! Terrific stuff! A real super event with a smashing bunch of chaps! The new members are all lovely and fitted in as well! I have to say it made me proud to be a carp angler again, after all the sordid nonsense with those other three last year; it rather reinstated my faith in humanity! Melodramatic thing to say, but it did! Like I said to you at the time shortly after that asylum seeker chap helped me change my flat tyre, I'd lost a lot of faith in some of our own people but the Fish-In helped restore it…"

Alan's words faded out of my head as I lowered the phone on a slack arm. My brain, so recently injected with Novocain, tingled with the return of feeling. My psychic hat trick had arrived. At the most unlikely of times, it had to be said, but there it was. It was clear what was going to happen, not unless I could stop it. The image of what was going to happen sat on the surface of my sea of personal torment like an oily slick, an oily slick that was calming the tempestuous water beneath it. There they both were, the two central characters, in a two-dimensional picture rolling and heaving on the surface of the water. I put the phone down and cut Alan off.

"I've got to go back to the pit," I told Sophie in zombie-like tones. "I'll explain, later."

I went over to her and kissed her on the forehead. "I forgive you," I said, not knowing if I did. "It's all my fault. We'll work it out, I promise. It won't be easy but we'll do it. Do it for ourselves and Amy."

I kissed her again, kissed Amy and Sophie gave me a hint of a smile.

I ran out of the house, opened up the back of the van and unceremoniously emptied the entire contents of my rucksack all over the cheap carpet I had laid in the back. I picked up the one item I needed at this precise time – and it wasn't a packet of boilie stops! I slammed the back door shut, opened the driver's door and got in, threw the Glock 17 onto the passenger's seat, cranked the van into life and drove like a man possessed to the pit. As I drove my anger welled up inside me until I was a seething ball of hatred. *Why* hadn't I done anything? *Why* hadn't I at least tried to smash Hollywood in the face as hard as I could? I had done *nothing*! I had just *stood* there, like a great big Jessie, and let him disclose his moment of triumph, centre stage, no heckling, without saying so much as boo to a goose. If it had been Rambo, he would be pulling up the patio slabs even now, in preparation for yet another body disposal. I gritted my teeth. All that would have to wait; my destiny was elsewhere, to see out the vision of my psychic hat trick. How could I be so perceptive, so insightful on these odd, amazing, infrequent occasions and yet be so blind the rest of the time? Pass. Whatever Wim's LSD tab had started I had no control over it. It came when it came and that was all there was to it. I was powerless to utilise it any better. I leaned forward against the steering wheel and put my foot down harder.

When I arrived at the upper gate my ferocity was undiminished. I leapt out of the van and undid the combination padlock and hurled the gate open and drove straight on, the front wheels squealing as I pulled violently away, not stopping to re-lock it. Anarchy! That was one fishery rule broken and I did the same at the next gate. I revved the van hard across the car park, glancing only fleetingly at the functional wooden clubhouse. Shards of gravel were ripped up by my tyres as I made a passable impression of a Friday night boy-racer out on the pose as I drove as fast as I dared across the rough terrain. Now was not the time to snap a leaf spring. The clattering of gravel stopped as I hit the grass track and the van slewed and snaked as the front wheel drive struggled for grip on the lush green grass. I yanked the steering wheel roughly to compensate – turn into the skid is the golden rule – and powered around the perimeter track. Luckily the rain Rambo had heard was on the way hadn't yet arrived. The old wood appeared out of my left-hand window; on I went, gradually changing direction from my northerly run until I had turned eastwards. I thumped my right foot onto the brake and I slid to a halt fifty yards short of the path to swim nine.

Stealth overtook the need for speed and I prayed I hadn't been heard. I *hadn't* been heard because the vision wouldn't have been the way it was, I reminded myself. I grabbed the gun and, after not shutting the van door, walked quickly and purposefully towards my goal. I strode up to the swim's entrance and then sneaked down, crouching into a stoop and inched down past the bushes until I could see all of swim nine. There before me was the scene I had imagined in my head. I accepted it. It was just as I had envisaged during the telephone conversation with Alan, when his innocent phone call had tripped… what? My *third* switch! Bizarrely, and yet at the same time totally acceptably – to myself – it was as if time had juggled itself so that however long I had taken to get from my house to the pit, was *precisely* how long it had taken the pair of them to get to where they were in their proceedings. My first sight of them had been *exactly* as the image had rolled and heaved in my head. But now time marched on, and if I didn't act quickly the scene would change for the worse, unspeakably for the worse.

The asylum seeker, who wasn't an asylum seeker, but who *was* the person I had seen walking near the pit one morning and who *was* the person to whom Alan was referring, had a gun. And his gun was pointing downwards, aimed directly onto the back of Rambo's head because Rambo was kneeling, facing the opposite way, with his hands clasped, fingers interlocked, behind his head. Those hands, as big as they were, would never stop the bullet.

I breathed deeply. I was what, twenty-five yards away? More to the point I was still unseen and fortuitously unheard. I raised the gun, grasping it in two hands. 'Just pull the trigger' Rambo had said, and I had seventeen goes to come, provided I didn't get killed before I could use them. My gun reached a horizontal plane. Heavily accented words, vengeful words, drifted on the south-westerly and into my ears. It was now or never or Rambo really would be dead, murdered by the same person who had killed Charlie. Bleakly I knew I now had once chance to assassin-8 him. I aimed at the bulk of the swarthy figure and squeezed the trigga.

The shot rang out and the swarthy figure jolted as the bullet found its mark. I shot again. The figure jolted again, a crimson patch welling up on his chest. Rambo was up in an instant and punched him full in the face with a Spunker-flattening right hand and kicked the gun from his hand. I walked down shooting coolly and hatefully at the figure. Rambo stood to one side, a look of complete amazement on his face, and watched me.

Three. Another slug ripped into Rambo's would-be assailant and the figure slumped down to his knees.

Four. In my head I counted the deadly projectiles.

Five.

Six. A bullet ripped into the swarthy figure's head and a splattering of snot, gore and brain came out the exit wound, the figure fell to the ground with an inert thud.

Seven. I was shooting at the figure's back now, as he was prone on the floor, limbs at ridiculous angles, in essence looking like a life size marionette.

Eight. I was right on top of the prone figure now and my hate for Hollywood and for myself was being released in every single finger movement.

Nine. Viciously I squeezed the trigger again, my face contorted with rage.

Ten. I pumped another bullet into the lump of meat at my feet.

Eleven. Tears poured from my eyes.

Twelve. "You *fucking bastard!*" I screamed.

Thirteen. "*Bastard!*"

Fourteen. "*Fucker!*"

Fifteen.

Sixteen. My vision was so hazy I could hardly see. My eyes were blurred like having swum in an over-chlorinated swimming pool.

Seventeen.

Click.

Click.

Click.

Sobbing hysterically I threw the gun down on my victim as hard as I could like a Superbowl footballer having made a touchdown. All done on the gun front, I flung myself hysterically onto Rambo's chest, draping my arms around him. My body sagged but Rambo hugged me tight and held me in his powerful arms.

"It's all right, Matt. It's all right, Matt. It's all right," he repeated, his voice choked with emotion.

I pulled back from him to see *his* eyes full of tears. He gave me a tender smile. "You *saved* me, boy! You *saved* my fucking life!" His brow furrowed in deep non-comprehension. "*How?*"

I let go of him and nearly fell to the ground because I was unsupported. I was shaking violently. All my anger was gone, I was an empty husk. "I don't know," I didn't explain. "I was at home, Alan phoned, mentioned the asylum seeker and I knew. I just *knew*... could picture it *exactly*. And when I got here... that's how it was." I said, my whole body now shuddering as if I was freezing cold. "It's like the thing with the mind-meld mirror and the ghost... I can't explain. Why did I even ask you for the gun in the first place? Was that a sort of premonition to the later vision?"

Rather self-consciously Rambo wiped his eyes and shook his head. "God knows, but I'm *mighty* glad you did! That's the closest I've ever come to buying it, you know." Rambo wiped both of his massive hands roughly across his face. "It keeps happening to you, doesn't it?"

I gave a tiny quivering shrug. It only *happened* to me, it wasn't as if I understood it or anything. "Is he dead?" I asked weakly and then spluttered a sort of nervous laugh through my stuffed up nose.

Rambo gave me a grin. "At a guess, I'd say he was, boy. Seventeen 9mm shells, good shooting by the way, are usually enough to put most people down. Permanently."

"Who is he?" I asked, my body juddering ever more violently with the shock of what I had done.

"Not too sure," Rambo admitted. "Certainly he's the bloke who killed and tortured Charlie to find out enough on me to find me and, I'm surmising, a relative of the bloke I duped into posing as me."

"W-what are we going to d-do with h-him?" I asked. I had two Kangos breaking concrete strapped to each leg now and it was making speech difficult.

"Get rid of him and every *trace* of him. That's what we've *got* to do," said Rambo.

"I w-wonder if Japp could g-give him a p-part in the p-porn video. He could p-play the b-big s-stiff," I said without humour, even if I was trying to be funny. I was stammering because my teeth were now clattering together and I shivered as if I had been locked inside a deep freezer for an hour

"Japp's making a *porn* movie, not a *snuff* movie!" Rambo pointed out. "We'll have to bury him somewhere. Somewhere he'll never be found."

"W-what? O-on the i-island?" I asked.

Rambo shook his head. "I *don't* think so! But we'll have to get rid of him somehow."

"D-do you f-fancy m-making it *t-two* b-bodies?" I said an idea formulating along with the need to off load my bad news.

"*Two?*" said Rambo.

I nodded bleakly. My teeth were chattering so violently I found it hard to speak. "I'm a-a-afraid H-H-Hollywood's r-r-run of r-r-revenge h-h-has h-h-happened," I said with difficulty.

Rambo's face changed to a look of deep concern. "What's that little shitbag done?" he demanded aggressively.

I told him the whole sorry saga with a stuttering speech impediment.

Rambo bristled with evil fury. "Don't worry, Matt," he said, his face as black as thunder, his huge fists clenched. "I'll fucking sort *him* out for you!"

I let out a heavy, tremulous sigh. "I-I-I d-don't know, R-R-Rambo. E-even i-i-if y-y-you d-do, w-w-what about a-a-all the m-mess it's l-left b-b-behind?"

Rambo stared at the ground. "I know," he said softly. "You were vulnerable because you had something other than yourself you really care for, and that bastard knew it. It's like I said before and why I'm a loner, and yet, and *yet*, there was smug old me, *equally* as vulnerable, although I shouldn't have been, all because I'd taken my eye off the ball and got caught with my trousers down! In more ways than one!" Rambo shook his head as if he couldn't believe how slack he had been. "Bad play, boy. Bad play," he said to himself as much as to me.

Rambo looked around at the pit and looked up to the sky, a sky full of dark clouds. Spots of rain started to fall.

"Shall we take him to taxidermist and have him mounted?" he asked, nodding at the grisly, bullet-ridden corpse.

I looked at the body, the body that had only minutes earlier been a living, breathing person. A living, breathing person *I* had killed. A wave of nausea washed across me, I had never even shot a bird before, let alone a mammal or a *human*.

"No." I said emphatically. Every muscle in my body was vibrating heavily and I felt sick. "I d-don't p-particularly w-want a photo, either," I said. "Let's p-put him b-b-back d-dead. N-n-ever to f-fight another d-day."

"I'll go find a shovel," said Rambo. "If we get our fingers out, I can have my baits back in the water by next feeding time. Then," he said, his lips thinning, "we can discuss our *strategy*."

"S-so ends another ch-chapter in our a-abnormal l-l-lives," I said looking in repulsion and fascination at the mutilated body. It had really hit me now, the magnitude of my action, especially seeing the exit wound to the back of the head so close up, the wound at which I was morbidly staring. I knew I was going to throw up shortly, just like I had at Pup's wedding.

Rambo looked up at me. "Going back to what we talked about earlier, I'd say this *was* the end of a chapter. And almost definitely the end of another book."

I felt the familiar churn of my stomach and saliva increased in my mouth. History had repeated itself. Hamworthy could claim *two* murders now. And *one* suicide.

I reached, my cheeks puffing like a trombonist's. If *my* murder secret was ever revealed, I thought, as I walked to find a spot to heave, *and* what with all the other shit hitting the fan, I could easily see the attraction of Michael's last session when compared to the possible alternative. I didn't want to go to prison again, not for killing the asylum seeker. I threw up onto the grass in an undignified Technicolor yawn. For killing Hollywood? I spat bile and food remnants from my mouth, oscillating my head quickly at the foul taste. I would have come back to you on that one.